A Dance Within the Darkness

Book Two of Within the Darkness Trilogy

Charley Black

First edition

ISBN: 979-8-9868877-3-9

Digital ISBN: 979-8-9868877-2-2

Cover art by MiblArt

Edited by Ashley Oliver – Enchanted Author Services

ALSO BY

WITHIN THE DARKNESS TRILOGY

Entwined Within the Darkness

Book One of the Within the Darkness Trilogy

To All My Fans,
Thank you for taking a chance on my stories.
It truly means the world to me.

TABLE OF CONTENTS

A DANCE WITHIN THE DARKNESS

BOOK TWO OF THE WITHIN
THE DARKNESS TRILOGY

PROLOGUE

Lucius

Evictus, 1859

"He wants her, Lucius. He will do anything to get her."

Tension surged through Lucius at hearing his wife's words while he carried her deeper into the intricate passage. The air was heavy and stagnant as the tunnel enveloped them in an eerie darkness, where only feeble rays of light managed to penetrate through the cracks and crevices in the rough-hewn stone walls. Dampness clung to every surface, lending a chilling moisture that saturated the air. The tunnel seemed to stretch endlessly as he let her words penetrate.

He acknowledged the truth of her statement, yet he couldn't afford to let his mind wander down that path. His focus remained steadfast on their escape, and he forcefully pushed aside those thoughts.

As they made their way through Ashmore's Cavern, Lucius fought the urge to stare directly at her, focusing instead on getting them out. The malevolent beast, Ashmore, who had stalked this cavern, hadn't been seen for centuries, but the tormented souls of his victims still lingered. Their anguished cries echoed off the walls, sorrow pulling at Mae and Lucius's essences, desperate to drag them into eternal suffering.

They could not remain too much longer.

His pace quickened, his feet carrying him with a renewed urgency as he glanced toward his wife once more, hating to see her defeated like this. His gaze roamed over Mae's filthy, torn white dress, stirring a deep-seated rage within him. The cuffs had weakened her, draining her, both magically and physically, to a point where she could barely lift her head. Not even his blood would help to rejuvenate her. A surge of helplessness washed over him, the realization settling heavily in his heart. His protective instincts intensified, fueling his determination to get them out.

A burning desire for vengeance consumed Lucius as he envisioned a fate of excruciating pain that would await the wretched demon at his hands. This was not the moment for his unbridled anger; instead, he needed to focus on getting them back to Eviathian, the human realm, to their home in Orendale. Lucius steeled himself, suppressing the fiery rage that threatened to consume him, directing his energy towards getting Mae back to Michael and their daughter, Sabine, who could heal her.

It had taken him weeks to find her, and he'd never expected to discover her in Valen, the Acidic Realm, known for its acid rain, where most of its creatures lived underground in caverns like this. Ashmore used to rule this realm, but now he was beginning to suspect what had happened to the creature. Thinking about it now, Umber had given him the information too fast. Too consumed in reaching his wife, he didn't even care that he could potentially walk into a trap. He had simply paid the ancient troll one astral coin and left.

So far, they had managed to evade any triggered traps, but he was still on full guard. They needed to reach the entrance where Canaan, a powerful draconian steed, waited. Canaan knew the safest routes through this treacherous realm and would lead them to the sacred Bastion Tree that held the key to their return home.

The entrance lay within reach, its exact location hidden from his sight. The light essence of Quary leaves intermingled with the delicate fragrance of Mense petals filled the air with a captivating aroma. Inhaling deeply, Lucius absorbed the intoxicating scent, letting it permeate his senses. While his eyes failed to see the opening, his senses and instincts urged him forward.

Just as a distant glimmer of daylight beckoned from the end of the tunnel, a sudden eruption of golden light burst forth from the left side of the cavern wall, enveloping the surroundings in its ethereal glow. Emerging from the luminescence stood Alazar, the half-demon, who materialized before Lucius in a grotesque display of power. Clad in his signature alabaster suit, the fabric clung to his form with unsettling precision, emphasizing the curves of his twisted physique. The pristine white hue of his attire contrasted starkly against the gloomy surroundings, a chilling reminder of the depravity that lurked within his malevolent soul.

Alazar's false presence exuded an air of wicked charisma, his façade a twisted mockery of beauty. His piercing gaze locked onto Lucius with a mix of amusement and malice, as if reveling in the torment that lay ahead. Just the sight of him filled Lucius with an indescribable rage.

"She is *mine*," Alazar drawled, his silvery voice dripping with malicious satisfaction, his devious smirk etched upon his face.

"Never," Lucius snarled as his fury broke through the surface, and his fangs sharpened in readiness. His sword, Luzia, hummed to life, casting a protective shield around him and his wife as a precaution. Though Alazar's presence was a mirage, Lucius refused to leave anything to chance, his fingers tightening their grip around his wife, pulling her closer to his chest. "She will never be yours," he seethed defiantly, his words resonating with unwavering determination.

Alazar's voice swelled with confidence as he proclaimed, "Odessa will be my queen, and I will be her king. Together, we shall reign over all the realms." His elongated fingers interlocked in gleeful anticipation while his red eyes glimmered with cruel amusement.

The temptation to set Mae down and rip out the half-demon's nonexistent throat surged within Lucius. Suppressing the violent impulse, he roared, "Our bond is unbreakable."

Alazar laughed with a delirious fervor, his lips curling into a cruel sneer. "Only for now. She will be mine. They both will."

Both? Their daughter. All his rage dissipated, and panic set in when Alazar's image began to fade. Black vines burst from the floor and walls, breaking through Luzia's barrier. They slithered up Lucius's legs and biceps, wrapping themselves around him. They pulled taut, trying to force his arms apart. Trying to get him to let go of his wife. His grip slackened, and he gritted his teeth at the pain rippling through his muscles.

He fought against the pressure, refusing to let her go even as the vines dug deeper into his skin, cutting into his flesh. The smell of his blood filled the cavern space as he struggled to keep Mae in his arms.

Just when he thought the pressure would be too much, the vines snapped, bringing him to his knees on the hard stone floor, but he still held onto his wife as she whimpered softly in his embrace, unconscious. The wicked vines slithered back into the walls as footsteps resounded behind him. He held onto Mae and calmed himself as he prepared to face whatever foe was approaching.

He had to be ready.

The footsteps came to an abrupt halt mere inches away from him.

Taking a deep breath, Lucius slowly stood, his gaze falling upon a figure with short silver hair and a sturdy build. Relief surged through him, intertwining with a heightened sense of panic, as his gaze locked with sharp silver eyes. Volt, a deadly Khedian and his most trusted friend stood in front of him. If he was here, something must have gone wrong. His thoughts went straight to his daughter as fear swelled within him.

"Tell me, Volt, what has happened?" he demanded.

Volt glanced worriedly down to Mae, then back to Lucius. The fearful look in his eyes told him everything he needed to know. This had never been a trap, just a distraction.

"You need to go home. Now, before it is too late." Volt's fingertips brushed the rough surface of the cavern wall. The stone quivered beneath his touch, shimmering with an otherworldly radiance as a dark void materialized before him. The stone gleamed, and then a black hole appeared, expanding itself. Shadows curled and slithered outward, expanding with an almost sentient will.

"Canaan is outside waiting for us," Lucius informed him as the hole was completed forming, and the image of their manor appeared within the portal.

"I will take care of it. Go *now*."

Holding Mae tenderly, Lucius stepped through with dread in his heart, frightened of what he would find once they were home.

When his feet made contact with the land, an unsettling sensation washed over him, signaling that something was wrong. The presence of the protective barrier, the steadfast shield that surrounded their beloved home, had vanished, leaving an eerie void in its wake.

Scanning his surroundings with apprehension and determination, Lucius inhaled deeply, drawing in the crisp night air. Its coolness filled his lungs, refreshing and invigorating. As he breathed, he couldn't help but sense the electric charge in the atmosphere, a palpable anticipation that seemed to hang around him.

The moon's soft glow bathed the manor in an ethereal glow, casting long shadows that danced across the grounds in silent vigil. Once a sanctuary of tranquility and security, it now seemed cloaked in an unsettling stillness. Its walls, adorned with ivy that wove intricate patterns, stood stoically against the night's embrace. The grand entrance, usually welcoming, appeared strangely muted and devoid of its typical warmth.

Lucius's keen eyes swept across the landscape, taking in the meticulously manicured gardens, now hushed and unmoving. The moon's gentle radiance kissed the ornate windows, their reflective surfaces offering a glimpse into the vacant halls. Yet an unspoken tension hung in the air, mingling with the quietude, whispering of a disturbance that had unsettled the tranquility of their cherished abode.

As he stood there, absorbing the hushed atmosphere, Lucius's heart braced for what lay ahead. The absence of the protective barrier and the eerie stillness that shrouded the manor signaled that he needed to prepare himself for what he might find.

Pure rage momentarily consumed him, making him want to rush forward, but he didn't know what lay ahead of him, and he still had to think of his unconscious wife in his arms. Mae's expression was slack, her weight heavy as he carried her. He would be no good to Sabine if he were dead.

Luzia's barrier wrapped around him as he forced his legs to move forward toward the old brown door he had always been happy to walk through. But now it laid off its hinges, askew.

Dread pulsed inside him with every step he took. He pushed it aside and stepped through.

He wasn't prepared for the devastation he found. The home they had filled with laughter, love, and joy now was filled with death, destruction, and anger. He slowly moved through the foyer, holding Mae close as he took in crumbling walls and black blood spattered everywhere. He walked past the dining room to find the furniture obliterated and glass shattered about. It was clear most of the fighting happened here. The silence was deafening, sending a shiver down his spine.

He sniffed the air, trying to determine what type of creature had invaded his home, but he couldn't pinpoint it.

A sound echoed in the distance, so faint he didn't think he heard it at first. He listened silently, finding only their heartbeats filled the space. The sound echoed again like a sword hilt hitting a wall.

Thinking of Sabine, Lucius climbed the stairs two at a time, pushing caution aside and running towards his daughter's room. He kicked open the door, and his eyes quickly searched the room filled with hundreds of shades of purple. To his relief, the space was eerily undisturbed, which gave him some semblance of hope.

He quickly moved to their room and gently laid Mae on the bed. He listened again for the noise, but the house lay silent.

Returning to his daughter's room, his hands touched the purple and black blanket at the end of her bed. She couldn't sleep without it. Mae had made it for her before she was born, using her magic to weave their love into it so her dreams would always be nightmare-free. Sometimes, those nightmares slipped through, which woke her during the night; instead of waking them, she would go into her cubby hole.

Lucius went to her closet. Stooping down, he moved a few pink dresses aside, revealing a small door. He slid his finger over the side, and four symbols glowed before the lock clicked.

He prayed he would find her curled up on her blankets waiting for him, but his hope vanished as soon as he pushed the door open. His stomach curled. Her purple bear and blue rabbit still sat in their tea chairs where she had left them a week ago; nothing had been disturbed.

Sighing and rubbing his hand over his face, he went back to his wife. So many possibilities spiraled through his mind, but hope bloomed again when he realized Michael and Ian could have run to protect Sabine. He had not found the bodies of any of them so far, so it was possible they could be safe. The fastest way to know where to find them would be for Mae to call Michael to let him know it was safe to return.

Calming himself, he returned to her and gently roused her from her slumber.

"Mae, baby, please. I need you to wake up for me. I know you must rest, but I need you to call Michael. Let him know it's safe to bring her back."

She moaned but didn't open her eyes.

"Baby, I know you're tired, but she is missing," he whispered.

Slowly, her eyes opened.

"Fuck," he cried. Her eyes gleamed with a fiery intensity, emanating a mesmerizing hue of vibrant red. The crimson glow seemed to dance within her gaze, casting an otherworldly aura upon her. "Mae! Can you hear me?"

Frustration and concern gripped him as he shook her, his grip firm and desperate. Yet her vacant stare persisted, her gaze fixed on some distant point beyond his presence. His words and actions fell upon deaf ears, failing to register in her consciousness. Determined to rouse her, he tried once more calling out her name and urging her to respond. But all he received in return was her passive resistance—a mere turn of her body, closing her eyes.

"Fuck." Lucius ran his hands through his hair in frustration, gripping the ends, torn between leaving his wife and finding his brother and Sabine.

Lucius stood, knowing they were a priority right now. She would do the same if their roles were reversed. He leaned over and left a lingering kiss on her forehead before making sure Luzia was secure on his back.

As he stepped out of the room, a sudden loud thud echoed from within their bedroom. Without hesitation, he turned on his heel and swiftly rushed back into the room. Near the foot of their bed stood a formidable figure—a faun-like demon adorned with fiery red skin and formidable black horns that curled menacingly. His presence exuded an aura of power and danger. But it was the sight within his arms that struck him to the core—his brother, Ian, lay motionless and battered, blood seeping from his wounds. Their eyes locked, and Lucius stared into the vibrant purple depths of the faun-like demon's gaze. It was a gaze that revealed his identity, shattering any uncertainty.

"Michael. Where is she?" he asked, dreading the answer but still holding on to hope.

Silently, the demon figure passed by Lucius, his steps cautious and deliberate, as he gently laid Ian on the bed beside Mae. Seeing his brother's disheveled appearance sent a pang of worry through Lucius's heart. Ian's once lustrous jet-black hair was matted with dried blood, and his usually vibrant complexion had paled.

Michael slowly rescinded back into his human form. Gradually, his purple eyes faded into a calming shade of hazel blue while his imposing black horns receded, transforming into short brown hair. Lucius asked him again, hoping to receive a response from him.

"Where is she?" He tried to keep it to a question, not a demand, but his patience was thin as he examined Ian more closely.

Seeing his brother in such a state devastated Lucius, and his heart sank with sorrow and admiration. It was evident from the open wounds that marred Ian's body that he had fought fiercely, refusing to yield. Black blood oozed from a few of the injuries. Lucius carefully touched one of the wounds, his fingertips stained with blood. Holding his finger to his nose, he inhaled deeply, his brows furrowing in concern and contemplation. The metallic scent filled his senses.

He still couldn't place the blade or creature that did this. He glanced over at Michael. Concern and guilt were etched into his features as he laid his hand on Mae's forehead. His hand glowed as Michael healed Lucius's wife, giving her some of her essence back.

As she took a deep breath, magic surged within her, filling her lungs. Once ablaze with a fiery red hue, her eyes became glistening silver. A dark, swirling mist materialized, flowing from her parted lips. It cascaded like a shadowy waterfall, gracefully spiraling and intertwining with the air around her. The inky tendrils seemed to dance with a life of their own, embodying the magic that coursed through her veins.

"Open the window *now*," Michael urged.

Lucius rushed to the window, opening it briefly before the black mist seeped out and vanished.

"She was poisoned," Michael revealed, then walked toward the door. "I believe I got it all, but I need to get the Water d'Silver."

The Water d'Silver, a precious and revered healing liquid derived from the mystical Silverlands, possessed extraordinary rejuvenating properties. This elixir could restore vitality, accelerate the healing process, and ensure the toxins had left her body.

Knowing this, Lucius still approached the door with a determined expression. He swiftly positioned himself in front of it, blocking the way. The presence of his determined figure did not surprise Michael, for he had expected this. Still, Michael remained silent, making no move to talk.

Lucius could not take it anymore, even though he knew the answer. His voice still cracked as he boomed, "Where is my daughter? What happened to her? Tell me *now*."

Michael took a cautious step back. Guilt was riddled all over his face, confirming Lucius's suspicions. "He has her. Estelle and Alecia came."

"Fuck. They took her." Lucius tried everything he could to keep himself calm, but he wanted to break Michael in half even when he knew he did everything he could to protect Sabine. He had his child to look after.

"We fought as hard as possible but had to protect Zarius."

"We will get her back," Mae promised from the bed as she sat up, her voice already stronger. She touched Ian, letting her magic flow and heal him.

Lucius went to her as Michael left to grab the water.

Ian gasped when the last of his wounds closed and opened his eyes. "Michael," he stammered, frantically searching the room.

"I'm right here." Michael handed Lucius the small bottle of ethereal water before moving to Ian's side.

Lucius opened the bottle and brought it to his wife's mouth, gently pouring it in.

"I know where she is and what he wants," Mae confessed through sips, defeated. "And I know you don't approve, but we must follow Arabella's plan."

"No," Lucius said adamantly. "Anything could go wrong. You know it's too dangerous. We can't trust her."

"We have no choice, Lucius. He will let her go if I go to him, and I will be able to get close enough to touch the orb to him. We can bind his powers and erase his memories, then lock him away with Lilith so they can be together forever."

"No, he must be destroyed." Lucius stood, walking over to the window to check his frustration and anger.

It would be fitting for Lilith, the mother of vampires, to rot together with her natural-born son. All this was done so Alazar could free Lilith and restore her powers. And what made it worse was his sick fucking obsession with making Mae his queen. He wanted him destroyed, not imprisoned. Mae and her damn kind heart.

"But you know we can't," she argued back. "It would offset the balance of the realms. It is the same reason Lilith cannot be killed. I know this is dangerous, but it is our only choice. Either way, I have to go to him to get Sabine back. She is more important than anything else. You know this."

Lucius hated it all the more because she was right. Their daughter was more important than anything, but that didn't mean he didn't hate *this*. If they went through with Arabella's plan, there was a chance he could lose Mae and Sabine forever. His heart would not be able to take it. He had heard of many who died of a broken heart when their families had died. He'd never fathomed such an idea until now.

"Where is Zarius?" Mae asked Michael.

"He is in Evictus with my parents. Safe."

Mae nodded, surely knowing he would not tell her the exact location. Alazar had stolen enough secrets from her, so they had to be cautious. "I am going to summon her."

Lucius helped her move to the floor to lean against the bed. "Are you sure?" He gazed into her eyes, needing to know. There was no turning back if this was the way they were headed.

She reached out to touch his cheek. Her hand warmed as she poured her love into him.

Trust me, love. This is the only way. Her words whispered through his mind before she moved her hand away.

"Michael, go to Zarius," she said before leaning back against the bed and closing her eyes.

Michael touched Ian, and they disappeared before him.

Mae's eyes fluttered open as soon as they were completely gone, revealing a radiant silver glow within their depths. Slowly, the magic within her awakened, and intricate symbols began to emerge, tracing a mystical path along her arms. They glowed with a soft luminosity, piercing through the room's darkness, casting an ethereal light upon her surroundings.

The symbols grew bolder, crawling upwards as if driven by an unseen force until her entire being was covered. They painted a mesmerizing tapestry upon her skin, a testament to the magical forces that coursed through her veins.

"I love you. We will find each other again. No matter what happens," she said as tears fell down her cheeks, and she grabbed his wrists. Magic shot through his body, paralyzing him.

Mae, no. This wasn't part of the plan.

She couldn't leave him behind. They were supposed to do this together like they always had.

His brows creased in panic. "Mae. *Mae*, what are you doing?"

"What needs to be done," she said before his world turned black.

Carmarthen, 1859

Lucius

"You will never find her. She is his forever," the white-haired witch cackled. Her silver eyes filled with laughter bore into Lucius's as he held his sword, Luzia, to her throat. The blade pushed against her smooth, tan skin, causing droplets of blood to run down her neck.

"Tell me where they are, and I will consider allowing you to keep your life."

He chased her across the realms for weeks, trying to capture her. His wife was missing, and the only person who knew where she had been taken was this witch, Arabella. They never should have trusted her.

Now, he had finally cornered her here, in the deep catacombs of Carmarthen, the Shadow Realm, where the Nasagals ruled—a dark, ghostly creature with hollow eyes and a ravenous appetite. Nothing lived in Carmarthen because of them. The only thing that kept them at bay was the power of Luzia and the blue gem that hung from Arabella's neck.

From the depths of the burial alcoves, the Nasagals lurked in the shadows. Their presence was felt rather than seen. Their dark forms blended seamlessly with the surrounding darkness. Observing with insidious intent, their malevolent eyes fixated on the unfolding scene.

Arabella now sat on her knees on the dirt floor, laughing at him.

As Lucius stood poised to strike, the Nasagals waited in anticipation, knowing that his act of violence would be the catalyst they sought. They hungered for the moment when he would snuff out her life force, and her body would become an offering to their insatiable appetite.

"Kill her. Drain her," Luzia whispered into his thoughts. Warmth poured from the hilt of his sword, caressing and encouraging him to lift his blade and swing.

The temptation to end it all in swift vengeance gnawed at Lucius's core. The power to snuff out Arabella's existence lay within his grasp, but he knew that he couldn't succumb to the allure of revenge just yet.

Every fiber of his being screamed for justice, for retribution against the one who had torn his family apart. Yet he understood that the key to rescuing his daughter, Sabine, lay with Mae, his wife. The desire for immediate vengeance battled fiercely against the burning urgency to locate Mae. Lucius knew that to save his family, he had to exercise restraint and patience.

His jaw clenched with determination, Lucius vowed to stay his hand for now, to bide his time until the opportune moment arrived. He knew that Arabella's demise would be inevitable, but first, he had to find his wife. Lucius steeled himself against the consuming flames of fury, for the well-being of their daughter hinged upon his ability to find and join forces with Mae.

Without Mae, all would be lost. *He* would be lost. And so, the witch's death must wait for now.

"I will give you *one* more chance. Tell me where she is," he gritted through his teeth.

"Never. Kill me, you filthy spawn of a demon. She should have killed all of your kind when she had the chance," Arabella spat, wiping the blood from her neck and then slowly licking it from her finger, exposing her rotten yellow teeth and black tongue. She smiled.

To humans, her beauty was no match. Her smooth skin, sensual lips, and alluring eyes captured males and females as she lured them into her nest and ate their hearts in an attempt to keep her youth. Her teeth and tongue were the only signs of her true age and corrupted heart.

Many moons ago, Lucius had cautioned his wife against her, but she chose not to listen to him, and now the bitch was responsible for kidnapping her and his child and giving them to *him*.

His grip on his sword tightened as he tried to control the anger simmering inside him. Lucius was trying to contain it, but the more she didn't tell him what he wanted to hear, the more it boiled beneath the surface, waiting to erupt.

He pressed his blade deeper.

Arabella's laugh erupted, a cruel and mocking sound that filled the air with its venomous tone. Her taunting words twisted the knife of jealousy deep within Lucius's chest, stirring a mixture of anger, frustration, and an overwhelming sense of helplessness.

"He must be having such a wonderful time with her," she jeered, her voice laced with malicious delight. "It's been weeks now. I'm sure Alazar's had plenty of fun with her. He is quite handsome and charming," she added, her eyes rolling in a cruel tease that sought to inflict maximum pain. A moan of pleasure followed by another bout of laughter punctuated her words as if reveling in the imagined pleasure Alazar might be experiencing.

The mention of Alazar's touch, his lips caressing Mae's body, sent a surge of fiery emotions coursing through Lucius.

Arabella's voice turned to a haunting whisper, a deliberate attempt to amplify his torment. "To run his lips all over her body," she breathed, her words laced with a wickedness that cut deep.

Distracted, consumed by the bitter sign of betrayal and jealousy, Lucius failed to notice the Orb of Gilean clasped within Arabella's hands. His focus remained fixed on the tormenting words that flowed from her mouth, and his sword raised defiantly in the air as he prepared to strike.

"Never!" he declared, his voice a resolute roar that pierced through the air, drowning out the echoes of Arabella's taunts. With unwavering determination, he swung Luzia downward, the weight of his emotions propelling the blade toward its target.

Unbeknownst to Lucius, the Orb of Gilean crackled with an ominous energy, its power pulsating in the witch's hands, waiting for the sacrifice it needed to begin its work.

"LUCIUS, DON'T!" a woman's piercing scream shattered the air, but it was too late.

The momentum of Lucius's swing could not be halted, his sword cleaving through the air with lethal intent. Arabella's head detached from her neck, tumbling gracelessly to the ground, while her lifeless body slumped, a gruesome fountain of blood gushed forth in a horrifying display. A wicked smile remained etched upon Arabella's face, frozen in a haunting expression of twisted satisfaction.

A heavy silence hung in the air, broken only by the steady flow of blood pooling beneath Arabella's lifeless body.

"Lucius. Oh no," the woman whispered.

That voice… He knew that voice. Lucius turned to find Alecia behind him. The Nyonian Diamond she held above her head illuminated her fiery red hair. Her green eyes lifted from Arabella's body to stare at him with sadness.

"What have you done?" she gasped.

Lucius gripped Luzia tighter. "Where are they?" he growled. He couldn't believe his luck. Arabella may be dead, but here was the woman who could take him straight to both his wife and child.

"All will be lost unless you remember…" she sighed.

A sudden tremor rippled through the room as Lucius stepped forward, jolting him off balance. He struggled to find his footing amidst the chaotic shaking, his muscles tensing as he fought against the disorienting forces.

A dizzying whirlwind of motion engulfed him, spinning the world around in a vertigo-inducing frenzy. The walls became a blur of colors and shapes, blending into a maelstrom of confusion. Alecia, too, was swept away in this swirling vortex, her figure fading into eerie chaos. His surroundings became a blur of fragmented images, a montage of memories and possibilities colliding in a cyclone of uncertainty. Time seemed to lose all meaning, and reality twisted and contorted with every passing moment until nothing was left.

Alecia

"There, there. You tried to warn him, but you were too late," Alazar snickered as he appeared behind her. Lucius lay unconscious on the floor as his memory was manipulated to fit the demon's new narrative.

She was too late. *Fuck*. She had gotten lost within the catacombs twice, and the Nasagals' hungry glares did not help.

Alazar picked up the Orb of Gilean, gazing at its intricate symbols and silver glow. "It still amazes me how such a small thing could be so powerful." He slipped it into his pocket.

This was too much. She needed to stop him. His promise to make them whole was not worth making him ruler of the realms. Too many innocent people had died already. She couldn't let him reach Odessa to manipulate her memory. Thankfully, she had escaped, but with the orb activated, he planned to create a world where he ruled, and she would have no place to hide.

"He is a stubborn fool and will always be. I plan to give him a terrible fate." Alazar laughed. "Come, we have much to do, and your sister waits. Or you can always stay and receive a fate worse than his."

He walked out the door, leaving Alecia to decide.

The thought of her sister, Estelle, vulnerable and entangled in Alazar's clutches made her cringe with a mix of fear and determination. Deep down, she knew she had to protect her sister, even if that meant protecting her from herself.

Waiting in Askaria like a wounded, misguided soul, Estelle stirred a whirlwind of emotions within Alecia's core. The image of her sister, once so vibrant and full of life, reduced to a pitiful figure longing for the return of a man who would only bring her harm, pierced Alecia's heart. Though a part of her whispered to take her chances and flee, to escape the clutches of this treacherous world, Alecia's love for her sister prevailed. She knew she could never abandon her sibling. She was the only family she had left.

It was a bittersweet realization, for in protecting Estelle, Alecia knew she would have to face the perils of Alazar's web once more. The danger that lurked in the shadows threatened to consume her, but she steeled herself, drawing strength from the bond she shared with her sister. She knew the journey ahead would be treacherous and the path fraught with uncertainty, but the unbreakable bond between sisters fueled her resolve.

Reluctantly, she turned to follow him out the door when a silvery glint caught her eye.

Luzia. She quickly bent down and said a spell she prayed would save Lucius from his fate before she walked out to deal with her own.

CHAPTER ONE

PATIENCE

"If it isn't Patty. Still trying to find your coven?" Annoyed silver eyes peered at Patience through the cracked dressing room mirror as she watched Selene wipe the makeup off her face.

After trying to burn the image of a naked Selene from her eyes and brain, Patience had finally gathered her strength and made her way backstage, mentally preparing herself to talk to the witch... turned exotic dancer.

She had easily passed their idiot security, who was too busy chatting up some blonde to notice her walk right past him. Selene wasn't hard to find, either. She was the only one with her dressing room, if she could even call it that, with the dingy brown couch in the corner, the vibrant array of cheap beauty products, and the ripped dressing screen. The only things that made it a dressing room were the clothes thrown about and the makeshift table made of a weathered wooden plank. It found support on mismatched milk crates, their rough edges contrasting with the delicate items displayed. A tattered red laced doily added a touch of femininity to the rugged setup.

The last time Patience had seen Selene was five years ago, and she was working as a waitress in a small diner on the west end. *How the hell did she get here?*

"No, but it seems to me you have found a new profession."

Selene sprayed her silver hair with some kind of hair product in a green bottle before turning toward Patience. "Well, waitressing wasn't cutting it, and here I get to set my hours, and I get paid triple what I was making at the diner. I needed to lay low for a while. What's it to you? What do you want?"

Her irritation was clear; she was not happy to see her, but Patience could do nothing about it. "I need your help."

"Look, Patty, I already told you. You are not a Silverlands witch. Trust me, you don't want to be one right now anyway."

Hearing Selene tell her she didn't want to be a Silverlands witch was almost funny when that was all she'd ever wanted. She still remembered when she'd told her she was not part of their coven. She knew her chances of being part of the Goddess's sacred coven were slim. However, she still had hope, which Selene had promptly shattered, albeit unknowingly, especially after so many other covens had rejected or failed to claim her.

Selene simply did not understand how wonderful or at least nice it was to be around people familiar to her. She wondered why she didn't want to be a Silverlands witch. Why didn't she want to be a part of a coven?

"If any other witch could help us, I would ask them, but they can't. We need you. So why wouldn't I want to be a Silverlands witch?"

Sighing, Selene stood, dropping her robe. Patience shut her eyes and turned away. She heard Selene moving across the room. Peeking cautiously through her fingers, she saw Selene's smooth olive-skinned butt disappear behind the pink flowered dressing screen in the corner.

"Because we are being hunted."

Someone was hunting Silverlands witches? Could it be the half-demon? It would make sense. "Hunted by who?"

Selene's voice came out over the dressing screen, "We don't know. That is why many of us have left this realm. There used to be at least thirty of us, and now we are down to six, myself included."

It *had* to be the half-demon, then. He must know that they needed a witch to keep Lilith locked away. "Do you know where the other five are?"

Selene stuck her head out from behind the screen and looked at her suspiciously. "Patty, why would you need to know that information?"

"Because I think I might know who is hunting you all."

Selene stepped out from behind the screen, thankfully, this time fully clothed. Sitting back down at her dressing table, she put on a pair of knee-high green stiletto boots. They looked sexy as hell on her. Patience wondered where she could get a pair like them.

"Are you just going to leave me in suspense, or will you tell me?"

Patience sighed, "Yeah, it's the reason I'm here. We found the King and Queen of Evictus. Not only were they being hunted as well, but they were looking for their missing son, who they found."

"Get to the point, Patty."

Patience really hated when Selene called her Patty, but she had corrected her too many times before. She had no effort to fix it now. Thanks to Alden, she knew her real name wasn't even Patience, so it didn't matter what she called her anyway. "My point is the creature who is hunting you is a half-demon believed to be the son of Lilith, and he is trying to set her free."

Selene looked at her for a moment and then laughed. "You expect me to believe that Lilith had a son? That would mean he would be as old or even older than the Goddess. Besides, the Goddess would have told us about this threat."

"Speaking of, where is the Goddess?" Patience asked as she strolled over to a gorgeous leather jacket that caught her eye. The Goddess had been missing almost as long as King Kieran, the Demon King. She realized she never asked Kieran if he knew where the Goddess even was. She doubted he would tell her anything, but you never knew until you asked. There was no harm in asking questions... Well, that all depended on who asked them, too.

Selene finished zipping up her boots. "You know I can't tell you that even if I knew the answer. How exactly do you need me to help?"

"Look, I'm not sure of all the details, but I know the King and Queen of Evictus need your assistance. The half-demon has taken over Askaria and may have found a way to Euphoria. He is trying to free his mother. If you come with me, they can explain everything."

Selene put on her leather jacket and grabbed her purse, making Patience hopeful that maybe she had gotten through to her. That was until she ran her hands through her hair, turning it fiery red, and then she put on her sunglasses with a smirk. "As much as I would love to help, I like my life more and have a date. If I am going to die, then I at least need to get laid first. Ciao."

She blew a kiss and vanished into thin air. So that's how it felt when she did that. Patience should have known Selene would not make this easy. She wondered for a while after first meeting her why the Goddess would have chosen to make Selene one of the first witches, but then again, she could ask the same question about herself.

Sighing, she closed her eyes and transported herself back to GreyJoy.

The Olde GreyJoy Bookstore is her favorite place in all the realms. The only place she could truly call home.

To humans, it looked like an old, deteriorating brick building, but to Etherians, non-humans, it was a treasure trove of knowledge.

While receiving information was free, a price had to be paid to take the information.

An Etherian could obtain any books if they exchanged them with something of equal value. It usually wasn't a currency. Whenever someone took a book from GreyJoy, he gave up a piece of himself and asked for the same—a fair exchange.

It was one of the things Patience loved about GreyJoy: He was free with his knowledge. He wanted everyone to have what they needed no matter who they were. To him, receiving knowledge wasn't dangerous because it all depended on how it was used. So, as much as she hated that he let any Etherian walk through his doors, she also couldn't deny his reasoning.

Taking a deep breath, she mentally prepared herself before walking back through his doors since she sort of... almost... had a small... minuscule mental breakdown before she left.

That damn vampire was the reason behind it, but she needed to push Lucius from her thoughts. She had other things she needed to concentrate on.

As soon as she walked through the door, his smell hit her. *Sandalwood.*

She looked around, thinking she would see him, but he was absent. *This bond must be finally getting to me.*

"GreyJoy," she called out, "I lost Selene. Do you know where she went?"

A note floated down; she caught it.

"Off the grid, as you would say."

Patience sighed and walked over to the counter, putting her head down. How had she gotten herself into this mess? Oh yeah, her one night of fun. She just had to have a night off. She had known that day would be different, but this was not what she was going for.

The urge to cry came at her in full force. Her feelings were still all over the place.

She still couldn't believe Lucius had created a blood bond with her, and the fucked-up thing was... she wasn't really mad about the bond. He had saved her life when they were in Calidium, but he knew what would happen if they had slept together, and he did nothing to stop them. What pissed her off the most was the fact that the damn vampire planned to break the bond without even telling her. He would not give her any choice in the matter. Not even discuss it with her.

"UGH! MEN!" she screamed to the ceiling, resting her head on the counter. She needed to wallow in misery just for a little while, and then she promised to get up. Right now, just sitting here sounded like a good idea.

She still wasn't even sure why she wanted to keep the bond. They didn't fit. Nothing about them fit... Well, not nothing. The sex was phenomenal. It was the one place they fit well, but unfortunately, that was not enough to base a relationship on.

The dreams. Their future. Their daughter.

Patience didn't understand any of it. Sometimes, she wished there was a cheat sheet to life where she could find all the answers and know how to prepare for the future. She could try to find a seer, but those were some cryptic bitches, and by the time a person figured out what the hell they were talking about, it either passed or already occurred. Besides, they were also a *bitch* to deal with. They always wanted something heart-wrenching in exchange.

No, she would figure this out. Maybe she should just break the damn bond. It could possibly make things easier for them.

Potentially, by breaking the bond with his "sworn enemy," his feelings of hate towards her might lessen. Though she had never been his enemy in the first place, maybe the removal of the threat to his brother's soul could pave the way for a platonic sexual relationship between them.

Ugh. Stupid tears.

"Thea. You've returned." Jafa, her mysterious friend from Calidium, appeared between the bookshelves, breaking Patience from her thoughts. She lifted her head, meeting his sympathetic green eyes as she wiped her tears, and he walked up to the counter. "Are you feeling better?" he asked, his tone brimming with compassion.

She noticed that in the brief time he had been here, his stubble had grown into a beard, and his short raven hair was trimmed. She wondered who had trimmed it for him. "No, but I will live, Jafa. Who—"

The scent of sandalwood hit her at full blast, distracting her from the question she was about to ask. Taking a deep breath, she searched around the area but saw the vampire nowhere. Her senses must be off.

She shook her head, trying to get herself together until warmth engulfed her. His scent, sandalwood, surrounded her again. An image flashed through her mind.

"Thea?" Jafa asked, concerned.

"Shhh..." Something was happening. The image flashed again, and pain shot through her, causing her to grab her head. Closing her eyes, an image appeared. It was... Lucius. He was sitting on a throne... a black throne with a devilish grin on his face—and staring at someone.

She tried to hold on to the image, but just as it slipped away, the angle of the image moved, revealing the person Lucius was staring at. The person was... was her.

Patience opened her eyes to find the same silver-gray eyes boring into hers.

"How did *you* get here?" Patience whispered to Lucius, shocked to see him standing before her. However, she shouldn't be shocked, considering how her days have been going lately. She wouldn't be surprised if the sky opened up and swallowed them all at this point.

"I should ask you. I was in the library; the next thing I knew, I was here. I'm assuming the damn bookstore brought me here with good reason." To prove his point, the book she had left him with was still in his hand. He was still looking for a solution to break their bond. The urge to electrify him was tempting.

"GreyJoy." He must have transported him here. She wondered why. Maybe he was finally growing on him. A note floated down to the counter.

"It was not I. You brought him here. Your pain."

She brought him *here? Holy shit.* She didn't know she could even do that like she summoned him to her side in her pain. Maybe it was the bond, though she didn't know a blood bond had that kind of power. Maybe seeking a seer won't be such a bad idea after all. She needed answers.

She passed her hand over the note, making it disappear. "Well, could you please send him back?" she requested.

"Send me back? No. You said we wouldn't find the answers in the books. Then where will we find the answer?" Lucius retorted.

That's all he could think about was breaking the damn bond. She guessed not even a bond could stop the hatred in his heart. Though, she did understand his hatred toward her kind. She never would understand his pain of losing his wife and child, but he also needed to understand that not all witches were evil. She had proven it time and time again in saving his damn life.

"We have more important things to worry about than breaking a blood bond. *We have bigger problems,*" she practically spat at him as she stood up. "The half-demon is hunting the Silverlands witches. That is why they have been so hard to find. He has been killing them off one by one. There are only about six left."

He looked as though he wanted to argue with her. Instead, he closed the book and asked, "And where did you get this information from?"

"From Selene. A Silverlands witch."

"And she is... where exactly?"

Finally, they could deal with this bond thing later. As long as they didn't sleep with each other again or exchange blood, they should be fine. Hell, it may simply fade away if they were lucky. But she was never that lucky.

"She disappeared on me and doesn't want to help us. At least, not yet. I need to talk to Estelle. I need answers that I hope she might give. Have she and Maxim talked?" She was so curious as to how their conversation was going. Finding your wife alive when she had been missing for over a century was crazy, but it gave her so much hope. Maxim didn't understand how lucky he was to have found her.

"Honestly, I don't know," the vampire confessed. She swore she saw guilt on his face before he masked it and added, "I have been too busy—"

"Trying to break the bond. I know." She wasn't at all surprised. Nothing else mattered to him other than getting untethered from her. The idiot vampire didn't understand how lucky he was to have a friend like Maxim, who put up with all his bullshit, including not even checking on him in his time of need. "Wouldn't you think checking up on your friend who just found out his wife was alive would be just a little more important?" she criticized, shaking her head.

His determination to get rid of her didn't surprise her, but she didn't think he would neglect his friend... It made no sense to her.

Maybe breaking the bond was best because she didn't think she could be with someone as heartless as him.

A note floated down from the ceiling, landing on the floor in front of him. He read it, then let it fall to the hardwood, stepping on it. It disappeared.

She smiled, glimpsing the note before he stepped on it. *She makes a good point.*

Goddess, she absolutely loved GreyJoy. He always knew how to make her feel better.

Seeing the frown on Lucius's face was worth it, even if it was a small victory, but one that surprised her, as he remained surprisingly calm. Perhaps, just maybe, he was turning over a new leaf.

"Keep it up. That contract said nothing about burning you to the ground," he threatened as he glared at the high ceiling.

She had spoken too soon, it seemed. "How about we check on your friend so I can talk with Estelle?" Walking over to him, she placed her hand on his forearm.

"So *we* can talk with her," he corrected.

His muscles tightened beneath his shirt, catching her off-guard. Unexpectedly, he placed his hand over hers, and although she shouldn't have relished the sensation, she couldn't deny the pleasure it brought. As he raised her hands to his lips for a kiss, her heart refused to remain steady. Her knees quivered involuntarily, and despite her best efforts, her gaze instinctively drifted to his lips.

Ugh... Her whole body betrayed her, especially when his silver-grey eyes brightened and his lips descended toward her.

Thump. A novel dropped to the floor, startling them from their daze.

"Sorry," Jafa blurted out, his face contorting with surprise and mild embarrassment as he picked up the book.

She had completely forgotten he was in the building, let alone standing next to them. Her cheeks flushed, and she quickly turned away.

"Umm... we should go. Jafa, do you want to come?" she asked, her voice tinged with a hint of mortification.

"I will stay here if you don't mind," Jafa replied, his tone gentle, a slight smile playing on his lips.

"Okay," she responded, a sense of relief washing over her. She closed her eyes, purposefully pushing out any lingering thoughts of the vampire beside her and focusing on her magic. Instantly, they were transported to his library within his grand castle.

Lucius

Vanilla with a hint of honeysuckle. Delicious.

Lucius wanted to bury his nose in her neck and inhale her scent all day. His fangs wanted to sink into the pulsing vein on her thigh and drink her sweet blood. His thirst for her consistently stayed with him. Growing worse when she was near. His control was wearing thin, but he had to remain strong. He couldn't let this bond become stronger than it already was.

Ever since she left, she was all he could think about. He couldn't even get through the damn book that was in his hand. The solution could have been staring him right in the face, but he could not see the words on the page. He could only see her face.

Lucius had never experienced a bond like this, but his instincts told him it was different... something *more*.

"Where do you think they are?" she said, breaking him from his thoughts. She tried to move her hand from his arm, but he kept his hand over hers, too reluctant to lift it. He wanted to be surrounded by her scent for just a little longer.

Her heated gaze rose to his.

He suppressed a groan that threatened to escape upon seeing the desire bloom within her golden eyes. Her heart rate picked up pace as his fangs pressed against his lips, aching to sink into her just as his cock wanted to push into her again... and again.

Controlling himself, he reluctantly pulled his hand away. He ignored the disappointment in her eyes and took a step back. "Not far. Come, we will find them together."

He almost held out his hand for her to take, wanting to feel her again. Instead, he walked toward the library doors, knowing she would follow.

Lucius stopped suddenly, turning and stepping close to her.

Curiosity shone in her eyes as she gazed up at him.

"We are not done. Once we deal with this, we *will* fix our little *problem*," he said with disdain before turning and walking down the torchlit hall.

The witch ran to catch up to him as they passed the empty rooms his wife had planned to fill and design long ago. She hated the mahogany wooden panels and dingy red carpet. They had planned to renovate the whole floor before that damn witch, Arabella, decided to take her life.

Lucius needed to remind himself of this constantly. It was her kind who had killed Mae. It was her kind who had killed their child. He had to break this bond no matter how strong it was.

They walked silently as they made their way to the grand staircase to the foyer. From there, they could reach the sunroom at the back of the castle. It was Estelle's favorite place, and knowing Max, he would take her there so she would be more comfortable and feel at ease.

Lucius kept his walk determined, but he listened for Patience's footsteps to make sure she still trailed behind him. As they approached the foyer to take the shortcut through the ballroom, he heard arguing instead of the moans of pleasure he expected, or at least an elevated heart rate.

"You have been gone for almost two centuries and can't even give me a good reason why you were gone so long with no contact?!" Max's voice boomed through the room.

"Max, it is more complicated than that. I wanted—I tried to, but… nothing worked. Please don't be mad at me." Estelle's crisp, clear voice was desperate.

Lucius slowed as he approached the stairs and stood to the side. He peered over the banister.

Estelle's blue eyes pleaded with Max as she knelt before him. She wrapped her slender arms around him and buried her head between his legs as she cried. Max's furious look slowly changed to sympathy as he ran his hand through his shoulder-length blond hair, his confused dark green eyes gazing down at her. His hand hovered over her head before he gave in, and his fingers sank into her light brown locks.

"I don't think we should watch this," Patience softly whispered into his ear.

He nodded slightly in agreement even when he was tempted to stay. He wanted to know what lies she would tell him. He didn't trust her.

The witch grabbed his hand and touched the wall, pulling them through and back into the library.

"We could have walked," he commented, even though he enjoyed the feeling of her hand in his. He still remembered the sensation of it against his chest as he entered... He let the thought trail off, not wanting to get sucked into it.

"But that's exactly what we did." She looked at him, confused, as she tried to let go of his hand. Instead, he turned her toward him.

"You pulled me through a wall." They now stood chest to chest. He stared into her beautiful eyes, searching for anything to repulse him, but all he found was hunger.

"Yeah, I did. And?" She raised a brow.

"*Witch.*"

Her eyes narrowed. "Oh, so we are back to that. *Vampire.*"

Such a snarky damn witch. He could shut her up. All it would take is a kiss to shut her sweet lips... No, he couldn't. No matter how deliciously tempting her lips were.

Her tongue darted out to lick her lips, causing his fangs to descend and press against his mouth again. His eyes glanced at the pulsing vein on her neck. Hunger sprang to life within him. It would be so easy to taste her. To taste her ambrosia. *Fuck. Stay focused.*

If they continued on this path, they would never break the bond, which couldn't happen.

Sighing, she moved away, picked up a book from the nearby table, and started flipping through it. "If you must know, it is difficult moving us from one place to another on my own. It consumes a lot of my magic, whereas the house has permitted me to move about freely; using minimum magic, I can easily get to where I need to go. Though, for some reason, this library—the one I'm not supposed to enter—is always the place it takes me to, most of the time without me even asking or thinking about it, which is quite interesting, don't you think? It must know this is my favorite room in the whole castle, even though I've only seen about half of it."

Her admission didn't surprise him at all. This library just had a way with the women in his life. Besides, she was friends with a damn bookstore, so it made sense. "The house gave you permission, like the bookstore."

This was his wife's favorite place, as well. He would always find her in here at all hours of the night when she couldn't sleep. Sometimes, she just walked up and down the aisle, dragging her fingers over some of the ancient titles. Most of the time, he would find her sleeping by the bay windows with a book in her hand or cuddled up on one of the chairs by the fireplace. He still remembered the many times he carried her back to their bed.

Patience rolled her eyes. "No, GreyJoy is a living entity or possibly a non-corporal creature, whereas the house is... the people who live here gave the house life. How long has this house been in your family?"

"Centuries. A local lord who thought it would protect him from our wrath gifted it to my great-great-grandfather. Though, it did not spare him the beheading when we found he was stealing from us," Lucius disclosed before he walked over to the table to find the book he was reading earlier, then realized he had left it at the bookstore. *Damn.*

"Let me guess, he then gifted it to you as a prize of some sort for defeating some Goddess-forsaken enemy?"

Lucius couldn't help but laugh. She had quite an active imagination. "No, he gifted to Ian, but he preferred the city. Then he gave it to us. For a while, I left this place but only recently came back after my..." he trailed off. *After my wife died.*

He hadn't wanted to return, but he was always drawn here. After killing Arabella, he never planned to return, but his brother and Max convinced him he needed to be here, that being surrounded by his wife's memory would help him.

All it had done was give him nightmares.

Ever since the witch had appeared in his life, Lucius realized he had only one nightmare. His dreams had been filled with the witch and their future. The image of the daughter they would have with silver-grey eyes like his and curly black hair like hers flashed before him. Over the years, the pain from the death of his wife and child had lessened.

The possibility of having joy, laughter, and... companionship in his life again didn't sound so foreign to him anymore. Being with someone and starting a family didn't seem so crazy and didn't feel like a complete betrayal.

But for that someone to be a witch?

No, that was too much for him to bear. He had already betrayed their memory enough by letting her into their home and saving her life. Allowing her into his heart would be a step too far for him. His greatest priority was breaking this bond, no matter how alluring the future seemed.

He closed his eyes and tried to shake the image.

"Got it. Touchy subject."

Opening his eyes, Lucius saw her bury her head in the book again.

He picked up another book and flipped through the pages, trying to concentrate when he realized he wanted her to ask him more questions. He wanted her to talk to him. He enjoyed conversing with the snarky witch. Despite all of his guilt, he couldn't help feeling this way.

Only if things were different if she were different... No, he couldn't think that way.

Grabbing another book, he searched through the pages, hoping to get his mind off of her and to find the solution he needed.

Although he knew, and he was certain *she* knew, they would not find the answer to their predicament in these books, neither seemed to care as they sat in silence, enjoying each other's company.

CHAPTER TWO

PATIENCE

Patience slowly glanced up from her book to find the *vampire* intently reading, still searching for a way to destroy their bond. Well, at least it looked that way. Upon closer inspection, she saw he was simply staring at the book, not actually reading it.

She wondered what he was thinking about. This was one of those moments when she wanted to peer into another person's head, even though she knew how dangerous such a power could be.

Patience wanted to see if he had buried memories of her. She thought back to the nightclub and when he had entered her mind. He'd assumed she had invaded his mind and that he was seeing his own memory, which was strange in itself because, in fact, it had been her mind he had invaded.

Now, she finally had time to think about it. It was confusing as hell and brought to the surface so many questions. Was it actually a memory or a glimpse of their future?

Her magical abilities grew every day, and she always learned something new, but to be able to see the future was a whole different ball game. It would imply that she was more than just a witch, but that was more than she could think about right now.

The real question was, how was Lucius able to access her memories? And could he do it again? She was tempted to spill it all to see if he would help her, but she still wasn't sure about him or his motives. Lucius could still be plotting her death after all, especially if they didn't find the solution to sever their bond. It would be the easiest way for him to finally break it.

Luckily for her, her best friend, Michael, was soul-bonded to his brother, Ian, whom he loved very much. She prayed nothing ever came between Michael and Ian because she believed this uneasy truce that she and Lucius were in would end in bloodshed, preferably his, if anything happened to Michael or Ian or them both.

Glancing over at Lucius, she resisted the urge to throw her book at his head to make herself feel better. But she felt he would catch it before it even reached him, which took the fun out of the notion.

The image from earlier suddenly surfaced in her mind.

Lucius lounged on a shadowy throne in a ballroom dressed all in black, looking devilishly handsome and bored. She could not tell much from the image except that the room was large and out of focus. He was the only thing that was clear.

She continued to stare, hoping to find a detail that would give her a clue as to when or where this was happening. Then, slowly, the image moved. Lucius sat up as though something or someone had caught his attention. A smirk formed on his face as mischief grew in his eyes.

Then the image shifted to her as it had done earlier.

She stood before him, a vision of elegance and allure. Her off-shoulder green and gold ballgown draped gracefully around her figure, accentuating her curves. Her curly hair was expertly styled in an updo, revealing the delicate curve of her neck. Every detail of her appearance exuded confidence and a touch of mystery.

As Lucius's gaze fell upon her, his hunger was unmistakable as the image returned to him. The intensity in his eyes was undeniable, as if he viewed her as his meal. The image of his desire flickered briefly, and in that moment, the image shifted back to her, and she swore she could almost glimpse the ghost of a mischievous smile on her double's face.

Maybe she was at a costume party, and Lucius was playing king. Keyword there: *playing*. If he were a real king, then she was screwed because then it would mean this was the past, but she highly doubted it. Even if it was the past, she knew he had never been king. She would have read it in the vampire history books. If she was seeing their future, then this had to be just a costume ball.

Because if it weren't, it would mean she would be his queen if he were king. A shiver ran through her at the thought. Now, that seemed too crazy even to consider.

If this image surfaced, maybe others would—just like in her dream—the beautiful little girl they would have together. Although she didn't see that future happening.

Lost in her thoughts, she didn't know present-day Lucius had stepped in front of her until his scent invaded her space, and his hand covered the page she was supposedly reading.

"Witch. *Witch.*" Lucius moved his hand when she finally looked up. "Witch, I have been calling you."

Her eyes narrowed, and she shifted away. "First, I have a name. And second, what do you want?"

Her heart skipped a beat as his expression mirrored the hunger she had witnessed in the image. In a blink, it was gone, replaced with annoyance.

"Perhaps we need to find this?" He placed the book he was reading on top of the one in her hands.

Huffing, she reluctantly looked down at what he was talking about.

The Blade of Sapience.

Created by Calla T'elair, a Stoven, Master of the Blade for Queen Nulna of the Fairy Trolls.

A purple double-edged blade was created to be used in the ceremony of Trolady to cut spiral herbs and to shed the blood of the Magna. Also, it can sever unwanted magical ties when used with the Spell of Seperatus.

"Okay?" She drew out the word, giving him a sidelong look.

"It says magical ties. We, you and I have a magical tie which is the blood bond. We need to find this blade and this spell."

Fuck. He was right.

"And where the hell do you expect us to find said blade and spell?"

"Well, you are a witch, and I know you don't use spells, but I am sure you can find a witch who does," he remarked matter-of-factly. "As for the blade, I know a fairy troll who at least could get us a location."

"You know we have an end-of-the-world problem going on right now, and we don't really have time to be gallivanting off to another realm in search of a blade and spell that could 'possibly' cut our bond." He rolled his eyes when she air-quoted possibly. She managed to control her laughter this time.

He growled at her.

"Don't you growl at me. We are in this whole predicament because of you."

"And you would be dead if it weren't for me!" he shouted, finally losing his cool.

Ian and Michael chose that moment to stroll into the library.

"Awkward," Michael whispered with a smirk. Patience glared at him.

"Oh, are we interrupting?" Ian asked, outright smiling. She leveled him with the same expression.

Lucius snatched the book from her and stormed off to the library's upper level. "We aren't done."

"Whoa. What did we miss?" Michael murmured to Ian.

Patience closed the book she hadn't even been reading and placed it on the table beside her. "Just another asshole moment from the enigmatic douchebag."

"Did you kick his ass?" Michael joked, but she wished she *had* kicked his ass.

"Unfortunately, no. At least, not yet!" she yelled the last part, eyes following Lucius's ascent up the stairs.

"Witch!" Lucius called down. She still couldn't believe they were back to this nonsense. She rolled her eyes, annoyed. "Tell them what you told me about the Silverlands witch."

Damn. She wanted to ignore him, but they needed to know this information.

"Shouldn't we wait for everyone to be here before I have to repeat myself?

Lucius grumbled, "They are coming."

"I am assuming this is about Selene. You found her?" Michael said, coming to stand next to her.

"Yes. I found her, but my poor eyes! I have seen more of Selene than I ever wanted to..." Patience trailed off, distracted by Max and Estelle coming in the door. Well... not Estelle.

An invisible barrier, like an ethereal wall, materialized between them. It stood resolute, denying Estelle's entry into the library. Maxim easily stepped back through, then attempted to hold Estelle's hand and enter again, but the barrier wouldn't even let one finger pass. Estelle's hand pressed against the unseen wall, her fingers meeting an invisible resistance as Max tried again.

"So, your ward does work?" Patience loved stating the obvious sometimes, especially when Lucius looked like he wanted to kill her as he walked back down the steps.

Did this mean he didn't trust Estelle? But what about Alden?

Or the ward above the library was truly broken. It had to be since it had let in his sworn enemies inside, her and Alden, but not his friend's wife. This brought up so many more questions. How could they all get into a place meant for the vampire's inner circle but not Estelle? This was all too much for Patience's brain at the moment.

"It has always worked," Lucius growled between clenched teeth.

The King and Queen of Evictus appeared down the grand hallway at that precise moment. They were a formidable couple, exuding an air of power and authority. The king possessed an intimidating demeanor, his visage marked by a menacing expression, matched by his deep bronze complexion and mane of auburn hair.

Standing beside him, the queen, of slightly shorter stature, emanated her own strength. Her brown skin glowed, accentuated by a head of curly blonde locks. Together, they embodied the essence of power.

"What is the matter?" Queen Circe asked, her voice echoing through the library's open doors.

"Nothing. We will just have to meet somewhere else," Maxim said, stepping back through the barrier.

"Wait." Patience was curious whether the king and queen could pass over the ward. "Could you both step into the library for a moment? It will only take a second."

Lucius's eyes were burning holes in her. She had a feeling he might just kill her this time, especially if her instincts were right.

The king and queen glanced at each other once reaching the threshold, communicating with their eyes as they often did. Ever since she and Lucius had found them in Calidium and they had saved her and Lucius's life, she felt like they knew something they weren't telling them. Now that they were trying to help them save their kingdom and potentially the realms, she prayed they were divulging all the necessary information they needed.

Sometimes, Patience wished she could read minds; it would probably make life easier, and secrets would be revealed faster. Unfortunately, she knew having that type of ability would be more of a pain than anything. And looking into someone's mind was dangerous and more exhausting than anything.

The queen looked away from the king and easily stepped through the doorway, which Patience wasn't surprised about. What she *was* surprised to see was the king's struggle to get through. At first, it looked like the barrier would reject him, but with some brute force, he entered. But was it because he was the King of Evictus, one of the oldest and most powerful beings in the realms, or did Lucius only trust him because of Queen Circe?

Seeing the king and queen walk through, Maxim and Estelle tried again, but she still could not get past the barrier.

"Fuck." Lucius must be wondering the same things she did, though he probably wouldn't admit to it. Also, the real question was, why wouldn't Lucius trust his best friend's wife? *Curious.*

Lucius

"I could just—" the witch tried to say, but Lucius wouldn't hear it.

Lucius

"No, we will just move this to another room. The parlor should fit us all." Lucius strode out the door, past Estelle, ignoring her. He wasn't sure how the witch was able to get past the ward in the library, but he knew the damn thing worked.

He didn't trust Estelle and would never trust her.

She was a lying, treacherous bitch. He just didn't have any proof of it. Disappearing for almost two centuries without a word. She said she was trying to get back to Max when she was summoned. *Lies.*

Max believed she had fled in the middle of the night to visit her sister. The truth was that he had caught her performing a summoning spell. She had been trying to summon a Zokarian from Enoch, the dark realm. Luckily, he'd stopped her before she could perform the last part of the spell, but she fled before he could question her, in turn taking all the evidence with her.

Zokarian were dangerous creatures who wreaked havoc on everything and everyone they encountered until they finally killed the ones they were summoned to go after. They were hard to capture and even harder to kill. Almost damn near impossible, in fact.

He also suspected she may have had something to do with his wife's death, but he could never confirm it, and so when she disappeared, Lucius was glad. If he ever found out that she was involved, Max would hate him, but he would kill her.

Now that she was back, he planned to keep a close eye on her.

Lucius went to the parlor, knowing the others were following him. He walked down the stairs and cut across the foyer to the old oak parlor with the gold-flower-patterned rug they should have thrown out long ago, but Max threatened Ian's life twice when he tried to remove it. Max was the only one who really used the room, anyway. He enjoyed reading his notes and, when he had the time, an occasional book.

Inside, Lucius went over to the mini bar and poured himself a glass of whiskey, then settled on one of the red plush couches as he watched his companions slowly enter the room.

He was admittedly surprised when the witch took a seat next to him. He should have sat in the armchair, but somehow, he knew she would find her way to him.

He cleared his throat. "Now that we are all comfortably in one room. Witch, tell them."

She sighed. "My name is Patience, and you should have the decency to use it, especially with the bind you put us in." She paused for a moment, perhaps thinking he would make the correction. It was better for him if he continued to call her witch, so he met her pause with silence. Giving up, she continued, "The half-demon is hunting the Silverlands witches. I met with Selene, and she said only six of them left, including herself. There used to be thirty."

"Where are they now? Are they safe?" Estelle asked keenly. Lucius wanted to order the witch not to tell her anything, but he didn't have to.

Patience nodded. "They are safe. Though, she doesn't know where they are. Even if she did, I wouldn't expect her to tell me. It still may be possible to get a message to them."

"Did Selene say she would help us? Especially with everything happening." Michael squeezed Ian's hand, looking at the witch with hope.

She hesitated. "Well... not exactly."

Lucius didn't realize he was holding onto hope as well until she said those words.

Lilith, his great-grandmother, could not be set free. The wrath and destruction she brought into this world almost killed most of his kind. As much as he wanted to concentrate on breaking this bond, he knew this was more important. He may not be the head of the vampire council, but he would not let his people suffer.

"Not exactly? Elaborate, witch." Lucius could swear he saw a spark come from her hand before she closed it into a fist.

Her lips thinned. "Selene can be a fickle creature and just needs some... persuasion."

"And do you think you can *persuade* her to help?" Estelle asked a little too eagerly for Lucius. She was up to something; he could feel it in his being. He didn't understand why the king and queen were working so closely with her, but more importantly, he wanted to know whether they trusted her.

"Possibly, though, I would need to find her again," Patience chimed in. "For now, we need to concentrate on convincing the councils to help. Especially the vampire council.

"If Lilith is released, she will want to rebuild her army and go after the vampires first. I will send word to Evangeline, the head of the witch council, that I am coming. Though, they may already know. Maxim, you should continue planning Michael and Ian's wedding. It might help to confuse the demon if he thinks we are not looking for him."

Smart. Lucius was going to suggest doing the exact same thing. Maybe Patience actually had some sense.

"I had some questions for you, Estelle. If you don't mind," the witch said, changing the conversation's trajectory.

Estelle looked surprised but prepared. "No, I don't mind."

"Can you tell me how exactly you were summoned and why you think it was the Goddess? Also, were other people in the Silverlands when you arrived?"

Lucius finished his drink, peering at Estelle over the rim of his glass. He wanted to know the answers just as much as the witch did.

"I was telling Max earlier. I don't completely remember everything, but I will try my best to answer."

I bet she doesn't. Lucius looked at Max's face, taking in his expression. To anyone else, he appeared calm and collected, but he was clearly pissed. The tick in his left eye always gave him away. Max didn't like the answers she had given him, and Lucius had a feeling he wouldn't like them either.

CHAPTER THREE

PATIENCE

"**I** was on my way home from visiting Alecia when a Hallow appeared. At least, I thought she was a Hallow. Jezabel was her name. She told me the Goddess needed me. She gave me this talisman, which then transported me to the Silverlands." Estelle took a pendant from within her blouse. It was a silver metal circle with red glass and a silver five-pointed star in the middle. The earth, fire, air, water, and magic symbols were etched into each star point.

"May I see it?" Patience asked, having the sudden urge to hold it to get a closer look. It seemed familiar. Although, she couldn't remember where she had seen one before.

"Sure." Estelle handed her the talisman. "When I got there, I found two Silverlands witches fighting the half-demon, Alazar I believe his name is, who was trying to get through a portal in the room I took you to. The witches tried to fight him off but failed. King Kieran and Queen Circe arrived just in time to save me."

There was a portal in the room. He was actually in the room with her. Patience's palms became sweaty as she gripped the talisman firmer and her heart pounded. *She had almost gone with him.* His words drifted through her mind. *I have always been with you.*

Her body shook as the talisman warmed in her hand. Suddenly, she couldn't breathe, like the air was being squeezed from her lungs.

Red eyes materialized before Patience, suspended in midair, their intense gaze seemingly penetrating her very soul. Her heart quickened with fear and anxiety. She couldn't tear her gaze away from the crimson orbs that called for her to come to him. A shiver ran down her spine as the red eyes pulsed with tense energy, whispering to her promises of love and power.

Her fingers went numb as pain blossomed in her chest.

"*Patience.* Look at me," a voice to her left called. She tried to turn her head but couldn't look away from the penetrating red eyes before her. "*Patience.* Look at me," the voice demanded again. They were no longer to her left but kneeling in front of her. Warm hands gently touched the sides of her face. "Open your eyes."

Cautiously, she obeyed, finding a bright pair of silver-gray eyes staring back at her.

"I need you to take a deep breath for me. Can you do that for me?" Lucius asked gently. She nodded, inhaling slowly, then exhaling. "Good girl. Now do it again."

She repeated the process until her heartbeat slowed, and the trembling stopped. After one more breath, she felt like herself again.

"I need you to let go of the talisman."

As Patience glanced down at the talisman in her hand, the red within the glass seemed to have seeped out. It had become a thick liquid and came to life, swirling and slithering like a sinister serpent, climbing its way up her delicate fingers. A mix of fascination and dread washed over her, causing her to instinctively release the talisman, her breath escaping in a gasp of shock.

"What the hell?!" The liquid continued to crawl up both her arms. The cold sensation caused her body to shiver. "Michael!"

Michael moved to her side and tried to touch her arm. When their skin made contact, a jolt of electricity surged through her veins, sending a powerful shockwave that forcefully propelled him backward. In the blink of an eye, Ian's swift reflexes kicked in, catching him just in time to prevent a painful collision with the ground.

"What the hell was in that talisman?" Lucius growled.

Patience's heart raced as she panicked. The red kept slithering up her arms. She tried to summon her magic but couldn't calm herself down enough. Fear gripped her as she turned to look at Lucius, pleading with him to save her... again.

Lucius

"Fuck," Lucius whispered.

He turned to glare at Estelle. Concern filled her face, but he didn't believe it for one moment. Then he focused back on Patience.

Her eyes pleaded with him to do something... anything. It squeezed his heart, causing him physical pain. He had to save her.

As the liquid crawled up her arms, he knew he had to intervene, sensing its potential danger. Without hesitation, he positioned his hands upon her, bracing himself for the imminent shock. In an instant, an electric current surged through him, traversing his body as he tightly grasped her biceps, forcing the crimson flow to halt its advance before reaching her shoulders.

Squeezing on her arms, he pushed down the red, trying to force it back out.

He looked at the witch and realized her eyes had rolled to the back of her head.

"Michael, if you have fully recovered, I could use your help," Lucius said calmly over his shoulders, pushing down his panic. "Max, make sure your wife doesn't disappear again."

Michael nodded to Ian, who helped him up.

"No worries. She isn't going anywhere," Max said, eyeing his wife suspiciously as she grabbed the talisman from the floor.

"What do you want me to do?" Michael said, standing near him.

"I need you to put your hands over mine and push whatever magic you would use into them so I can push it into her. We need to get this out of her."

Michael obeyed. Lucius felt his hands warm and then glow as magic traveled through his palms and into the witch, moving lower and lower down her arms.

"Where is the talisman?" Lucius demanded. He needed to get whatever the hell this was back into the damn talisman.

"Give it to me," Max commanded Estelle, barely keeping control of the anger in his tone. "*Now.*"

"It is harmless. I don't know what she did to it," Estelle said innocently.

"Estelle," Max insisted one final time. Reluctantly, she handed over the talisman. "Where do you want it, Lucius?"

"Place it in her hands."

Max kneeled, then looked over at Ian. "Make sure she doesn't go anywhere."

Ian nodded, shifting closer to Estelle.

Max then uncurled Patience's fists and placed the talisman in her hands.

"Alright, Michael. We will do this in one push because this thing is fighting me. Are you ready?"

"Yes."

"On a count of three. One, two, three... push." They moved together and pushed the red liquid down into her hands, where it seeped back into the talisman.

As the crimson liquid receded, a sense of relief washed over Lucius. Immediately, Lucius removed it from her hands and placed it on the carpet, distancing the talisman and the witch. "Patience. *Patience.* Snap out of it. Wake up." Michael tried to shake her awake, but her eyes stayed white.

"Shit. Patience. Wake up." Lucius shook her, trying to get her to move.

"Let me see if I can help," Estelle said, moving close to her. Lucius snarled, forcing her to sit back down.

What the hell did this female do to her? Think. Lucius raked his brain for any spell that may work, but it was hard when he didn't exactly know what the hell that thing did to her.

Michael placed his hands on her head and closed his eyes. His hands glowed as he gently rubbed her temples.

Lucius wasn't sure how long they stayed like that, but the wait was killing him. He hated seeing her like this. Hurt. He shouldn't care, but he couldn't help the worry that rose in him. He was about to move when her hand shot out, grabbing him before she gasped for air.

"You're okay. Take a deep breath," he directed gently. His worry wasn't going to stop until he knew she was okay.

She took two deep breaths before she visibly calmed.

"Are you okay?" he asked.

"I am. Thank you," she whispered, not letting go of his hand.

"What happened?" Lucius enjoyed the warmth of her skin, despite the situation. He rubbed his thumb over the pulse of her wrists, reminding himself of the hollow ache in his stomach. He would need to feed soon, or else he would find his teeth sinking into her sooner rather than later.

"I am not sure. Can I see the talisman?"

His expression darkened. "That is not a good idea."

She shook her head. "I don't want to hold it. I just want to see it."

Lucius relented, letting go of her hand, picking up the talisman, and displaying it in front of her.

"Can you flip it over for me?"

He turned it in his hand.

"It is a Dolem Talisman. It is used to spell a specific bearer." Patience gazed over at Estelle. "It paralyzes the bearer's magic and lulls them into a deep sleep. Only the one who spelled the talisman can wake the person."

"And where did you say you got this talisman?" Maxim asked her, the tick in his eye twitching.

"From—" Estelle cleared her throat before she said, "Jezabel."

"Jezabel Elixiaire," the ever-quiet king spoke. "She was the admiral in Lilith's army. It was said the Hallows killed her." He stood, taking the talisman from Lucius's hand. Circe shifted over to get a closer look.

"It is definitely her work." Circe examined the talisman closely, then turned to look at Estelle. Her eyes narrowed. "You said that she gave this to you, and you were transported to the Silverlands?"

Estelle nodded slowly, biting her lip. "Yes."

"It could have been spelled twice. It's not unheard of, but how did she know she would give it to Patience?" Circe pondered to Kieran, then asked, "You haven't seen her since she gave it you?"

Estelle shook her head.

"And no one else has come in contact with it?" Circe said as she turned it over in her hand.

"No, I always keep it on me. I thought it would be my only way back into the Silverlands," Estelle explained, her voice tinged with disappointment and frustration. She extended her hand, attempting to reach for the talisman, but Circe instinctively moved out of her grasp, keeping the artifact just beyond her reach.

"Can you place it on the floor for me, please?" Patience requested.

Circe gently set the talisman on the floor near her. Patience simply waved her hand over it. In a breathtaking flash, the talisman vanished from sight.

Lucius raised a brow toward her in question, but before she could react, Estelle's scream pierced the air, her voice laced with desperation and hysteria.

"NO! Bring it back!" Her movements were frantic as she rushed towards the vacant spot on the floor, her hands grasping at empty air, desperately yearning to retrieve what was lost. Her eyes filled with wild intensity. She searched, her fingers clawing at the void, unable to accept the absence of what she sought.

Max ran over to her, wrapping his arms around her shoulders. "Calm, Estelle, calm."

The witch moved over to her and placed her fingers onto her forehead. Estelle slumped into Max's arm, unconscious. "Do you have anything of hers from before that she really cared for?" Patience inquired.

"Yes, I believe I do."

"You should give it to her. I think that talisman became her lifeline, and she needs something to replace it."

Max nodded in understanding before he lifted Estelle into his arms and left the room.

Patience moved back to the chair and glanced at Lucius. From her look, he and the witch were on the same page about Estelle. They didn't trust her.

Michael touched her shoulder, gaining her attention and letting her know he was there for her. She patted his hand to let him know she understood.

Just as she was about to turn her attention back to him, she grabbed her head and screamed in pain.

CHAPTER FOUR

PATIENCE

Patience closed her eyes as unimaginable pain pulsated and a new image appeared of Lucius.

He was no longer on his throne. Instead, he stood in the middle of a ballroom bowing in a dance. She concentrated, ignoring the pain, when the image suddenly moved, and music played as he stood upright. *Her* hand reached out toward him. He took it, sweeping her up into his arms, then twirling her around. She laughed when a warm smile graced his lips as he gently lowered her, setting her delicate form down onto the hardwood floor. The tender moment lingered, an unspoken connection between them, as their eyes locked in a shared understanding.

Then he led her into a dance. She watched as they conversed. Lively classical music played around them, drowning out their conversation. Whatever she said to him made him laugh, and it was a truly beautiful sight. He looked like an entirely different person.

Patience never wanted this memory to end.

She wanted to be there already. With him. In the future.

Someone touched her head, and the image began to fade as the pain dissipated.

"Wait, no! Stop!" she cried as she pushed the hand away, but the image was already gone.

Opening her eyes, she found Michael standing over her with his hand hovering over her head. He must have healed her.

"What happened?" Michael asked, tilting his head to the side with concern.

They were all staring at her intently, waiting for her to explain, but she wasn't ready to.

All she wanted to do was go back to the vivid image that had captured her heart. It called to her to come back, begged her to make that her reality.

She wanted to make it real.

As her eyes sought out Lucius, she glimpsed the genuine concern etched in his gaze, and in that moment, an overwhelming desire surged within her—a yearning to seek solace in his embrace, to lose herself in the reassuring warmth of his presence, finding comfort amidst the chaos.

Instead, she said, "I-I don't know. I need to lie down." She stood and was about to walk toward the door when her world spun, causing her to stumble.

His hands were there to catch her.

"Thank you." She gazed into his eyes, seeing nothing but concern. He reached up and touched her cheek to wipe away the tears she hadn't known were falling. "I need... I need to go."

She stepped out of his arms and touched the nearest wall, walking through it. Though this time, instead of taking her to the library, it brought her to the room that was given to her.

Patience threw herself onto the bed, inhaling his scent. It was still on the sheets.

That was all it took for the dam to break. The tears wouldn't stop coming. All she could think about was being in Lucius's arms and seeing him smile knowing that would be the only time she would see it if they broke this bond.

Everything in her was telling her not to break the bond, but they didn't fit.

Nothing about them went together, which made her heart heavy because she knew she would have to face reality and let him go. Even when all her instincts told her not to. She wanted to blame it on the bond, but it was more.

She and Lucius were connected. They just needed to find that missing piece that would fit them together.

She tried to stop the flow of tears, but they just kept coming, especially when she knew that in order to find that missing piece, they would have to actually get to know each other and most importantly, they *both* would need to want to take that next step.

She just didn't understand how he could deny this, deny her. When even now she could feel him standing right outside her door wanting to come in, but would he?

Lucius

Lucius stood outside her door.

Michael had tried to follow her, but she held him back. He assured him he would check on her, which unexpectedly came tumbling out of his mouth.

He shouldn't be standing here in front of Patience's door. He should be interrogating Estelle; her story was missing too many details, and he wanted to know more. To fill in the gaps. Instead, he stood there listening to the sadness pours out of Patience and warring with himself.

His heart and mind were at war, and he was at the point where he didn't know if it was the bond or... whether it was something more.

He could hear the tears flowing down her russet cheeks, the heart-wrenching sobs, and he could feel her pain. He knew he was the cause of it all. All he wanted was for her pain to go away.

These conflicting feelings were slowly killing him. Part of Lucius didn't want anything to do with her, but the other part... the other part wanted... her.

It wanted to be *near* her, see her laugh and smile, and hold her.

That other part of him, the one that didn't want her, kept whispering to him that it was just the bond, nothing more. That these feelings would go away as soon as the bond was severed.

Then he remembered the dream of the child. Of the little girl with silver eyes and curly black hair just like hers. A dream of a possible future, even though he knew it wasn't real. It was the possibility of having that again after everything that had happened. The temptation to put all his hatred and fear aside and reach for it was there.

He placed his hand against the door. She was just on the other side, and all he had to do was walk through the door.

Lucius tried to summon an image of his wife and child to stop himself and to bring about all the fury and hatred he knew he should feel for the witch, but it didn't work. The image that surfaced was of the witch holding their dream child.

His heart... his heart had already made the choice for him, but his mind was in complete and utter denial even when he knocked, and his hand twisted the knob, and he found himself stepping over the threshold.

Patience stared at him as he cautiously approached the bed. Her shoulders shook as she continued to cry and gape at him, pleading with Lucius for something he wasn't sure he could ever give her.

Not being able to take it anymore, he joined her on the bed, gathering her in his arms as she continued to cry. He held her tightly, blindly saying words to comfort her. He wanted—no, needed her to stop crying. Her wrenches of pain were doing damage to his heart that he couldn't quite take. The sight of her suffering tore through him, leaving behind lasting marks of pain that resonated within his soul. He longed to alleviate her torment, to shield her from the relentless throes that threatened to consume her.

He wasn't sure how much time had passed until he realized her sobs had turned to whimpers and then finally, silence. Her heart had slowed to a steady rhythm. She had fallen asleep.

Gazing down at her, he moved a curl from her face.

She was a beautiful creature. Looking at her like this in such a vulnerable state, no one could tell how determined and proud she was. She had no fear of him at all. Almost all witches he encountered would tremble at his approach. Witches used the tales of his hunting days when he was the Ragana Zidikas to scare their children, and that was what he preferred. But Patience merely laughed at him outright or with her beautiful almond-shaped eyes crinkling at the corners in amusement.

All he wanted to do was suck on her soft and luscious lips as he buried himself deep inside her. The sound of her moans filled his head. *Maybe one kiss wouldn't hurt.*

Lucius leaned down and was about to kiss her when a soft knock sounded on the door. He gently laid her down, hating himself for leaving her. If he could, he would lay here with her all day and night, if only things were different.

Another knock sounded, this time just a tad louder.

He got up and practically ran to the door, not wanting to disturb her. As he swung the door open, revealing Ian and Michael on the other side, a flicker of annoyance crossed his face.

Their presence didn't come as a surprise. They still harbored suspicions, believing him to be a threat to her life. At least, not at this moment. A different reality consumed his thoughts, distant from the notion of harm. Though, the prospect of killing her to alleviate his troubles always lingered in the recesses of his mind.

He met Ian and Michael's gaze with a weary expression, his eyes betraying a hint of conflict and contemplation. The weight of his predicament hung heavy in the air, overshadowing any immediate confrontation.

Lucius stepped from the room, shutting the door softly behind him. "She is asleep. We shouldn't disturb her. She needs her rest."

"See?" Ian announced. "I told you he wouldn't kill her. The bond wouldn't let him kill her even if he eventually wanted to," he explained to Michael like it was no big deal.

He shook his head as he walked past them, rolling his eyes. "If you wake her up, I will kill you both. Brother be damned."

Lucius returned to the parlor, hoping that Estelle was awake and calm so he could ask her some questions. Arriving, he found Estelle embracing her sister, Alecia. Max must've sent word to her. They pulled apart, and Lucius saw she had a silver chain with Max's wedding ring hanging around her neck as he walked into the room.

"Alecia."

She nodded in greeting.

"You are just in time. I just had a few more questions for your sister."

"I also have questions for you, starting with why the King and Queen of Evictus are in your house?" Alecia snipped, narrowing her eyes.

Lucius stiffened. "Well, that is something your sister can answer since, from what I am learning, she has been working with them for over 150 years."

Alecia swiveled to face Estelle. "What? Is this true?! You have been with them this whole time? I've been worried sick and looking for you everywhere!"

When Estelle disappeared, Lucius wanted to confide in Alecia about what he had seen Estelle doing that night, but he wasn't sure just how much he could trust her. She was still part witch, and he knew how witches loved to play their games. Well, except one witch it seemed.

Estelle and Alecia were once close, and if he wouldn't betray his own brother, she wouldn't betray her sister, even if she didn't like what she was doing. No matter how many years had passed.

Loyalty could be a real killer if you gave it to the wrong people.

"I am sorry, but the Goddess needed me, and now we may have found a Silverlands witch to help us. I will be able to come home," she retorted, walking over to Max and taking his hand. He still didn't look so happy with her.

"You found a Silverlands witch? Patience?" Alecia looked toward Lucius to answer the question.

He cleared his throat. "No, but she was able to find us one. They are being hunted. Many have been hiding, so it hasn't been easy to find them. It could also be why we haven't heard from the head of the witch council."

No need to give her any more information than necessary. It was bad enough that Estelle would tell her anything they divulged anyway. He was going to have to explain to the witch about Estelle and Alecia, that as long as they were together, she shouldn't divulge anything vital. He didn't trust Alecia not to tell her sister essential information. Though, part of him knew she already had her guard up.

"It's good that you are here, Alecia. You will be able to help Lucius and Silas to convince the council members to help in our plight to stop the half-demon from freeing Lilith."

Lucius glared at Max, who merely raised an eyebrow at him. Apparently, Lucius was going to have to tell Max as well.

"Huh? What the hell is—" A dagger sliced in front of her face, silencing Alecia.

Lucius tensed, turning just in time to see another dagger head toward him. He quickly moved aside, almost evading it right before it struck the fireplace. A drop of blood ran down his face, as it still managed to cut the side of his head. *Shit.*

He saw a Hokima, an Askarian assassin, looking toward the doorway, staring at him with its luminescent eyes. Max grabbed Estelle, twisting her out of the way as the king and queen dashed to the side of the room out of their line of sight. Lucius acted quickly, jumping behind the couch as the assassin threw another dagger his way. Alecia joined Lucius behind the sofa, placing her hand on the ground to erect a shield around them.

"That won't hold him," he blurted, his voice tinged with concern.

Alecia's brow furrowed, her eyes narrowing as she looked over the edge. "You mean them? Who exactly is them?" she questioned with disbelief.

Them? Lucius peered over the edge of the couch. His eyes widened with surprise and annoyance as two pairs of radiant white eyes now stared back at him. Two Hokima assassins, clothed in black attire from head to toe, used their menacing red daggers to expertly pierce through the shield. The barrier slowly weakened under their relentless assault, threatening to crumble within seconds. In a desperate act, he pressed his palm against the floor, channeling his magic to reinforce the defense, buying them a few more minutes.

"Do you still have the Blades of Flux?" Queen Circe said calmly as she and King Kieran joined them behind the couch. *Where were Max and Estelle?*

"They are back wherever Max keeps my other weapons hidden. Only he can get them. Did you see where Max and Estelle went?"

Alecia cautiously looked around the edge of the couch, her eyes widening in alarm as she focused on the other side of the room. "They are hiding behind the clock," she whispered, her voice filled with fear and urgency. "But we have another problem. They have gotten through," she added.

Lucius peered over the edge of the couch and saw the shield disappear as the two assassins stepped into the parlor. Behind the Hokima assassins, a sinister presence emerged, revealing the lurking Tral'goth demons that had remained hidden until now. Adorned with scales and sharp fangs, their reptilian forms sent a shiver down his spine. The ancient yellow eyes of the demons scanned the room with a predatory intensity, and their gaze fixated on the surroundings as they searched for their targets.

He watched intently as the Tral'goth demons slithered with serpentine grace, their elongated bodies undulating in a chilling dance. The sound of their slithery tongues brushing against the floor echoed in his ears, evoking a primal instinct within him to act until they vanished before his eyes.

Damn, he needed the witch and his sword.

"We need a—"

A bloodcurdling scream came from near the clock. They all stood to see Estelle being thrown over one of the Hokima's shoulders as Max fought the other. The assassin was trying to stab him. King Kieran flew past them, gripping an invisible entity and flinging it toward the wall. The Tral'goth momentarily appeared as it slid down the wall, only to scramble back up and disappear again. *At least they had someone who could see them.*

Lucius moved to help Max as Alecia and Circe went after Estelle.

It wasn't easy pulling the assassin off of Max. "Damn, these sons of bitches are strong."

"And fast. Move!" he exclaimed, his words laced with a sense of command and a hint of panic.

Lucius swiftly dodged to the side, narrowly avoiding the assassin's lunge as their blade sliced through the air. But before the assassin could recover, Kieran sprang into action, moving with unparalleled speed. In a blur of motion, he intercepted the attack, stopping the blade with his own weapon and thwarting the threat with swiftness.

Before he could grab the dagger, a searing pain sliced through his leg, then up his back. A sinister tongue snaked its way around his neck, aiming to seize hold of his chest. He grasped onto it, desperately attempting to pry it off and break free from its grip.

Max reached down to retrieve the red dagger. A piercing scream escaped his lips as he involuntarily released the weapon, causing it to clatter to the ground. A veil of smoke swirled from his left hand, permeating the room with the acrid scent of burnt flesh. Grimacing in pain, he cradled his singed hand against his chest, his focus now shifting to helping Lucius.

Max scrambled to his feet, doing everything in his power to assist in freeing Lucius from the relentless grip of the creature on his back.

The demon only dug its talons deeper, causing him to fall to his knees. The pain was excruciating.

The Tral'goth was almost as strong as the Hokima, which made sense since the creature was its counterpart, except an Anduril Blade, which was the only thing that could kill a Tral'goth. It was one of the reasons why the Hokima were so deadly. If they didn't kill you, their Tral'goth would.

The deeper its talons dug in, the more Lucius's strength gave out. He almost wanted to give in until his sword, Luzia, clattered to his feet. Without a thought, Lucius picked it up and sliced the tongue off.

The demon cried out as it released its talons. He turned to see Max holding the Anduril Blade in his uninjured hand. *It had to be the witch, but where was she?*

"Max, we need the Blades of Flux."

The king was still fighting the Hokima. So far, he had prevented them from taking out the double-edged Blade of Valhal. If they managed to get it out, he had a feeling they would be no match for the king.

"The other one may still be around here." Max handed him the Anduril Blade before he walked out the door.

Lucius went to join King Kieran in holding off the Hokima, praying Max would get back in time to kill this thing. Or maybe the witch would take this opportune moment to help them.

CHAPTER FIVE

PATIENCE

"Michael! Move!" Patience screamed as a Hokima assassin appeared in the bedroom doorway with one of their black Gutrend spikes ready to strike just as Michael was about to leave.

She slammed the door in time right before the spike embedded itself in the wood, then threw up a shield, knowing it would only buy them a few minutes if not seconds. She had no clue how they were getting past the damn barrier around this place. What was the use of having a protective barrier if it didn't protect?

She had woken with a start, feeling a shift in the air. Michael told her it was remnants of the trauma she experienced, but this was different. Her spidey senses were sending her a loud and clear warning. She couldn't ignore it. And thank Goddess, she didn't because she saw the Hokima as soon as it appeared. She had almost thought it was a mummy from how it was wrapped in black cloth until she saw its luminous white eyes and the Gutrend spike at the ready. As soon as her brain kicked in, she reacted.

With her shield in place, she seized Ian's arm, who then grabbed Michael, and together they ran to the closest wall. She touched it and stepped through, but instead of taking her to the library, it brought her to the foyer just in time for her to find Circe and Alecia trying to pry Estelle from yet another Hokima assassin.

Patience used her magic to create a looped rope and threw it around the Hokima's legs while it was distracted, tripping it and forcing it to release Estelle before it hit the floor. Patience managed to catch Estelle midair with her magic, but before she could put Estelle down, the Hokima was already back on their feet.

Summoning more magic, Patience lifted the Hokima into the air and then slammed it into the wall, knowing it would barely stun the damn thing. What she needed was the Truesilk. It was the only thing that could slow them down long enough for her to kill it. She had sent it back to her vault after the last attack. It would take her a moment to summon it. Without it, that damned vampire was her best bet. Fuck, she really needed Lucius.

Estelle still hovered in the air, strangely calm as she watched the scene below. Patience kept slamming the Hokima against the walls, hoping to keep it occupied.

Michael stood behind her, touching her shoulders, giving her strength and pushing his magic into her while Ian stood ready to protect him if the Hokima came for him.

"If anyone has any bright ideas, now would be the time to share them!" Patience yelled in the direction of Circe and Alecia.

"Keep it occupied. I might have a spell that may work," Alecia hollered back, moving to grab a broken candle on the floor.

Patience sometimes forgot that other witches needed to use spells and she only needed to use them for certain things. Magic came naturally to her and took her less than half the time. Though, she still drained magic like other witches.

She needed to put Estelle down. Thinking quickly, she threw the Hokima up the stairs and then opened the front door. Before the Hokima hit the bottom step, she picked it up and tossed it through the door, slamming it and putting up her shield. Then she placed Estelle on the ground.

"That won't keep it for long!" Circe shouted as she helped Estelle up.

"I know. Shhh... I just need a moment." Patience closed her eyes, summoning the Truesilk. A soft thud sounded on the hardwood floor, letting her know the Truesilk was before her.

A thunderous boom rumbled behind them as the front door croaked. They only had seconds left. Quickly, she summoned Luzia, Lucius's ancient sword, and sent her to him as well as the Anduril Blade because she had a sickening feeling he would need it more than they would.

When she opened her eyes, Estelle screamed as another Hokima jumped from above and landed in front of her. Unsheathing a pair of lethal red daggers from its back, it stalked toward Estelle.

In the same moment, the other Hokima smashed through the door and her barrier. Its white eyes glowed brighter as it swiftly moved toward them. *Damn, two assassins.*

They needed the Blades of Flux. The only thing that could actually kill them. They were made from a flux metal that was found in their birthplace, under the Askarian Mountain, Vasteri. *Maxim. He has them.*

As though she conjured him out of thin air, Maxim grabbed Estelle just as the Hokima was about to snatch her again.

Patience only had one Truesilk net and two Hokimas. *Damn, decisions.* She chose to throw the net at the Hokima currently moving toward Michael. Using her magic, she wrapped the net tightly around it and lifted the Hokima before tossing it out the door again. She slammed her shield back in place.

As her gaze swept across the room, Patience's eyes fell upon the chaotic scene unfolding before her. Circe, Ian, and Maxim fiercely struggled against the relentless Hokima assassins. Rage surged within her, and she swiftly harnessed her magic, summoning a potent ball of crackling electricity and throwing it at one of the Hokima, sending the assassin crashing through the wall.

Alecia's words echoed through the air as she finally finished her spell, erecting a shield around them. Patience moved toward Maxim.

"Where are the Blades?"

He hesitated, eyeing her and the others warily.

"You don't have to tell me. Just grab my hand and think of them." She held out her hand, and he grabbed it. Within seconds, the blades were clattering at their feet.

Queen Circe picked them up and ran toward the Hokima, who was about to slash the shield with their red dagger. Without any hesitation, she stabbed the assassin between the eyes. They all watched as it froze in place and abruptly shattered, crumbling into a cascade of ash scattered across the floor.

Circe turned and tossed the blade toward her just as the other assassin came crashing through the door. Patience caught it with her magic and sent the blade right into its chest. The resonating sound of the blade hitting the floor echoed within the foyer as the Hokima halted, and its body disintegrated into a swirling cloud of fine dust that scattered across the hardwood.

Relief rushed through her, but it was fleeting. Dread followed just as swiftly. She summoned the blade to her and went to the nearest wall, walking through it and heading for the parlor.

She glanced around and found the Demon King on the ground, unconscious, with a deep bloody slash across his chest and Luzia in his hand. She moved over to him and checked for a pulse. He was alive; his double hearts were still beating. She grabbed a nearby cloth from a table and placed it over the wound. It wouldn't do much besides buy her time until she could heal him.

Grabbing Luzia, she stood and searched for Lucius. A loud crash came from the hall, startling her.

She made her way toward the sound just in time to see Lucius being pinned by the remaining Hokima as she rounded the corner. *Damn.* She stopped in her tracks and quietly stepped back, hoping it didn't see her. She cautiously peered out. It hadn't noticed her yet.

She had to do something because it was strange to see the vampire in such a vulnerable position, especially after him being so aggressive toward her. Part of her wanted to bask in the glory of seeing him pinned until his pain vibrated down their bond.

Fuck. She had to help him.

He continued to fight off the Hokima with the Andruil Blade, but his movement was causing the spike to tear his shoulder blade. The pain intensified as the Hokima pushed the spike in further, causing Lucius to shudder as it drained him of strength and magic. She blocked out his pain before a scream tore from her lips.

Patience peeked her head out further. Finally, seeing her, relief crossed over Lucius's face momentarily before sudden horror took its place. With the last of his strength, he threw the Andruil Blade at her feet. There was a Tral'goth demon nearby. She called the blade to her empty hand as she leaned Luzia against the wall.

Grabbing the Hokima with her magic, she threw it down the hall and erected a shield, then she looked at Lucius and followed his eyesight.

Glancing up, she saw the demon was visible above her, ready to pounce. She turned the sharp end of the blade toward the ceiling. She had to time this right, as she would only get one chance. She let the Andruil Blade fly from her hand at the same moment she took a step back, and it pounced.

The Tral'goth dropped from the ceiling, meeting the blade, then exploded midair.

Patience tried not to think about the guts and blood that splattered on her as she hurried toward Lucius.

"See, this is me saving you... again."

"*Witch*," he growled.

"Yeah, yeah. I know. You are lucky I need you or else I would be tempted to leave you hanging like this."

She could swear she heard him chuckle, but she saw a face filled with pain when she glanced at him. It was strange to see him like this. Defeated and drained. He gazed down at her, giving her a weak smile as she reached up to pull the spike from his shoulders.

"Patience, watch out," Lucius warned.

As soon as she gripped the spike, the Hokima assassin came running at her down the hall, knocking the wind out of her as she crashed into the wall. It removed the red double-edged Valhal sword from its back and was about to bring it down to slice Lucius when Patience grabbed the Blades of Flux from the small of her back and flung them at the Hokima between its shoulder blades, causing its blade to drop to the floor. Its arms fell to its sides as it slowly dissipated into ash.

"Saved you... again. I'm not counting or anything, but I seem to have a knack for saving you, which most people would take as a sign to stop trying to kill that person. But I know you are different and need more time to process such details."

Lucius's nostril flared as he snarled, the only sign he showed of the pain he was actually in as he reached up to grab the spike. Agony vibrated down the bond. Even with it blocked, small bouts came through as he tried to pull it from his shoulders.

"If it were that easy to remove, they would not use them," Patience said sarcastically, rolling her eyes. Just as she was about to help Lucius down, a sharp pain spread through her right shoulder. She looked over at it to see the point of a black spike being quickly removed from her shoulder. Glancing behind her, she found another Hokima assassin holding the bloody spike.

She huffed, "Shit. I forgot one."

Using her last ounce of magic, she picked up the assassin, threw it into the nearest room, and erected her shield. Buying time.

Exhaustion and pain spread through her as her back hit the wall, and she slid down to sit.

Her magic was drained. She needed rest, but she had to kill the last Hokima. At least, she prayed it was the last one. She didn't have the strength to fight another.

When this was over, she had to find the flaw in the protection spell surrounding the house. Otherwise, they would be vulnerable to further attacks.

She reached out to summon the Blades of Flux to her. Nothing came or appeared. Her magic was depleted. They needed more help. She closed her eyes, trying to reach out to Michael, but all she could do was feel him.

"Ugh... I think we are shit out of luck," she said as the Hokima struggled against her shield. "I guess you finally get your wish after all." She didn't have the heart to look at Lucius. The only problem would have been the fact that he didn't get to kill her himself, but it would be something he would have to live with.

She touched the wound in her shoulder, brushing the necklace. *Alden.*

Touching the silver pendant at her neck, she said the word: *Apparitor.*

He would help. They were friends...

Alden materialized in front of her just as fatigue forced her eyes to close.

Lucius

She had saved him…again. If she kept on saving him like this, he would never be able to pay his debt to her.

Lucius's emotions were tangled and uncertain, his thoughts caught in a web of conflicting feelings, but he didn't have the luxury to dwell on in the present moment. He pushed aside his inner turmoil and redirected his thoughts. He needed to get down off this damn wall. The witch looked as though she was about to fall over, and he wanted to catch her. As she was trying to pull the spike from his shoulder, he did not see the assassin behind her as he was too occupied with helping her. Her gruntled sound made him look up as the Hokima pulled the spike from her shoulder.

Turning, she used her magic to lift and throw the assassin into the small sitting room nearby before erecting a shield over the door. Her back hit the wall just as her knees gave out.

"Ugh… I think we are shit out of luck. I guess you finally get your wish after all."

His wish? Fuck. The Hokima was going to get through the barrier.

Using the last of his strength, Lucius pulled on the spike one more time. It didn't budge. She was right; the blade wasn't coming out. The spike had stolen both his strength and his magic.

Lucius hated being vulnerable like this. He could barely speak as the spike's magic continued to drain him. He gazed at Patience, wanting to tell her these would not be their last moments. And… that… that he didn't wish her dead. He needed to tell her.

"Patience," he croaked out. "Patience."

She didn't respond.

Shit. She must have lost consciousness. Damn, where are the others?

Alden suddenly materialized in front of her in his usual immaculate all-black suit. His sleek black hair, expertly tied in a ponytail, accentuated his polished appearance, except for a single stray strand. The only hair that was ever out of damn place. The witch must have summoned him. How?

"Odessa." He stooped down, reaching out to touch her cheek.

Lucius thought back to that night. The *fucking* night when of the son of a bitch tried to kiss her. He must have given her something to summon him. Why? He still didn't understand what he wanted from the witch. A shudder of pain rolled through him, causing Lucius to groan out loud, gaining Alden's attention. *Fuck.*

Surprise filled Alden's golden-brown eyes as he stood and walked over to him. "It seems you have yourself in quite a predicament. What did you do to her?"

Gripping the spike, he twisted it.

"If you would look to your left, you would see it was not I who hurt her," Lucius grunted through clenched teeth.

Bang. Alden and Lucius glanced over to find the Hokima assassin trying to escape the barrier. Alden let go of the spike and pulled out a dark blue handkerchief from his pocket, wiping his hands with contempt.

Putting his handkerchief away, he walked over to the barrier, leaving Lucius just to hang there.

Alden stood in front of the barrier as the assassin tried to break through with no fear, just watching with curious eyes until the barrier dropped. Moving quicker than Lucius could see, Alden ripped off the Hokima's arms before it could reach for its blade. The assassin let out a horrendous screech as Alden grabbed it by the neck, bringing it over to Lucius.

"I am assuming," he grumbled as the Hokima struggled in his arms, "you have a way to kill this thing."

Lucius looked down at the Blades of Flux below him. Alden held out his hand, and one of the blades flew into it. *So, it's true. He does have magic.*

Alden swiftly stabbed their attacker in the head. It stopped struggling before it disintegrated.

"What did you do to piss off the King of Evictus?" Alden asked as he brushed himself off, even though they both knew there wasn't a speck of dust anywhere.

"I wish it were the king who sent them. At least he could be reasoned with."

Alden stared at Lucius skeptically. Lucius braced himself for the pain as Alden reached up to grab the spike. He paused, staring at Lucius, giving him time to prepare before he quickly pulled the spike from his shoulders. The vampire gritted his teeth as pain tore through him. The spike clattered away as soon as his feet hit the floor.

Not having the time or care to deal with Alden, Lucius rolled his shoulder back, already feeling it beginning to heal as his strength restored itself.

Magic flowed back through his veins as he moved toward the witch and took in her disheveled appearance, her short, tousled curls cascading around her like a wild halo. Her face, usually adorned with a confident expression, now bore the signs of exhaustion and weariness. She had used too much magic. Always too busy taking care of others before herself.

Her heart beat strongly in his ears. He checked the wound on her shoulder and found that it had stopped bleeding.

Picking her up, he walked into the parlor and placed her gently on the couch before moving to check on the king. Kneeling next to him, he listened for his heartbeats. They were beating strong, but he would need to be healed.

"The Demon King? Is he alright?" Alden asked, kneeling next to him. "His own assassins attacked him?"

"He should be fine, but he needs to be healed." Lucius stood. "Yes. It is a long story that I do not have time to explain."

"The gist of the story being that the rumors are true. You have been trying to solicit the council's help in breaking into Askaria. Have you been working with the king this entire time? You should have come directly to me with this."

Alden went over to the witch and kneeled beside her. It took all of the strength and willpower Lucius had in him not to run Alden through with Luzia. Alden moved a curl from her face, then checked the wound on her shoulder before standing.

Before Lucius lost the battle with himself, Max appeared in the doorway, disheveled and bloody. Relief washed over his face when he saw Lucius, but he still asked, "Are you alright?"

"Yes. Where are the others?"

Max stepped into the room to come stand near him. "They are making their way back here."

Multiple footsteps could be heard coming down the hall toward the parlor. Queen Circe appeared first, running to King Kieran with worry etched on her face.

"He needs to be healed," she cried as she kneeled beside him.

Alecia came over to examine the king and the damage done to him. "Estelle and I can heal him, but we need to move him."

"I can help."

Everyone but Lucius turned toward Alden, surprised to see him.

"The witch summoned him," Lucius informed them as if that was all the explanation they needed. He walked over to the king and stooped near his shoulders. Max joined him on the side. Alden and Ian grabbed a leg as Michael supported his middle. They all grunted and groaned as they lifted him.

"Fuck, he's a heavy son of a bitch. Circe, what the hell are you feeding him?" Max exclaimed. Lucius shook his head, but the queen smirked.

They slowly brought him into the dining room and laid him on the large mahogany table.

As Alecia and Estelle began their healing spell, Lucius slipped out of the room. He needed to check on Patience. Needed to know that she was alright. He wanted to blame his concern on the blood bond they shared, but he knew it was more than that. There had always been a deep connection between them. He didn't understand what it meant, but it was something he refused to acknowledge. If he did, he knew in his heart that he would give into her, and that was something he was not ready for.

He grabbed Luzia on the way into the parlor, not liking her sitting in the hall away from him. He laid her against the side of the couch before sitting down on the edge of it to observe the witch's shallow breathing. She continued to save their lives. *His* life... even when she knew he hated her kind, witches.

He didn't want to admit it, but she amazed him. Her strength and her selflessness. In a way, he admired her because in some ways he reminded her of his wife, Mae.

He reached down to gently touch the side of her face, tracing her cheek-bone until he reached her lips.

"I believe it is rude to touch a lady when she is unconscious."

Lucius snatched his hand away and stepped back from her. "She isn't a lady."

Alden took a step toward the witch, but before he could reach her, he found Luzia at his throat.

"Do... not... touch... her," Lucius drawled slowly so he could understand each word. He knew it was stupid and dangerous to have a sword at the throat of a council member, especially the head of the vampire council, but if Alden touched Patience, he would kill him.

Their connection was becoming dangerous. His feelings were becoming dangerous.

Still... "I am going to need you to back away from her."

Alden made no move to do so. Lucius pressed Luzia harder into his neck.

"I am afraid you will need to do what he says. They have blood bonded," Max said from the doorway.

Alden looked suspiciously at the both of them, then at the witch.

"Unfortunately, it is true," Patience said. Lucius glanced at the witch, finding her now awake. Alden took a step back as she sat up.

It took several more moments before Lucius finally lowered the sword.

Patience rose to her feet, then glanced at Lucius before she walked over to Alden. She was standing too close for Lucius's liking, but she kept enough space between them to keep his anger at bay.

"Thank you for coming," she said, a coy smile playing on her lips as she glanced at Alden.

"Anytime," he replied, grinning back at her.

Lucius felt a surge of irritation as he noticed Alden's hand almost rising, before he thought better of it and returned it to his side. The urge to punch him in the teeth gnawed at Lucius, but he held back. Barely.

"I take it you were able to kill the Hokima," Patience observed. "Since we all are still alive."

"Yes, easily," Alden confirmed. "Why was there one here in the first place if the king didn't send it?"

"There were four... I believe." She glanced toward Lucius to confirm.

He nodded, too irritated to speak.

"So do you want to tell him what is going on or should I?" Patience smirked, raising a brow at him in question.

"I can explain," Max interjected, but Lucius held up his hand to stop him. He would explain since he wanted to make sure Alden only got the necessary information.

"Since we have time now. The long story is that Askaria was invaded and taken over by an unknown half-demon and the king has requested help to get back into his kingdom. We planned to make a formal request to the council, but as you see, we have been distracted," Lucius explained. "But it appears as though you already knew this."

Indeed, not a hint of surprise showed on Alden's face. Lucius raised his brow, prompting him to explain.

"A few council members may have approached me in passing and told me of the matter, but in not so many details. You should have come directly to me as the head of the council," Alden said defensively.

"You were our next stop until this happened," Max chimed in.

"How long has this half-demon been in Askaria?" Alden questioned. He gazed at Patience for too long before moving to look at Max. Jealousy rushed through Lucius as his hands balled into tight fists, trying to control himself.

"For the past century, from what we are told," Max responded.

"Why is he sending the Hokima here to attack you?" Alden directed toward Lucius. If they didn't need his help, he wouldn't have told him anything. Unfortunately, they did.

"He wants Michael, my best friend, and King Kieran's son. He wants to free Lilith from Euphoria so they can take over the Silverlands together," the witch supplied. "Though, the Hokima were after Estelle. We need to continue to question her."

They were both on the same damn page. That Hokima went straight for her, so the question was why did the demon want her? She could be working with the half-demon for all they knew. Maybe it was time he spoke with the king and queen to learn how they truly met her.

"I couldn't agree more." Lucius moved toward the door when suddenly, his brother, Ian, came rushing into the room. "Patience, we need you! The king is dying."

CHAPTER SIX

PATIENCE

Dying? This may sound silly to say, but he was too old to die. Rushing into the elegant dining room, Patience was shocked to find Circe pressing a knife to Alecia's throat.

"Whoa, what the hell is happening?" she exclaimed, freezing in the doorway, her eyes wide with shock and confusion. As she stepped closer, the scene unfolded before her. Kieran lay on the sturdy mahogany dining table, his body stretched out, motionless. The rich wood grain beneath him contrasted sharply with the pallor of his skin. A hushed urgency filled the air as Michael and Estelle knelt beside him, their hands clutching white cloths pressed tightly against the gaping wound on his chest. The pristine cloths were quickly becoming saturated as black blood filled them, staining them.

Patience didn't remember him bleeding so profusely. It would have left a trail. She glanced down at the floor but only saw the few drops that had spilled from the table.

"What happened?" Lucius demanded, coming up behind her.

"She tried to kill him!" Circe shouted angrily as she pressed the knife deeper into Alecia's throat. *Why would she try to kill the king?*

"Don't kill her, please! She was just trying to help," Estelle pleaded.

Alecia stood there, stock-still, letting the queen press the knife further against her. A drop of blood dripped down onto her shirt. *So, she doesn't deny it?*

Patience moved toward King Kieran, examining him. Perhaps she could heal him. "I've never healed anyone but Michael," she whispered to no one in particular. It hadn't always been easy to heal Michael. It took practice, especially since she didn't use spells. She had to let her magic be the guide, and it would be harder this time because she was also completely drained.

"You can do it, Patience. Please help him," Michael begged.

Taking a deep breath, she was going to need help. Her powers weren't fully restored yet. She turned to glance at Lucius, and then she saw Alden standing behind him.

"I'm going to need your help." Lucius almost stepped forward until he realized she wasn't talking to him. Guilt filled her, but she needed Alden's magic. Other than the king and probably herself, he was the most powerful being in the room.

"What do you need from me?" Alden said, moving around Lucius toward her.

"I need your magic," she told him, then peered around him at Lucius. "I am going to have to hold his hand. Will you be able to control yourself?"

Anger marred Lucius's face. "Yes," he snarled. "But not for long."

"Okay. Alden, just relax. I'm not sure how much I'll need. It may drain you," she informed him. He nodded.

Michael came to stand on the other side of her. He placed one hand on her uninjured shoulder and the other on his father.

As soon as her hand touched Alden's, she could feel the surging power emanating from him, pleading for her to embrace it. It both thrilled and frightened her, the intensity of his magic's eagerness to merge with her own. She hesitated, momentarily unsure of what to do, until his enchanting magic began to weave around her, coaxing and enticing her to surrender. The king's fading complexion reminded her of the limited time they had.

With a deep breath, she closed her eyes and made a choice. She dropped her protective barrier, allowing Alden's magic to flood into her being. It surged through her like a tempest, an exhilarating and overwhelming force. The contrast between their powers was stark. Where her magic was ethereal and delicate, floating like a feather on a gentle breeze, his was pure yet shadowed, heavy like that same feather being dragged through deep waters. His magic weighed her down and surrounded her in darkness, where his magic was the only light.

Concentrating, she reached out and touched the king's shoulder. She focused on each wound, letting their magic flow from her hands into the king. With each touch, she willed their powers to mend what was broken and restore everything to its former state of wholeness. At first, his magic would not move beyond her fingers until she gave it another stern command.

The feeling was heady and intoxicating as so much undiluted power flowed through her. She had never felt anything like it before. Though, what made it strange was how natural it felt.

The power moved through every inch of her body, caressing her and begging her to let it stay. To open her heart and soul to it. The temptation was too great.

"Patience," Michael called. "Patience, he is healed."

Odessa, stay with me, Alden whispered through her mind.

Taking a deep breath, Patience pushed Alden's magic out, closing her barrier to all that power. Estelle and Michael moved the cloth away as she opened her eyes to find the king's wounds had closed but he still had not gained consciousness.

Circe laid her hand on his smooth chest and looked at Patience with gratitude.

Then, Alecia finally said, "I did not try to kill the king." She dropped to her knees near the queen. "Please forgive me if you thought otherwise. I was only trying to help."

So, she did know how to grovel. That was surprising. She didn't want to help Alecia, but curiosity got the best of Patience. "What spell were you trying to use to heal him?"

"Xalenial, the Basion spell of healing," Alecia muttered.

"No wonder he was bleeding out. You can only use that spell on hallowed ground. We are not." She looked over to the queen. "This happens all the time. They forget to read the fine print," Patience assured her before she reached out her hand to help Alecia.

She was trying to be the better person since they started off on the wrong foot when she tried to check on Michael earlier and got zapped.

Alecia stared at her hand momentarily, then glanced at the queen before taking it and standing. "Since you are Estelle's sister and Patience claims you made a simple mistake, I will forgive you, but I will be watching," Queen Circe said to Alecia before turning to Patience. "Thank you," she said, picking up a cloth and wiping the blood off of the king's chest. Her hardened gaze softened. "He is just resting now. He will wake soon."

Patience nodded and looked at Alden. This would have been impossible if not for him. "Thank you."

He smiled. "The pleasure was all mine. Now, let me heal that shoulder."

Her shoulder. She had forgotten all about it. The wound barely stung, but she couldn't walk around with a hole in her shoulder. He placed his hand over the wound and sent soothing magic into it. It warmed as pleasure moved through her. A moan unconsciously escaped, surprising her. Hunger burned in his eyes as his magic caressed her again, pleading with her to let him in.

Before Patience could step back and thank him, Lucius gripped her upper arm, snatching her away from Alden. Anger blazed in his eyes as he glared at her. His eyes were a reflection of her own. She didn't understand what his damn problem was. He was the one who didn't want her, so why this act of jealousy?

She could feel everyone's eyes on them, especially Alden's.

"Leave me alone," she said through clenched teeth.

Feet moved toward them, and Lucius growled, grabbing her arm and whisking her out of the dining room. The world around them became a whirlwind of motion as they moved through the halls, their footsteps moving with a silent urgency.

They flew past the grand parlor, its opulent furnishings and elegant tapestries mere glimpses in their hasty escape. The magnificent staircase blended into a cascade of steps as they ascended to the upper floors, each room they passed blending into a blur of colors and shapes. Time seemed to warp as they ventured deeper into the manor, leaving behind a trail of fleeting images.

A door opened then slammed before he pushed her against a wall in a darkened room.

"That is enough. Send him away before I kill him for touching you," Lucius's deadly voice whispered before his lips crashed into hers, silencing any retort she would have had.

Pulling her sweater aside, he moved down to kiss her newly healed shoulder. The tip of his tongue darted from his mouth, tracing her shoulder blade. Pleasure moved down her spine, causing an involuntary moan to escape from her. His tongue slid up to her neck, distracting her as he ripped the front of her sweater open and exposed her breasts.

Reaching into her bra, he pulled out her left breast. Her nipple hardened to a peak as the cold air hit it. She unconsciously licked her lips as wetness pooled between her legs. His hand caressed her breast, slowly running his finger over her left areola before tightening around the nipple and sending a burst of pleasure straight to her core. His tongue slowly trailed down her chest, past her rapidly beating heart, to her breast.

Patience gasped in pleasure as his warm, wet mouth sucked generously on her nipple. The sharp points of his fangs pressed against the curve of her breast. Part of her hoped he would break the skin.

She moaned, running her hands through his hair. Lucius growled, ripping her sweater and bra completely off. Moving to the other nipple, he sucked it deeply into his mouth.

Her moans filled the room as he moved between her breasts. Frigid air cooled her heated lips as her pants opened. His hand reached in, finding her completely soaked. He groaned as if in pain, then whispered into her ear, "You are going to kill me."

Then he was gone, leaving her cold and vulnerable as the door opened and slammed closed.

She ran her hands down her face, then buttoned her pants back up. She summoned Seckor, her little ball of light, and glanced down at the damage he had done to her clothes. She fixed her bra, grateful he hadn't decided to rip that, then pulled the sweater together. She used what little magic she had left to mend it back together.

How dare he? He talked about witches and their games, but all he did was play this game of hate then want.

She'd had enough. She was done. He had no right to play with her feelings like this. *Damn their connection.* She would get rid of this bond and maybe pursue someone who actually wanted her. If he only knew that he wasn't the only one who made her wet.

Once she felt calm enough, she went over to the wall and stepped through right into the dining room. Michael came over to her.

"Are you alright?"

"No. The bastard. I am going to kill him when I see him."

Michael raised an eyebrow, sensing her anger and frustration.

She searched the room for Alden, but Circe caught her eye. She was bending near the king and whispering something in his ear as she stared across the room. She followed her eye line to Alden standing by the window. It wasn't just that she was looking at him, but it was the suspicion on her face that made her take a pause momentarily before she headed in his direction, leaving Michael standing there.

Alden gazed out at the forest in the distance. The moon shone high over the land, and the stars twinkled brightly in the night sky. They still had hours before dawn would come.

"Thank you for helping us," Patience said as she walked up to him.

Alden turned around and smiled at her. "Thank you for calling me. You can do so anytime... and for anything, but I see that I am not welcome here," he said, looking behind her.

Lucius had walked into the room. She could feel his eyes burning into her back.

"I'm sorry. Until we get this bond thing figured out—"

"I know how the bond works. I take it was an accident and that you are trying to find a way to break it?" Alden offered.

"Yes, we are trying to break it," she said loud enough to make sure Lucius could hear. "You don't happen to know where we could find the Blade of Sapience and the Seperatus spell to go with it, do you?"

He raised a brow. "You are serious about breaking it?"

"Yes, absolutely."

"I will see what I can find out about it."

"Thank you. And like I was saying, until we get it figured out, it is best that you leave even though I would really like for you to stay, because I do have so many questions you still must answer for me."

"How about next time you are alone, you summon me, and I will answer any question you want me to," he said, then bent closer to her and whispered, "for as long as you want me to."

Patience wasn't quite sure how to respond to his comment as a shudder went through her. She nodded, and then he disappeared right before her eyes.

As soon as he was gone, she could feel Lucius breathing down her back. "Don't summon him here again."

She turned around to stand face-to-face with him. "Fine, next time I will just let them kill you."

"I would have survived," he threw back at her. Fury consumed her as she saw red. Her hands itched to zap him. Just one good electrical shock until he turned to ash.

"Lucius, admit it. She saved our asses *again*," Max called out.

She had the sudden urge to stick her tongue out like a child, but she restrained herself. Patience was so grateful for Maxim. He was always the logical one she could count on to make sense of the situation for Lucius since nothing she said got through his thick skull.

"They were adamantly trying to kidnap Michael and my wife… but why?" Maxim questioned, looking at Estelle.

"Well, we know they need our son to set Lilith free. As for Estelle, I understand why they would be after her since she has been protecting the Silverlands and only she knows how to get past the wards that are in place," Circe said, still hovering over the king.

"That would make sense. They would also want to know about how she got there in the first place," Patience wondered aloud. Then a thought resurfaced. "How the hell did the Hokima get past the ward around the house?"

They all stared at her, wondering the same thing. She walked over to the dining room wall and placed her hand against it. Closing her eyes, she reached out with her magic, extending outward in search of the protective ward that surrounded them. As her magic swept over the boundaries, she could sense its presence, but something felt off. A faint tinge of weakness emanated from a particular spot, like a subtle fracture in an otherwise solid barrier.

Her magic revealed the exact location of the breach, situated near the outskirts of the enchanted forests. It was right near the outskirts of the forests where Alden had put together a picnic for them. Interesting... it had to be pure coincidence.

Opening her eyes, she shared with the others what she had found. "Who put up the ward? Lucius?"

Confusion muddled Lucius's face before he remembered: "It was Alecia and Estelle who put this ward around the property."

They all turned to look at Alecia and Estelle. "You sure it was us?" Alecia said as she looked at Estelle. "We don't remember putting it up."

"It was Mae who put up the ward," Maxim confessed.

"Who is Mae?" Patience asked, her gaze fixed on Lucius as a sense of familiarity stirred. Deep down, she knew the answer to this question.

"My wife."

"Your wife knew magic?" Patience asked, surprised.

"Yes..." He seemed unsure but then continued, "I taught her a few of the spells that I knew, and she dabbled in magic here and there. She wanted to learn it to protect our child." Lucius said the last words pointedly as his eyes bore into her.

Sometimes she wished she just kept her mouth shut.

"Maybe it just needs to be reinforced, which I can do so the Hokima won't be a problem for us," she said, moving away from Lucius. She wasn't ready to go back to him trying to kill her. "I will fix it. Then we can focus on getting Selene, but I need to rest. I think we all do after that ordeal."

"Agreed. Let's meet back here in an hour. No one leaves the property," Lucius said sternly. "Max, you keep a close eye on your wife. We don't want her being stolen from us again. Especially since the ward is damaged. Anyone can slip through. The safest place would be the library."

"I can get Estelle through the ward," Patience interjected.

"Fine, let's move there," the asshole vampire said, not even glancing over at the king as he walked out the door.

Patience moved over to Circe. "I can send him to the library, if you want to meet him there."

Circe gazed down at Kieran, then back at her, biting her lip in thought. "Okay."

"I will wait a few minutes, then send him to you."

She nodded before following them out.

Michael and Ian stayed behind with her.

"Your brother is an ass," Patience told Ian, who merely smiled at her.

"I think she is finally going to kick his ass," Michael said excitedly.

"Yes, I am, and I am going to break this bond. I don't need someone so Goddess-damn confusing in my life right now," Patience ranted, thinking back to earlier and how he had left her like that. Vulnerable and alone. "One minute, he wants me. The next, he doesn't. I don't get it. We have a connection, but that connection means shit unless we plan to acknowledge it and at least try to get to know each other. The sex is phenomenal, but it is not worth this trauma. From here on out, I am done with him. I will get that damn blade and cut him out of my system."

Ian handed her a drink. She didn't even see him pour it, but she drank it down anyway. It felt good to get that out of her system the same way it would feel good to get Lucius out of her.

Enough was enough. If he wanted her, he would have to prove it. If not, no matter how much it hurt, she would end this trauma.

Placing her hand on King Kieran, she waited for Michael to put his hand on her shoulder sending his magic through her as she sent Kieran to the library, hoping he landed on the window seat and not the floor.

As soon as he disappeared, they made their way to the library. Estelle stood right outside the doors. Patience walked past her into the library to find out if the king had landed in the correct spot. Circe was putting a few cushions behind the king's head. He had landed on the windowsill bench, thankfully.

"Is he doing okay?" she asked, walking up next to Circe and observing the king.

She smiled kindly. "Yes, he is resting. He will wake when he is ready."

"Good. I will let Estelle into the library, but you should keep a close eye on her. I know she is your friend."

"I will keep an eye on both sisters," Circe replied curtly.

Patience wasn't sure if keeping them all in the same place was the best idea, but until she fixed the barrier around the house, it would be the safest.

Leaving Circe and the king, she returned to the library door and placed her hand against the frame.

"I will lift the ward only enough for you to get into the library. You will be unable to leave it. At least, not without my help," she said, her voice laced with authority and a hint of caution.

She would only lift it so she could walk through, not remove it. She turned to look for Michael, but he was already behind her. He touched her shoulder and poured his magic into her, giving her the boost she needed to lift the ward.

Estelle stared at Patience, shocked. *My eyes must be glowing*, she deduced as the magic seeped from her hands into the doorframe. The words of the spell ward glowed above the door as the barrier appeared, shimmering.

"Part." The barrier slowly opened. "Estelle, come through."

She cautiously stepped inside. As soon as she was fully in the library, Patience removed her hand and the barrier slammed closed.

She could feel the heavy weight of exhaustion weighing down on her bones, each step becoming a struggle against the relentless pull of sleep. It called to her, its seductive embrace tempting her to surrender. She knew that if she didn't find her bed soon, she would inevitably succumb, collapsing under the weight of weariness.

Turning to Michael, she mustered the last remnants of her energy and managed to utter, "I... I need to sleep." Her voice trembled with fatigue.

"Come, I will show you back to your room," Ian said.

Michael wrapped his arm around her as they trailed behind Ian. They walked until they reached the grand staircase, but instead of going down them, they walked across to the other side, to the newer part of the castle. The part that actually had electricity. When the ass had first brought her here, he had stuck her in the older part of the castle. The only light and heat had been from the damn fireplace. Luckily, Maxim was gracious enough to find her an actual room with electricity.

Sighing, she rested her head on Michael's shoulder.

Patience was so exhausted. The burgundy carpet was starting to look really good.

She was so tired she didn't even realize they were already back in her room. The dark grey walls greeted her happily as she laid back on the black comforter. She really wanted to take a shower, but she didn't think she would have the energy to stand.

Maybe Lucius could help me stand. As soon as the thought formed, she regretted even thinking of him.

Ian lit the fireplace as Michael tucked her in and kissed her forehead. "You are doing good. I know you are tired and today was too much, but get some rest. We will watch over you."

He ran his finger down her face, putting her to sleep.

———◄O►———

His icy gaze pierced her right in her gut as soon as she stepped into the ballroom.

Lucius sat on his throne with three men behind him. Maxim stood to his left with a grim look on his face that didn't mask the desire in his eyes as he watched a young woman with crimson hair dance. Silas, a warrior assassin, stood directly behind him. His auburn eyes searched the crowd, looking for any threats. The scar across his face made him look menacing and scared most away, but the deadliest of them all was the one on his right.

Volt's silver eyes looked upon the crowd with boredom, but she knew he was also assessing the crowd for threats and opportunities. Always by his damn side.

Circe's brother, Silas, would not be an issue tonight. He would help to get him alone when the time was right by distracting Maxim and Volt. Though, Volt was who she needed to be most cautious of. Khedians were dangerous, especially to witches, with their ability to drain a witch of her magic and to become undetectable. Though they weren't an enemy to witches, only Lucius was. Volt's loyalty to Lucius was what made him dangerous.

She took another step into the crowded room, purposefully ignoring his gaze. Everyone was here to pay the king his dues. Disgusting. No creature should have such power.

She focused on making her way across the ballroom. She moved around the edge of the room, passing by vampires already drunk on blood wine. She had to be careful not to run into trouble tonight. She had one goal, and nothing could stop her. Finally making it to the table with the wine, she picked up a glass.

Turning her back on Lucius's captivated gaze, she surveyed the room. Dancers twirled on the marble floor as the orchestra played a lively tune.

His stare bored into her as she kept her back to him.

"Well, aren't you a breath of fresh air."

"Alden, what are you doing here?" She turned toward the voice with a warm smile.

He beamed back. "I could say the same to you, Odessa."

"I am here to meet an old acquaintance. You?"

Silvia had introduced her to Alden a few weeks ago. He was how she managed to get invited to the Moonharvest, the annual gathering of vampire clans, and introduced to Lucius.

"I am here to pay my dues just like everyone else here. Dance with me? Let's make your acquaintance jealous."

She wanted to say no, but Lucius watched. Alden and Lucius were old friends, after all. No better way to get him to trust her.

"Gladly." She placed her glass on the table and took his hand.

He led her onto the busy dance floor just as the orchestra played another song. Once he had her in his arms, he said, "I take it you're here for Lucius." For a moment, she thought she had been found out, but then he revealed, "It is quite obvious since he has not taken his eyes off of you since you walked into the room, and you have been avoiding him."

She smirked. "How observant of you. I actually came here to pay my dues, the same as you. Besides, I don't kneel before men on thrones."

He pulled her closer, moving them out of the way before a drunken couple collided with them. Alden grinned, then asked, "But you do kneel?"

"Wouldn't you like to find out?" she countered.

He laughed and spun her. Right into Lucius's arms.

Enveloping her in his embrace, he remained silent, their bodies swaying in perfect rhythm to the gentle melodies playing in the background. His eyes, filled with a mix of curiosity and intensity, studied her intently, as if he were attempting to unravel the depths of her being, peeling back the layers that concealed her true essence.

All she needed to do was convince him she was a vampire and that she wanted him to ravish her. She tried to start a conversation, but the longer he stared at her the more self-conscience she felt. Her confidence was plummeting with every second the clock ticked by.

Everything she had prepared to say was slipping out of her head.

Damn, why wouldn't he speak to her instead of just staring at her? Men.

She wished she could conjure her pinnacle dagger and stab him through his treacherous heart, but if she did, it would cause an all-out war that her witches could not afford. He had killed too many of them, weakening their forces.

He had killed so many daughters and sons yet here he stood, alive without punishment. She would make him pay for all the deaths he had wrought. Spilling his blood would be too easy.

Her mission was to seduce him, then kill him. They would get their revenge.

CHAPTER SEVEN

ALECIA

Alecia grabbed her sister's hand while Max was distracted by the queen and pulled her between some bookshelves where they could be seen but not heard.

"Estelle, what the hell is going on?" she asked, confused. "You weren't supposed to come back here."

"Plans change. Lecia, you know this. I thought he explained what was happening." Estelle glanced over her shoulder as she playfully patted it.

"Is that the reason for the talisman?"

"Yes. Jezabel created it specifically for her. It will be able to bring her to him." She glanced over her shoulder again, making Alecia want to know what she was looking at.

"But Lucius stopped it?"

"He thinks he did," she whispered.

Alecia raised a brow with curiosity, and Estelle peered over Alecia's shoulder once more before pulling her a little bit further into the shelves.

"All I needed was for her to touch the talisman. He removed the vessel but not the poison. The poison will begin to work soon and do its job. She will give in to it, and we must be ready. They will be waiting for us."

"Where? And no one told me the plan about trying to kill the king." Alecia hated being left in the dark, but she had no choice but to play go along with this foolishness.

"You shouldn't have stopped me. It may have been the only opportunity we had."

"Then you should have told me beforehand. Now the queen suspects me," she argued, her voice laced with frustration and anger. The omission of crucial information infuriated her, but it was the feeling of being left out, excluded from the plans, that gnawed at her. She had to find a way to contact Daphne. Maybe she would be able to give her some clue about their plans.

Her sister shrugged. "You apologized, so the plan will still work."

Alecia wanted to ask her more, but then she heard footsteps behind her, and Estelle smiled. It had to be Max.

"Estelle, can we talk?" his voice rang out.

"Yes, of course. Alecia and I were just catching up. More like I was being scolded, so thank you," Estelle said sweetly.

Alecia rolled her eyes before Estelle moved around her to get to him. She had forgotten how good of an actress her sister could be. Playing the kind, delicate thing when she was anything but.

The memory resurfaced with vivid clarity of when she had first approached her years ago, revealing the deal she had made with Alazar. The promise had been tempting, dangling before them like a glimmering gem of hope. Alazar had whispered words of power, enticing them with the prospect of a transformed existence. They had been promised restoration, a return to wholeness, in exchange for aiding him in reclaiming his kingdom. The weight of that decision had settled upon her shoulders, knowing that their lives would be forever altered.

Estelle had dabbled in magic she did not understand when summoning Alazar. She wanted more power, and Alecia didn't understand her. Time and time again, she tried to convince her to embrace her vampiric side and join the Drath, the clan of half-vampires, but she refused. The power of magic seduced her. She chose to be an Aberrant, a witch without a coven. She said she would find her true coven one day, but until then, she would learn and gain as much power as she could.

Such was how she found Alazar and fell into his allure. Estelle fell for all his promises of power and... love. More like they needed a descendant of a Silverlands witch, a stupid and susceptible witch like her sister, to get into the Silverlands to kill the Goddess.

"Sashee, Iloren sus glilanshe?" (*Sashee, what did she say?*) Circe asked in Novarian as she approached the bookshelf's other side.

Alecia sighed. "The plan has changed. She has not revealed how, but it concerns the talisman."

Centuries ago, Alazar sent her on a mission to steal a child. Instead, she met the end of Queen Circe's blade. She was the reason she tried to stop Lucius from killing Arabella and making the mistake that changed their lives. For these past years, Alecia had been working with the king and queen to right the wrong that had been done so long ago.

She had been trying to save her sister, but as time passed, she began to see her sister's true colors, especially when she killed her Ezekiel.

"Was I too rough with the blade?" Circe moved closer, gazing at her neck.

"No, Sashini. I am alright. It was the only way for us to cast suspicion away from her. I stopped her before she could do any damage. There is a plan in place that I have been kept out of, so we must be cautious."

Alecia could see Max still talking to Estelle in the far corner of the room, but Estelle's gaze was on her. She knew she could not hear her, but she would have to go through the motions so she would not suspect. Alecia slowly bent her knee and kneeled in front of the queen.

"She is watching," she said softly before bowing her head in shame.

"I understand. You are forgiven but only because we trust your sister," Circe said loud enough for everyone to hear. "You need to ask the king for forgiveness, as well."

Alecia lifted her head and nodded before standing. Queen Circe walked past her and led her over to the king, who to her surprise had his eyes open.

"Sashee."

"Mi malani, doveche si?" (*My king, how are you?*) Alecia asked as she moved closer.

"I will recover. I did not suspect he would send more Hokima so soon. They were trying to kill Lucius." Kieran moved to sit up. "They also tried to take Estelle. He must want her returned to him."

"Plans have changed. We need to find the Silverlands witch now. Estelle has poisoned the witch somehow. Whatever was in that talisman affected her, which is not good since they are losing each other. They were away from each other for too long, and not even the blood is working." When Circe had told her the night of Michael and Ian's ceremony that they had blood bonded, she thought it was good news, but seeing them now, you would never know they were bonded other than the clear sexual tension between the two.

"I know," Kieran admitted. "I don't know what kind of poison it was. We will have to watch her closely to see how it will affect her. It is possible that her magic is defending her against it."

The queen nodded. "We will keep a close eye on her. But there is no need to worry her unnecessarily. Let us go and convince her to find the Silverlands witch. You will stay here and talk with Lucius. He has listened to you once before. Maybe you can get through to him again."

Kieran gazed at his wife before he nodded, and then he pulled her toward him until she was standing between his legs.

Alecia stepped away and turned her back, wanting to give them some privacy. She glanced around the room in time to see Michael and Ian walk through the door.

"Has anyone seen Patience?"

CHAPTER EIGHT

PATIENCE

Patience followed Maxim as they walked past the grand staircase back toward the library. He led them to the winding steps that took them back to the second floor.

An hour ago, she woke to his horrific red eyes staring down at her as the shutters lifted from the windows. Panic set in before she realized where she was when she saw Michael and Ian lying on the carpet near the dying embers of the fireplace.

Energy rushed through her when she sat up. Her magic had been fully restored. Leaving Michael and Ian to sleep, she went and found Maxim, who was already on his way to her. She asked him to show her to the center of the property so she could fix the barrier.

As soon as they were back on the second floor, she had a feeling she knew where he was leading her, especially as they walked past the lit wall torches.

They reminded her of the dream she had.

Surprisingly, it wasn't the future she had dreamed of. The scene unfolding before her eyes resembled more of a haunting memory from the past. Doubt crept in, casting shadows of uncertainty over its authenticity. Could it be real, or was it merely a projection of her conflicted emotions? Maybe it was simply a dream projecting her feelings, especially since she did plan on killing him in it.

Who knew? It didn't matter either way. It was just a dream. What she needed to concentrate on now was getting the barrier fixed before any more surprises showed up.

Seeing the door where she had found the necklace, she hoped Maxim would walk past it, but when he started to slow, she knew exactly where the center of the house was.

"Lucius sealed this place off when his wife... Mae died," Maxim imparted, his voice tinged with a mix of sorrow and reverence. His expression softened, his eyes filled with a distant sadness as he recalled the painful memories. "This is the center of the house," he added, his voice dropping to a hushed tone.

This is where Patience had found the necklace. His *wife's* necklace. The one she wanted back even though it wasn't hers. She didn't want to go back in there. When she had first entered, she had no clue it was Mae's room. It felt strange returning, now knowing who the room belonged to, but she had to fix the barrier or else Michael wouldn't be safe. None of them would be safe.

Maxim placed his hand on the knob, but before he could turn it, Lucius shoved him away and stood in front of the door, glowering down at him.

"What the hell do you think you are doing?" Lucius yelled. His face was red with fury. "You know this room is off limits."

"You know she needs to fix the barrier around the house, so we aren't vulnerable to attacks. Stop being *stubborn*." Maxim tried to stay calm but ended up shouting the last word. Lucius wasn't budging.

Patience was debating whether or not to tell him she had already seen the room, but she wanted to keep her life a little longer.

"Fine, be an ass, but it will be on your conscience if someone gets killed because of your stubbornness and resentment," Maxim snapped before storming off.

"Look." Patience walked up to Lucius until they were chest-to-chest, attempting to keep her tone level. "I won't touch anything. I need to sit on the floor. You can watch me the whole time if it makes you feel any better, but I need to get into that room so I can keep us all protected. Please."

She could see him fighting himself. He knew they were right and that he would have to put aside his pride... and stubbornness. Patience was aware his wife died over a century ago, but time moved differently for vampires. For them, a century ago could feel like a decade. She couldn't help but wonder if he was still in love with his wife.

Stupid question. Of course he is. Why else would he be so protective of her things?

And maybe that's one of the reasons why he was rejecting their bond so hard. She really wanted to peek inside his brain to know what the hell he was thinking.

It didn't matter either way. She shouldn't be upset by it because she planned to sever this bond as soon as she got the chance. Though, she still couldn't help the sadness that seeped into her heart. It was just this stupid blood bond. That is all it was... just the blood bond. Maybe if she kept telling herself that, it would help the pain to go away.

"Fine," he whispered. She was surprised by how easily he gave in.

Turning his back to them, his voice barely above a whisper, he incanted a spell. Three silver interlocking circles, adorned with hues of blue, red, and purple, materialized on the surface of the door. Placing his hand over the radiant symbol, he exerted a gentle pressure, causing the door to unseal and open.

The lock clicked, and then he placed his hand on the knob. It took a moment before he turned the handle and the door opened.

Lucius made no move to go through.

"I can go first. Like I said, I just need to sit on the floor. You can watch me from the doorway if you want," Patience offered as she moved to stand next to him.

Lucius didn't budge for a second, then took a step back to allow her through. She pushed the door slightly, opening it more. She glanced at him one final time before going inside.

Shivers ran down her spine just as they had before when she entered. The familiar perfumed scent hit her nose. The room seemed dustier than she remembered, but then again, she was only in there for a few moments, taking things that didn't belong to her. Her eyes immediately went to the three-mirrored wooden vanity table near the corner window, hoping to see the necklace lying amongst the dust.

No, GreyJoy had the necklace. She would need to remember to ask him about it when she had the time.

Glancing around the room, Patience allowed her gaze to sweep across the dilapidated space, her senses taking in every detail now that she knew whose room it was. The air felt heavy with neglect, and a musty odor hung in the stale atmosphere.

Her eyes scanned the decaying remnants of what was once a grand chamber. Thick curtains, now moth-eaten and frayed, barely clung to the rusted curtain rods, their once vibrant colors faded by time. The bed sheets, once luxurious, now bore the marks of decay, their fabric threadbare and riddled with holes.

Against one wall stood a wooden armoire, its once sturdy frame now warped and rotted, with doors hanging askew on their broken hinges. The vanity table, a relic of forgotten beauty rituals, displayed a cracked and dusty mirror, its reflective surface marred by time's cruel touch.

A tilted dresser caught her attention, standing precariously on three legs while two others were completely absent. It seemed to teeter on the brink of collapse, its worn drawers gaping open, revealing the remnants of forgotten treasures and memories.

In a corner near the fireplace, two chairs stood as the remains of forgotten comfort. The first chair lay on its side, devoid of legs, its toppled form a testament to the passage of time. The second chair, although upright, bore a gaping hole right in its center, a void where its former upholstery had once offered respite.

Patience's gaze shifted to the floor, covered in a thick layer of undisturbed dust, obscuring any trace of the carpet's original color. The room seemed frozen in a state of abandonment, where the vibrant hues of its past had been swallowed by the relentless march of neglect.

Contemplating her seating options, Patience hesitated. Sitting on the dusty floor was less than appealing, yet the vanity table that held a rusted metal chair seemed like a better option.

"Don't even think about it. You said the floor. The floor it is," Lucius growled as he stepped into the room.

"Fine." She wasn't even sure it would hold her weight anyway.

Just seal the barrier, Patience, then you can go take a nice, warm shower. The thought helped her focus.

Patience plopped down in a very unladylike fashion onto the hardwood floor, causing a cloud of dust to waft up. She stifled a cough. A small smile grew on her face when Lucius sputtered, clearing his lungs.

"Okay. I need complete silence for the next five minutes."

Closing her eyes to try and focus her thoughts, footsteps approached her. She knew it was Lucius. Her blood called to his.

Opening her eyes, she saw his legs in front of her. She slowly lifted them, loving everything she saw as she met his steely gaze.

"You know I don't like tricks or games. Fortify the barrier and nothing more. Do you understand me?" he commanded.

She would be lying if she said she wasn't turned on at this very moment. She loved how his presence towered over her. Commanding her. Her arousal must have shown in her eyes because his illuminated, and his nostrils flared.

His hand reached down to cup her cheek, and warmth spread through her as he stared down into her eyes. Hunger burned in them, but something else was there. Something she knew could be hers if she just reached out for it.

Slowly, his lips moved toward hers when a sudden pain sliced through her mind.

Grabbing her head, the pain moved until an image emerged right before her eyes as the pain stabbed her temporal lobe, causing her to slam her head back against the footboard.

"Shit. *Patience.* What's wrong? *Patience.*" Lucius grabbed her head and called her name, but all she could do was concentrate on the image as it came into focus.

The image was distant. It was a crowded ballroom.

An orchestra sat in the corner on a small, raised platform playing a soft tune as couples swayed slowly to the rhythm. People drank, laughed, and chatted as they stood on the edge of the marble floor. Pink champagne flowed from a tower through a set of oak doors that people left and entered with small plates of food.

Gazing down, she realized the room was filled with purple flowers from pansies to lilacs. Her favorite color. A soft night breeze blew in from the open terrace doors, spreading the scent of the flowers throughout the room.

Haughty laughter drew her eyes to the couple in the center of the room dancing under the three–tiered crystal chandeliers glittering in the soft light.

She recognized herself right away. Though, she looked different. Her unruly curls were pulled back into a nice, elegant hairstyle, beautifully gold-tiered earrings hung on her ears, and she wore the most sensual dress of lavender and crystal beads. Though, it was the warm and loving smile she wore on her face as she gazed at her partner that made the biggest difference.

He leaned in, whispering something in her ear. She threw back her head and laughed with such joy. His ravishing dark hair was familiar, but it wasn't until they turned that she knew it was *him*. Lucius.

Then she was no longer watching from above. She was there in his arms, and he was smiling down with such love in his silver-grey eyes.

Patience threw back her head and giggled. "Dragoste, behave."

"Zeita, I only tell you what I desire to do to you later," he whispered to her as he nipped at her earlobe, causing a shiver to go through her.

She gave him a wry look. "Lucius, we are in a room full of people. Behave. Or you will get nothing later."

"As you wish." He smirked, then twirled her around until they made their way to the edge of the dance floor, where Lucius gave her a mischievous grin before moving her behind a corner pillar.

"I will only behave if you kiss me." He leaned down, caging her in.

"Oh, dragoste, you promise?"

"No." His lips devoured hers as the music and people continued to move around them.

When he finally let her up for air, the last thing she wanted was for him to behave. "I think we should take this somewhere more private."

"I couldn't agree more, Zeita." Grabbing her hand, they made their way out of the ballroom, ignoring all those who called after them.

They moved through the house so quickly she did not get a chance to look around. The only thing she had eyes for was him until he reached a door.

Patience's recognition sparked a surge of anticipation within her. She observed intently as he turned the familiar doorknob, revealing the room they had entered before. With a swift motion, they tumbled into the room, their bodies intertwining on the soft expanse of the bed. The door slammed shut behind them, sealing them in. Every inch of the room appeared pristine; there wasn't a speck of dust anywhere, and all the furniture looked new.

"Lucius, we have a house full of people here to celebrate us. We can't abandon them. Max is going to kill us."

Lucius grinned as he pulled off his shirt. "Then we better make this quick."

"Oh, you wicked man." She laughed as he nuzzled her neck.

"My apologizes for interrupting your nuptials, but we have an urgent matter to discuss." Volt appeared at the door with his back turned.

Lucius cursed. "Fuck, Volt. You couldn't have waited ten minutes?"

"I doubt it would have taken that long."

Lucius glared at his back as he pulled on his shirt. She tried to muffle a chuckle, earning a menacing glare from him.

"What is happening?" she asked as she moved from the bed.

"He has found it." Volt turned to look at them. "He will be coming for you next."

The image started to fade as the pain subsided. She tried to hold onto the image, but it slipped away out of her grasp.

Opening her eyes, she found a furious pair of silver-grey ones glaring at her.

"What did you do?" Venom poured from his voice.

Patience sat up confused, then looked around. The room had changed. Like the image, the dust was gone, and all the furniture was fixed... No, not fixed, more like restored.

Somehow, she had restored everything in the room. Even the pale lavender walls and the red oak floors. She absolutely loved the different shades of purple and gold. Her favorite was the carpet that sat in front of a blazing fireplace. It was thick, purple, and fluffy. It would be the perfect place to cuddle up and read a book.

But the one thing that caught her eye was the purple and black blanket with strange colored flowers woven into it. She couldn't pull her eyes away. She got up from the floor and walked over to it, ignoring the glare from Lucius.

Her hand reached out to touch it when he snatched it away.

"Change it *back*," Lucius growled, placing the blanket on a chair. "Change it back *now*."

Did she do this? Sometimes her magic did have a mind of its own but this... this would have taken too much magic, and right now she didn't feel like she used any magic.

"I don't think I did this," she whispered.

"Witch, I watched you. The magic came from you. Change it back."

Her eyes widened in shock. "What do you mean it came from me? Tell me what you saw."

He continued to glare at her but reluctantly spoke, "The floor changed around you first, then the magic moved throughout the room changing everything."

Shit, so it did start from her. "Is this how your wife's room looked before?"

"Yes," he growled out.

"Down to the very last detail?"

"Yes, this was how my wife's room looked the day before she died." His face remained blank, but the pain in his eyes spoke volumes. She had fucked up.

"I didn't mean to do this. Sometimes my magic has a mind of its own," she admitted as guilt consumed her. "I will try to change it back, but I am not exactly sure how I was able to do this."

In a way, she had helped keep the memory of his wife alive by restoring everything, but she also realized she just brought so many painful memories back for him. *Damn.* She had to tell him about the image. The memory. Maybe it would help him understand.

"I—"

"I don't care what you are about to say," he snapped. "Change it back, *witch.*"

He wasn't even going to give her a chance to explain. The bastard. It would be so easy to set him on fire. One thought and *poof.* Then she could dance around his ashes.

The rose desonite stone on his damn neck would protect him from her magic, but she was so tempted to try.

Closing her eyes, Patience stooped down and put her hands to the oak. Concentrating, she tried to summon her magic back, but it wasn't working.

She tried again but still nothing.

Great. Now, he would try to kill her, and she would have to run. Though, she was so tempted to fight him. Actually, itching to.

Opening her eyes, she stood. "I can't," she spat, steeling herself to hear the hatred in his voice. "It's not that simple."

"*What?* Witch, no games." He reached out, grabbing her. "Change it back!" he shouted as he shook her.

"I *can't!*" she yelled as she lifted her hands and shoved him away from her. His back hit the unlit fireplace with such force that it caused the ornaments on the mantle to fall to the purple carpet.

When he dropped to the floor, his eyes glared up at her with pure rage. Patience knew she should run, but if she did it would mean she was guilty of something. She didn't mean to do this, and she just needed time to fix it, but the rage in his eyes told her he wasn't going to give her a chance to.

Calling forth her magic, she stood her ground. She was done running.

Lucius moved fast, but she was prepared for him as he tried to grab her from behind. She pivoted before he could get his arms around her. She pushed him with all her strength onto the bed. He swiftly rolled off and stood.

"You need to stop this madness. You won't win," she seethed, manifesting a ball of electricity in her hand.

Ignoring her, he ran toward her, trying to reach for her neck when her barrier erected around her. Her magic, finally, protected her against him. She lowered her electric ball, extinguishing it.

He stood outside her barrier, glaring. The fury burning in his eyes made her tremble, but only on the inside. She would not show weakness to him, not in this moment.

"You can't hide from me. I know you're afraid." An evil grin formed on his face as his hand began to stroke her barrier.

Fuck, the bond. She wished she could tear it out and rip it apart.

"I am not afraid of *you*."

He continued to grin and stroke her barrier until, much to her surprise, his hand slipped through, grabbing her. She cursed her magic for betraying her as he gripped her throat.

"Change it back or this will be the last breath you take, witch."

"Then kill me, Lucius. Kill me because I can't change it back." She waited for his grip to grow tighter as he stared into her eyes. She dared him to do it. She wanted him to. Then she would have all the proof she needed to break this bond and be done with him.

His grip slackened, surprising her, then fell away entirely. "Get out." The anguish in his voice killed her inside. "Get out *now*."

Patience hadn't realized she was moving until she had shoved past Maxim, who was walking back toward the room. She ran, not being able to hold back the tears any longer as an agonizing pain rushed through her, crushing her.

It wasn't hers. It was his.

Lucius

She was in his grasp.

His fingers were wrapped around her fucking neck. He could have *so easily* snapped it and been done with it all. The bond would have been gone, and his life would go back to the way it was.

His hand should have squeezed the life from her. Her eyes would have rolled to the back of her head as her last breath left her body. It would have been glorious.

Except he found his grip loosening and his hand slipping from her neck.

He couldn't do it.

Fuck. It would have been so easy, but all Lucius wanted to do was kiss her luscious lips.

He screamed for her to get out. As soon as he was sure she was gone, he fell to his knees, ashamed of himself for wanting... craving another woman while he stood in his wife's room. He couldn't even get himself to think of her name.

He glanced around and saw everything looked the same as it did on the day she died. Even her smell was everywhere, in everything.

The feeling, the pain, was all so overwhelming as tears poured from his eyes. He let the anguish course through him, thinking he deserved the pain for sullying his wife's memory... Mae's memory for wanting a witch. For wanting to lay the witch down on her bed and make love to her. For wanting to taste her sweet blood again. For... For wanting to let it all go and to begin a life with her.

The image of the daughter they would have had emerged in his thoughts. Her smile warmed his heart as she ran into his arms.

He disgusted himself. To be sitting here in his wife's room thinking of his future with a witch. He wished he could reach in and tear the memory out, erase it, and sever this bond.

A hand touched his shoulder. It was Maxim.

"Lucius."

He looked up at Max's outstretched hand. He wiped his tears away before he grabbed it and stood. "Where is the witch?"

"I don't know. She ran past me. What happened? Did she do this?"

"Yes." He took a deep breath to get a grip on his emotions. "She wo—can't change it back."

"Can't. How did she change it in the first place?"

Lucius went to the vanity and picked up Mae's silver hairbrush she bought when they were in Athenios all those years ago. It looked like it did the day she bought it from the old lady on the street.

"This would take immense power," Max said, touching the curtain.

"I know." Lucius moved over to the purple and black blanket the witch had been staring at. He had completely forgotten about it. Mae had made it for their unborn child. He had thought the flowers were the strangest hue of lavender and white.

When he had asked her about it, all she said was it held their love so the baby would always feel it even if they weren't there. She would lay it across her belly.

Lucius ran his fingers over it before bringing it to his nose and inhaling her vanilla honey scent.

It almost smelled like Pat—*no.* He put the blanket down and walked away from it.

"She needs to figure out how to change it back. I will not stand for her changing Mae's things," he hissed. "If she doesn't change it back, her time is up, Max. Bond or not. To hell with the debt."

He didn't need this. He had sealed this room off long ago for a reason. When they had died, he sat in this room for hours... sometimes days without eating or drinking. Too consumed in the pain of their loss to even think about functioning, except to kill. To kill witches and make them pay for the pain they caused.

When the councils, both the vampire and witch, had decreed over a century ago that the killing of each other was outlawed, Lucius had locked himself in here for almost a month. It was his brother and Max who finally got him to leave their memory behind. To seal off this room. To leave the pain in here.

Now, it was all back because of *her.* And now, being in this space, instead of thinking of his wife and their child, all he could think about was *her.* Patience ruined it.

"I see nothing has changed," Volt's smooth voice spoke as his body filled the doorway. His silver eyes assessed the situation, not daring to enter the room.

"And I see you finally decided to make an appearance." Lucius glared, not able to contain the anger in his voice.

"Umber was being difficult and would not answer all my questions about the witch. Tried to demand two, which was unusual."

Umber demanding two Astral coins for one question was unheard of. "What did you ask him?"

"I think this conversation would be more appropriate in your office and not our current setting." Volt nodded towards the room.

"You are right," Max said, his voice tinged with concern. "We can move this to his office so that he can calm down."

It was a good idea, but he was reluctant to move. It had been so long since he had let himself be in here, and now the thought of leaving Mae's warmth and scent was painful. He closed his eyes and took it all in. Let her warmth soothe and comfort him as her scent surrounded him, cooling his blood.

When he opened them again, his rage was palpable. Patience had gone too far. To touch his wife's things... her room.

A fury so pure washed over him, igniting every nerve in his body. He needed to find her and kill her so this pain would go away. He wouldn't live with this agony again.

He stormed past Volt and Max, determined to find the witch and end her life once and for all.

CHAPTER NINE

PATIENCE

Patience ran and ran, having no clue where she was going.

She slammed her hands into the wall, asking it to take her somewhere safe. The wall shuddered, and then she fell through, landing on a purple carpet. Glancing up, she realized she was back in the room. *Shit.*

Thankfully, Lucius wasn't here anymore, and the door was closed.

Why would it take her back here?

She moved to the door and placed a barrier to exclusively keep Lucius out. He was going to try to kill her again, and she wanted to be prepared for it. "Please keep me safe from him," she pleaded with the house. The walls groaned in response. She smiled. Her and the house had a connection. She still wasn't sure how, but just as she and Lucius were connected, so was this house.

Taking a deep breath, she calmed herself and wiped away her tears. The pain had subsided. Now, all she could feel was his rage.

She blocked the feeling as best she could. Though, strong bouts of it came through the bond every few minutes.

This wasn't her fault. The only way for this to be possible would be for her magic to have intentionally poured out from her. Except restoring an item wasn't that simple. To restore an entire room as old as this one would take a lot of power and would have drained her immensely, yet she didn't feel drained at all.

Patience walked around the room, trying to figure out how she could have done this.

She thought it would feel weird being in here alone, but surprisingly, she didn't feel that way. It had been stranger being in there with Lucius than being alone which, eerily, felt comfortable. Her fingers itched to touch and explore every corner of the space.

She controlled herself. She didn't need him being angrier than he already was. If that was even possible.

Patience moved back over to the foot of the bed where she had plopped down. She searched around the area for something, anything she may have triggered. Sometimes spells were cast on objects that could only be triggered by a specific person touching that object, like when she came into contact with the talisman.

Dropping to her knees, she searched the floor to see if she may have touched something unexpectedly. The only object close enough to her was the bed. Could that be the trigger?

She sat back down on the floor and slowly moved herself into the position she had opened her eyes in. As soon as she laid down fully, her leg touched the left peg of the bed. Was the bed enchanted? Was she the trigger? Or did Lucius touch the bed?

If only she could ask the damn male. She shook her head as she sat up. *The stubborn fool.*

The only way she may be able to reverse it was by finding the trigger object and resetting it to disable it. Though, it was strange that someone would put a trigger to restore an old room unless they planned to come back. Patience had heard of dead people coming back to life, but these days it wouldn't surprise her if people did come back from the dead.

She would have to contemplate that more later. If the vampire wasn't in such an uproar and would have given her a moment to think without the pressure, she would have been able to change it back. But she was pretty sure she needed him, and she was not about to risk her life to help him. The barrier was the priority. If he calmed, she would come back to fix it.

Sighing, she prayed to the Goddess that the house would keep its promise and protect her from Lucius. Wiping the last of the tears from her eyes, she sat against the bed and centered herself. She planted her hands on the floor.

Her magic seeped into the wood, spreading out into the walls. It slowly moved until it filled every crevice. Then she asked the house to lead her to the barrier. She swore the walls groaned in response as her magic was pulled by an unseen force toward the outer perimeter of the house.

The ancient magical barrier surrounded the property. She let her magic seep into it to assess the damage. It was thin and weak. There was also the huge hole in it near the forest edge. Thankfully, she would be able to easily fix it.

The magic in the barrier seemed familiar to her. Simply because it was similar to hers yet different in its own way. She used her magic like a thread to sew the hole closed. As soon as it sealed, the barrier shuddered, becoming thicker and stronger.

Before pulling her magic back, Patience took a moment to examine it.

There was ancient magic here and more than one person's. Interesting. Maybe it was her magic that had triggered a spell long forgotten. It would make sense why she wouldn't be able to absorb the magic back because it wasn't hers to begin with.

She could absorb it. Though, she wouldn't have any idea what kind of ancient magic she would be taking into her body. She wished she had time to examine both the barrier and the room more, but she knew Lucius would be beating down the door at any moment. Maybe another time.

Patience moved to get up when shivers ran up her spine at the sudden chill in the air. Her eyes searched around the room, trying to figure out where it was coming from, when she felt *it*. The pressure of eyes boring into her back.

A whispered echo filled the room, *Come to me, my love.*

Red eyes materialized, shimmering before her, causing her to freeze. The half-demon was here. How? How was this possible? She wanted to run, but she couldn't get her limbs to move. This time, neither Michael nor Lucius were here to save her. *Fuck.*

I am waiting for you, Odessa. Come to me.

A warm, gentle breeze swept through the room, surrounding her and caressing her cheek. *Home* was all she could think of. The same way she felt when she first encountered him in the vault, and he had appeared before her in his signature alabaster suit.

She didn't understand what he wanted from her. Maybe it was just a ploy for him to get closer to Michael. For some reason, she doubted it. This demon clearly knew her, and she wanted to know how.

Pushing down the scream that threatened to burst from her throat, Patience reached out her hand toward the red eyes.

Yes, my love. Soon. Happiness shone within the red eyes as they faded away.

Should she have reached out before instead of always running? Did this mean he was coming for her?

A knock sounded at the door before it opened. "Patience, are you in here?"

It was Michael. She instinctively got up and ran into his arms.

"Is everything alright?" he asked. Concern and worry for her was written all over his face. "Maxim told me to find you before he stormed after Ian's brother."

Shit, her time was up here. Lucius was on a war path, and nothing would stop him from getting to her. *Damn.* She wanted to tell Michael what had just happened, but she couldn't stay here a moment longer.

"I need to go. The only safe place I will be from him will be GreyJoy's."

"No, you stay with me. Ian and I can protect you."

"It's okay. I will be fine. GreyJoy will protect me. Plus, he needs some time to calm down. I messed up, and I need to fix this," Patience said to Michael as Ian walked through the door. Circe and Alecia silently entered behind him, glancing at her with concern. "Besides, brothers should not be fighting. I will just stay with GreyJoy for now, and I still need to find Selene. I promise I will be fine."

"So, *this* is what he is upset about. You restored her room?" Ian questioned, glancing around. "Shit. This isn't good."

"No, I didn't, but I believe we may have triggered a spell which restored the room. Your idiot brother is upset that I can't instantly turn it back into the shambles that it was in. And I know."

Ian nodded as he walked further into the room to the footboard, running his hands over it. "A spell? You think this room was spelled?"

"Yes. I think Lucius was the one who triggered it. I need him to change it back, but of course he is being his irrational self."

"Now I see why he is so pissed. He had sealed off this room to close off the memories and the... pain of *their* memory. It has been decades since this door was opened," Ian divulged with a grimace. "This is most likely more painful because his fee—"

"I don't have time to deal with this," she said, cutting him off before he said something that would make her feel even more guilty. "I am going to leave for a few hours to try and find Selene."

"I'm sorry. I believe you," Ian said, moving to stand next to Michael. "You're right. We don't have time for this. Brother be damned at this point. We need to find Selene and get to Askaria."

"He is right. We have bigger fish to fry," Alecia commented. "He will have to wait to kill you."

"Are you sure?" Michael asked, both he and Ian ignoring Alecia.

"Yes, Max managed to distract him by hiding Luzia, but he will find her, so we should move quickly."

"I agree with Ian. We must concentrate on getting back into Askaria. It is only a matter of time before he finds another way to free her," Circe stated.

"What about the king? You shouldn't leave him in the state he is in," Patience directed toward Circe.

"The king is up and has made a full recovery. He is aware that I will go with you."

Patience glanced at Michael for reassurance before she held out her hand and Michael grabbed it. "I'm going to need everyone to touch me, preferably on my arm or shoulder."

Ian grasped her other hand while Alecia and Circe grabbed her shoulders. Making sure everyone had a firm grip on her, Patience transported them to the bookstore.

Jafa was sitting at the front desk reading through a magazine on home decor.

His eyes widened when he took in their appearance. "Thea, you are back. Did you find her?" he exclaimed, putting the magazine under the counter. "We have been busy, busy, busy waiting for your return."

"You have?" she asked curiously, wondering how many customers were coming in when she normally only saw three to four a day.

"Yes, something has everyone stirring and looking for magical weapons."

"You don't think that word got out about Lilith?" she said, anxiously looking at Michael and Ian.

"It is possible that one of the people my brother visited may have let it slip out on purpose?" Ian replied, pondering out loud.

"This is good. We need more people to know about what is going on," Circe said adamantly.

Hopefully, the more people who knew about it would give the councils the proof they needed to actually help. At least if people began to voice their fears and concerns, the councils would actually listen and do something about it. They needed this type of panic to show the councils that this threat was real.

"I couldn't agree more," Silas, Circe's brother and their friend, said, coming from an aisle with a book in his hand.

"Ugh, that is all we need—a panic on our hands. Next thing you know, the humans will be up in a tizzy," Patience huffed, a little annoyed but knowing he was right.

A note floated down; she caught it:

"Good evening, Thea. We have seen more than our usual customers, but the most curious customers want to know more about who Lilith is."

Interesting. So, word may have gotten out. Remember to deal with one crisis at a time. Michael was now safe to go from the mansion to GreyJoy's, but anywhere else was dangerous. She needed to speak with Ian because she knew he would be the only one to really get to Michael, especially since he wasn't going to like that he wouldn't be able to go with them to find Selene, but first...

"Silas, where the hell have you been?" Patience demanded, more annoyed than surprised to see him.

"I have been researching a way for us to get into Askaria," he stated, leaning against one of the bookshelves. He had on his usual worn leather jacket, but he also had a gold-hilted sword strapped to his back, which was unusual since he typically preferred daggers. "I tried to tell you earlier before you disappeared in a frenzy. No worries, Michael filled me in on your issue."

My issue. Patience rolled her eyes. *This fucking bond.* She didn't need a reminder.

"I may have found a way to get into Askaria." Silas handed her the open book. She looked down at the open page and read, then glanced at Silas. He was serious.

"Michael, could you go check the vault for Truesilk for me? We may need more. Take Jafa with you."

Michael reluctantly nodded and tried to pull Ian along.

"Ian, stay," Patience told him. "I need you to look at something for me."

Michael cast her a suspicious look before continuing down the hall. Circe followed behind them. A note floated down.

"Would you like me to keep them occupied?"

"Only for a few minutes, GreyJoy. Nothing crazy."

"And should I even ask what is on that page?" Ian said, walking over to her as Alecia kept herself busy browsing shelves.

"Silas wants to use Michael to open the doors to Askaria. We would have to take Michael into Evictus, and he would have to place his hands on the city doors to declare himself king."

Ian tensed. "Not happening."

"No worries. Silas has missed a lot like the fact that we were attacked by, let's see, *five* Hokima assassins."

"What? When?" Silas gasped, his eyes widening.

"Not even twelve hours ago." Patience knew he would blame himself for not being there. She didn't want to lay on the guilt, but she needed for him to see this plan wasn't feasible. "The demon has sent the Hokima to kill him. He knows that Michael is the only one who can challenge him for the throne and win. Plus, Michael is the only one who can open Lilith's prison. You are supposed to be here to keep him safe. This will not keep him safe."

Patience held up the book to emphasize her point before throwing it on the counter.

"He was with his family who clearly protected him, since I see he is alive and well," he said pointedly.

For a minute, Patience thought he was only talking about the king and queen, but his stare conveyed he included her as his family, as well.

"Not the point and no, I will not be getting my best friend killed to get into a kingdom to kill a demon. We will find another way," she said flatly, walking up to Silas and poking him in the chest so he completely understood her.

"Fine," he growled, grabbing the book from the counter.

"Now, Ian, I need you to do two things for me."

"Which are?" Ian still glared at Silas.

"First, I need you to convince Michael to stay within the mansion's grounds. I was able to fix the barrier, so he should be safe. He is also protected here because no one but your idiot brother would try to go against GreyJoy."

The frown fell from his face as he chuckled, knowing she was right. "I can definitely figure out a way to convince him," he said with a mischievous smirk.

"The second thing is I need you to protect Michael."

Ian raised an eyebrow at her.

"I know it sounds silly since you both are soul-bonded, but Michael can be reckless sometimes when it comes to protecting the ones he loves."

"He's not the only one," Silas grumbled.

"And," Patience continued, ignoring Silas, "he would sacrifice himself to save you. I need you to remind him that it would kill you both, and you want to live."

He waved her off. "No worries. I understand what you are saying, and I will try my best."

"That is all a girl can ask for. Now, let's find ourselves a witch. GreyJoy, where is Selene?"

"He says she is still off the grid, but he may be able to get us in prox-prox-im—" Jafa stammered, coming from in between the bookshelves with Michael behind him.

"Proximity," Michael chimed in.

Jafa flushed. "Yes, proximity of her."

Michael placed the Blanket of Hildan and the Silks of Neadle on the counter. "That is all the Truesilk we have."

She wished they had more, but this would have to do. It was possible that maybe she could create a reusable rope out of it. She laid the silk on the counter and began to roll it together so she could create a rope.

"So, what's the plan? I know you have been formulating one," Michael said, knowing Patience too well, but he wasn't going to like her idea.

She bit her lip. "I do. You and Ian are going to go back with Silas and distract a crazy witch hunter while Alecia, Circe, and I go and find Selene."

"Noooo, we are going with you!" Michael argued.

She could see Michael getting visibly upset, but Ian swooped in.

"Soțul, we just want to keep you safe. You will be safer with me at the mansion." Ian grabbed Michael's head and put their foreheads together. "If he captures you, it will be the end of everything we know, and we don't want that."

Michael still looked tense until he whispered something to him that Patience could not hear, but from the smile on Alecia's face, she clearly did.

"Fine, I don't like it, but he has a point," Michael said before grabbing her hands. "You be careful. Don't trust anyone and get back to me. Promise."

Patience smiled. "I promise. You can stay here with Jafa if you like and GreyJoy can send you back to the mansion, but you must not go anywhere else."

Michael nodded in understanding.

Letting go of his hand, she moved over to the counter and found the Truesilk had been turned into a reusable rope. Perfect.

"GreyJoy, you beautiful being. I love you," she beamed. "Now, all we have to do is locate Selene, and then maybe we will be just one step closer to getting into Askaria. Do you happen to know where she is?"

"He says she has popped up," Jafa replied, still behind the counter. His home décor magazine was long gone and had been replaced with a men's fashion magazine. "He knows where she is, but he is not sure how long she will be there."

It was still strange to Patience that he could hear GreyJoy speak and she couldn't. It was another reason why she was eager to get her memories unlocked. She wanted to hear his voice and know what her friend sounded like.

Unlocking her memories now seemed like such a distant dream. Patience still believed Lucius was the key, but at this point, it didn't seem worth it. She was starting to think maybe she had locked her memories away for a good reason. Besides, she would have no time to talk with Alden now. Maybe when all of this was over, she could just get him to tell her about her past and be done with it from there.

No matter how well she believed she understood herself, merely hearing it couldn't compare to truly knowing and feeling who she was.

"So, what's the plan? I take it this won't be easy," Alecia said, pulling Patience out of her thoughts and running her hands over the rope. "This is nice and will work beautifully."

"Selene definitely wasn't eager to help. I think she is afraid since she has been on the run for quite a while, and I don't blame her after watching all her brothers and sisters get killed," Patience said, taking the rope and then summoning her satchel. She curled the rope up and placed it in the bag before sending it back to the vault.

"How about you try speaking with her again? Tell her you have proof and then you can use my memories to show her," Circe explained.

"That sounds like a good plan," Patience agreed.

"Sounds like the only plan," Alecia retorted as a matter of fact.

"Alright, let's get this done before Selene really goes into hiding," Patience said, holding out her hands. Alecia and Circe each grabbed one. "We will be back hopefully with a Silverlands witch. Silas, try not to sacrifice Michael until I get back. GreyJoy, take us to her."

"What the hell?" Michael exclaimed.

Silas glared at her. Patience only smiled.

"He says stay safe!" Jafa shouted as they disappeared.

The smell of pine, alcohol, and another pungent smell Patience didn't want to think about assailed her nose. A log cabin bar stood between the edge of a forest and a long, dark road. Music, drunken shouts, and the knocking of pool balls could be heard from its open windows.

Two busted outdoor lights illuminated a variation of old Harleys to new Yoshimura motorcycles that lined the gravel lot. The sign that flashed from above the door read Tootsie's.

Patience scanned the outside walls of the building for the magical symbol that would tell her what creatures they would encounter.

She found it on the upper left corner of the entrance. A twisted circle with two intertwined Xs. *Fuck.*

Trolls and goblins.

CHAPTER TEN

Lucius

A red haze clouded Lucius's vision. A maelstrom of emotions stirred within him. It felt as though the anguish of Mae's death was resurfacing, plunging him back into the depths of that haunting memory. The recollections rushed to the surface, overwhelming him with their intensity.

The scene replayed in his mind, vivid and visceral, as if it were happening once more. The sight of blood splattered everywhere, the metallic scent that permeated the air—each detail etched into his consciousness, refusing to be suppressed.

The turmoil within Lucius intensified, torn between conflicting emotions and impulses. He harbored a deep-seated desire to exact vengeance upon the witch, holding her responsible for the resurfacing pain he believed he had buried long ago. Though, another part of him, a small flicker of reason, acknowledged her innocence and recognized that she bore no responsibility in the death of his wife and child. However, his rationality was being obscured by the overpowering presence of the Ragana Zidikas, the ruthless witch hunter residing within him.

The insatiable thirst for blood coursed through his veins, threatening to overwhelm his better judgment.

"Lucius, I need you to calm down. Killing the witch will not help you," Max pleaded as he practically ran beside him to keep up.

Lucius had already searched the library and followed her scent to the bedroom she was using. Not finding her there, he was on his way back to his wife's room. If he found her in there, he wasn't sure what he would do, but he guaranteed it would end in bloodshed.

"Give me Luzia now, or you will not survive this night."

Lucius was so focused on finding the witch that he failed to sense Volt behind him before it was too late.

Volt grabbed his shoulders then transported them to Lucius's office. They appeared in the middle of the room. Embers from the dying fire were the only light until Volt turned on his desk lamp. His office was scattered with little trinkets he found over the years in various realms from his witch hunting days. They were trinkets of different hues of purple that his wife would have loved. These precious mementos adorned every available surface, adorning the fireplace mantel and lining the bookshelf, creating a kaleidoscope of purple hues. His desk and chair remained untouched, except for one single purple gem that was meant for his child. Being in his space grounded him a little.

"You need to listen to my questions and Umber's answers. You may find them interesting. May I let you go now?"

Lucius took a deep breath and nodded. Volt let him go.

He went over to the fireplace and put two logs in it. Then he took the poker, moving them around until they caught fire. He shouldn't give a shit what answers he found, but he did use an Astral coin and it was very fucking interesting to learn Umber demanded two coins to get an answer for one question.

Lucius went over to his crystal bar globe and grabbed a bottle of whiskey. He poured himself a drink before sitting in his leather chair. "Speak before I change my mind."

"You wanted me to find out more information about the witch." Volt stood in front of his black oak desk with his hands behind his back. "The first question I asked was simple: Who is Patience Harrington? He told me what we already know. She believes she is an Abberrant whose memories are lost to her."

"Yes, we know this. What is the next question?" Lucius took another sip of his drink and tried to keep focused.

Volt pierced him with a curious look before he told him the next question. "I asked what coven does she belong to? The answer to this question I didn't understand, but he said she belongs to all covens, and she was once accepted into most clans."

"That makes no sense. A witch that belongs to all covens and is accepted into most clans." Lucius rubbed his chin, then downed the rest of his liquor. Accepted by both witches and vampires? Who the hell was this female? Lucius ran his hands down his face. "What was the third question?"

"Who was she before she lost her memories?'"

Lucius raised a brow. It was a very good question, and he was quite curious to know the answer to this.

"He wanted double for this answer, but I refused to pay it, so I was allowed to ask another in which I simply asked him, why does that question cost more? I was told that there is dark magic at work that prevents him from revealing anything without greater cost and exposure to himself. He says we must protect her at all costs and that if she dies, all will be lost. *You can't kill her*," Volt said, emphasizing his point.

"Protect her? From what?" Lucius sputtered, rage gleaming in his eyes.

"That I am not sure of. It could be from the half-demon, Alazar, who has taken residence on the throne in Askaria."

It did not surprise Lucius one bit that Volt knew the half-demon's name or what was happening in Askaria. "You think the half-demon is after the witch?"

"She is powerful, and if he were to convince her to join his side, I think she would be hard to take down."

Volt made a good point. She was indeed powerful, even if she had no idea how powerful she truly was. If the half-demon did somehow convince her to join his ranks, they would be fucked. In his heart, Lucius knew that would only happen if she had no choice.

"Or I could just kill her now and then he would not have anyone to convince." Even as he said the words, he knew he would never follow through with them.

He'd had the chance to end her life earlier, yet his mind was consumed with the desire to taste her lips, to lose himself in her. He closed his eyes, images of her flooding his thoughts, the memory of her scent haunting him. His fangs pressed against his lips, a pang of hunger gnawing at his gut as the forbidden allure of her blood invaded his mind.

"Lucius," Volt said to bring him back. He opened his eyes to see Volt gazing at him with a knowing look. He knew his feelings for the witch ran deeper than he let on. "I know you are upset about her bringing back unwanted memories, but I need you to put aside those feelings and think logically. This witch is important, even though we are not sure of the reason. You met her for a reason, and what have I always told you?"

"There are no coincidences. Fuck. Okay." Lucius ran his fingers through his hair, knowing that Volt was right. He needed to push aside his feelings and think logically about this. "Hokima assassins attacked the house. Twice.

The first time they were after the witch's friend, Michael. This second time they tried to kill me, and they went after Alecia's sister, Estelle."

"They also were after Michael again," Max said, strolling in the office.

"None of them went after the witch?" Volt asked, raising a brow.

"She never gave them a chance to touch her," Max added like a proud father.

"Where is the witch now? We have to talk with her."

"Well, this *one*,"—Max pointedly glared at Lucius— "scared her off. She is probably back at her apartment or at the bookstore."

"Or she ran due to guilt," Lucius scoffed.

The witch had left. The realization crashed upon Lucius like a tidal wave, dousing him in a mix of regret and anguish. The weight of his actions settled heavily upon his shoulders. Of course, she would have run from him, as any sensible person would have. The sting of her absence pierced through him, and the desolation of her departure echoed in his heart. He ignored them, pushing the feelings aside.

Max walked purposefully toward him. "You are being a complete ass!" he shouted, his dark green eyes illuminated with fury. His hand balled into a fist and slammed against the desk, cracking it in half. It fell to the ground, along with all the paper and pens on it.

Lucius stood, pushing back his desk chair. He had never seen his friend so upset with him before. They'd had plenty of arguments, but the anger in his eyes made Lucius take pause.

"She has nothing to feel guilty about!" Max's voice thundered through the room, his rage shaking the very air around them. He didn't give a damn about the desk as he forcefully shoved it aside, closing the distance between himself and Lucius. His nostrils flared, drawing in deep breaths, while his fangs bared in a menacing display. His fists remained tightly clenched, coiled with the anticipation of a brawl, his entire being poised for a fight that seemed inevitable.

"As much as this is fun to watch, we have bigger problems on our hands. I am not sure what Patience did to piss you off, but it will have to wait," Silas said, leaning against the doorway. "And Patience is actually off searching for the Silverlands witch. Though, we may have found another way into Askaria."

"Which is?" Lucius asked curiously.

"I think it is best for King Kieran to explain." Silas stepped aside to let the king pass.

"Michael and Ian have returned and told me my wife has gone with Patience to find the Silverlands witch. This would be the best time for us to go and find the back entrance," King Kieran explained.

Lucius's brows furrowed. "Back entrance?"

"There is no time to explain. We must go now."

Fucking Demons. This was his house, and no one told him what to do in his own house, especially not a demon. King or not.

"No one will be going anywhere until you explain. You. Are. Not. My. King. I bow to no one. You can either explain or get the hell out."

"I may not be your king, but you will obey me." King Kieran stood at his full height and pinned Lucius with his stare.

Challenge motherfucking accepted.

Lucius was already too far gone, and Max knew his intent. "Lucius don't!" Max yelled seconds too late as Lucius's hand connected with King Kieran's jaw.

King Kieran dodged his next fist but backhanded Lucius, sending him hurtling through the air.

Lucius crashed into the nearby furniture, causing it to tremble and topple. Splintered wood and shattered glass exploded in all directions, adding to the chaos of the room. The impact reverberated through the space, leaving a trail of disarray and sending a shower of debris cascading to the floor.

"Clearly, he has some tension and anger he needs to get rid of. Maxim, please quickly fetch two swords. Let us see if we can get him to let some of his anger go," King Kieran said, flexing his muscles, getting ready to do battle as Lucius climbed up from the floor and watched as Volt faded away with a smirk on his face. *The bastard.*

Lucius charged, but the king easily deflected.

"Leave us alone," Kieran directed at Silas as Lucius rushed him again.

Instead of deflecting, the king caught him, lifted him, and threw him against the wall behind his desk. He landed against it with a hard thud, causing the water lily canvas to drop. Silas swiftly left, closing the door behind him.

Lucius jumped to his feet, ignoring the ache in his back. He was going to kill the king, then Silas, then Max, and finally the witch—all in that exact order. They all deserved to die. It wouldn't make him feel any better, but it would take away the pain until he could bury it deeply again.

Lucius picked up a chair and broke it apart, taking the leg of the chair for a temporary weapon. He knew the king was fast, so he had to be faster.

They both locked eyes, their gazes unwavering, as Lucius contemplated the most effective way to end the king's life.

"You will never best me, not in this state. You are weak and not yourself, but give me the best that you've got," the king taunted.

Blinded by rage, Lucius took the broken chair and charged at the king, trying to pummel him with the chair leg, but Kieran easily dodged him, then grabbed him from behind before tossing him across the room.

"Enough of this nonsense. You will not beat me. Od—Patience is not here. Whatever she did to upset you, you must put it aside —"

Ignoring the king's words, Lucius picked up a small table and threw it at the king. The king blocked it and sent it flying into the fireplace, where the flames consumed it.

"Lucius! *Pesteum.*"

Every bone in his body froze, paralyzing him.

The king slowly stalked over to him, narrowing his eyes. "Funny, that would have never worked on you before, but that is what happens when you are apart from each other."

Lucius didn't understand what the king was talking about. He tried concentrating on moving any inch of his body, but nothing happened.

"You will not be released until I say so," King Kieran said sternly, but then his deep voice softened with sympathy. "Now, I need you to listen. I understand that you are in pain, I can feel it coming off of you, but I need you to know it's not real. I wish I could tell you more, but the damn spell he has in place has not allowed me to. There is so much you and Patience need to know, but we can only say so much. What we *can* do is kill the bastard. Do you understand?"

Lucius wanted to understand, but this didn't make any sense. What spell prevented him from speaking, and what did he mean his pain was not real?

Lucius tried to move his body again. He was completely at the demon king's mercy.

A knock sounded, and Maxim entered.

He glanced between Lucius and Kieran.

He kneeled before the king and handed him both swords, including Luzia.

The traitor.

"Thank you. Leave us."

Maxim glanced at Lucius again, then turned and left.

The king laughed. "You all have changed so much, except for her. She is the same fiery woman who still has a soft spot for you."

He gripped Luzia, swinging her back and forth to test her weight and balance. "She has also not changed one bit, still a formidable fighter just like the day I gave her to you."

Liar. It was his grandfather who gave him that sword.

"I know you don't believe me, but it doesn't matter at the moment. Are you ready to fight? *Glandran.*"

The king tossed Luzia at him, and he caught it right before blocking the king's sword. He was faster, but Lucius knew this dance. Dodge, deflect, attack. Repeat. It was as though his body was waking up and his muscle memory was kicking in.

"Ah, yes. Finally, your body is remembering. The Dance of Flames. Your mind will soon follow. Unfortunately, you will forget most of this conversation."

Faster and faster, they moved to a non-existent rhythm. Dodge, deflect, attack. Repeat. Dodge, deflect, attack. Repeat. Until they became a blur of movement. Lucius became so concentrated on keeping the rhythm that when the king changed the pattern, he became caught off-guard. The king took the opportunity to trip him, causing Luzia to slip from his hand and fly across the room as he landed flat on his ass with the king's sword at his throat.

"Here is the deal. You will help me get back into my kingdom, and you won't have to ever see me again if you so choose. I may have a way for us to get back into the kingdom undetected that doesn't have to do with sacrificing my son. Though we must do it now while my queen is distracted. Do we have a deal?"

Lucius shouldn't trust him, but the thought of never having to deal with another damn demon again was appealing and at this point, he knew he had no choice. The only way to get the king out of his life would be to help him get back into Askaria, which meant he would need to kill the half-demon.

As the rush of adrenaline subsided, Lucius's clarity returned, and with it a sense of humility. He couldn't help but acknowledge the stupidity of his initial assumption, believing he could have triumphed over the formidable demon. In his heart, Lucius understood that the king had likely restrained himself, showing mercy to a lesser opponent like himself due to his youth.

The true extent of the king's power remained cloaked, a hidden force that he never fully unveiled. In truth, the king possessed the ability to effortlessly end Lucius's life, but the witch's influence distorted his reasoning. Lucius realized the magnitude of his luck in securing the initial deal with the king who, despite his immense power, saw reason and offered him an opportunity for redemption.

"Fine. We have a deal."

The king moved the sword away from his neck and held out his hand. Lucius grabbed it, and Kieran helped him off the floor.

"Good. Now, let's go find the others."

CHAPTER ELEVEN

PATIENCE

"Well, ain't this just peachy," Alecia grumbled. They were seated at the bar made of an old metal container between a bearded goblin and a green-faced troll.

In the dimly lit tavern, an old hard rock song blared from a jukebox nestled in the corner, its raucous melody intertwining with the boisterous laughter of goblins gathered around the two pool tables. The air was thick with the scent of ale and tobacco as these small, mischievous creatures indulged in merriment and revelry. Amongst them, trolls huddled together at scattered tables, their gaze fixed upon a human sports game playing on the flickering television screen.

The eclectic mix of beings created a lively atmosphere, filled with clinking glasses, uproarious cheers, and the occasional clash of pool balls. It reminded Patience of the few times her and Michael had actually had fun instead of trying to save the world.

They still hadn't found Selene, but Patience knew she was here. GreyJoy wouldn't have directed them wrong. *She's here, but where?*

"Are you sure this is the right place? I don't see any silver-haired witches," Circe muttered as she dodged the fourth male who tried to grab her ass. "My tolerance wears thin."

Patience wanted to reach out with her magic, but witch magic wasn't allowed here, and as soon as she did anything to reveal it, she would be kicked out. She didn't have Michael to help her suppress her magic, so she had to be careful here.

"What will it be, sweetheart?" the barmaid asked for the third time.

Patience didn't want to drink anything, but they couldn't leave until they found Selene.

"Ummm… I will have three rumites. Captain Morganna, if you have it."

The bolrag, a cross between a warthog and a rhino, fixed her drinks before placing them on the filthy bar, then moved on before she could bombard her with any more questions about a silver-haired female.

"So, what's the plan?" Alecia asked as she took a sip from her drink and then cringed. "That is not a rumite."

"I don't know. I have no clue where she could be. We could head back to GreyJoy's and see if he can find her again," Patience said before she took a sip of her drink and almost spit it out. It was sweet. That was definitely *not* Captain Morganna. She had no clue how Circe was even still drinking it.

The queen shrugged. "Tastes like Aurlin. Is that her?" Circe pointed over to a female with long black hair who was cleaning up the tables while trying to fight off all the grabby hands.

Patience wasn't sure until the female turned to slap the back of one of the male's heads.

"Yes, that's her. She changed her hair color." Her hair color would have stood out too much here. "Let's stop staring before she gets spooked."

They all looked away. Though, Patience kept her eyes on her as she finished clearing the tables then headed into the back of the bar.

"I'm going to follow her. Follow behind me in five minutes."

Circe and Alecia nodded as Patience slipped off her stool. She took one last sip from the cup as she forced down the sweet drink. Then she cautiously made her way to the door, trying not to be too obvious as she crept through.

She found Selene in the back opening a box of liquor. The Silverlands witch took out a bottle of Ol'Redbane, goblin whiskey and took a swig.

"Ah. The sweet burn." She smiled, then turned and spotted her. "Took you forever to find me, Patty. I know that damn bookstore is helping you. As I told you before, I won't help you. I've got my own problems."

"Your problems are my problems. We have the same goal," Patience said, grabbing the bottle from Selene and taking a swig herself to wash away the taste of that awfully sweet rumite.

"I have to say I like your spunk, Patty. How are our goals aligned?"

Patience took another sip before she handed it back to her. "We can stop the demon who is hunting you, but I need your help."

"Do you even know what type of demon it is or what his other half is?"

"Well... no, but together we can figure it out. Before that, we need to get him out of Askaria, so he doesn't set Lilith free."

"So, in other words, you have no real plan." Selene took another drink from the bottle.

Patience flushed. "We—"

"I know you don't. There is no need to make one up, but since you seem so persistent, I will come with you." Selene flashed a confident grin. "It's probably mostly the alcohol talking, but I'm tired of running. I watched him kill another of my friends yesterday, and I am ready to take him down."

She uttered the words with such nonchalance that it sent a shiver down Patience's spine. Yet as the realization dawned upon her, she understood that

Selene had witnessed the deaths of numerous friends, perhaps rendering her numb to the pain that accompanied such losses. "Selene, I am so sorry," she whispered to her, not knowing what else to say. She could only imagine what she was going through to see her friends murdered like that.

"There is nothing to be sorry about. Just promise me you will kill him when you get the chance," Selene said as she drank the last of the whiskey, then shook out her hair. It turned from black back to its original color, silver. Patience needed to remind herself to ask her how she did that. It would make her life so much easier.

"I promise you I will kill him as soon as I get the chance."

"That's all I ask. I take it these are your friends." She nodded towards the bar.

Patience turned to see Circe and Alecia walk through the door.

"Yes." This time, Patience addressed the others, "No worries, she will be coming with us willingly."

"Aw, so I won't be able to tie her up," Alecia said sarcastically when she reached them.

"Well, if you ask nicely, I still might let you," Selene teased.

"Alright, let's go. We need to get back and hopefully, the damn vampire's head has cooled," Patience said as she grabbed a bottle of liquor from the box, hoping to use it as a white flag for the vampire.

"Let's go out the back. It will be faster to get away from the no-magic ward."

They all followed Selene through the dingy kitchen out the back door of the bar. As soon as Patience stepped outside, Selene pushed her to the ground.

"Shit, they found me, Patty."

Patience looked up to see two pairs of smoldering eyes staring back at her from the darkness. Tarnok. They were shadow demons that carried sickness and death wherever they went. Eight thick horns adorned their rugged heads as they emerged from the shadows. Their hard, fibrous bodies were riddled with gaping wounds showing the infernal fire that burned inside them as their whip-like tails snapped behind them.

"Damn, he's really trying to kill you," Alecia said as she geared up to fight. "Alright, witch, show us what you can do."

Erecting a barrier wouldn't stop them. Patience tried to think of what she read about the Tarnok, more like what Michael had read to her about them. *Ah, yes,* she remembered. *They need light.* Only if she could raise the sun, but maybe she had something better.

"I am going to need you to distract them for a few minutes, but anything made of light will help," Patience informed the others.

The shadows began to slowly surround them, swirling menacingly. Alecia held out her hand, and Patience watched as a pink double-bladed sword materialized. She sliced the sword through the air with a vicious smile.

"You wouldn't happen to have another one of those?" Circe asked as she admired the way Alecia swung the sword through the air.

Alecia held out her right hand, and a gold spear appeared. She threw it toward Circe, who easily caught it.

"You have five minutes, so make it quick," Alecia said as her and Circe walked forward to meet the Tarnok.

The shadows were moving closer to Patience and Selene by the second. She needed to act quickly because if those shadows touched them, they would drag them down to their lair, where she would have no power.

"Give me your hands. We need to make light." She reached out and grabbed Selene.

"I know a spell."

"No, I just need you to trust me and let me in, okay?"

Selene gave her a skeptical look but nodded.

"Okay, just relax. Take a deep breath. I know you are scared, but I need you to concentrate. We can do this," Patience reassured her, also trying to take her own advice.

The shadows were right on their heels now. She summoned Seckor, her pathfinder, but also her little ball of light. The illumination helped to push the shadows back, but they needed *more*.

"Close your eyes and think of light surrounding you. The feel of it on your skin."

Selene's silver hair began to glow, giving off light.

"Yes, Selene, just like that," Patience encouraged as she pushed magic into Selene and Seckor. She could hear the clashing of swords behind her.

The grunts and groans brought worry to her mind, but she ignored it. She continued to concentrate on pushing more magic into Selene. She grew brighter and brighter. Her skin began to glow, and symbols similar to the ones on her vault appeared one by one on Selene's arms. As she grew brighter, Seckor grew in size and its glow spread wider, feeding off her.

"Yes! That's it. Keep it going. More light!" Alecia yelled. "Damn. Circe, I didn't know you could do that with a spear. Teach me."

Circe laughed, and the clashing of swords continued.

"You are doing well, Selene. Keep going. This is almost over." Patience squeezed her hands, encouraging her. The symbols glowed brighter, and she took a moment to look at Selene to see her beauty and her power.

This was a Silverlands witch. This was the power of the Silverlands and direct power from the Goddess. It was beautiful.

Seckor grew until light burst from it, and Selene lifted off the ground as luminance filled the air and surrounded them. Just as quickly as it appeared, it dissipated.

Selene fell into Patience's arms. "Are you alright?" she asked with worry.

She stared at her strangely. "Your eyes. They glow silver."

"Yeah, I know. It will fade in a moment, but are you okay?" Patience urged, but it still took Selene a moment to respond.

"I am fine. What about the other two?"

Patience turned around to find Circe and Alecia sitting in the dirt, exhausted. She noticed a few bruises on Alecia's arms and a claw mark on her side, but that was all. The queen appeared to be unscathed.

"Are you both alright?" Patience asked.

"I think that is the most fun I've had in a long time," Alecia said, laughing as she moved to get up.

"It has been a while since I fought with a formidable opponent and had a real fighter by my side," Circe added, walking over to Alecia to help her up.

"I'm glad I could be so accommodating to you both," Patience retorted with an amused eye roll.

They both laughed.

"Now, let's head back to GreyJoy's so we can rest and gather a plan."

They all moved around her and touched her arm or shoulder before she transported them back to GreyJoy's. She just prayed Lucius would not be waiting for her there.

◆○◆

Patience

The witch needed to rest. He could feel her exhaustion. Whatever she was doing was draining her.

The bond was getting stronger. He was beginning to feel her emotions. Soon, he would be able to reach out through the bond and force her to come to him.

The question would be to either kill her or kiss her? He was still deciding.

The information Volt gave him earlier still swirled in his head. *No such thing as coincidences.* In a way, he was right. If the half-demon, this Alazar, did manage to lure her to his side. She would be a formidable foe to go up against. If it ever did happen, he would look forward to fighting such a foe, but secretly, he hoped that it would never come to that.

The pain is not real... you and Patience.... Dance of Flames... spell. You will forget this, the words echoed through his mind. It was the king's voice. Pieces of a conversation that he didn't remember having but felt familiar.

"Lucius. Lucius, are you listening?" Max called out to him.

They had moved this conversation into the library since they had destroyed Lucius's office and Max did not want to risk them destroying his own.

"*What?*" His eyes snapped back to his friend.

"Are you paying attention?" Maxim asked. King Kieran had been explaining how a portal was built as a back door into Askaria.

"Yes, I am. Where is this door?"

"It is here." King Kieran pointed to a map of Evictus that Maxim had taken out. Lucius glanced over to where he pointed and almost wanted to laugh. No wonder he waited to reveal this when his wife left. The back door to his kingdom was in the city of Amare, the city of the selkies, more commonly known as sirens.

"So let me guess, your wife doesn't know about you and Azalin. I guess she would be even more pissed if she knew about this backdoor," Lucius said, trying to stifle a laugh at the king, who was glaring daggers at him.

"Exactly why we must take this opportunity to go now. We will need weapons," the king said to Max, ignoring Lucius.

Volt materialized near the fireplace.

"Nice enough for you to join us," Lucius drawled sarcastically.

"I thought it would be best to stay out of the way," Volt replied.

"I still think my plan would work," Silas spoke up. "We can keep him safe."

"If Circe heard you talk that way about her son, you would no longer have a tongue, brother or not," Kieran snapped as he continued to look over the map. "Time moves differently there, so we should have a few hours before they return. Once we have weapons, I will summon a portal to take us there."

Maxim left the room, Lucius assumed to find weapons.

Lucius walked to the window alcove. The moon illuminated the forest that surrounded the perimeter of the house. He told himself he went here to look out the window, but it was to be closer to the witch. He didn't want to think about her, yet he needed to know if she was okay. He still could only feel so much through the bond.

As much as he wanted to hold on to his anger, his concern for her was outweighing it.

The memory of her in his arms resurfaced.

"Are you alright?" he whispered.

"Keep me safe."

She had buried her head in his neck and wrapped her arms around him. Her scent had surrounded him, penetrating not only his senses but also his mind. It was the moment she broke through, piercing the shield around his heart.

Reflecting on it now, he realized he'd let his anger get the best of him. He was never going to kill her. He didn't have the heart to, which answered his questions about whether he wanted to kiss or kill her. Kiss was definitely the answer. *Fuck.*

He wasn't sure if they could ever be anything more. He wasn't sure if he would ever be able to get past her being a witch. His wife and child still meant so much to him. It was why their memories were so painful. He would thank her for giving him back something he thought he had lost for a long time.

Sighing, the one thing he could admit was that he did care for her well-being, and he hoped she was alright wherever she was at the moment.

"I hope I am not interrupting, but I am looking for the witch. I have something she wants very badly," Alden called out from the upper level of the library.

Alden. An unbridled rage surged within Lucius upon hearing his voice. The desire to tear him apart still burned fiercely within him, fueled by a mix of anger and jealousy. Even though the witch was not here, Lucius couldn't help but imagine Alden touching her, their magic intertwining in a way that should have been his alone. Lucius felt his feet move toward Alden, but the king caught his arm before he could even reach the stairs.

"Alden, it has been a long time," King Kieran replied, keeping his voice level.

"Yes, it has indeed, my king." Alden spoke as he made his way down the stairs until he stood in front of Lucius and the king. Lucius struggled against the king's grip, but Kieran only clamped down firmer on his arm.

"I heard you helped to heal me. Thank you," the king said evenly.

"It was my pleasure, but it is Dessa who helped to heal you." Alden glanced at Lucius's arm, and then at Lucius, raising a brow in question.

Dessa? "Who the hell is Dessa?" Lucius asked, confused, ignoring Alden's quizzical look. He felt like a child.

The king squeezed his arm as if to tell him to behave before he let it go and continued to speak with Alden. "You are not affected?"

Lucius rubbed now sore limb in anger and stepped away from Kieran. Affected? What the hell was he talking about? Lucius glanced around the room. Everyone looked as confused as him, except for Volt, of course. He made himself comfortable on a nearby chair staring into the fireplace.

"No, I am not," Alden revealed.

"How?" the king asked suspiciously.

"The same as you. I believe." Alden moved away from the stairs and began to peruse the books on the table, not making eye contact with the king.

"I am still censored from speaking certain things. Are you?"

"I have broken past that." Alden smirked.

Lucius tried to follow along with their conversation, but he didn't understand. "What the hell are you two talking about?"

"Nothing," the king said quietly. "Just two old friends catching up."

Lucius glanced between the two again, suspicious of their confusing conversation but not in the mood to pursue it. He looked at Alden, keeping his anger in check. "So, you are here for the witch?"

Alden stood straighter. "Yes."

"Well, she is not here. Now get *out*," Lucius sneered, walking away because if he stayed near him, he would start another fight, except this one he would win. He was certain.

A loud clash sounded near the door. "Weapons." Maxim dropped a few swords and daggers onto the hardwood. "Take your pick. Alden?"

"Maxim, do you know where the witch is?"

"No, but sorry about this, how did you get in here?" Max scanned the library until his eyes landed on Estelle.

"Because some things never change, even when time moves on, and minds become blind. Trust has not been broken," Volt replied.

The king stared at Volt as though he was seeing him in a different light. Lucius hated it when Volt became cryptic. It didn't explain how the fuck he got in his library. Maybe the witch was right, and the damn ward was flawed.

"We waste time. We must go now." The king chose two swords and placed them in the sheathes on his back. "I am ready."

Michael and Ian took that moment to come strolling in, appearing freshly fucked. Lucius ignored their mischievous grins and said, "Max and Silas will come with the king and I. Michael and Ian, you will stay here with Estelle." He turned to look at Volt. "You will watch them all."

Silas and Maxim grabbed swords and sheathed them on their backs as the king pulled a pouch from his pocket. He revealed a blue bottle of shimmering liquid.

"I believe you should take Alden with you," Volt said, surprising them all.

"No," Lucius spat. As much as he valued Volt, this was one of those moments he wanted to murder him. Alden had no business going with them. He had no business being here in the first place.

"Where exactly are you going?" Alden inquired.

"They are going to Amare to find a way into Askaria," Volt informed him in a casual tone, as if he were discussing the weather rather than sharing important information. His posture exuded a sense of ease and nonchalance.

"Amare? There is a back entrance there." Alden could not help the grin that appeared on his face. "And I take it the queen doesn't know about this."

It wasn't a question. Lucius couldn't even fault him for it because they all knew. He withheld an eye roll. "What is the plan?"

"There are eyes and ears everywhere in Amare. It will be nearly impossible but this,"—the king held up the blue shimmering bottle— "will open a portal right outside the gates of Amare. She will grant me an audience and welcome us because I am her king. But forewarning, she is pissed at me, so I am unsure of how warm her welcome will be. To appease her anger, I will offer you as gifts to her daughters."

"You will *what*?" Max didn't seem so happy with the idea.

"The door is in the Atrium. It is where they will take you. Do not eat or drink anything. If you do, you will become lost to us, and I will kill you myself. The daughters will try and seduce you with their siren call. You must sneak away before that happens. The sirens will leave you to become vulnerable. So before that happens, you need to sneak away."

"Vulnerable?" Silas asked, confused.

"Naked. We must leave before they get us naked," Maxim supplied with a scowl.

King Kieran said without missing a beat, "Once you sneak away, on the southern wall of the Atrium, you will find the mirror set in stone with the words, Πόρτα στο Βασίλειο του Βασιλιά."

Max snickered. "The door to the King's Kingdom. You couldn't have made it more obvious. I'm guessing the other side says, door to the King's Mistress."

The king glared at Max with such intensity, it made Lucius realize he might just lose his best friend because if the king didn't kill him, he would.

"Someone must have a death wish," Alden whispered.

"Max, shut it," Lucius muttered.

King Kieran continued, clenching and unclenching his jaw, the only sign of his growing annoyance, "You need to say *Acasia* to activate the door. Once through, you will appear in the fallion, and you need to find the false wall, which will lead you to the throne room. Hopefully, the bastard will be sitting on it, and you can kill him right then and there, but if not, you need to search for him. I will join you as soon as I can."

"Do you think it will be that simple?" Silas asked as he sheathed the dagger that was twirling in his hand.

"No, but we have an opportunity here, and I say we take it. You do not have to go if you do not wish." The king looked into the eyes of every one of them. No one looked away.

"The Maladrias, Nikita and Ennes, are your greatest threats. The queen will take me to her bedchamber, and that is where they will stay until the queen leaves, so they should not be a problem. If they are, do not let their small sizes fool you. They are deadly. Use this to knock them out." The king handed Silas a small clear glass ball filled with pink gas.

Lucius grabbed Luzia and sheathed her on his back. He was ready to do this. Hopefully, they would be able to kill this half-demon before the night was over.

Kieran moved to an open space within the library and poured the shimmering liquid onto the floor. As soon as the first drop hit the hardwood, a large portal opened.

"I will join you," Alden finally spoke.

Rage instantly spiked in Lucius. He turned to face Alden, speaking through his teeth, "You make one wrong move, you are dead, head of council or not."

Alden nodded slightly and smirked.

The king stepped through first, then Silas. Maxim followed, then Alden and Lucius were the last ones through.

Before them stood enormous black gates, looming in their presence, as the portal behind them closed with a faint whisper, leaving them isolated in a desolate realm. The gates towered above them, their imposing structure radiating an aura of foreboding. The surrounding atmosphere was suffused with an eerie silence, broken only by the sound of their own breathing. They stood on the shore of a pitch-black sea, its lifeless waves crashing against the sandy shore.

As they waited, the gaze of the selkie guards fixated upon them, their grey eyes piercing through the darkness. The crystal spears they held glistened ominously, poised for action. Positioned atop the curved walls, the guards remained vigilant, their presence adding to the air of tension.

Suddenly, a dreadful sound pierced the stillness—a resounding blast of the bluegrog horn. It echoed through the surroundings, sending shivers down Lucius's spine. He couldn't discern if the chill that coursed through him was from the frigid breeze or the unease that enveloped him.

With a gradual creak, the massive gates began to open, unveiling what awaited them beyond.

"And here we go," Maxim said. "Let's all try to stay alive."

CHAPTER TWELVE

Lucius

As they stepped beyond the towering gates, a breathtaking sight unfolded before their eyes, immersing them in an overwhelming sense of awe. Nestled gracefully in the heart of a vast lake, the city emanated an ethereal beauty that was nothing short of enchanting. From the majestic mountain peaks of Askaria, crystalline streams cascaded with graceful abandon, merging with the tranquil waters below.

The buildings, crafted with exquisite artistry, stood proudly, fashioned from a rare and captivating dark purple crystal. Bathed in the soft glow of light refracted through the transparent structures, an array of vibrant hues danced playfully upon the city's surfaces. The kaleidoscope of colors, a testament to the city's unmatched splendor, seemed to be a celebration of the harmonious union between the crystal edifices and the shimmering lake. Lucius had a feeling that if the witch were here, she would absolutely love it.

He shouldn't even be thinking about her. He needed to concentrate in this moment so he didn't get anyone killed. All he needed was another unnecessary death on his hands.

As they followed the king across one of the bridges, their path intersected with that of a striking female selkie. Her pale gray skin contrasted with her full, sensual red lips, accentuating her allure. Her voluptuous body was complemented by long curls cascading like silk down her back, adding to her delicate beauty.

"Mistress has been eagerly waiting your return, my liege. This way."

"Nice to see you too, Nikita. I am sure eager is not the correct word usage," the king commented as Maladria Nikita began to lead them through the quiet streets.

The Maladrias were the commanders of the Amarian army and the personal guards of the queen. It was strange for one of them to be greeting them. Lucius wondered where everyone was. The selkies were not known to hide, especially within their own kingdom.

A movement caught his attention in the distance. The water rippled, and a tail fin disappeared under the water. He was an idiot. The vastness of their city was underwater. If he remembered correctly, they could shed their skins anytime, but they did so the most during the full moon. He'd heard that their festivals were divine, but the many who were invited were often never seen again.

He was once invited long before he met his wife, but he missed it due to hunting a witch. He had made her pay dearly for it. Thinking of that particular witch's death brought a small smile to his face until the image of his witch came to mind.

His... He meant *the*. Damn.

They walked until they reached a building in the city center made of black marble. Statues of past selkie kings and queens adorned each side of the staircase as they ascended.

The doors at the top swung open, and another selkie waited for them. She was more sensual and seductive than Nikita. Her silky magenta curls flowed over pale gray shoulders, her plump purple lips screamed *kiss me,* and her lavender eyes drew him.

Lucius could practically already see them entangled together. Everything about her screamed *take me.*

Take me now, Lucius, a seductive voice whispered through his mind. He pushed the voice out, shutting his mind to any intrusion.

"The king finally returns with guests. Must be our lucky day. We were starting to think you had forgotten about us. Especially since we heard you have a new wife," the female selkie said as they reached the last step.

"I could never forget you, Ennes. I apologize for being away for so long. Ruling a kingdom does have its sacrifices," the king said, caressing her cheek.

Ennes spoke to the other selkie, "I can take things from here, Nikita. This way. She awaits your arrival."

Nikita nodded and left them, but not before brushing Max's shoulder. Lucius watched him shiver before getting a hold of himself. Maybe that witch did them a favor by having them miss out on the festival. Maxim may not have returned.

They followed through the quiet marble halls. Water silently flowed down the walls into connecting rivers. Occasionally, they heard a splash and a tail fin disappearing under the water. They were being watched, Lucius noted.

Finally, they reached silver doors that opened as they approached.

The throne room was vast. Braziers illuminated the room in a blue glow of dancing shadows. Paintings of seas from different realms adorned the domed ceiling while stone sea animals and selkie sculptures looked down upon the aqua marble floor.

A ruby carpet met them at the door and trailed all the way to the foot of the imposing silver throne. Large statues of two selkie maidens sat behind a throne covered in glided engravings, and fixed on each leg were blue crystals. The cushions were deep coral, the same as the curtains that adorned the stained-glass windows of a stormy ocean. Large dark pools of water sat on both sides of the carpet, and a small pool sat on the left side of the throne.

"She will be with you momentarily," Ennes said before she left, closing the doors behind her.

"Well, this isn't eerie at all," Maxim remarked as they heard a splash in the far corner of the right pool.

"Remember they have eyes and ears everywhere," the king told them.

From the pool near the throne, a distinct splash echoed through the chamber, drawing everyone's attention. As the ripples settled, a figure emerged, her lustrous copper hair cascading down her shoulders. With piercing emerald eyes that seemed to penetrate each individual in the room, she locked her gaze onto the king.

Clad in a form-fitting green satin dress, it accentuated her alluring curves, leaving little to the imagination. Every step she took exuded an air of pure seduction, swaying her hips with captivating grace as she made her way towards her throne. Surprisingly, she appeared completely dry, without a trace of a tail. Every male present couldn't help but be entranced by her presence, their eyes fixated on her as she gracefully settled upon her throne, crossing her long and exquisite legs. It was undeniable proof that they possessed the ability to transform instantly.

"Now, to what do I owe this pleasure, my king?"

"Azalin." Kieran went to one knee, and the others followed. Though, it took Lucius a moment longer since he hated bowing to royalty. The selkie queen's gaze bore into him until he felt compelled to get on one knee.

"I see you brought your distant offspring here. May I ask why?"

"I have brought them to you as a gift to your daughters. They come seeking pleasure," the king said, keeping his head bowed.

"Gift?" Max exclaimed, faking surprise.

The queen laughed as her gaze roamed over each of them. "And you, my lord, do you come seeking pleasure?" she asked curiously.

"Only to *give* pleasure. I have been gone a long time, and I have a lot to make up for."

"And what of your wife? How does she feel about you being in my kingdom?"

"I have grown bored of her." The king raised his head and stared into her eyes. "I seek to warm your bed again, if you will have me."

Azalin moved from her throne and walked over to King Kieran. She ran her hands over his shoulders, then bent to whisper something in his ears that caused his knee to drop and to shiver visibly. The king's reaction told Lucius just how powerful her seductive charms were and made him think this plan wouldn't work.

"You lie, my king. You have come to use your treacherous door. The one in which you barred me from all those years ago when you chose her over me."

"Azalin, I never meant to hurt you," the king grunted out.

"Nikita." The throne room doors opened. "Please take our lovely guests to the Pools of Eden where they can find the pleasure of your sisters. The king and I have some catching up to do."

"This way, gentlemen."

Pools of Eden? They need to go to the Atrium. *To hell with this.* Lucius stood, pulling Luzia from her sheath. "No, we need to get through that door."

The king's eyes landed on him, pleading with him not to do this. Their plan was not going to work, so Lucius had to improvise, and this was the best he could do. The others continued to bow, not intervening. It should have been his warning against his foolish plan.

The queen laughed. "You will not make it anywhere near that door."

"You underestimate my sheer will and determination." Lucius moved slowly toward the queen. "You will tell us where the atrium is."

"Oh, Lucius, you have not changed one bit." Azalin smiled, locking eyes with him. Distracting him with her comment when he was no more than two feet from her. The cold metal of a dagger was at his throat.

Changed? What the hell was she talking about? He had never met her before. How did she know him? As curious as he was to know the answers, he needed to get them out of here.

"I would not do that if I were you," Nikita said as she pressed the knife deeper. "Sheathe your sword or meet your death. The choice is yours."

"Now would be a great time to use it, Max," Lucius muttered under his breath, hoping his companion would catch the hint. At first, it seemed like his words went unnoticed, but then Lucius observed as the small pink ball soared through the air, colliding with the wall. A brief cloud of pink smoke materialized and swiftly dispersed.

"Well, shit. That was a bust," Max exclaimed, his tone tinged with frustration. So much for that damn plan.

"Clairingil? Naughty, naughty boys." Azalin sauntered back toward Lucius, pushing his sword down until she moved closer. "Ah, now you are interesting." Queen Azalin touched Nikita's arm, and she moved away, leaving a small scratch on Lucius's neck. "Quite stubborn and defiant. You would be a nice challenge for me but unfortunately, I have,"—she glanced back at the king— "other plans. Nikita and Ennes, escort them to the Pools. Let's give them a nice warm welcome."

"Sheathe your sword or you will find it taken and not returned," Nikita warned.

"Lucius, do as she says. Go to the Pools. Enjoy your pleasure," the king groaned.

He was tempted to fight it out, but the Atrium must be near the pools if the king still insisted they go. Reluctantly, Lucius sheathed Luzia.

"Now, be good little boys and do as your king says," Queen Azalin said as she moved to stand in front of the king, who remained kneeling.

As Lucius turned to follow the others out, he looked to the king and watched a visible shudder go through him as the queen whispered into his ear.

He was tempted to grab Luzia and see how good these Maladrias were.

No, he had to stay focused on the bigger picture. The king knew what he was doing, and Lucius had his own part to play. Kill the demon.

He glanced back one more time, observing the doors closing behind them, sealing off the chamber they had just exited. He followed Ennes down the stone steps as Nikita took the lead. The city remained eerily silent as they veered left, trailing behind Ennes with cautious footsteps along the deserted streets. The rhythmic hush of their movements persisted until the shimmering pink pools came into view, glistening in the distance like eerie mirages.

"It has been so long since I have heard the sweet sound of the sirens," Silas purred.

"Their song... it's... beautiful," Max drawled in a stupor.

Lucius glanced at Silas and Max as though they had lost their minds. "What song are you talking about?"

They all turned to look at him, including Nikita and Ennes.

"I just knew there was something special about you." Nikita reached out to drag her dagger over his shoulders in delight.

Lucius flexed his fingers and took a deep breath. Time to test their skills. He moved fast, grabbing Nikita by the waist and flipping her to the ground. Before she fully hit, he snatched the dagger from her hands and held it to her throat.

"I knew you wouldn't be a good little boy." Nikita smiled and raised one finger.

Lucius turned to see Ennes with two knives at the ready. Max and Silas swayed to the silent song he could not hear. What took him by surprise, however, was the sight of Alden wielding his sword, its blade pointed directly at Ennes.

"It seems we find ourselves in quite the predicament," Nikita stated.

"Quite," Alden agreed.

Before Lucius could blink, both Nikita and Ennes were gone. "What the hell?"

He stood and pulled Luzia from his back, moving closer to Alden. "Where did they go?"

"Not far. Be ready."

Haughty laughter surrounded them. "Now, boys, you are in our realm. There is no playing fair here," Nikita's voice whispered through the air, sending a chill down his spine.

Alden and Lucius stood back-to-back, searching their surroundings for some sign of them. The water rippled nearby.

"We should move away from the edge," Alden hissed.

They inched away from the edge, but no matter where they stood, they were still surrounded by water.

Lucius had the sudden urge to laugh. How the hell did he get into this situation with Alden?

For a solid moment, he thought about dropping his sword and walking away because none of this had to do with him. This all started with the damn witch and even now, as he was in the middle of a fight, all he could think about was her.

She was calm but worried. Worried about him. He had just wanted to kill her, and yet she worried about him. There was something clearly wrong with them both.

"What's the plan?" Alden murmured with his eyes on the water.

"Plan?" Lucius sputtered. He didn't have a damn plan.

"Since you put us in this predicament, I *assumed* you had a plan."

He snarled, "Yeah, get to the damn door."

Alden sighed, then muttered, "Still the same hotblooded Lucius."

"If we can get Silas and Max to snap out of their spell," Lucius began, his voice filled with determination. But his words were abruptly cut off by the sound of Alden's sword hitting the ground with a loud clatter. "What are you doing?!"

Then he felt a knife at his throat. "Oh boys, your time to play is over. Drop it."

Lucius turned to move but then felt another blade pressed against his back. If he wanted to reach that door, he would have to give in. He dropped Luzia.

"Good boy. Ennes, take them to the Pools. This one, take to Adrienne. She will know what to do," she said, talking about Alden. Then her gaze shifted to Lucius. "This one I will take to Mira."

She removed the dagger from his throat and placed it to his back as she picked up Luzia. "Move."

Patience

"They went *where?*" Circe asked Michael in disbelief.

Men are idiots. Why did they think going to a city full of sirens without them was a good idea?

"They went to find another way into Askaria," Ian said in a panic as Circe pointed a spear at his balls.

"*Where* exactly did they go?" She moved the spear closer as he stood in front of Michael, who tried to move him out of the way, but Ian wouldn't budge.

Circe wouldn't hurt him because that would mean hurting her son, but it was suspicious that they were very reluctant to tell them where they went. Even Estelle was quite close-lipped about it.

The queen's grip tightened on the spear as she inched closer. "It only takes one of you to give me grandchildren, so if I were you, I would talk."

"You will find them in Amare," Volt said, appearing beside her.

"So, he was smart enough not to leave him alone with her?" Patience whispered, side-eyeing Volt.

"Amare." Circe pulled the spear away, and the look of relief on Ian's face was comical.

"I was told to keep a close eye on a certain someone," Volt said, his gaze shifting towards Estelle with a hint of suspicion. "All has been quiet until you arrived."

"Patience, I need you to open a portal to the City of Amare. I need you to open it *now*," Circe said in a deadly voice.

Anger blazed in Circe's eyes, her brows furrowed, and her lips pressed into a thin line. Clearly, she was pissed. They went to the city of sirens to find a door to Askaria. It didn't make... any... sense...

Holy shit.

There was a door that the king didn't disclose to them that was in the City of Sirens. No wonder Queen Circe was pissed.

"Selene will have to do it since I drained a lot of my magic back there." When they arrived back at the manor, Patience was grateful Lucius was not there. She didn't have it in her to put up a fight with him, but since he was gone, she had hoped to get some rest. She needed to recharge, but it looked like she wasn't going to get any rest today. "We are going to need a mirror."

As if on cue, a square mirror appeared in front of her. She searched the room, confused, until Volt said, "You're welcome."

"I am going to kill that male when I see him. I'm going to tear him into shreds piece by piece," Circe grunted out, and her hands gripped the spear.

"So, the City of Sirens. What are we walking into? I am not sure where this portal is going to put us," Patience said, effortlessly summoning the tome of spells from the safe at GreyJoy's.

"My book," Selene exclaimed as the book dropped onto the table near her. She flicked her finger, and the pages opened to the spell they needed. A bottle of Veridian appeared on the table next to the tome. Patience glanced over at Volt, who smirked at her.

She really needed to know what the hell he was, that he could do magic as she could. She turned to look at him. "What are you?" As soon as she said it, she realized how rude it sounded and flushed. "I am so sorry."

"No, it is a valid question."

"He is a Khedian," Alecia supplied. "They make the best damn spies, but they are hard to find, and their price is always too high. Still not sure how Lucius got this one to commit to him."

"What exactly is a Khedian?"

"Something we don't have time for you to find out," Circe interjected. "Selene, open the damn portal."

Selene grabbed the bottle. "*Aperi ad notum ostium in Amare realm Evictus*," she said, then placed a drop of Veridian on the mirror. The mirror rippled, showing the waters of Amare.

"Alright, let's go get these idiots," Alecia said, flexing the sword still in her hand.

Circe was the first one through the mirror. Alecia followed, then Selene.

Patience stepped up to the mirror and stared at Volt, conveying a message to continue to keep an eye on Estelle. He nodded before she looked at Michael. "We will be right back. Hopefully, with the idiots in tow."

"Be careful," Michael urged as she walked through the mirror.

CHAPTER THIRTEEN

Lucius

Lucius didn't like that she was separating them, but this was not the time to fight, especially as he saw several heads and fins move through the water. They were heavily outnumbered. He would have to find another way back to the door.

Silas and Maxim druggily followed Ennes like puppy dogs as she kept her dagger firmly on Alden's neck, forcing him to move forward. Nikita pushed Lucius toward a path to the right. It led past a few rooms with different-colored pools. They moved down two flights of stairs until they came across a cave-like room, its walls adorned with ancient markings and moss-covered stones. In the center, a pool of water shimmered with a clear, ethereal light, casting a gentle glow that bathed the surroundings in a mystical ambiance. The water itself glowed with a mesmerizing blue hue, illuminating the room with an otherworldly radiance. The air held a sense of serenity and magic, as if time had stood still within this sacred space.

"Undress and get into the water. Mira will help sort your chaotic thoughts and uncorrupt your clouded memories," Nikita whispered as she pressed him closer to the water's edge. "Now I see why the siren's call does not work on you. It is said that those who are deeply connected to someone will not even hear the call. Those in love."

"Ha-ha, I am not in love with anyone." Thoughts of the witch immediately flooded his mind. *Never. No.* He pushed them away, but his treacherous heart swelled at the possibility. A possibility he would never be able to admit.

"I did not say you were. I said deeply connected. It goes beyond love. Love can be manipulated. This cannot." Nikita placed Luzia near the poolside. Then she dragged the dagger up his back. "Undress."

He glowered at her, narrowing his eyes. "No."

She moved around him, dragging the dagger over his shoulders until she stood in front of him. "There is no need to struggle. You will obtain what you came to find. You must enter the pool in order to do so."

Lucius looked into her eyes to see if she was lying, but all he saw was truth. She must have seen when he gave in because the dagger melted away and she began to unbutton his shirt.

Lucius gripped her wrists, stopping her. "What are you talking about? My wife has died. I hold no deep—"

"You do, whether you chose to acknowledge it or not."

He knew she was talking about the blood bond he temporarily shared with the witch.

"The connection you speak of is only temporary and will be broken soon."

She merely smiled at him and continued to unbutton his shirt until he was bare. "The connection you have cannot be broken. To break it could kill you both or cause one of you unimaginable pain."

She reached for his belt, but he gripped her wrists again.

"Blood bonds have been broken before. Although they are not easy to break, they can be broken. I can take it from here."

"Stubborn indeed," she tsked, taking a step back from him. "Mira will know if your connection is true and break any false ones." Nikita laughed as she walked away, leaving the room. Lucius listened to the echoes of her footsteps fade before he buttoned himself back up.

He bent to pick up Luzia but found her gone. He searched around him, but he could not see her until a gleam from the water caught his attention. She must have pushed her in when she was unbuttoning his shirt.

Grunting, Lucius unbuttoned a few before pulling the shirt over his head and taking off his shoes. He hated it when they played games like this. If he knew that it wouldn't start a war, he would kill Nikita.

Jumping in the water, he dove to the bottom, but before he could grab Luzia, something grabbed his leg, pulling him back. He looked around but saw nothing. He tried to grab Luzia again but was tugged away, this time more forcefully.

He searched around, angered. Lucius was alone. He went to the surface but found he couldn't break through.

What the hell?

He tried again to no avail. He pulled back his fist to punch the water, but his might had no effect. He swam around looking for another way out, but every time he tried to get to Luzia, a force pulled him back.

Hush. Do not panic. I am here to help you, my child, a powerful feminine voice said, surrounding him. A calmness rippled through the water, causing his muscles to relax and become paralyzed. *Do not fight,* she whispered. *I am Mira. This is my home. I will help you.*

"I don't need your help," Lucius replied in his head as he tried to fight, even though he knew it was useless.

You do, my stubborn child. She will need you. Let us begin. Relax, " Mira said as the water moved him horizontally in the pool.

A current enveloped him, first slowly, then faster and faster until it penetrated his body through his mouth and nose. The water surged through his body, its presence intensifying with each passing moment. Starting from his feet, it flowed steadily, making its way upwards, inch by inch. It traveled along his legs, embracing his muscles with a cool, fluid touch. Rising further, it enveloped his torso, tracing the contours of his abdomen and chest. The sensation was both exhilarating and unsettling as the water coursed through his veins, reaching his shoulders and arms.

But it didn't stop there. The water pressed onward, steadily ascending towards his head. He could feel its persistent movement, like a gentle but insistent tide rising within him. The current swirled around his neck, a watery embrace that carried a hint of anticipation. Gradually, it approached his face, caressing his cheeks, his lips, and his nose. As it continued its ascent, his senses heightened, the sensation becoming more profound.

The water was on a relentless journey, seeking entrance into his mind. It pulsated through his thoughts, swirling around his memories and stirring his emotions. It sought to explore the deepest corners of his consciousness, driven by an unknown purpose until it reached the crown of his head. Though he resisted, it persisted, relentlessly battering against his defenses until his walls cracked and water trickled in.

It moved through his memories, exploring every corner, until it stumbled upon an enigma—an unfamiliar sight—a red door. The water, determined to breach the door's seal, pounded relentlessly, but it remained steadfast. The relentless assault continued, but the door refused to budge.

Then, finally, it discovered the keyhole and swept inside, flooding his consciousness.

Moon Harvest, 1693

Stepping into the ballroom, the smell of blood and laughter assailed Lucius. The party was already well underway. He could already see the empty bottles of blood wine piling up on the tables as crowds of vampires arrived from all over the world. Sometimes he forgot how many of his kind there really were. Their numbers were massive and growing, but they blended in well with the human civilization of Eviathan. This would be their home.

He made his way through the room, passing by vampires already making use of their human companions. It was going to turn into a blood fest soon.

Lucius wanted to hit the card tables so he could loosen this bloody bow tie. He hated how wearing this tux always made him feel like a damn penguin. He wished he hadn't promised his mother he would stay for the performance.

If he left, she would know, and he wouldn't hear the end of it. His mother could be a pain when someone didn't do as she said, especially when that someone was one of her children.

"From the look on your face, Mother is making you stay for the performance as well." Ian passed him a glass filled with blood wine as he joined him in a matching tux at the edge of the ballroom.

"Do you know what is so special about this performance?"

"It's the woman. I'm told her dancing is divine." Max came to stand next to Lucius, also in the same suit, except his was blue, not black. "She dances and selects her companion for the night. I was also told she is seeking a mate. It might be why your mother is so eager for you to watch. Come, your mother is looking for you."

Lucius sighed and downed his blood wine, then he and Michael followed Max as he led them through the crowd to the table at the front of the room where his mother and her friends were sitting.

"Ah, my sons have finally decided to join us this evening," she said, the picture of perfection in her diamond-encrusted sweetheart gown.

"I apologize, Mother, but my dreams were more interesting than I care to admit, and I did not want to leave them." Lucius came around the table to kiss her cheek, then took a seat next to Max as the music began, signaling the show was about to begin.

The lights dimmed in the ballroom for a dramatic effect as all the torches lined around the room lit up at once. The crowd parted as Silvia, the hostess, slowly walked into the middle of the ballroom with the most beautiful female at her side. Her silky brown curls fell past her russet-colored shoulders as an elegant silver mask hid most of her face, except for her golden-brown eyes.

Silvia smiled and lifted her right hand, signaling all the eligible bachelors to stand up, meaning all those who were not bonded or married. Lucius, Max, and Ian reluctantly obeyed. All the males gathered in a circle in the middle of the ballroom.

"Now, I am going to say this once and only once," Silvia spoke loudly so everyone could hear. "You may not touch her. Only she may touch you, and when she plants her hand firmly over your heart, then you will know she has chosen you. I repeat one more time, you shall not touch her, and if you do, the penalty is death by my hand, unless she has chosen you. Is that understood, gentlemen?"

All the males in the circle nodded their heads, and even some at the tables nodded as well.

"Now with that understanding, we shall begin."

The young female moved into position as the music changed and the dance began.

Lucius could not tear his eyes away from her as her body moved to the rhythm of the music. She mesmerized him, like she was dancing only for him alone. He wanted her to remove her mask so he could see her face. He *needed* to see it.

Moving in sync with the beat, she used the entire dance floor to enthrall the crowd and enchant the males. The rhythm grew faster and louder as she twirled and spun with the beat in a sensual dance. Lucius found himself wanting her to choose him if only to see her face. The music began to slow to a steady beat as she slid into a split. The room erupted in applause as she stood, moving back to Silvia's side.

Silvia whispered something into the young female's ear, and she nodded. Silvia raised her hand, and the crowd quieted. "Now, remember what I said. She is ready to choose."

The young female slowly made her way around the room, gliding to the slow rhythm of the music, making every male want to touch her as she swayed her hips to entice them.

Lucius's heart began to race as she walked closer to him. His hands formed into fists as she flirted and teased the males as she passed by them.

The closer she got to him, the more he had to control himself.

The desire within him was unmistakable, and his hands trembled with anticipation. It was his turn now. He prepared himself, ready to seize her as she approached Max and him. A flood of hope coursed through him, his outstretched hands eager for her touch. But as she drew near, she smiled at Max, bypassing him with deliberate slowness.

Every step she took toward Lucius felt like a promise, until her fingers hovered just inches away from him. A wave of disappointment crashed over Lucius as she continued past him, coming to a halt in front of his brother.

He watched as she placed her hand on his brother's cheek, then continue to move around the room until she got to the very last male and stopped. Lucius had the urge to kill the male if she laid one finger on him, but she didn't.

Instead, she turned around and walked back across the room straight to him. Before Lucius could comprehend what was happening, she placed her hand over his heart, indicating that she had chosen him.

"She has chosen!" Silvia announced.

The entire ballroom went up in cheers. Silvia quickly came and swept the young woman away. Music began to play again, and the blood wine began to flow. As all this was happening, Lucius still had not moved an inch, too shocked by what just happened.

"Lucius, are you alright?" Ian asked, concerned. He put his hand on his shoulder, startling him. "Whoa, are you okay?"

"I don't know. What just happened?"

"You were just chosen. You know you cannot refuse."

Lucius let that sink in as his brother handed him a glass of blood wine.

He didn't understand where this urge to see her face was coming from. He had never seen this female before, not that he could really say that since she was still wearing the mask, but he never experienced such a strong urge to possess a female before. Whoever this beauty was, she was dangerous. He had too much at stake now that they were winning against the witches to become vulnerable.

Max placed a glass of whiskey in front of him. "You look like you need something even stronger, even though I am not sure why." Max slapped his back as he took a sip, spilling a little on his shirt. "You are the luckiest male in here tonight."

"Then take my…" he trailed off as he caught sight of her mask stepping back into the ballroom. She slowly made her way over to them. Her aura was powerful and alluring, causing every male and some females to stare after her.

Lucius still couldn't believe she had chosen him, but he wondered who she was.

"I believe you owe me a dance," she said, taking his whiskey out of his hand and drinking it down. "Thanks." She handed it back to him with a serene smile.

"He does, but I believe my brother wants to—" Before Ian could finish, Lucius swept her up into the next dance.

"I believe your brother was speaking," she said as he pulled her closer.

"Nonsense. I'm Lucius. And who may you be?" He was being forward, but he didn't care. They could skip the pleasantries. He needed a name.

For a moment, she seemed hesitant, but then she said, "Odessa. I'm Odessa."

CHAPTER FOURTEEN

PATIENCE

Murky water filled her lungs as Patience sank deeper into the abyss, drowning until a hand plunged in, grabbing her arm and pulling her up to the surface. She flopped onto something hard. "You are all right. I have you," Circe said, patting her on the back as she coughed up water, clearing her lungs.

They were in what appeared to be a house except they had just emerged from a small pool in the middle of their living room. They were in the City of Sirens, so she guessed it made sense.

"We must be quiet. There are eyes and ears everywhere. They would have taken the males to the Pools of Eden, except for Kieran. I know where to find him," Circe whispered.

Pools of Eden. She had heard about where the sirens took males to seduce them then... kill them. She read somewhere that they liked to bathe in blood to keep themselves young. She wondered if it was true. Guess she would find out. Idiot males.

Of course, they would go to a city filled with powerful women who could fuck and kill them at the same time.

The image of some random siren straddling Lucius surfaced. She imagined sending a bolt of electricity into the siren and watching her turn to dust. Fuck. She didn't need her jealousy to surface right now.

Goddess, please don't let me find him with a siren. I can't be held responsible for what I might do. She sent the prayer up, hoping that it was heard.

Selene touched her clothes and whispered a spell. They instantly dried. Patience wished she hadn't depleted her magic so much. She could have made them invisible, but they would have to rely on stealth. Her reserve was teetering on empty, and she would need to use it sparingly. Those males really were idiots.

They made their way out into the quiet streets, and Patience's eyes widened in awe. The sight before her was unlike anything she had ever witnessed. The architecture of the buildings was a marvel to behold, crafted from the purest crystal she had ever encountered. The structures exuded a mesmerizing radiance, diverting the ambient light and casting a brilliant glow upon the surroundings.

As they proceeded through the streets, gentle streams of water cascaded down the sides of the crystal edifices, creating a stunning display of shimmering beauty. The water droplets danced in the air, catching the soft glow and transforming it into a kaleidoscope of colors. The entire city seemed to glisten and sparkle, as if adorned with countless precious gems.

Patience couldn't help but imagine how breathtaking this spectacle would be in the sunlight. But even in the absence of sunlight, the ethereal charm of the crystal city captivated her. Its tranquil streets and luminous architecture filled her with a sense of wonder and reverence. Each step she took was accompanied by the gentle melody of water, as if the city itself whispered secrets of its enchanting existence.

"The Pools of Eden are down this road." Circe pointed to the left. "Keep going straight until you come upon pink pools. You should find the idiots there. We will meet back here in thirty minutes. If we are not back here, you leave without us, do you understand me?" she whispered intently.

"Understood," Patience said, hating the idea of splitting up, but she knew it was the best option. The faster they found those idiots, the faster they could get out of here.

"Stay away from the water's edge and remain as quiet as possible and hidden," Circe urged before disappearing down the road off to the right.

Alecia led the way as Patience took up the rear. They moved stealthily through the streets, avoiding guards and trying to stay away from the water's edge. Any time they ventured too close to the waves, Patience could have sworn she saw a pair of glossy pearl eyes and coral-colored hair disappear below the surface. Circe was right, they had eyes and ears everywhere.

Just as they were beginning to see the pink pools, they heard heavy footsteps walking toward them.

"Move back quickly. Hide," Alecia hissed. Patience obeyed but Selene, in a panic not to get caught, tripped over her silk cloth, almost falling. Patience caught her just in time. Though as she righted them, Patience could not tell whether she accidentally slipped off the edge or if something pulled her down, but either way she fell into the water.

Expecting to be met by darkness, she was taken aback as a warm, inviting light emanated from below her. The sight that unfolded before her eyes left her momentarily speechless. The glow illuminated the surroundings, revealing a breathtaking scene. Movement danced and weaved amidst the radiant crystals, captivating her attention. It took a moment for her to comprehend the enchanting spectacle.

As she focused her gaze, she noticed vibrant hues of blue and green, shimmering with life and vitality. The graceful tails of selkies swiftly darted through the water, vanishing into openings within the crystal structures. It dawned upon her that these magnificent creatures were the very fabric of the city itself, their homes intricately intertwined with the crystal formations.

The Selkie City, hidden beneath the surface, was a thriving world brimming with energy and activity. Curiosity sparked in the pearl-like eyes that peeked out from behind the crystal buildings, observing her presence from below. The selkies, with their majestic presence, held her captive with their otherworldly beauty.

The desire to plunge into the depths and join them in their underwater realm tugged at her, tempting her to explore the city firsthand. However, before she could give in to her impulses, a hand plunged into the water from above, breaking the spell of fascination.

Join us, Ceamae. We have missed you. Swim with us, voices whispered to her, tempting her to join them as eyes began to stop and look at her.

She was about to swim down when the hand grabbed hold of her and pulled her up.

Patience climbed back onto the road with the help of Alecia. "You are alright. Don't worry."

"Thank you." She coughed to remove the water from her lungs. There were no guards surrounding them, so they had not been caught. She took a moment to catch her breath before Alecia motioned for them to move on.

Using what little magic she had left, Patience managed to dry herself. Yet her eyes still wandered to the placid water wanting to go back and explore the city. The things she would discover...

Reluctantly, she followed behind her companions, but her eyes kept returning to the waves. She didn't understand why she was so drawn to this place... to the city. Maybe she had been here before. Was it possible someone may remember her? But who? The need for answers surged within her, but as usual she pushed it down, knowing she needed to save those idiots first before she could even entertain that possibility.

They finally arrived at the entrance of the shimmering pink pools. A magnificent archway adorned with intricate carvings of underwater creatures stood before them. The archway was crafted from a delicate, iridescent material that glimmered in shades of pink and lavender, reflecting the gentle light that emanated from the vibrant hues of the pools beyond.

As they approached, their eyes fell upon the two selkie guards standing watch, their expressions alert. Alecia swiftly moved into action, her movements fluid and calculated. Her steps were light and agile, barely making a sound as she closed in on the guards. Shadows seemed to dance around her, concealing her presence from their watchful eyes.

With a series of precise strikes and well-timed parries, Alecia engaged the guards with expert precision. Her movements were sharp and controlled, each strike aimed to disable rather than kill. Her hands moved like a blur, her body seemingly a seamless extension of her lethal skills.

Despite the intensity of the encounter, Alecia fought with a quiet determination, her actions purposeful yet silent. The clash of weapons was muffled, barely audible amidst the tranquil ambiance of the pink pools. Her efficiency and skill allowed her to quickly incapacitate the guards without alerting any unwanted attention.

"Clear," Alecia announced, her voice carrying a sense of triumph mixed with determination.

They moved past one petite selkie who was hiding behind an onyx column. Alecia simply turned in its direction and it scurried off. They found two of the idiots, Silas and Maxim, lounging in a large pink pool on the far east of the building getting rubbed down by two selkies each. Eating grapes and sipping wine like they had no cares in the world.

"Of course, they are enjoying themselves. This doesn't look as though they are searching for a door," Patience whispered angrily.

"Patience, don't you hear it?" Selene asked her.

"Hear what?" Patience listened, but all she heard were the selkies moving through the water as they washed the males.

Selene looked at her strangely before answering, "The sirens are singing. They have the males enthralled."

Now it was her turn to look at Selene strangely. "I don't hear a thing."

"Look, see the sirens' mouths are moving."

Patience looked closely and saw that Selene was right, their mouths were moving, but Patience could not hear their song of seduction and allure.

"Why aren't we affected?" Patience asked curiously.

"There could be several reasons, though I am no expert in selkie knowledge. I believe they say those in love can hear the siren but aren't affected, and those who are married can't hear the call at all."

"Selene, I'm not married. Are you in love?"

"No. Shit, Patty, I don't know. I said I wasn't an expert. What are we going to do?" Selene asked, gnawing her lip in worry.

Patience's mind raced, contemplating their next move, but before she could voice her thoughts, Alecia sprang into action. With swift and calculated movements, she stealthily approached one of the selkies, her hand quickly covering the unsuspecting selkie's mouth. A glint of steel flashed as Alecia pressed a knife against the selkie's throat, eliciting a tremor of fear in her body.

In the tense silence, Alecia leaned in, her voice a low and commanding whisper that sent shivers down the selkie's spine. The selkie's eyes widened, her expression a mixture of terror and realization as Alecia's words sank in. The selkie nodded.

As Alecia released her hold, the selkie wasted no time, scurrying away to relay the urgent message to the other selkies within the room. Patience and

Selene observed in awe as the selkie hurriedly approached the others, her urgent words exchanged in hushed tones. A wave of frantic activity ensued as the selkies reacted, their movements quick and purposeful. Their expressions carried a mix of fear and urgency as they hastily vacated the room.

Patience's mind buzzed with questions, curious about what the hell Alecia whispered to them until a splash drew her attention.

"No, come back. We are not finished here," Maxim demanded, almost grabbing one of the selkies, but Alecia kicked his hand away.

"Patience, Selene, get in here," Alecia bellowed. "Fix them before I kill them."

Selene looked at Patience. "I don't know how to fix them. I don't have my spell book."

Patience sighed, realizing it was up to her to remedy this. They totally owed her for doing this. "Selene, give me your hand."

Taking a hold of Selene's outstretched hand, she absorbed some of Selene's magic, then placed her hand on Maxim's head. She could now see the siren's aura clouded around his head. She placed her hand in the green aura and pulled until it gave way and disappeared. She did the same for Silas.

"They should be back to themselves in a few minutes." As the fog slowly cleared from their heads, Patience glanced around, searching for a sign of Lucius. Maybe he was in another pool, but she had a feeling he was not there. She groaned, "Great, we have another problem."

Both Alecia and Selene looked at her, already exhausted. It had been one hell of a night, but Patience knew she still had to save that idiot no matter how much she just wanted to leave him to go cuddle in her bed.

The bastard better not even think of lifting one finger toward her after this.

Lucius

The memory made no sense to him. Lucius remembered that night, and the witch was not there. This had to be a trick.

This is no trick. I do not lie. These are your memories. Locked away in your mind, Mira's voice resonated through the water, its melodic timbre carrying a depth and power that vibrated in the liquid medium. Each word she uttered seemed to ripple through the surrounding water, creating a mesmerizing symphony of vibrations that echoed and danced around him.

"*NO.* It is not real!" he shouted back to her in his mind as he struggled against the water. "You *lie.* Let me go."

He remembered the Harvest ball and how she danced, enchanting him. It was the night that changed his life because he had met Mae. He had swept Mae into his arms, not the witch. He would not let them manipulate his memories like this. They would not take his wife away from him. He needed to get out of here. He fought against the current, wanting out, breaking his paralyzed state. He began to move his arms and legs.

Stubborn fool. You will lose her forever, Mira chided.

Lucius ignored her and continued to flail around, trying to find a way out. With his arms and legs finally free, he tried to break the surface until he saw a hand reach into the water. He swam towards it like his life depended on it until he grasped it.

The hand tugged him up out of the water, and onto the edge, then he pulled himself the rest of the way out of the pool.

He cleared the water from his lungs and looked up to see who his savior was. He met golden-brown eyes and wanted to curse the fates. It was the witch.

"Well, gee, don't jump for so much joy to see me," Patience said, getting up from the wet stone floor. "You chose an opportune time to go for a damn swim."

"Witch—"

"Yeah, yeah. Save it. We don't have time. You can kill me later," she muttered before he could threaten to maim her or whatever. "We need to go to the others and find Circe and Kieran. Unless you know where Kieran is?"

Lucius hated that she was right. He grabbed his shirt and shoes, put them on, and took the moment to reorient himself.

Whatever the hell that was had to be a trick. A manipulation of his memory, no matter how real it had felt. He couldn't think about it now. The implications, the reality of it, were too much.

Right now, he had to concentrate on reaching Kieran and getting out of there. He turned to look back at the bottom of the pool. Luzia glinted at him. *Shit.* He needed to get her. As he prepared to leap back into the water, the witch suddenly appeared by his side, extending her hand over the shimmering surface. Her voice carried a note of impatience.

"Here, so you don't waste any more of our time."

Luzia emerged from the depths of the glowing pool, rising swiftly and breaking through the water's surface, before gracefully descending into her outstretched hands.

"Let's go," the witch urged, her tone firm. "Lead the way."

Lucius bit back a scathing response and silently led her back to the throne room.

Alecia's fingers clenched tightly around the hilt of her double-edged sword, her grip betraying her mounting frustration. Silas and Max continued their oblivious conversation, seemingly ignorant of her seething presence, while a woman with silver hair and silver eyes stood by, just watching the show. He assumed this was Selene. The doors to the throne room were closed.

"Patty!" Selene exclaimed as she saw them approach.

"About time," Alecia uttered. "Do you know where they took Alden?"

"Alden is here?" Patience looked surprised and asked, "Did you kill him?"

Lucius wanted to laugh but realized they were all looking at him seriously, waiting for an answer. "I wish. Maladria Ennes took him to someone named Adrienne. We don't have time to find him if he is not here. Whatever situation he is in, he will have to find his own way out."

Patience scoffed at him, then reached for the necklace. "I'm not even sure if this will work, but it's our only chance without separating again."

Lucius shook his head, ignoring her attempt to rescue Alden. He walked over to the throne room doors and tried to push them open, but they wouldn't budge.

Fuck. They would have to find another way in.

Lucius tried to ignore Patience, but he glanced out of the corner of his eye as she took off the necklace. Grabbing Selene's hand, she took a deep breath and whispered, "Apparator."

As Alden failed to appear, a conflicting mix of relief and disappointment washed over Lucius. A part of him wished Alden was dead, but that would make life too easy.

Just as the witch took a breath to say the word again, Alden materialized in front of her, dripping wet with a smile on his face. "You saved me," he said softly as he reached out to touch her face.

It wasn't the touch that angered Lucius. What sent him over the edge was when she stepped into it, clearly enjoying the feel of him. Without thinking, he moved toward them.

"Good, you're here," he said to Alden, then grabbed the witch, snatching her away. He pushed her toward the door. "Now, *witch*, help me open this."

"Well, that was rude," Selene muttered under her breath.

He didn't care what they thought. Ignoring them, he tried pushing on the door again.

She huffed, "Obviously, that's not going to work."

He glared at the witch and gestured for her to try.

Stepping back, she examined the door, then placed her hand against it. Nothing happened at first, until she said, "*Sii*".

Blue light emanated from her palms, rippling over the door. As soon as she removed her hand, it swung open.

"See? Easy."

Lucius's control was hanging on its hinges. He just needed to get through this.

Walking into the throne room, they found it vacant. Only the sound of flowing water echoed through the vast marble hall, not even a splash.

The queen's throne stood empty, and the large dark pools remained placid.

Where the hell is everyone?

"Where are they?" Patience asked, walking further into the room.

"I don't know. This is where I last left him."

"Do you think the queen got him out and is waiting for us?" Patience turned and asked Alecia and Selene.

"If she did, this place would be swimming with guards," Silas answered, making a face. "No pun intended."

Patience couldn't help the laughter that burst from her lips.

"Ennes and Nikita have not appeared. They must be standing guard," Alden added.

"Standing guard where?" Patience gazed at him, letting her eyes flicker over Silas, Max, and Alden. They were all reluctant to speak.

"I am guessing they guard her bedroom, since you all seem reluctant to supply an answer." Selene shook her head, rolling her eyes. "Typical males."

"Okay, so where is her bedroom?" Patience asked.

No one answered, but Max shrugged his shoulders.

"Must I do all the work?" The witch's gaze slid to Alden's, but she walked toward Lucius. "Since you have a tizzy every time I touch Alden, you are going to have to let me use your magic."

Lucius had to admit she had a point, and it was either he let her use him or Alden. His mind told him she could use Alden all she wanted, but his foolish heart lifted his hand for her to take.

As soon as she touched him, warmth spread, and his palm tingled as she drew magic from him. She held out her other hand, and a little ball of light appeared. He remembered she called it Seckor.

"Hi, friend. Can you help me find King Kieran?" The light glowed brighter in response, then zoomed off. "Come on."

The witch followed after it. It led them to a hole behind the throne filled with murky black water. Seckor disappeared under the waves.

"Ladies first," Lucius mocked as he held out his hand, gesturing for her to dive in first.

"I knew you would say that since you are *such* a gentleman," she said with sarcasm dripping from every word.

Without hesitation, she jumped in. Not having a choice, he followed after her. It was surprisingly warm and pitch-black; he could not see a thing. Not even his night vision was working. A hand touched him, pulling him forward until he saw Seckor's light. He could see the witch swimming toward it. He followed her until another hole came into view.

She climbed out and reached out her hand to help him. He refused and lifted himself out, much to her annoyance. She sent the ball of light back into the water and looked around.

It was an underground cavern, embellished with exquisite ancient markings. The walls, smooth and glistening like polished pearl, were adorned with intricate carvings that told the tales of the selkie lineage. The detailed patterns, reminiscent of flowing water and swirling currents, seemed to come alive in the soft glow of luminescent crystals embedded in the walls. The symbols depicted the rich mythology and history of the Selkie people, their connection to the sea, and the wisdom passed down through generations.

The air was tinged with a faint scent of salt and mystery as if the very essence of the ocean lingered within this sacred space. It was absolutely enchanting.

The waterhole rippled seconds later, and Silas emerged from the water, followed by Selene.

"Wow, this is beautiful," Selene said, amazed as she walked over to the pink crystal walls and ran her hands over them in wonder.

Max came next, followed by Alecia and then Alden.

Patience marched over to Lucius and grabbed his hand.

"I'm going to dry us," she mumbled, avoiding his eyes for reasons unbeknownst to him. Pulling magic from him, a glowing halo appeared above them, slowly moving down over their bodies, drying them.

"If it's okay with you, can we dry the others?" Her gaze lifted to find his eyes illuminated. Her eyes immediately dropped to his lips, and he looked away.

"Witch," he murmured, not realizing she was leaning toward him. "Step back."

She stepped back, not letting his hand go but shaking herself from whatever spell had wrapped around them. She dared not look around the room to see who had caught their moment. Instead, she asked again, "Can I dry them?"

She glanced into his eyes to find the glow was gone.

He nodded, then said, "Quickly, witch."

She took his hand again, enjoying his warmth. "Alright, everyone, don't move."

Looking around, she made sure everyone was still as she pulled magic from Lucius and sent it toward each of them. A halo appeared above each of their heads, then moved down their bodies, drying them.

"Thanks," Alden whispered, and she smiled.

Jealousy ripped through Lucius when he realized he wanted her to smile at him. As soon as the thought occurred, he let go of her hand. "We have to move. We are not sure what we are walking into, so everyone be on guard."

Seckor had been hovering over the water, but the witch grabbed it and gently let it go. It zoomed around the room until it found a path forward. They followed Seckor silently until they caught sight of a door up ahead.

"Where are they?" Lucius asked, more to himself when he didn't see Nikita or Ennes at the door.

"They are over there. Right by the door."

"Where?" Lucius searched the area near the door, but there was nothing there.

"Standing by the door," she whispered.

"The only thing near that door are pictures of two selkie guards."

Patience looked at him like he had lost his mind.

"Obviously, she can see what we cannot. What are they doing?" Alecia asked.

"Watching us," Patience stated.

"Fuck."

"Well, there goes the element of surprise," Alecia muttered, standing with her weapon at the ready. Lucius followed her lead and pulled out Luzia.

As they moved closer, the images on the wall moved, and they watched Nikita and Ennes slip from the walls with spears in hand.

"Look, sister. Mira let him go. This must be his lover," Nikita said to Ennes as she pointed to Alecia.

"She doesn't look like his type," Ennes said, looking Alecia up and down with pity.

"Now I am *really* going to kick your ass. He is not my lover," Alecia sneered.

"Oh, look, he brought friends. This will be fun. It has been a long time since we had fun," Ennes said as she moved toward Alecia.

Nikita placed her hands against the wall, and ethereal figures began forming, emerging like water taking shape. These water-shaped warriors materialized with grace and fluidity, their translucent bodies shimmering with hues of aquamarine and sapphire. Their features mirrored the ebb and flow of the ocean, their forms ever-changing yet retaining a sense of unity with the watery realm from which they emerged.

"Oh shit!" Max exclaimed.

Then Nikita charged him. Lucius easily blocked her. Ignoring everything around him, he focused on deflecting her stabs and lethal plunges until his back hit a wall.

"You are very good, but not good enough," Nikita smirked before she pulled back and tried to strike him in the chest. At the last second, he brought his sword up, deflecting and rolling out of the way.

Without thinking, he looked around the room, his eyes searching for the witch. She stood with Selene behind Alden. She held both of their hands, seeming to be channeling their magic. Silas and Max protected them, fighting back the warriors.

Nikita's footsteps sounded behind Lucius as two water warriors charged toward him from the sides.

As the footsteps of Nikita echoed behind Lucius, the serenity of the cavern was abruptly shattered. Like torrents unleashed, two formidable water warriors surged forth, charging at him with relentless determination. Their liquid forms took on distinct shapes, resembling imposing warriors molded from the very essence of water. He stood at the ready as the rhythmic sound of splashing water accompanied their advance, creating an ominous symphony of impending confrontation. With a swift and precise motion, Lucius sliced through the air, his blade cutting through the watery bodies of the approaching warriors.

The clang of metal against water reverberated through the cavern, creating a symphony of echoing clashes and splashing droplets. Lucius moved with a practiced grace, exploiting the vulnerabilities in the warriors' forms. His blade swept through the aqueous adversaries, slicing through their liquid bodies with precision and determination.

As Lucius struck down the water warriors, their liquid forms began to tremble and waver, shattering and cascading down in a torrent of droplets, pooling on the cavern floor.

With a swift pivot, Lucius intercepted Nikita's spear just moments before it could strike him. He quickly pushed her back against the wall, where two more warriors appeared.

Her lips curled back in a cruel smile. "Looks like you are outnumbered."

Lucius growled, hating that she was right. He was about to move away from her to cut down the warriors when a chill went through the room and the warriors froze, turning into ice before crumbling to the ground.

"It seems the tables have turned," Lucius said with glee as he raised his blade to strike, but then he saw the stunned look in her eyes. He turned to follow her gaze.

It was the witch. Both Alden and Selene were touching her shoulders as she rose from the ground, but what made him pause was the glowing blue aura around her.

"Ceamae," Nikita said softly before she dropped her spear and fell to her knees. "Forgive us. We did not know it was you."

Lucius looked over to Silas to find Ennes on her knees with her head bowed as well. Silas kicked the spear from her reach, and he did the same to Nikita's.

Lucius didn't understand. Maybe she had put them under a spell. He stepped toward the witch as the glow faded and her eyes turned back to her normal brown.

"Witch, what did you do?" he asked when he stood in front of her.

She glanced around, confused, until she saw Nikita and Ennes on their knees. "I'm not sure. I just wanted to freeze the warriors."

"Well, let's not look a gift horse in the mouth," Alecia said, striding over to the door. Nikita and Ennes made no move toward her, even as she touched the door and tried to open it.

When it wouldn't open, she tried to kick it. She didn't even make a dent.

"Open the door, witch."

She rolled her eyes. "Why don't you open the door? I am drained."

He walked over to the door and placed his hand to it, repeating the word she said earlier, "Sii."

It remained locked.

The witch came up behind him and placed her hand on the door over his. "Sii."

Blue light rippled over the door before it swung open. He glared at her.

"I think we have bigger problems than you wanting to kill me," the witch said, pointing toward the scene that laid before them.

Queen Circe had Queen Azalin on her knees on the blue oceanic stone floor with a knife to her throat as King Kieran lay naked on the bed.

CHAPTER FIFTEEN

PATIENCE

With a deep breath, Patience scanned the queen's bedroom, her gaze tracing the intricate patterns of shimmering sea pearls adorning the walls. It was a sight of otherworldly beauty that both captivated and unnerved her. As her eyes wandered, they settled upon the grand mirror framed with delicate seashells and coral motifs, reflecting her own determined expression. The room held a hushed stillness, broken only by the sound of her own thoughts.

In the center of the room, the large, canopied bed carved from coral and adorned with seashells cradled the unconscious form of the king, lying naked and vulnerable. How the hell was she going to convince Circe not to kill Azalin? Queen versus queen.

As much as she would love to see this epic battle play out, she was too exhausted.

Her magic was completely depleted. She would have felt better if Michael was here, but it was too dangerous. Instead, she would have to push through it. Selene and Alden's magic were helpful, but his magic lingered, forcing her to push it out every time. His magic enticed and seduced her, drawing her closer with an irresistible allure.

Its potency was palpable, like a surge of raw energy resonating deep within her. It possessed a purity that surpassed anything she had ever encountered, radiating an aura of immense power. And yet, this very purity instilled a sense of fear within her. The untamed force held an unpredictable nature and a potential for creation and destruction. It was a delicate balance between fascination and trepidation, as she found herself simultaneously drawn to its allure and wary of its untamed potential.

She still had so many questions for him and for some reason, she felt like time was running out, but she wasn't exactly sure why. She had to push the thought away and focus on the situation in front of her.

"Wake him up or you die," Circe said to Azalin as she pressed the blade deep into her throat.

"As I told you, he is mine now. He touched the stone and made the deal. You are free to use the portal to get into your kingdom. That was the exchange," Azalin said causally. She almost looked bored as she kneeled on the stone floor in her aqua nightgown.

"What's the plan?" Patience whispered to the idiot vampire beside her. He pulled out Luzia, gripping her in his hands. She should have known. Always violence. "How about we try to talk before we slay?"

He rolled his eyes. "Fine, but Luzia will be at the ready. Lead the way."

Shaking her head, she walked into the emerald-colored room as Circe looked over at her. "What are you doing here? I told you to leave without us."

"And you really want me to tell your son, whom you just found, that I, his best friend, left his parents in danger? Oh, hell no. I know you may not know your son that well yet, but he will never let me live it down."

Queen Azalin slowly turned to gaze at her as they entered her bedroom. "Ceamae?"

There it was again. *Ceamae.* Did they know who she was?

Circe pressed the knife deeper into the queen's throat, silencing her as a drop of green blood dripped down her neck.

"We have to wake the king," Circe urged.

Patience ignored her instincts, which told her to talk to Queen Azalin and moved over to the bed. She grabbed his shirt and quickly covered his nether regions, not wanting to get a glimpse of her best friend's father, even if he was a fine specimen.

Patience gasped when she saw that his eyes were open.

"Is he enthralled?" Selene asked, coming to stand next to her.

"No. She said he touched the stone and made a deal." Patience tried to remember what she read about the selkies, specifically Queen Azalin. She made deals with creatures who sought her help. Fair exchanges that were struck once the Stone of... Stone of... *Trite* was touched. It hung around her neck and was sealed with a kiss.

Patience strode over to Queen Azalin and searched her neck for the green crystal. She saw the silver chain and followed it until she realized the crystal lay between her bosoms. "So sorry about this."

Queen Azalin smirked as Patience gently reached for the chain and pulled the crystal up. She laid it in her hand, examining it. Okay, she could figure out how to undo this. She just had to think.

She reached up and tried to remove the necklace, finding it sealed. She whispered the word, "Sii." The necklace fell into her hands. Azalin narrowed her eyes and struggled to get free, but Queen Circe pressed the knife harder against her throat, causing another drop of blood to run down her neck. "I'm sorry," Patience said before she moved back over to the king.

"You cannot undo our deal, Ceamae, not without causing him harm," the selkie queen warned.

She was right; Patience couldn't undo their deal, but she could make a new one. She had no clue if this would work, but nonetheless, she put the necklace on.

"Are you sure that is a good idea?" Alecia questioned, coming to stand on the other side of the bed.

"No, but do you have a better one?" Patience was met with silence. "Alecia, you might want to move back."

Alecia took a step away from the bed. Patience leaned down over the king and grabbed his hand, then whispered into his ear. "Hi. I know we are not the greatest friends, and I am not sure how this exactly works, but here is the deal. I promise to protect your son until my last dying breath if you take back the deal with the queen and wake, so we can go to Askaria and kill the half-demon together."

She leaned over and kissed his forehead. The stone on her chest slightly burned as it glowed.

I accept, Zeita, the king's voice whispered through her mind as she pulled back.

A burning sensation moved from her chest down her arm to their interlocked hands, then the sensation disappeared as their hands glowed, then faded. She let go when he blinked.

Circe came to his side and kissed him. Patience turned back, only to find Lucius with his sword at Queen Azalin's throat.

She didn't seem surprised by the turn of events as Lucius demanded, "Take us to the Atrium."

"Please," Patience added. Sometimes, being polite could go a long way.

"For you, Ceamae, I will."

"Lucius, let her go." For a moment, she thought he wasn't going to listen, but then he removed his sword from her throat.

"You make one wrong—"

"I believe she understands. No need for the threats." Patience glared at Lucius; her exhaustion was beginning to affect her mood, which was never a good thing when she was agitated. She was reaching a deadly point.

Azalin moved out of Lucius's reach and strode over to her. "It has been forever. I have missed you."

Patience was stunned and silent, especially when Azalin embraced her. Missed her? *Do I know her?*

She had read about Queen Azalin in books but didn't think they were friends. Or were they? There was no way she was friends with the Queen of the Selkies. This was the time when she hated her memory loss the most. Now it was about to be awkward.

"I am so sorry. I don't remember you. I am having some memory issues. How do we know each other?"

Azalin pulled away and stared at her strangely. "Memory issues? Ceamae, you jest. We have been friends for hundreds of years. You are the one who helped me gain this kingdom."

"We have? And... I did?" Patience tried not to let hope seep into her voice. Maybe she would be able to tell her who she really was. She couldn't help but turn to look at Alden, who nodded, letting her know this was real.

"We don't have time for this, witch. Lead us to the Atrium."

Queen Azalin looked over to Patience with sadness, then glared at Lucius as she walked over to the wall on the side of the bed. The king was now fully dressed, which Patience was thankful for. Queen Azalin and the king made eye contact, but no further exchange was made as she moved to the wall and placed her hand against it.

"Sii." Green light emanated from her palms, and a hole opened. "This way."

She stepped through, and Alecia trailed right behind her. Circe and King Kieran followed. Patience moved toward the opening, expecting Lucius to be right behind her, but instead she found Alden, who helped her down the few slippery steps that led into a cavern hallway. She could see Alecia up ahead behind Queen Azalin with her sword ready. She glanced behind her to see Silas helping Selene through and Max and Lucius following.

"You need rest," Alden said as he walked beside her. "It must be even more exhausting pulling magic from us."

"It is, but I will push through if it means this will end soon. It will be one issue down, and then I can concentrate on the next."

"But when will you get time for you?" he asked her seriously. It was a good question she didn't have an answer to.

She heard people say they would sleep when they were dead, but she'd always thought those people had a death wish. She didn't, but at this point, she might have to wait till she was dead. Ugh, she was being morbid. She definitely needed to rest; fatigue was starting to affect her thinking now, too.

"No worries. I have something that will solve at least one of your problems," he said, looking back at Lucius.

"You found it?" She tried not to sound too excited but couldn't help it.

"Yes," he said with a smile.

She wanted to ask where the Blade of Sapience was, but then she got distracted by the commotion up ahead.

"If you do something like this again, I *guarantee* you will regret it," Queen Circe said to King Kieran vehemently before she walked through the opening Queen Azalin and Alecia had disappeared through. *Someone was in the doghouse.*

King Kieran rubbed his forehead in frustration before following through the opening. Patience and Alden glanced at each other, and he smirked before helping her through.

When she entered, she was hit by the most mesmerizing fragrance—deliciously divine. She glanced around the Atrium as the others came through. It was a garden atrium.

Water poured from stone flowers into the crystal-clear pool that was in the middle of the room. Plants formed chairs and tables that lined the outside of the space, closer to the pool. More fauna made up lounge chairs scattered about. What drew Patience's attention were the shimmering flowers on the wall. She found herself moving toward purple flowers.

"They are called Ceamallia. They were named after you," Azalin explained, stepping behind her.

"Did I really help you obtain this kingdom?" she whispered.

"Yes, you did, Ceamae." Azalin gently touched her face. "You have not visited me in so long. Now, I know why."

Azalin knew her. This was her chance to learn about herself. It was time.

"Can you tell me what my name is?" she asked, eager to hear what she had confirmed in her heart.

Azalin smiled. "Of course, it's—"

"Witch, we found the door. Time to go."

Her gaze hardened. "No."

"Witch, we don't have time for your games. Let's go," Lucius demanded.

Azalin raised a brow in surprise.

How dare he? Enough was enough. She was tired of him. Not knowing if he wanted to kiss or kill her. Always interfering when it came to her past.

Anger boiled to the surface like Patience had never felt before. It spread throughout her body at her core until a blue fire sprung from her palms, surprising her.

Lucius looked at the flames. "Witch."

With no hesitation, she flung it at the vampire with so much force it pushed him across the room. She wasn't sure where this surge of magic was coming from, but it felt so damn good.

"Fuck," Max whispered loudly, "she is going to kick his ass."

"Should we interfere?" Silas asked, confused as to why no one helped.

"Not unless you want her to kick your ass, too," Alecia retorted, moving to the side out of the way.

"Witch!" the vampire yelled as he stood. "How dare you?"

He pulled Luzia from his back. Patience flicked her hand, causing Luzia to fly out of his grip across the room. Then she held out her palm, summoning Luzia to her.

Lucius stalked toward her, but she put up a barrier to stop him. It would only hold for a few seconds, but that was all she needed to cast her illusion. Closing her eyes, she pulled from this newfound magic. Throwing Luzia to the ground, she moved her hand over it. Then staring Lucius in the eye, she slowly melted it down.

Her barrier cracked as anger illuminated his eyes, and he furiously beat against it.

She sealed her fate when the melted liquid absorbed into the floor. The barrier broke as he stormed toward her. A darkness inside herself swelled at the sight of the pain she saw in his eyes. It was his turn to suffer.

Patience let him rush toward her before her magic took hold of him and slammed him into the thick glass ceiling before she let him drop to the ground.

Laughter sounded behind her. "Did I tell you how much I have missed you, Ceamae?"

Using her magic to pick him up once more, she smashed him against the wall. She reveled in the blood coming from the open wound she'd created on his forehead. Patience sent magic into it, causing it to slow its healing rate. She wanted a scar to be left so he would be reminded of this moment.

"I think we should interfere now," Selene warned. "Look at the necklace, it's pulsing."

Patience quickly erected a barrier around them, sealing them in together. "*Stay out of it.*" Her voice echoed through the atrium.

Too busy enjoying her triumph, she didn't see Lucius's magic snake out his fingers and wrap around her legs. Yanking, he pulled them out from her, then dragged her across the stone until she lay before him. He used his magic to lift her, then wrapped his hands around her throat.

"You had your fun, witch. Now it's my turn." He squeezed until her air began to cut off.

NO. I will not let this happen again.

She withdrew her hands, summoning all her strength, and delivered a forceful punch to his ribs. "You will not lay a hand on me anymore. You are a fucking piece of shit," she declared, her voice filled with anger and defiance.

He immediately released her, but that didn't stop her from punching his face with all her might, earning a pained grunt. Straddling him, she pinned him down, relishing in the satisfying thud of her fists against his chest. She reveled in the sound, driven by her desire to hear him scream in pain. With each blow, the sickening crack of his ribs breaking only intensified her determination to deliver even harder punches.

As he attempted to unleash his magic, she intercepted his intentions by placing her hand firmly on his chest, siphoning magic from him. With each passing moment, he grew weaker, his powers diminishing. Using her own magic, she forced his hands to the wall above him, binding them with an invisible force. Helpless and restrained, she launched a relentless assault, striking his body with fierce blows. Her fists pounded against him, delivering a punishing onslaught that left him vulnerable and at her mercy.

This violence was empowering. Seeing the blood coming from his mouth made her want more.

Patience had to stop herself. She was spiraling down a hole that if she went too far down, she was going to kill him, but she couldn't halt her blows. This was all his fault. He should have just listened to her.

"ODESSA, STOP!" Circe's piercing scream reverberated through the room.

But Patience's frenzied assault continued unabated. There was an uncontrollable rage consuming her, a bloodlust she couldn't comprehend. It was a force she had never experienced before, an unfamiliar darkness that threatened to consume her very being.

Azalin's laughter filled the room, her taunting words echoing in the air. "You will never reach her that way. She has tasted blood, and she wants more."

Patience fought against the torrent of emotions flooding her mind. She knew she had to stop herself before she went too far, before she crossed the line into irreparable harm. But the fury within her refused to subside. It was all his fault, she thought, seething with resentment. If only he had listened, if only he had understood.

The battle between her instinct for vengeance and her dwindling sanity waged on. She stood on the precipice, teetering between the desire to inflict harm and the need to regain her composure. It was a delicate balance, and the outcome hung in the balance, threatening to tip toward irreversible consequences.

Reeling back to hit Lucius once more, a blade appeared in her hands.

"What are you doing, Alden?!" Alecia yelled.

You can be free from him. Break it. Cut it out, Alden whispered through her mind.

A tender touch brushed against her cheek, a gentle caress that she instinctively recognized. She knew it was him even though he was nowhere near her. She turned her gaze in search of him, only to discover him on her left. He extended his hand, pouring his magic into her protective barrier, his eyes shimmering with an intensity of affection that both enthralled and unnerved her. It was a love so profound that it sent shivers down her spine, evoking a mixture of awe and fear within her soul.

She turned back to Lucius.

This was it. The Blade of Sapience. Its slender, razor-sharp blade, forged from a rare alloy of starlight and tempered steel, shimmered with a radiant glow, beckoning her to use it.

Severe the bond. Be free, Alden encouraged.

Using her instincts, she used the blade to make a small cut on his chest, and then she cut her palm, placing it on him. She called their bond forth, then slowly pulled her hand from his chest. As she did, his aura changed, flickering between red and purple. She ignored it and avoided his eyes, afraid of what she would see.

The thick purple ethereal cord was beautiful. Their bond was beautiful.

She felt wetness on her cheek as a tear fell from her eye. She wiped it away. No, she would not let this get to her. Lucius didn't want this. He didn't want *her*. She brought the blade close to the cord and felt him begin to struggle. Her eyes moved to his of their own accord. The world faded.

It was just the two of them.

Mae, I love you. Don't do this, Lucius's voice said gently through the bond. *I need you.*

No, it was a trick. It wasn't real. She wouldn't listen to his lies. She closed her eyes and pushed him out. She would be free.

Before she could think, her trembling hand grasped the hilt of the Blade of Sapience with determination. With a decisive motion, she brought the blade down upon the cord that connected her to him. A searing pain sliced through her chest as if a part of her soul had been cleaved away.

The sensation was indescribable, an agonizing mix of anguish and liberation. As the cord was severed, a rush of emotions surged within her, raw and unfiltered. It was as if the world around her momentarily blurred, and she found herself suspended in a realm between connection and detachment.

The pain, though intense, was accompanied by a rush of emptiness... and loneliness, as if the act of cutting the cord had taken away a part of herself. Then, amongst the darkness, a glimmer of something unfamiliar began to bloom, taking the place of what was lost.

As her thoughts swirled in confusion, a haunting whisper echoed in her mind, drawing her attention. It was Alden, his voice a seductive lure amidst the turmoil. "Now, kill him," he whispered, his words resonating with a sinister promise. "...and the pain will stop."

It would cease, the emptiness would dissipate if only she took that final step.

Her heart pounded in her chest as the temptation to end it all rose within her. It seemed like an easy solution, a way to rid herself of the agony and ensure that he could never hurt her again. The thought of plunging the blade into his heart held a vicious appeal, promising an end to her suffering and a twisted sense of justice.

But amidst her turmoil, a spark of resistance flickered within her. It was a faint voice, a sliver of her own conscience urging caution and questioning the allure of such a violent act. A battle raged within her, torn between the desire for release and the flickering flame of her own moral compass.

As she stood at the precipice, contemplating the irreversible choice before her, she felt a rush of conflicting emotions as tears filled her eyes, and she decided. Raising the knife above her head, ready to plunge it in, hands wrapped around her wrists, gripping them tightly.

Then a voice whispered in her ear, "You can't kill him, love. Not yet."

His sultry voice weaved around her, filling her with a sense of warmth... and home. Her grip loosened, and the knife dropped to the side. That voice. She knew that voice.

"Now that's a good girl."

She turned to meet red eyes. No, it couldn't be. This couldn't be real. Her nightmare was coming to life. Patience glanced down at the only person who could save her, but the half-demon lifted her chin, forcing her to look into his red gaze.

"Do not be afraid, my love. I would never harm you."

He ran his finger over her eyes, forcing them to close. His magic twisted around her, mesmerizing her and seducing her with its dark allure.

"That's it, my love." This time, when she opened her eyes, she didn't want to scream. Somehow, she knew he wasn't there to harm her. "Good girl."

"The pain," she whispered.

"I can heal your pain." He held out his hand to her. "All you have to do is come home. It is time."

She gazed down at Lucius. Blood spilled from the corners of his mouth as he stared back at her. *What have I done?*

"Nothing he didn't deserve, my love. Come, we must go."

She stared up at the half-demon. Long brown curled horns protruded out of his head, but this time, he wore a bright blue suit which made his black skin even darker, if possible.

"I don't understand what is happening," Patience confessed, confused by the events unfolding. Nothing made sense anymore, and everything was a blur. She glanced back at Lucius. She needed to heal him.

"He will live unfortunately, but we must go now so we can unlock your memories."

He had finally gained her attention.

"You can unlock my memories?" Patience asked, praying it was true. She needed hope.

"Yes. But we must go now."

The barrier vibrated. She looked to see Alden banging furiously, his magic no longer able to get through. The half-demon stared at Alden and then grinned.

"Love, let us go." This time, when he held out his hand, she took it. He helped her off of the vampire, who desperately grabbed her leg, bringing her attention back to him.

"I have to heal him first."

"Azalin will make sure his friends get him home. He will be fine. Come."

She pulled her leg away easily as the half-demon led her over to the Damascus, a full-length magical stone mirror. Its reflection rippled as they neared.

"Where are we going?"

"Home, love. Home"

Patience glanced back at Lucius one more time before she stepped through the mirror, the half-demon following after.

CHAPTER SIXTEEN

LUCIUS

Everything hurt. His ribs were broken, puncturing his lungs. It was one of the times Lucius was grateful he couldn't breathe. He was sure that both his arms were broken, as well as one of his legs, and he wasn't healing as fast as he usually did.

The worst part of it all wasn't the pain from his wounds. The most excruciating pain was from his chest, where Patience had severed their bond. He had never felt anything like it before, like someone had reached into his chest and pulled out his very heart.

Alecia kneeled before him as the mirror became solid and shattered. "Lucius. Lucius. Fuck. Selene, can you heal him?"

Selene kneeled on the other side of him. "I need my tome. I have a spell that will speed up his healing rate, but we have to get him back."

Lucius could hear the rushing of footsteps as Maxim and Silas came to stand before him. He tried to talk, but all he could concentrate on was the agonizing pain rippling through him.

"Fuck. Shit, Lucius." Max ran his hands through his hair as Lucius saw the guilt in his eyes.

"Max, don't fall apart on me right now," Alecia pleaded, her voice tinged with urgency and determination. "We have to get him back."

"Patience," Lucius croaked out, blood spilling from his lips.

"Shhh. Don't talk, idiot. Save your strength," Alecia scolded, grabbing a long cloth from Queen Circe, who kneeled near him.

"We have to wrap this around his ribs before we can move him."

Lucius's eyes searched the room until they landed on Queen Azalin, who stared at him. *I am so sorry. It was the only way to save my kingdom, but you must remember in order to save her, Zidakas.*

The queen's words echoed through his mind. Anger coursed through Lucius as he began to understand her words. He glared at her, pushing all his anger into his stare so she would know he would be coming for her.

"Don't lift him. You may damage him further, even with the bandages around his ribs," Ennes said as she kneeled beside him. "Here, drink this. It will not fully heal you but give you substance and strength." Ennes pulled a small green vial from her pocket and tried to pour the liquid into his mouth, but Maxim stopped her.

"How do I know it will not kill him or if this is another trap?"

Alecia snatched the vial and poured it down his throat. It was candelilla, exactly what he needed at the moment. It took a few seconds for the effects to take hold. It dulled his pain, except the one in his chest. Pushing through it, Lucius tried to speak a few words.

"Max." No blood came up. He continued to speak. "Where is Alden?"

"The bastard disappeared as soon as they went through the mirror," Max muttered, barely in control of his own fury.

"Did he lift the curse from your daughters?" Kieran asked Azalin.

"It lifted as soon as the mirror shattered."

"Good." Kieran said as he went to stand by Circe, who was clearly pissed at him. "I think it is time we left," the king announced.

"Curse?" Silas questioned with a curiously raised brow.

"The demon, Alazar, cursed our sisters. They have not been able to transform into their humanoid form for over a hundred years," Ennes disclosed.

"A deal was made that if I helped him capture the king, he would return my daughters to me. That deal changed the moment Ceamae stepped foot back into my kingdom. In exchange for my daughters' freedom, all I had to do was get her here to the atrium. He no longer wanted the king. He wanted her," Queen Azalin confessed.

Pure rage spread through Lucius, fueling him enough to try and stand.

"We have to get her back." He spat blood.

"The portal is closed. There is no way through now," Nikita informed them as she stood by the shattered glass.

Selene stood by the mirror as well, examining the glass. "I think I may be able to recreate this portal. Was it the half-demon, Alazar, who created it?"

"No, the portal was there long before that thing existed. The Queen Yarlya of Amare and King Nyx of Evictus used the portal originally, and Ceamae is the one who created the portal for them to continue their illicit love affair," Azalin supplied as she glanced at the king. "And before he found his queen, King Kieran used it quite often."

"I can feel the Silverlands magic within it. I think there is a spell in my book. We must go." Whispering a spell, the witch summoned a satchel and placed a few of the glass pieces inside before securing it over her shoulder.

"We need to get her back," Lucius whispered weakly, his voice barely audible yet filled with determination.

"We can't do anything until you rest and get some blood in your system. Once you are back to full strength, we can go rescue Patience, the witch you hate, if I must remind you," Max retorted sourly.

Lucius scoffed, ignoring his comment. The pain in his chest reminded him how much he didn't hate her. It was like a part of his soul had been ripped from him.

A hollow feeling spread through him. Even with the bond gone, thoughts of her still consumed his mind. He didn't want to think about what that meant, but the weight of the truth pressed heavily on Lucius's heart, causing it to ache with a mixture of sorrow and longing. Deep down, he knew what it meant, even before his mind could fully comprehend it. Their connection, once so strong and vibrant, had been severed, leaving an empty void that echoed with the pain of loss.

His heart cried out in mourning, each beat a melancholic melody of what they had shared and what had slipped through his fingers. He wished he could say that the intensity of his feelings surprised him, that he hadn't fully grasped the depth of his emotions until now. But the truth was, he had always known. From the moment he laid eyes on her, he had known that she meant more to him than he dared to admit.

The realization hit him with a crushing force, threatening to overwhelm him. The feeling of her absence was like a gaping chasm in his soul, an emptiness that couldn't be filled by anything else. It was as if a vital part of him had been torn away, leaving behind an ache that consumed his being.

He closed his eyes, taking a shuddering breath as he tried to find solace amidst the torrent of emotions. The pain was too much, but he couldn't deny it. He had to confront it, to face the reality that Patience, the woman who had captured his heart, was no longer by his side.

Alecia moved to a wall and spoke a spell, using her blood to write symbols on it until a portal opened. "This will take us back. Let's go."

She walked through first, followed by Circe and Selene. King Kieran whispered something into Azalin's ear, causing her to frown before he, too, went through the portal.

Silas and Maxim helped Lucius to his feet. They slowly began to walk him forward to the portal when Nikita touched his chest, stopping them.

"I have a gift and a message from Mira." She placed a small bottle filled with a shimmering silver liquid into his pocket and whispered in his ear, "Look to Luzia for the key, and the rest will follow. Ustafa will know the way. Drink to remember, or all will be lost." Kissing his cheek, she stepped away.

He didn't understand. Luzia was gone. The witch destroyed her. Anger should be boiling up inside of him at his loss, but he didn't have the strength. *Look to Luzia for the key, and the rest will follow. Ustafa will know the way. Drink to remember, or all will be lost.*

Who was Ustafa, and what key did Luzia hold? To what?

He could not dwell on this now; he had to focus on healing. They continued to inch towards the portal. Silas went through first, and then Max and he walked through together.

Surprisingly, King Kieran waited on the other side with Silas to help him through.

The king urged, "Let us bring him to his room so he can rest. Silas, he will need blood."

Silas nodded before disappearing toward the kitchens. The king and Maxim guided him up to his room and helped him into bed.

Lucius loathed being this helpless. Patience had barely used magic on him, yet she had caused so much damage. His body began to shut down. He needed to heal.

Selene and Alecia walked into the room.

"We will try and help, Lucius, so stay still."

As they chanted the spell, their magic surged through him, weaving its way through his body with purpose. The wounds that marred his flesh began to close, the aches and bruises fading away under the mending power of their combined magic. But amidst the physical healing, there remained a deep ache within his chest, an emptiness that resisted the mending touch of their spells.

A groan escaped Lucius's lips, a sound that carried the weight of his anguish and the frustration of an unhealed pain.

"There is nothing we can do about that particular pain. Lucius, you have to let yourself feel all of it," Alecia said before she kissed his forehead.

"Let's leave him. He needs rest." Kieran nodded, then left.

Maxim placed another log on the fire, then glanced at Lucius before departing.

As Lucius sat in solitude, the weight of his emotions bore down upon him, threatening to consume him whole. He no longer held back the floodgates that held his pain at bay, allowing the rawness of his grief to wash over him like a torrential storm. Each wave of agony crashed against his being, threatening to drown him in its relentless intensity.

As the excruciating pain threatened to pull him into the depths of unconsciousness, Lucius's eyelids grew heavy, each blink a struggle against the overwhelming weight of his sorrow. But before succumbing to the darkness, his fingertips brushed against something cold and unyielding. He turned his head slightly and glanced down.

Luzia sat on his bed next to him in all her glory, fully intact. She hadn't destroyed her.

He gripped her tightly before the pain took over, forcing him to close his eyes.

⬤

Patience

"My love, don't be afraid. I have been waiting for your return. I have the key to unlock your memories so you will remember me and our love."

The half-demon spoke to Patience, but she didn't really understand what he was saying. The fog in her head hadn't cleared, and her whole world felt off, like she was missing something. All she wanted to do was go back and heal Lucius.

He needed her. She didn't understand why or how she got here. It was all confusing.

"Take me back, please. I need—"

"You have been through an ordeal. You need to rest. Then we can talk."

They stood at the bottom of a large black marble staircase that had a white velvet carpet running down it. A chandelier hung above them, illuminating the stone walls and floors.

Where the hell am I? I have to get out of here.

Patience tried summoning her magic to create a portal. Nothing came.

"Your magic will not work here until I deem it so," the half-demon whispered in her ear.

She tried again, ignoring his words. Closing her eyes, she looked deep into herself, focusing on her magic. Searching for it.

Love, it will not work here. The words resonated through her head as red eyes popped in front of her within her mind. Her eyes shot open.

He was standing right in front of her now. His red eyes peered into hers. The same red eyes which had been haunting her were right before her, and now she was defenseless.

Her magic had abandoned her in this place.

"Now, now. Don't look so sad. All you have to do is love me and obey me in every way, and I will return your magic to you, love. For now, let us get you some rest," Alazar said, his voice laced with a twisted sense of possession and desire, further unsettling her fragile state.

The offer he presented, tainted with manipulation and control, offered a seemingly simple solution: to love him, to obey him unquestioningly, in exchange for the restoration of her magic. It was a tempting proposition, but Patience knew the price she would have to pay.

The burden of her exhaustion weighed heavily upon her, her weary body longing for respite. Yet deep within her core, a flicker of resistance burned. She refused to succumb to him. Even in her weakened state, a spark of defiance ignited within her. She would never bend to his will.

The demon's grip tightened around her waist, his touch suffocating and oppressive. Patience felt herself being pulled along, walking up the staircase under his forceful guidance. The path ahead seemed ominous, each step heavy with uncertainty and trepidation.

As they ascended, the air grew heavier, the atmosphere thick with an unsettling energy that seemed to emanate from the demon himself. Patience's heart pounded in her chest, her mind racing with a whirlwind of emotions. Fear, anger, and defiance mingled within her, creating a storm of conflicting sensations.

The staircase stretched before them, its darkened steps illuminated only by the faint glow of malevolent energies that swirled around them. Patience's every instinct screamed at her to resist, to break free from the demon's grasp, but she found herself ensnared within the inescapable hold of his power. As the demon led her down the dark hallway, torches lining the walls burst into life, their flickering flames casting an eerie glow upon the surroundings. The light they provided was feeble, barely penetrating the obsidian expanse of the black marble walls that enclosed them. The corridor seemed to stretch endlessly, each step echoing with an ominous hollowness.

Patience's senses heightened, her heart pounding in her chest as she strained to discern any hint of what lay ahead. The torchlight flickered and danced, casting disorienting shadows that played tricks on her mind. The air grew colder, carrying with it a faint scent of decay and foreboding.

The walls, devoid of any ornamentation or relief, appeared to absorb the feeble light, swallowing it into an abyss of darkness. The black marble seemed to possess an otherworldly quality, emitting a sense of malevolence and confinement. Patience's skin prickled, goosebumps rising as a shiver ran down her spine.

They stopped in front of the only thing out of place. A silver door.

It stood in stark contrast to the surrounding black marble walls, its lustrous surface reflecting the dim torchlight in shimmering waves. Patience's gaze fixated on the door, its presence inexplicably captivating yet tinged with a sense of trepidation.

"I prepared this room, especially for your return."

The half-demon rummaged through his pocket and produced a silver key. As he stuck it in the lock, Patience peered uneasily down the hallway, weighing her chances of escaping. She had a feeling that once she was in the room, there would be no return for her.

The torches had extinguished behind them, leaving complete darkness in their wake. She would be running blind, and he would catch her before she even hit the stairs. It would be better for her to wait and figure out where the hell she was.

The lock clicked, and he pushed the door open. As it swung inward, a breathtaking sight unfolded before them: a bedroom adorned in an ethereal palette of silver and white.

Soft, silvery light cascaded from ornate chandeliers, casting a gentle glow that danced upon the pristine white walls. The floor, adorned with plush, snowy carpets, invited barefooted steps, its fibers sinking beneath the weight of each tread. Delicate lace curtains framed the expansive windows, allowing a stream of moonlight to filter into the room, casting a serene ambiance upon the space.

The centerpiece of the bedroom was a grand, four-poster bed, draped in opulent silver and white fabrics that billowed like clouds. Its intricately carved wooden frame bore exquisite detailing, displaying craftsmanship that spoke of timeless artistry. Nestled within this haven of comfort and refinement, the bedding beckoned with its promise of rest and solace.

Every detail was meticulously arranged—a vanity adorned with gleaming silver accessories, a chaise lounge draped in plush velvet, and delicate flower arrangements that exuded a sweet fragrance, infusing the air with a sense of serenity. The interplay of silver accents and pristine white hues created an atmosphere of tranquility and sophistication, captivating Patience's senses and briefly easing the turmoil within her.

In that moment, Patience couldn't help but acknowledge the sheer beauty of the room, despite the circumstances surrounding her.

Her feet moved forward into the room of their own accord. Her eyes were drawn to a silver crown sitting on the mantle above the large fireplace. Her fingers reached out to trace the intricate design.

"Yes, you found your crown."

Her eyes widened. "*My* crown?"

"Yes. So much for you to learn. For now. You sleep."

He placed his hands to her temples, and she collapsed into his arms, falling into a dreamless slumber.

CHAPTER SEVENTEEN

DAPHNE

"And where have you been?" Alazar, sitting in his demon form at the white wooden table, asked Daphne as she walked into his queen's bedroom. He was angry with her. She was late. He hated it when she was late.

"I was with Jezabel, helping her with a spell. I am sorry for my tardiness." Daphne kneeled at his feet on the white carpet, knowing it was always the quickest way to appease him. She had been imprisoned with this man for over a hundred years. He was so manipulative that she couldn't tell what was real or not.

Even though her power was vast, she still couldn't get away from him. The gold and black bracelet encircling her ankle, the Cuff of Anu'un, gave him complete control of her and the magic she could wield. She had tried so many times to get it off, but only the owner of the bracelet could remove it. Or she could cut off her foot? Which she had contemplated many many, *many* times and almost attempted one night long ago in her desperation.

Now she had hope that she would soon be out of this situation and back where she belonged. Daphne glanced over to the woman from the bookstore, his queen.

"Has she awakened yet?"

Alazar's anger changed to longing as he stood, moving around her toward the woman.

"Does she remember you?" Daphne whispered, getting up from the floor and moving to stand next to Alazar as he watched over the sleeping woman's body. He said her name was Odessa and that she would be his queen.

"No, but they will be looking for her, especially him." Alazar bent down and adjusted the blanket over her. He slowly ran his hand down her cheek.

"The Ragana Zidikas. He won't stop looking for her. How are we going to protect her? Are they still bonded?" Daphne questioned as they walked out of the room, shutting the door softly, so as not to disturb her.

"He will never find her here. We are safe."

Safe. Daphne wanted to scoff. Of course, they would never find her here in Askaria. No rescue mission was coming to save them with all the wards he had in place.

"As for the bond, no, they are no longer bonded, which Alden will be happy about, but she was never his to have. She is mine and has always been mine. Once she remembers, we will bond, especially since I have the spell now. You will help me cast it."

Daphne gaped at him in shock. "You found the spell?"

She had honestly hoped he would never find it, the bonding spell. That woman did not belong to him. He wanted to use her powers just as he had used Daphne's. She sensed Odessa's power was far greater than hers, as well.

"Yes, I did. All thanks to Jezabel and the death of an old friend." Alazar stopped in front of his office door.

She wasn't allowed in there, save for one time in the past. It was the first time he brought her here to his castle of onyx. He forced her to create two portals. She wasn't sure where the portal went because she didn't understand the words of the spell then. But now that she was older, she knew one of the portals led to the human realm, Eviathan, and the other she believed led to Enoch, the dark realm, but she wasn't sure.

She needed to take another look at the spell, but he always kept it locked away. And she was too afraid to try and take the key hanging around his neck. She didn't want to be locked in the dungeon again. Too many things lurked in the dark down there.

Her hope was that Odessa would be able to help her escape. She had the feeling he wanted to imprison her too. Maybe with their combined powers, they could escape together.

"A bond like theirs can't be broken."

He eyed her suspiciously.

She scrambled to fix her mistake, "What I mean is that bonds are very hard to break, especially one like theirs. Are you sure it is broken?"

"Yes, I watched her cut the thread, but to be sure the spell will work, we are going to try it out first. I know the perfect couple to start with." He chuckled to himself, causing Daphne to cringe. *That poor couple. I wonder who it will be?*

Looking away she said, "And if I refuse?"

"Then you already know the consequences. We wouldn't want me to get angry now, would we?" He grabbed her face, forcing her to look into his cruel red eyes. "Now, would we?" he repeated.

She swallowed over the newfound lump in her throat. "No."

"Good girl. Now, go and finish your chores, then gather the ingredients from Jezabel and meet me in the tower so we can begin."

Daphne walked away, eager to leave his presence. She heard the echo of the door closing when she was almost halfway down the hall.

Freedom was close. She just needed Odessa to wake with her memory intact. She hadn't seen him use anything on her to manipulate her memory, but she wasn't sure since she wasn't always around. Nevertheless, she prayed to the Goddess that even if he did, she could still convince the girl to help her escape. If not, the foot cutting idea would start to look appealing again.

CHAPTER EIGHTEEN

Lucius

Lucius woke to blood being forced down his throat.

"You're going to kill him, Michael. Stop," Ian snapped, trying to snatch the blood from his hands.

"He's been sleeping for three straight days, and we still have no clue where the hell Patience is. I can't feel her, and it is freaking me the hell out. GreyJoy said we need to wake him, or else she will be lost forever." Michael kept Ian at arm's length as he continued to force the blood down Lucius's throat.

The blood sped through his body, strengthening and rejuvenating him.

"See? He finished this one," Michael said in triumph, showing Ian the finished bag of blood before placing it next to the other empty bags. "Give me another." He held out his hand, waiting.

Another blood bag was pushed into Lucius's mouth. Finishing it off, yet another was pushed toward him, but he reached up, grabbing Michael's hand and forcing him to drop the bag.

"Enough," he croaked.

Ian walked over to Lucius's bed and grinned. "You're awake."

Lucius glared up at him, then glanced around his room to see Michael cleaning up the empty blood bags from his side table. He looked toward his window to see what time of day it was. His red curtains were drawn, meaning the shutters were closed. *The sun must be up.*

"You have been sleeping for three days straight."

Three days. He had slept for three days.

He sat up abruptly. *The witch.* He had to get to the witch. Lucius closed his eyes, searching for the bond. All he found was a hollow emptiness and pain. He was about to open his eyes to get away from the agony when he felt it.

A small tug where the bond had been.

Drowning out the sound of Michael and Ian's movements, he reached into the emptiness inside him. He wasn't sure what he was hoping to find, but he searched until he felt the soft pull again. He raced toward the pull, reaching out—grasping for something, anything. Then it was gone.

Sadness crept through him. Somehow, he knew Patience was alive. He couldn't find the right words to describe it. He was sure their blood bond was gone, but she was there within the hollowness and pain. He wasn't sure if it was really her or just his imagination... or worse, just hope. He felt like he was going crazy, but one thing he absolutely knew was that they needed to find her.

He opened his eyes and tried to get up.

"Woah, take it easy. You are still weak," Ian said with concern, placing his hand on his shoulder.

Lucius reluctantly sat back, clearing his throat as Ian passed him some water. He took a sip before he spoke, "Have you found her?"

"No, Selene has been trying to recreate the portal into Askaria, but she hasn't been successful."

Three days. He needed to get up and move. He had wasted too much time already. The pain in his chest had lessened, but it still pulsed.

She was gone.

Lucius placed his hand on the bed, pushing down to sit himself up when metal touched him. He turned to see Luzia. He had forgotten she had appeared at his side when they had returned. The witch hadn't destroyed her.

"Leave me," he said softly.

"What?" Michael asked.

"Get out! Leave me."

"Come. He needs a moment. Leave the blood on the stand," Ian said as he moved off the bed. Michael placed two more packs of blood on the stand, then followed behind Ian.

When the door closed, Lucius laid back against the headboard, thinking about what had happened that night. He wasn't sure if he actually understood. Her anger was real. Her punches were real. Patience had wanted to hurt him, and she did. She had severed their bond.

He closed his eyes, searching for the cord within him and finding it drifting alone in the dark. Hollow like his heart. The pain would ache, then dull, and then he would never know she had been there. Sadness crept into his heart at the thought, but he pushed it away. This was what he had wanted, and she had given it to him.

She could have killed him with one blow and instead, she had only injured him. Now, the half-demon had her. Lucius needed to find the strength to get her back.

He didn't want to question why he wanted her back, but the most plausible answer his head would accept was that he didn't want her to give into the half-demon and be on his side. His heart had a completely different answer for him. Pushing it away, he thought back to what Nikita had told him.

Look to Luzia for the key, and the rest will follow. Ustafa will know the way. Drink to remember, or all will be lost.

He pulled the small bottle of liquid from his pocket then picked up Luzia, examining her. She looked the same as she always did in all her glory, just as she did the first day he held her. She was forged by a Stoven, a dwarven descendant, and gifted to his grandfather, who then gifted it to him.

He examined her long, thin, slightly curved silver blade. She held the same engraving that was written on his family's crest *Prin cenusa, ne vom ridica din nou (From the ashes, we will rise again).* Lucius continued to examine her handle, looking at her twisted cross guard and her leather grip. The only thing he found off was the pommel. It took him a moment to figure it out as he rotated her in his hands. Her pommel was slightly bigger, which would mean her weight would be off.

Lucius stood and balanced her in the palm of his hand, then swung her through the air a few times. Her balance was not off. He examined his family crest on the pommel closer. It appeared different, as well. He grabbed a cloth from inside his side table and began to wipe it, hoping to make it clearer.

A small crack appeared. He wiped harder and the crack grew wider, revealing a sliver of red. *What the hell is in there?*

Scrubbing harder, he pushed against the crack until more red was revealed. It looked like it was a gem. He reached under his bed and grabbed the dagger that was there. He continued to scrap off the silver until a red roman gem was revealed.

Lucius tried to recall if it had always been there or whether it was something he later added to her. No memory revealed itself.

Is this what they were talking about? Is this the key?

Nothing about the gem was familiar, so it begged the question of how it became part of his sword.

"Your moment is up. We need to talk," Maxim said as he strolled back into the room.

"Do you remember Luzia having this before?" He held her up for Max to examine.

Confusion marred his face. "Did this just appear now? Your family crest has always adorned the pommel."

"I know." Lucius glanced down at the silver on the hardwood. "I scraped it off."

"And this was under it? Interesting." Max stooped down to look over the silver. "Its silver metallic paint hardened. You think the witch added it?"

"No, it would make no sense for her to add this."

"What made you remove the paint?" Maxim asked curiously as he continued to examine Luzia.

Lucius recounted some of the details of what happened within the waters of Mira, excluding seeing Patience, and then showed Maxim the vial Nikita gave him and told him the words she'd spoken to him.

"Ustafa. Who the hell is Ustafa?"

"It is what Jafa calls GreyJoy," Michael said as he entered the room with Ian in tow.

"The bookstore is Ustafa?" Lucius asked.

"Yes. Why?"

"I need to see him so he can explain this to me," Lucius said, grabbing Luzia from Max's hand and showing it to Ian.

"What the hell did you do to her?" Ian grabbed the blade and looked at the pommel. "You scraped off the family crest?" he asked incredulously.

"Yes, that was underneath."

"You need to see GreyJoy. He may be able to explain what is going on," Michael told them.

"I agree. Where is the witch?"

"I assume you are talking about Selene," Maxim stated.

No. He had momentarily forgotten Patience was gone, but they didn't need to know that.

"Yes, where is she?"

"She is in the library perusing through her tome of spells, trying to recreate the back door to Evictus."

Lucius grabbed Luzia from Ian and headed to the library, not caring if anyone followed. The fastest way to the bookstore would be to be transported there by the witch. He just hoped this witch would have the means to do what he asked.

As he reached the library, a bright light seeped through the cracks in the door before he heard a loud boom. He opened it and rushed into the library to find the witch Selene, Alecia, Circe, and Estelle sprawled on the floor like they had been thrown about by an explosion.

He checked Alecia first. "Alecia. Alecia, are you alright? What happened?" He lifted her head to cradle in his hands.

She opened her eyes and smiled. "I think that witch made you soft."

He immediately dropped her head and stood.

"Ow! Bastard."

Circe was already up helping the witch to her feet, and Estelle sat up, rubbing her head.

"Well, clearly that didn't work, just like I told you it wouldn't," Alecia directed at Estelle as she stood.

"What the hell is going on here?" Lucius demanded. "What are you doing in my library?"

"We are trying to recreate the portal," Queen Circe explained. "Selene said she would be able to recreate it, but so far we have only come close once."

"Which just exploded. No thanks to Estelle," Alecia added, annoyed.

"I'm sorry, Lecia. I thought if we added a little spruce oil, then it would work."

Alecia rolled her eyes, ignoring her sister's apology as she stood. "We have been at this for days. I think we need a break." She strode over to the wall and opened Lucius's liquor cabinet. Taking out a bottle, she took a swing.

Well, shit.

"Two hundred years of sobriety down the damn drain," she said as she consumed the bottle like water.

He didn't have time for this. "I need to go to the bookstore."

"You do realize we are in a library. Why do you need a bookstore?" the witch, Selene, said with a strange look. "I feel like I have seen you before."

"You do realize we just rescued them from the City of Amare, right?" Alecia remarked.

"I know, but I think I have seen him somewhere else."

"He is the Ragana Zidikas," Alecia added.

"I know this, but his aura is off as well. Can't you see it?" Selene strode over to him and walked around him in a slow circle. "It is like they are fighting each other, and the red is winning at the moment."

Alecia came over to him with a different bottle in her hand this time. "Yeah, you are right. I knew his aura was off before, but then it was only a flicker. Now it seems as though it is trying to take over him. What happened in Amare before we got there, Lucius?"

"What the hell are you both talking about?" Lucius asked, bewildered by their comments. He had no clue what the hell they were talking about with changing auras. "I don't have time for this. I need to go to the bookstore."

Maxim strode through the door. *Finally, someone to help me get through to these females.*

"What happened, Lucius? Spill," Alecia said, taking another swing from the bottle.

"He encountered Mira," Maxim imparted, moving to stand near Alecia. *The traitor.*

"Mira? As in, the Spirit of the Waters? Let me see the bottle." Selene held out her hand.

"What bottle?" Lucius questioned. He crossed his arms, feigning ignorance.

"Give her the bottle, Lucius," Max commanded him.

"How do you know about the bottle?" he demanded.

"Because of your aura," Alecia retorted. "Give it to her."

Reluctantly, Lucius pulled the bottle from his pocket and offered it to Selene.

Selene took the bottle, looking closely at it. She glanced at him, then back at the bottle. "You need to drink this?"

"Obviously, but what is it?"

"They call it Elixir du Trouvé. Did you find something that was lost?" Selene asked.

Lucius looked down at his sword's pommel, his eyes lingering on the gem. "I don't believe I lost it, per se, but I did find this."

"What was said to you exactly?" Selene questioned.

"She said, 'Look to Luzia for the key. Ustafa will know the way. Drink to remember, or all will be lost,'" Maxim volunteered.

"Who is Luzia?"

Lucius lifted his sword for Selene to see.

"We must find this Ustafa."

"Finally, someone on the same page. I need to go to the bookstore, and you are the fastest way to get us there," Lucius said, annoyed by this whole conversation.

"I do not know how to find Ustafa," Selene retorted, handing the elixir back to him.

"We know where he is. He needs you to create the portal."

"Do you have anything that belongs to him?"

Lucius went over to the table and picked up the three books he borrowed from GreyJoy. "Will these work?"

He handed them to Selene.

"Yes, give me a moment."

Selene placed the books on the floor, then placed her hand on top of them. The books shimmered as she used her finger to burn a circle into the floor.

"That better not be permanent," Lucius growled.

"It's not," Alecia assured him as she took another swig from the bottle.

They all watched as Selene began to chant a spell and the circle grew bigger, but her finger stayed in a steady rhythm. "Aperi nexum ad Ustafa."

A bright light burst from the circle, then spread through the room until it disappeared. An image of the bookstore emerged in the circle.

Selene smiled, pleased. "Come."

"I need those books." Lucius gave her a pointed look.

She lifted them and handed them over to him before she dropped through the circle. Alecia followed behind with her bottle in hand. She smiled and saluted before hopping in.

"There is no way I am missing this," Maxim said before he also went through the hole.

Ian grabbed Michael and ran for the portal. "Remember, safest place for us," Ian yelled before they also went through.

Estelle calmly walked to the edge of the circle. "So, I guess we all are going."

"No, Kieran, Silas, and I will stay here," Circe announced. "So will Estelle."

"I will stay as well," Volt said from above. He sat balanced on the banister, reading a book.

Lucius absolutely hated the idea of leaving strangers in his home, but he felt better with Volt here, and he needed to get to the bottom of this all. He prayed this would shed some light on what the hell was going on and where the hell the witch was.

The fact that he even cared about where Patience was made him want to pull his hair out. This was what he wanted. Their bond was severed, and she was gone, so why did he care so much? His heart was screaming at his brain to catch up, but he refused to acknowledge what he knew it was telling him. His heart was already past the point of no return, and if his brain decided to let go, there would be no turning back.

The library doors opened behind him. Silas and King Kieran stepped through. Kieran nodded toward Lucius in acknowledgment.

"We will keep your home safe. Do not worry," Queen Circe said, walking over to King Kieran.

Lucius had no choice in the matter. He nodded before he proceeded through the portal, landing right outside the bookstore.

Everyone was already inside when he stepped through the front door.

A note floated down. He caught it.

"Cutting it close."

Lucius incinerated the note.

"Alright, *Ustafa*, tell me what the hell is going on and how I can find the witch."

CHAPTER NINTEEN

PATIENCE

Three days.

Patience had been stuck in this damn room for three days. She had been staring at these damn immaculate white walls for just as long.

Her magic didn't work. At all. She tried every hour on the hour but nothing. Not even a damn spark. Magic surrounded her, but she couldn't absorb it or use it. She hated being vulnerable.

Her favorite meals would appear on the deep oak table by the fireplace, tempting her to eat. In the morning, the aroma of French toast with strawberries or banana pancakes would fill the air. In the afternoon, grilled cheese and a small pear salad or a tuna sandwich would make her stomach grumble, and at night, it was the most delicious lobster macaroni & cheese or a juicy cheeseburger with potato wedges. Each dish would disappear within an hour, whether she touched it or not.

The first day she woke up there, she realized everything it served was her favorite, down to the glass of red wine that would appear every night at midnight.

She never touched the wine, but she was curious as to why it appeared at that specific time every night.

Pulling the room apart every day, she searched for a way out, but every time she closed her eyes, the room would put itself back together.

She screamed at the top of her lungs in frustration when she broke the window and figured out the view she was seeing of rolling hills was just an illusion. She was only able to glimpse the city lights of Askaria before the window immediately fixed itself, shifting to a new illusion.

The only good thing about this was that she no longer dreamed of red eyes. Now that the half-demon had her, she guessed there was no real reason to haunt her dreams. Though, she wondered if he would return her memories now.

What was even crazier was that her concern for herself was minimal. She just wanted to know that Lucius was alright. She couldn't feel him through their connection, which scared her the most. Though, the stranger part was that she swore she could feel Lucius slightly tugging on their bond every once in a while, even though she knew she had severed the bond. There was a hollowness within her, but she didn't feel any pain. She wasn't sure if it was because he numbed it or if it was still there.

She had tried to tug back a few times, but it was always gone before she could grab it.

Unfortunately, he was never far from her thoughts. More like he never left them to begin with, always lingering on the edge, waiting for her thoughts to quiet.

When she first felt the phantom pull, she couldn't stop the relief that spread through her, knowing he was alive and that she hadn't killed him. Part of Patience hoped he would be trying to find a way to her, especially since the tug was stronger about an hour ago, though still as fleeting as ever.

Patience stared into the fireplace, running her fingers through the flames that produced warmth but did not burn.

A knock sounded on the door. She ignored it, continuing to caress the fire. Whoever it was knocked again. Reluctantly, she stood and walked over to the door.

"Come in," she called out, hoping someone would answer and actually open the door. She knew it couldn't be the half-demon since he never knocked.

She moved closer to the door, placing her ear against it to see if she could hear breathing or maybe retreating footsteps.

All she heard was silence. "Strange."

Patience waited a few more minutes before she moved away.

She turned just in time to see a beautiful dark velvet off-shoulder gown appear on the bed with a note on top.

I will see you at midnight. Dress appropriately.

She threw the note aside and lifted the dress.

Dress appropriately? Did he think she would put on the dress? Well, that wasn't happening. Even if it was a gorgeous dress that would hug her curves just right.

Putting the dress back on the bed, she went back over to the fire to sit and wait for her twelve o'clock meal.

She stared into the fireplace so long that her stomach began to grumble. She glanced up at the clock on the mantel. It read twelve-thirty.

Her food was late. In her three days here, that had never happened before. She went over to the table to see if she had missed anything, but there was no sign of any food.

Interesting.

Ignoring her grumbling stomach, Patience began her endless scouring of the room, hoping she had missed something in her earlier searches that would help her escape.

Of course, she had no luck, and her stomach grumbled louder.

She decided to take a nap in order to distract herself from the raging hunger pains. She got on the bed, throwing the dress aside and closing her eyes, letting the sound of the crackling non-burning fireplace lull her to sleep.

A few hours later, she woke to another knock on the door. This time, she didn't bother moving from the bed, but she did wait to see if the door opened. It did not.

She scrubbed the sleep from her eyes and looked at the clock. It was six o' five.

Glancing at the table, she still saw no food. Patience turned around, thinking about lying in bed for a few more minutes. Then she abruptly sat up when she realized the dress had been neatly draped across the table.

Patience cautiously slipped off the bed, walked over to the table, and picked up another note that had the same message but in a different order this time.

Dress appropriately. I will see you at midnight.

It was going to force her to put the dress on or starve her. She rolled her eyes and grabbed the dress. Going into the bathroom, she showered but as she was putting the dress on, she realized Alden's necklace was gone and so was Queen Azalin's. He must have removed them. Strangely, she had completely forgotten about them. She should have put an invisibility spell on the jewelry. *Damn.*

Gazing at herself in the mirror, she absolutely loved how the dress hugged her curves. She only wished Lucius could see her in it. She sighed at her foolishness.

As soon as she stepped out of the bathroom, food appeared on the table for her.

Her stomach grumbled loudly as the aroma of baked chicken filled the room. As much as she wanted to just shove the food down her throat, she took her time sitting down and arranging herself so no food would get on her dress. She painstakingly ate her chicken, mashed potatoes, and green beans as well as a slice of chocolate cake.

After she finished eating, she climbed back on the bed and waited for midnight so she could finally confront her captor. Even though her first instinct was to find a weapon, she decided against it. She was in his domain for now. She had to bide her time and really plan her escape because she knew it would not be easy.

Patience wasn't sure how long she stared at the fireplace, but just as her eyes were about to drift closed, a cup appeared on the table, which didn't surprise her. What surprised her was the second cup appearing.

She sat up and waited for her gracious host to appear.

After about five minutes, no one showed, so she laid her head back down, and as her eyes were about to close again, she heard him.

"Sorry I am late, my love."

Lucius

"You have returned!" Jafa exclaimed, his emerald eyes filled with excitement as he rushed over from one of the aisles. "See, Ustafa? I told you he would come."

He seemed strange in his black jeans and grey sweater instead of the brown robes he had originally worn in Calidium. Even his raven hair seemed different. Maybe because it wasn't filled with sand anymore.

"Jafa, do you know what is going on here?" Lucius asked, trying to keep his anger in check long enough to get some answers. Luzia itched to taste blood.

"Ustafa asks if you have the gem and the elixir from Mira?"

"You can understand him directly?" Lucius asked suspiciously. "Did she know this?"

"Yes. Yes, she did."

"How are you able to understand him directly?" Lucius gripped Luzia tighter.

"I know you have many questions, and all will be answered as soon as you drink the elixir. Do you have the items?"

"I do." He pulled the elixir from his pocket and showed him the pommel of Luzia. He still didn't understand where this was all going, and he honestly didn't have time for this. "This was a mistake," Lucius confessed. "We don't need her. We have a Silverlands witch who can recreate the portal."

Alecia laughed out loud, then took another swig of her alcohol. "Lucius, we need her. Trust me. It has been three days of hell trying to create the portal, and we are no closer. We need her power, whether you want to admit it or not."

Fuck. She was right. "Fine. What do I need to do?"

"Excellent. You must return the books and then we can begin."

Lucius grunted but placed the books on the counter. His wife's necklace appeared, as well as another identical necklace, but instead of a blue pendant, this one had a purple pendant. He picked up the purple one, curious about whom it belonged to.

"Only the blue is mine. The purple one does not belong to me."

"Ustafa says the purple one is needed."

His brows creased. "For?"

"Ustafa says this is where you need to trust. You need to take both pendants."

Trust. He had to trust a damn omnipotent bookstore. He should walk out the door and say to hell with all of this. The hollowness and pain in his heart told him differently.

A note floated down in front of him. He caught it.

"You need her more than you will ever know. Trust."

The damn bookstore knew more than it was letting on. Lucius would go with this for now, but if anything felt off, he was going to torch the place.

"Fine. Let's get this over with. What do I need to do?" Lucius grabbed both the necklaces and placed them in his pocket.

"This way. Follow me." Jafa gestured him down one of the aisles with his arm. When Maxim tried to follow behind Lucius, Alecia stopped him.

"Only him," Alecia told Maxim. "He doesn't need a babysitter for this. Promise."

Maxim grunted but did not follow.

Lucius continued after Jafa until they reached a spacious, open area bathed in an otherworldly glow. The air felt charged with a mysterious energy as his eyes fell upon a pristine white circle etched into the ground with a white star in its center. On the left side of the room, a majestic pedestal stood, adorned with intricate carvings and embellishments. Its soft, ethereal light drawing his attention, Lucius cautiously approached.

Atop the pedestal rested a round orb, emanating a calm blue light that danced across its surface. Its luminescence seemed to hold secrets and possibilities, casting mesmerizing shadows on the surrounding walls. The orb appeared to pulse with a subtle energy, as if it possessed a life force of its own, radiating a sense of both enchantment and trepidation.

"Please place the gems on the star inside the circle," Jafa directed him.

Lucius took the purple necklace from his pocket and placed it in the circle directly on the star. Then he took out his wife's necklace and reluctantly placed it on the circle on the star as well. Luzia was the last to be placed before he stood.

"Now, he needs you to place both hands on the orb."

"This will not harm the items?" He didn't want this to destroy his wife's necklace. The very idea nauseated him.

"No, the items will not be harmed, I assure you."

Walking over to the orb, Lucius examined the blue marble ball before placing his hands on both sides.

Shackles extended, cuffing him to the pedestal. They felt tight around his wrists, especially when he tried to pull. Rage immediately swelled within him. The bookstore was going to burn. "What the hell is this?"

"Ustafa says it is temporary but necessary."

Lucius tried to pull his hands off the orb, but it was as if they were glued.

"Let me out. Let me out *now*!" he roared.

Jafa stepped back into the aisle, leaving Lucius alone. He continued to struggle to free his hands to no avail as a low hum began.

The circle on the floor lit up. Then rhythmic chanting surrounded him as a small light appeared in the middle of the orb.

The light grew bigger as the chanting grew louder.

A deep voice penetrated the chanting. "Kynigos, remember. Remember your wife. Remember your family. Remember."

The gem on Luzia's pommel lit, and sharp, throbbing pain began at the tip of his spine and grew. He cried out in agony as a thousand needle pricks made their way up to his cervical axis. He fought hard against the chain and tried to rip his hands from the orb, but the shackles held steady even as the pain subsided.

"Let me go *now*. Or I will burn you to the ground."

Stone walls erected around him as his wife's necklace became aglow and pain shot from his spine into his skull, starting at the back of his head and creeping its way to his temporal lobe. It was as if the spell had ignited a burning fire and was trailing it across his mind.

Lucius tried to control the pain by holding it in, but when the first scream escaped there was no stopping the others from following.

The agony went on and on for what felt like hours before it suddenly stopped. He slumped against the pedestal.

"Let me go... please."

"You are almost there. You are so close, Kynigos," the deep voice whispered to him. "This is the last step. Hold on."

Lucius gradually lifted his head and moved his feet until he stood upright. He searched around the room to find where the voice was coming from, but there was no one in the area except him. His head still throbbed in pain. It was possible he imagined it.

He tried to pull free once more when the purple gem lit. Light stretched out from all three gems, filling the circle. Once the circle filled, light traveled up the pedestal into the orb, which grew brighter. He felt pricks on his fingertips before light entered into his veins and traveled rapidly up his arms, then neck, entering his skull.

A sharp pain stabbed his skull before his mind went blank and the world faded away.

Mae appeared before him and gently touched his face. "Lucius, my love. I know this is hard, but it is the only way for you to get back to me. You cannot let him win. You must remember so you can save me."

She placed her hands on both sides of his head and stared straight into his eyes, pouring all her love into him. Then before his eyes, Mae changed. More like a fog lifted and his blurred vision became clear. Mae turned into Patience, like they were one in the same.

Lucius didn't understand. Nothing made sense except her love for him. He felt it down to his soul.

"Remember. Remember me. Remember us." Her lips pressed gently against his, sending a jolt through him. Sights and smells, music and laughter sped through his mind as images and sounds rushed around him. Spinning and going faster and faster.

Then silence.

"Lucius, love, wake up," Mae called from the distance. Lucius slowly opened his eyes and found Patience gazing at him. Strangely.

"There you are. I thought you would never open your eyes." She smiled.

He hesitantly sat up and looked around the room. They were in his bedroom.

"Lucius, are you okay?" She touched his arm gently as she kneeled on the side of the bed, gazing up at him with love in her eyes.

"What is going on?"

"You are remembering, my love. You are remembering us."

Lucius's world spun. *My love? What the hell is going on? Is someone playing a trick on me?*

"Come. They are waiting for you." She gently pressed a kiss to his head, then faded away.

Images and sounds all rushed forth, spilling out into his mind. His memories transformed right before his eyes. Things he thought had happened became different.

It was a trick. It was all a trick, he thought until the feelings came. The overwhelming feelings forced him to his knees as tears fell from his eyes when he watched the image of his wife change.

Shock ran through him as it all came rushing back to him. The way she smelled, the sound of her laughter, and the look in her eyes when he made love to her.

Everything made sense now. Anger swelled within him as he remembered everything.

CHAPTER TWENTY

Patience

The demon appeared before the fireplace in his double-breasted alabaster suit and a cocky grin on his face. His red eyes gazed at her with happiness.

"I had a few things I needed to take care of so that I could be with you for the next several days." He moved over to the bed, but Patience quickly removed herself, not wanting him to get any ideas. "You look absolutely beautiful."

"Why am I here? And who are you?" Patience demanded.

"Love, who am I? I am your lover, partner, and... husband," he said, taking another step toward her.

Patience kept backing away until she hit a wall. *Lies.* They had to be.

"I don't believe you."

"Of course you don't. I would not believe me either if I were in your situation." His hand reached up to gently caress her face. She turned her head away, and he pulled back. "I am sorry for causing this. I never meant for things to be this way."

He took a step back, giving her some space.

"I know you are not used to seeing me this way yet, so maybe I will have to go back to the way you first met me."

The once obsidian-black skin gradually shifted, morphing into a rich, warm shade of brown that seemed to glow softly under the ambient light. The imposing horns that once adorned his head retreated, giving way to a cascade of short, vibrant auburn hair that framed his features with a touch of earthly charm. His sharp, predatory teeth, once a formidable sight, now seamlessly transformed into a set of ordinary, human-like teeth, adding a sense of normalcy to his countenance. The only thing that did not change were his luminescent red eyes and pristine alabaster suit.

"Do I look familiar now?"

Something about him did look familiar, but only slightly. He did look less imposing, so she was grateful for the small things in life.

"No," she admitted truthfully.

"How about we have a little wine and just talk? I promise you I am not here to harm you. In fact, I am here to do the complete opposite. I want to give you your life back. Then I can get *mine* back." He picked up the wine from the table and handed her a glass.

Hesitation gripped her before she took it. "You know nothing you are saying to me makes any sense."

Taking a sip of wine, he smiled and gestured for her to sit at the table.

Patience sat in the chair farthest away from him.

"I know you don't trust me. I have you locked away with no way to escape. I would not trust me either," he said as he took a seat in the chair across from her. "But I am asking you to trust me. I am doing this for your protection."

Her eyebrow couldn't help but raise as she took a small sip of wine.

"Dessa, there is a reason you locked away your memories."

Her forehead creased in confusion. "Dessa?"

"Yes, Odessa is your name. Not this Patience you have been calling yourself."

She knew it, but hearing it confirmed the matter. Gave her such joy. She took another sip of the wine. It was delicious. "So, it was me? I locked away my own memories?"

"Yes, you had information you need to protect. Unfortunately, the spell did not go as planned and more than the memories you wanted to be sealed away were forgotten. That same night, we were attacked and became separated. I have been searching for you ever since. Your dreams have been my only connection to you."

The words—*I will kill him. You are mine. Forever*—came to her mind. If this were true, then he would know the words.

"If what you are saying is true. What did I dream of every night?"

"Sometimes it was a different dream, but most of the time it was the same two dreams. One was of you being chased by them the night we separated, and the other was of us together dancing under the moonlight. Both dreams ended the same way. Me promising to kill him for you, and you being mine forever."

"Kill who? Who did you promise to kill?"

"Lucius, of course."

It didn't surprise her to hear him say what she already knew. She placed the wine glass on the table, afraid she would drop it. No one, not even Michael, knew the words she heard almost every night. Who was this demon to her?

"I know this seems unbelievable, but I have something that may be able to make you believe." He went into his pocket and pulled out a clear glass sphere filled with a red mist.

Her mouth fell open. "This is a—"

"Aurora's Sphere. A memory keeper."

He placed the sphere in the middle of the table. "It will show you who I am and who you are."

Memory keepers were tricky. They could be manipulated, but they would have to change the memory before it was stored within the sphere, which was not easy to do or a guarantee that the memory would stay manipulated once inside the sphere because the owner of the memory would have to think the memory was true beforehand.

She could be looking at a lie, but it could also be true. Either way, she needed to find out. Maybe it would bring her one step closer to the truth.

Her hand reached out toward the sphere, then pulled back. "How do I know this isn't some kind of a trick or illusion?"

"Trust." He stood and came to stand behind her.

Patience tensed until he placed his hand against her cheek. A familiar warmth spread through her.

"You have to trust me, Dessa, or we will never get our life back. Trust me, please," he pleaded as his hand moved down to her neck, causing the warmth to spread all over her.

He was right; she had to trust him. If she didn't, then she would never know if this was real or not.

She reached out her hand and touched the sphere. The red mist moved toward her fingertips, gluing them to the ball. An electric shock flowed through her, paralyzing her. She felt pinpricks on her fingers. Her eyes watched as the mist entered her veins, traveling up her arms.

Patience tried to struggle, but the paralyzing shock continued to keep her body still. This was not Aurora's sphere. This was attacking her bloodstream.

"Shhh... relax. Let it do its job. It will all be over soon, and you will be mine. *Forever*," the half-demon said as he laughed into her ear.

Patience continued to struggle until redness filled her eyes and they slowly closed.

Alazar

Alazar lifted Dessa and placed her on the bed. He knew the sphere would work. Easily cloaked to look like something familiar to her. The Sphere of Erogonian would implant the memories he created of their life together.

It took him over a hundred and fifty years to painstakingly weave the memories from the dream realm. He visited her often in her dreams, knowing she would not remember. He made sure she never found the ability to unlock her memories.

The fates hated him when she found Lucius. It was bad enough when she found Michael, but he knew that was bound to happen because he was her familiar. He was surprised she lasted as long as she did without him, but then again, he knew how strong she was.

Gazing down at her beautiful face, he could not wait until she opened them, and they filled with love for him.

"It has been too long, my darling," he said, gently stroking her face. "Sleep and dream of us."

He kissed her forehead before he left to allow the mist to do its work.

He needed to go prepare for their wedding and deal with his brother.

Patience/Odessa

Odessa walked out on the terrace to breathe in the night air. She didn't realize how hot it was inside until the cool breeze brushed against her skin. She stood there watching the waxing moon and the stars. This had been the most wonderful night, and she never wanted it to end.

She sighed as a pair of arms came around her at the same moment. Alazar's warmth surrounded her as she snuggled into him. Nothing could be better than this.

"You look absolutely beautiful. As beautiful as the moon," he whispered into her ear as she leaned back to get closer to him. She loved it when he held her like this.

"Let's take a walk in the garden."

"Must we?" she asked, not wanting to leave his warmth.

"Yes, we must," Alazar said as he nuzzled her neck.

He took his arms from around her and turned her.

She smiled as she gazed into his red eyes. She put her hands into his short, auburn hair and touched his lips for a much-needed kiss.

"Now, you see why we need to go for a walk." He held out his arm for her to take. Reluctantly, she took it, knowing she would get what she wanted by the end of the walk.

Silently, they strolled through the garden until they found a small pond hidden behind some tall hedges. They would have missed it had Odessa not heard something splash into the water.

"This is so beautiful. I wonder why it is hidden?" Odessa murmured, mesmerized by the beautiful goldfish swimming within the pond.

"I think you already know the answer to that question," he said, engulfing her in his arms again and kissing the back of her neck.

"Alazar, did you take me here to ravish me?" she laughed as she slowly turned around. She found herself staring into his loving red eyes. She was so happy she could just burst with the joy that filled her. She never thought she could fall in love with someone like him, but he made her feel safe and loved. She couldn't imagine where she would be without him.

"Yes and no," he chuckled as he tucked a loose curl behind her ear. "I actually took you here to make you mine. "

"You silly man, I am already yours," she said, placing her hand against his cheek. He took it and gave it a loving kiss.

"I know you are, but I want to make it official so everyone in the realms knows."

Odessa's heart began to race at the same moment her brain realized what he was doing. He got down on one knee and pulled a red velvet box out of his pocket.

"Dessa, we have been through a lot over these past few years. When we first met, you wanted to rip my guts out and almost did, but you took mercy on me. You saw something in me that no one else did, changing our lives forever. Now, I can't see my life without you. By becoming my wife, will you make me the luckiest being in all the realms? To have and to hold forever?"

Tears stung her eyes as happiness spread through her. She didn't think this moment would ever come for her.

They were already soul-bonded. She didn't need a ring from him to know he loved her. A wedding wasn't needed. She told herself time and time again that she didn't need marriage, but deep down, she wanted it no matter how much of a human thing it was, and he knew.

"Yes," she said, hugging him. "Yes, I will marry you."

Odessa opened her eyes to find her love gazing at her. She remembered everything.

CHAPTER TWENTY-ONE

Lucius

"Lucius. *Lucius.*"

Lucius opened his eyes to find Alecia standing above him.

"Lucius, are you alright?"

He reached out grabbing her throat, squeezing. She wrapped her hands onto his arm, trying to stop him.

"Mincinos. *Trădător,*" (Liar, Traitor) he spat as he tightened his grip.

"I had to. I had no choice," she sputtered as she tried to loosen his grip. "I can help."

"Kynigos. You cannot kill her. You will need her," a deep voice boomed. GreyJoy.

"Do I?" Lucius grunted out. Unfortunately, Grey was right. He did need her. He loosened his grip, and she fell to the floor. She crawled into an aisle, disappearing from his sight.

"Kynigos," Jafa said, coming from one of the other aisles. "You are back."

"Yes, my friend. I am back. Tell me where my wife is." Lucius walked to the middle of the circle and picked up Luzia, as well as the two necklaces before slipping them into his pocket.

"He has her," he declared, with a mixture of determination and profound sadness.

He growled. "How long ago was she taken?"

"Three days ago."

His wife was within his grasp *three days ago* and he had foolishly let her go. What the hell happened to him?

"Grey, I need to remember this life he created for me."

A vial of red liquid appeared before him.

"You will not like what you see," Grey informed him.

Though, he already knew that sick bastard made him do something horrible and made his life miserable. He just didn't know specifically what, but he would find out soon.

He picked up the bottle and quickly swallowed its contents.

Red glazed over his eyes before memories of the present surged forth.

Anger boiled up inside of him as his mind showed him all the lies and the male the half-demon had forced him to be. Though, what almost brought him to his knees were the memories of his cruelty toward his wife and his senseless need to break the bond that could never be broken.

Lucius wanted to kill that version of himself for giving her that look of sadness. Now that he had these wretched memories, he wished for them to be gone.

"They wait for you, Kynigos. What will you tell them?"

"As much as I can without frightening them. We have to get her back. Lilith is still imprisoned, and Michael is still with us, so we are safe, but if he gets her on his side, she will destroy us." Lucius took a deep breath and was about to walk forward when Luzia vibrated in his hand.

Maestru, she sang. *You have awakened.*

It had been so long since he had heard her voice. "Luzia, you have protected me well. You have been here even when I did not know it. I cherish you, *Sabia*."

She vibrated with joy as her pommel glowed and her handle warmed. Her leather sheath appeared near him. He picked it up and put it on, then placed her in it before he walked down the aisle.

As soon as Lucius saw Ian, he walked over to him and hugged him tightly. The last memory he had of his brother was of him stabbing that bastard in the side before he was flung away out the window, not knowing if he was alive or dead.

"What the hell did they do to my brother?" Ian laughed nervously, hugging him back.

"It is good to see you, brother. It has been so long."

Ian pulled back and looked at Lucius, eyeing him warily. "You just saw me. What is going on?" he asked seriously.

"He has gotten his memory back," Jafa informed them.

"Memory? What memory? I don't understand." Ian took a nervous step out of Lucius's arms. He didn't blame him. He would have done the same.

"There is a lot I need to explain but precious little time. I need to get to Odessa or as you know her, Patience, back from Alazar. We need to get the portal to Askaria open. I know what you are missing, Selene."

"Wait. You can't just reveal all of that without explaining," Maxim interrupted. "We all need to understand what is going on here. You could be under a spell or an imposter for all we know. If you really are Lucius, tell me something only I would know, like how we first met."

"Max, how I have missed you. I don't believe you would want me to say this out loud." Lucius strode over to Max. He glanced at Alecia, who peeked out from her aisle, then whispered into his ear, "Fucking a whore against a nice oak tree in the forest of Bankura. You also hide your peanut butter behind a potato substance."

Max pulled away and really looked into Lucius's eyes, then broke out into a grin. "It really is you. I need a better hiding spot. I don't understand what is going on."

"I know. I promise to explain it but first, Selene must take me back to the house. We need to get the king and queen. They are not safe there with Estelle."

"Estelle? Why would they not be safe with her?" Max probed, growing suspicious even with proof that Lucius was truly himself.

"Grey, make sure no one leaves, especially her." Instead of wasting his breath explaining again, Lucius went over to Selene. "Take me back now."

Selene nodded, taking his hand and transporting him home.

As soon as he appeared, he felt the sharp point of a dagger in his back.

"You are late," Queen Circe hissed, pressing the dagger deeper into his back. "She tried to take him."

Lucius turned his head to the left to find King Kieran nursing a wound on his side.

"Bătrâne, eşti din ce în ce mai încet cu fiecare vârstă." *(Old man, you are getting slower with each passing age.)*

Kieran grinned. "Cel puțin încă nu îmi pierd memoria." *(At least I am not losing my memory yet.)*

Lucius laughed. "True."

"He has returned, Circe."

"Finally." She removed the dagger from his back.

"Selene, heal him," Lucius directed. "What happened to Estelle?"

"After she stabbed Kieran, Volt grabbed her and tried to drain her, but then she spoke the Spell of Iliad and jumped into the illicit demon's arms as soon as he appeared. Silas and Volt chased after them. She tried to slip this into Kieran's drink." Circe opened her hand and showed him a small clear marble filled with red mist.

"What is it?"

"It is mist from the Orb of Gilean. She was trying to manipulate his memory." Circe closed her hands and placed the marble into her pocket. "We have to keep Michael from him because if he gets that in him..."

"He won't," Lucius asserted, his words carrying a sense of conviction. "They are with Ustafa. We came to get you."

"Umm... Mr. Lucius, sir. He's not healing," Selene said with concern.

"We need to get him to Grey." Lucius walked over to Kieran to peer at the wound. "She must have stabbed you with a Victus Blade." He touched the laceration, causing the king to grunt in pain. "It looks like they used omicron poison on the blade in an attempt to paralyze you, but they didn't get enough in you. We will need to remove the poison, but it's too dangerous to stay here. Selene, take us back to Grey."

Selene nodded. Lucius and Circe placed their hands on Kieran, then Selene transported them back to GreyJoy's bookstore.

As soon as they appeared, Lucius helped Circe lay Kieran on the floor.

"What happened, and where is Estelle?" Maxim demanded, rushing over.

Lucius ignored him. He needed to make sure the king was healed. "Grey, he has been poisoned and can't fully heal until the substance is removed."

Circe took a step back as Kieran began to sink into the floor, disappearing from view.

"Grey will remove the poison and heal him, but it will take a few hours," Lucius assured.

Max grabbed him by the shoulders and turned him. Anger clouded his face. "You need to explain what the hell is going on right *now*. Or we are going have the fight of the century and I don't plan on losing."

Lucius placed his hands on his shoulders. "Calm, my friend. I will explain as much as I can, but it will not make much sense to you since your memory has been altered."

"Altered? Like Patience?" Michael said, finally breaking his silence.

"No, Odes—Patience's memory is not altered. She purposely locked her memories away so Alazar would not get to them."

"Purposely. You mean all this searching she has been doing has been for nothing? She has always had her memories." Michael's face contorted with a mixture of distress and bewilderment. His brows furrowed, and his eyes darted around, searching for answers in the midst of his emotional turmoil. It was evident that the situation had left him feeling deeply unsettled and uncertain about what was happening.

"It was not nothing. She thought she was looking for the key to unlock her memories, but she was really looking for me and a way to unlock my memories." Catching his mistake, he quickly added, "She was actually looking for all of us."

No one spoke, so Lucius continued trying to explain.

"Alazar, or the half-demon as you know him, who has taken over Askarian has had control over the throne for over a century," he revealed.

They all looked to Circe to confirm. "He is right. Alazar forcefully took the throne from King Kieran."

"He did not take it from him alone. My great-grandfather Dracul helped him. His eagerness to free Lilith and his hatred for Kieran caused him to work with that backstabbing son of a bitch. He killed my great-grandfather as soon as he was able to take the throne in Askarian."

"Lilith is his mother?" Michael gasped.

"He killed your great-grandfather? No, great-grandfather was killed by Thalia," Ian stated, confused. "How was he able to change everything?"

"No, he killed grandfather, not Thalia." Lucius sighed before he continued, "Alazar has been using the Orb of Gilean to change reality and alter our memories."

"The orb was lost in Enoch long ago. How was he able to find it?" Max asked, his voice tinged with concern and curiosity.

"It was never lost. He only made it seem that way. He has had the orb this whole time." Lucius should tell them he was the reason he found the orb in the first place. If he hadn't pushed her to find it, then it would still be sealed away. But they did not need to know that information right now. "What matters now is that we get into Askaria and get my wife back and destroy the orb. He can't get to Lilith without Michael."

You know he no longer needs Lilith now that he has her, Grey whispered through his mind.

I don't want to stress them. They will not be able to handle that kind of information, he countered.

"I know this is a lot to take in. What you need to focus on is getting into Askaria. Selene, you will need another Silverlands witch to help you create the portal."

Selene's eyes widen. "Shit, you are right. I should have thought of that. I will be back." They all watched as she faded away with grim determination on her face.

"I know you want us to focus on that, but you just dropped a huge bomb of information on us. How do we know if anything you say is real? How do we know this whole situation is not being manipulated? The orb is powerful and should have been destroyed as soon as it was made. And where the hell is Estelle?" Maxim was pissed, and he had every right to be.

Lucius wanted to tell him everything, but he could not risk it. Not until they got Mae back.

"He speaks the truth," Circe said. "The orb has no effect on my, Kieran's, or Alecia's memories. We all know the truth. He trapped us in Calidium with that bitch. Fortunately for us, she began to become senile, and our plan was to convince her to give us her army. Thankfully, Lucius and Odessa showed up and got us out of there. This situation is not being manipulated, only your memories. For some have been completely taken and others have been altered." Circe walked over to Max, touching his shoulder. "Estelle called upon a demon to take her back to Alazar now that he has Odessa. He no longer needs her to spy."

Max's expression shifted to one of surprise as he processed the information. He turned his gaze towards Lucius, seeking confirmation and validation. He nodded.

It would be a lot for him to process, but he would come to terms with it.

"Why haven't your memories been altered?" Michael asked, stepping out from behind Ian.

"Because you can't manipulate Novarians. That is why he had our people killed," Circe said. "It was the only way he would be able to make sure his plan worked. It was King Kieran who saved me from the fires."

"What about Silas?" Michael asked. "Isn't he Novarian?"

"Unfortunately, Silas is not full Novarian. He is only half," Circe disclosed, her lips a thin line. "He could not fight against the spell."

Out of the corner of his eye, Lucius saw Alecia moving through the bookshelves. Tuning out the rest of the conversation, he focused on her.

Does she still have her powers? Lucius asked Grey within his mind.

Yes, but I have not granted her permission to use them within my domain.

Lucius smiled as he moved fast through the shelves and captured her.

"Lucius," she exclaimed as he gripped her neck, dragging her to the front of the store.

"You all want to know the truth. The truth is that you cannot trust Alecia or Estelle. They have been working with Alazar all this time," he spat. "I am sorry you have to learn the truth like this, Max, for the second time, but you need to know now before she tries to contact you again. And trust me, she will."

"Lucius, all I have been trying to do is help," Alecia choked out as she tried to grab his arms. "I'm the reason you are able to remember in the first place."

"I'm afraid she is right, Kynigos," Jafa spoke up.

Lucius knew she was right. He remembered that night he killed the witch. Alecia was there. She made sure his memories were locked away into the gem before the spell took full effect.

He let go.

"He has an army, Lucius. He built it with the prisoners from Euphoria. Over the past century, he has been releasing them and making them swear fealty to him."

"Shit. How many prisoners remain?" Lucius growled out.

"Just Lilith," Circe answered. "Alecia has been working with Kieran and I to learn about each creature and their weakness. She is the reason we stayed in Calidium to try and gain Sucora's army."

Alecia's betrayal was always the hardest for him to take. He had trained and counseled her. He even helped her to find Drath like her to start her own clan. Over the years, she had become family, even becoming the godmother to his daughter. Their daughter. He couldn't think about Mae.

It wasn't until Estelle arrived and begged her to help her that she turned against her. Then again, he didn't blame her. He would have done the same for his brother, but the betrayal still hurt, especially when Alazar kidnapped his wife.

"Alecia." He stooped down in front of her. "I will give you one. Last. Chance. If you betray me, I. Will. Kill. You." He emphasized every word to make sure she felt the venom in his voice. "Do you understand?"

"Yes," she gasped, quivering as she stared in his eyes.

"Good." Lucius stood. "Now, I know this is hard and confusing, but we don't have time for handholding. We need to get Odessa back. Max, you will work with Alecia and Circe to learn as much as you can about this army he is building. I will be back. I need to go see an old friend."

Lucius reached behind him and touched Luzia's handle, then transported himself to a very familiar office where a pair of brown eyes lifted to meet his.

"It's been a long time, Alden," he snarled, barely containing his rage.

Alecia

"I didn't know he could do that?" Michael said under his breath.

"He can do a great many things. The witch has taught him a lot," Alecia said, exasperated as she picked herself up off the floor.

Max came to stand in front of her. Surprisingly, anger didn't mar his face. Just determination and maybe a hint of curiosity. "You and Estelle are traitors. Let me guess, Estelle hadn't been missing all those years?"

"No, she had been in the Silverlands trying to find a way to weaken its barriers," Alecia revealed.

Max's face turned pensive, his brows furrowing as he contemplated the situation. Suddenly, a spark of realization lit up his eyes, as if something dawned on him.

"Wait, so you're not married to Lord Christian?" Max asked curiously.

"Is that all you can think about at a time like this?" Ian demanded, looking at Max like he had lost his mind.

"No, I am not. I am afraid no female should be married to that male." Alecia rubbed her neck, still feeling his tight grip. She glanced over at Max, who was still looking at her strangely. She wondered if he knew. No, it had been too long. There was no need to go down that road.

A cup appeared on the counter. Jafa told her, "Ustafa says this will help soothe you."

"Thank you." She picked up the cup and took a sip. The herbs instantly eased the pain in her throat.

"Why can't I feel her?" Michael finally spoke. "I know she is alive. I just can't *feel* her."

Sighing, Alecia finished her drink. "Because Alazar has been perfecting her prison for a very long time. He has complete control over it. Only he determines what she can see and feel. He has her completely isolated and vulnerable. She has no connection to the outside world. Even more so now that she has severed their bond."

"What? She broke their bond? How?" Michael glared at Maxim, who clearly hadn't told them.

"The only bond that was broken was the blood bond," Circe said as she came from one of the aisles carrying a large, ancient leatherbound tome. She placed it on the counter just as Silas walked through the door.

"Brother." Circe went to him and pulled him into an embrace. "Are you alright?" she asked, worried.

"Yes, I am fine. The Iliad not so much, but she still managed to escape." Silas moved further into the bookstore and glanced around. "What happened?"

"Lucius's memory has returned," Circe admitted.

"Finally," he cried. They all turned to find Volt lounging against one of the bookshelves. "Where did he go?" he inquired, moving from the bookshelf to stand near Silas.

"He said he was going to see an old friend," Max answered, placing a book back on one of the near shelves.

Volt smirked, nodding toward Silas before he disappeared.

"I must go find him as well," Silas mentioned, heading toward the door.

"I will come with you," King Kieran said, fully healed from the aisle.

Volt reappeared behind Max. "We are going to need him, too."

"*What?*" Max yelled as Volt grabbed him, and then they both disappeared.

"I take it you know where to find him?" Silas asked Kieran.

"Yes, I am pretty sure I can guess, but you will drive us," Kieran told him before turning to his wife. "I must go, but I will be back. Teach them as much as you can." He kissed her and then he and Silas left.

The queen waited until they walked out the door before she spoke, "Alecia, we have to prepare them. He will make his move for Michael soon, and we need him to be ready."

"We need them *both* to be ready." Alecia opened the tome filled with all the knowledge she had gathered from the demon over the past century about the prisoners in his armies and the magic he used but most importantly, bits and pieces of his plan and weaknesses.

"Ready for what, exactly?" Ian asked, pulling Michael over to the ancient book.

"Readying you both to take the throne," Circe said proudly.

CHAPTER TWENTY-TWO

DAPHNE

Daphne watched as Odessa tried on her third wedding gown. This one was even uglier than the last, but she didn't want to burst the happy bubble she seemed to be in.

She was surprised when Alazar found her in the dining room and told her to help Odessa get ready for the big night. Daphne thought this would be her chance to convince the girl to help her. Unfortunately, Odessa had been nothing but a lovesick puppy.

Do you think he will like this? Should I change my hair? Do you think he will like this style? On and on... She would rather go help Jezabel train the Gorgons, pesky little creatures who were always trying to touch her inappropriately. It would be better than this torture of picking out gowns and linens.

"Daphne, are you listening?"

Her head snapped back to her. "Huh?"

"I realized I need shoes! Shoes are the best. Should I do stilettos for the ceremony and flats for the reception?"

Daphne stood, not being able to take it anymore. "I am going to see if Jezabel needs any help. I will be back."

"Wait no, don't leave! I'm sorry. I am just excited. Alazar and I have just been waiting forever to be married. I have never planned a wedding before, so I just want everything to be perfect," Odessa said, grabbing her arm and pulling her back to the chair she was sitting in. "Also, I hate being here alone. Alazar says I shouldn't wander the manor by myself since it's not completely secure and knowing me, I will get completely lost. Let us be friends, okay?"

Inwardly, Daphne cringed, but taking a deep breath, she said, "Okay."

The truth was she wanted to be friends with Odessa after hearing about her and watching her after all these years. She believed her and the old Dessa would have made great friends, but this new one was annoying as hell. Still, she was going to be her ticket out of here, so Daphne realized she would have to play along.

"I'm sorry. I am not into all of this. The only person I grew up around was Jezabel, and if you see how she dresses..."

"Oh, Daphne. I didn't think. Come, let's have you try on this one." She picked up a frilly green one, and Daphne almost threw up. "Wait, no. This one will probably be better." She threw down the green gown and picked up a beautiful, elegant off-shoulder satin gold dress. "This would be perfect for you. Please try it on. Please."

Reluctantly, Daphne got up, took the dress, and went into the bathroom.

"This was stupid," she muttered to herself as she took off her clothes and put on the dress. She was about to walk out when she caught a glimpse of herself in the mirror. The female who stared back at her scared her. It had been so long since she had gazed at herself.

She pulled out the elastic that imprisoned her black curls and let them fall. Jezabel had just cut it short for her, and she was really enjoying it. Easier to manage. She ran her hands through the unruly locks until she liked the way they looked. Then she took one final look into her silver-gray eyes. "I can do this. She will help me. I just need to get through to her. If this is the way, then I will just have to play along."

Feeling better after her little pep talk, she opened the door and walked back in the room. Odessa looked at her, stunned, until she blinked.

"You are beautiful, Daphne," Odessa said softly as she walked over to her and grabbed her hands. "This is the dress for you." She smiled.

Daphne surprised herself when she smiled back.

"Now we just have to find you some shoes." They both looked down at her old black combat boots. These were her favorite. "Have you ever worn heels?"

Daphne raised a brow.

"I am going to take that as a no. No worries, we will practice. Let's take these off." Odessa bent down and began to untie her laces.

"You don't have to do that," Daphne argued, trying to stop her.

Odessa swatted her hand out of the way. "Don't be ridiculous. Sit."

Daphne sat and tried to think of an excuse to get out of this. She did not want to wear heels. She had seen a few of the humans wearing them, and they looked painful. She still had no clue why females tortured themselves, especially since they were not practical for combat at all.

Odessa pulled off her left boot, and the black and gold cuff slid down her leg.

Fuck. She tried to pull her leg under the dress, but it was too late. Odessa saw it. She didn't say anything for a moment. Daphne held her breath.

"That's the Cuff of Anu'un," she stated. Odessa touched it and then glanced up at Daphne. When their eyes met, Daphne's heart sank.

"Ah, there you are," Estelle said, strolling into the room. Daphne snatched her leg out of Odessa's hand and hid it under the dress.

"Estelle? Oh my God! It's been so long," Odessa exclaimed, rising from the white carpet and running over to Estelle, embracing her. Daphne took the opportunity to slip into the bathroom to take off the dress.

Once she got back into her original clothes, she sat on the toilet with her head in her hands. There were no emotions in her eyes at seeing the cuff. No anger, no disappointment, just a blank stare. A small part of her had hoped that she would recognize the cuff and instantly help her formulate a plan to escape. It was dumb.

She would just have to find another way. The pity party was over. She would have to find a way to trick her into helping her. After what she saw, it shouldn't be that hard.

Feeling a little better, she stood and walked back into the room. Estelle and Odessa were chatting away like they were old friends. *The bitch.*

She would have to figure out how to warn Odessa against her because she would stab her in the back the first chance she got now that she was back. She wanted to be his queen, and she would do anything to get the title.

Odessa stood and came over to her. "Estelle told us she knows a great place to find shoes."

If she was going to do this, she would have to fully commit, and there was no way she was leaving Odessa alone with her. "Awesome. When can we go?"

"Yay!" Odessa hugged her excitedly.

Estelle looked pissed. Daphne smirked.

Lucius

"Lucius," Alden said tensely as he reached for the small crossbow under his desk, "you are alive."

"I wouldn't do that if I were you," Volt said as he tapped his shoulder with his blade. "Slowly bring it out and place it on the desk. You really thought you would be safe in the council office? Oh, Alden, how weak you have grown." Volt shook his head, keeping the blade close to his neck.

"I see you are still devious as ever." Lucius sat in the seat in front of the desk as Alden placed the crossbow on the desk. Volt handed it to Max as King Kieran, and Silas walked through Alden's office door. "Ah, it is nice to finally have the gang all back together."

"I take it your memory was returned," Alden said, his tone laced with curiosity and concern.

"Oh yes, it has, and you have a lot to answer for," Lucius seethed as he turned to look at Kieran, who sat in one of the black chairs in front of Alden's desk. "He has had his memory intact this entire time?"

"Yes. He even told me that he could break past the curse," Kieran informed him.

"So, he could have told me the truth this entire time but chose not to." Lucius glared at him, ashamed of the male who sat before him. The one he had once called a friend.

"I believe he chose to go after your female instead. Even gave her his amulet to summon him," Volt added, placing one hand on Alden's shoulder as he balled the other into a fist.

"I was waiting for the right opportunity," he muttered.

"Was that before or after you kissed my wife?" Lucius remembered their fight and the way he had held his wife. At least his former self had the sense enough to know she belonged to him, even though he was an idiot for trying to hurt her.

Let me taste him, Luzia hummed through his mind. *I crave blood.*

"Ah, even Luzia wants a piece of you," Lucius growled. "You just wait, my sweet. You will get your taste."

"Lucius," Alden croaked, "I thought if I got her to trust me, I could explain it all to her and we would unlock your memory together."

Lucius scoffed, not surprised by the falsehoods spilling from the bastard's mouth.

"Alden, enough with your lies," Lucius said firmly, his voice filled with resolve. We need to know where your brother took Odessa and what his plans are." As he spoke, Lucius made it clear that he was aware of the connection between Alden and the unfolding events, demanding the truth from him.

"You know I don't know the answer," he stammered. It was strange to see Alden so unhinged, which made his guilt all the more clear.

"So we are going to play this game. You know how much I love games. Silas, did you bring the cuffs?" he called over his shoulders to Silas, who stood near the window.

Silas pulled out a pair of Zirconium cuffs from his jacket pocket.

"Lucius, there is no need for this. We were friends. Can't we still be?" Alden pleaded.

"Alden, you had your chances to prove your loyalty. And repeatedly, I ignored the warnings and almost lost a friend." He glanced at Max, who smirked, not knowing what he was talking about. "But I will not overlook you this time. I remember everything. Silas."

Silas placed a cuff on each of Alden's wrists, then stepped back.

"Lucius, I love—" Alden tried to say, but Lucius cut him off, not caring for the words he would say.

"You were supposed to find her and protect *her. Not* fall in love with her!" Lucius yelled.

He was trying to keep himself calm, but that gets hard when the male who was supposed to be one of your closest friends tells you he is in love with your wife.

Lucius pinched the bridge of his nose in frustration. "Alden, what happened? How did we get here?"

"I never meant to fall in love with her. It was never in the plan, but I did. I saved her that night, Lucius, and I saved her fifty years ago. I have been trying to keep her from my brother with the help of Alecia."

"More like you were trying to take her for yourself," Max interjected.

"What happened, Alden? This is your only chance to talk," Lucius growled.

"That night when she arrived, she had Jezabel and Estelle hold her down and try to get her to inhale the red mist of the orb, but it didn't work because I replaced the mist. When he locked her away, I caused a distraction and helped her to escape. I thought she would return to you, but when you came to me looking for her, I couldn't tell you the truth because he was there in the room, listening behind the wall. That's why I directed you to Arabella."

Lucius hadn't known his wife had escaped, but it didn't make sense why she didn't come to him. Unless...

"Did she have our daughter with her?" he asked, even though he already knew the answer.

"No... Jezabel took your daughter to the Anthralls," Alden said sadly.

Lucius closed his eyes, pushing through the pain of hearing that his daughter might be dead. No one survived the Anthralls, and if they did, they became mindless slaves.

"And you found her fifty years ago?"

"Jezabel found her fifty years ago. I had been keeping tabs on her because I know they were still looking for her, and I had been tasked with—"

"Let me guess. Tasked with watching over me," Lucius guessed with a roll of his eyes.

Alden nodded. "I managed to get there in time before Jezabel cornered her, but she didn't trust me. She drank a potion and then jumped from the roof. I don't know how she reached the steps of the academy. That is all I know."

Lucius didn't know if he could believe him. There were only two people who could corroborate his story. One currently didn't have her memories, and the other he didn't trust.

He needed to find his wife and determine what happened to their daughter. The only way to do that was to get into Askaria, and he knew who would help him.

"We will see if you are telling the truth. Volt, drain him."

Alden's eyes widened in fear and disbelief at Lucius's command. He tried to protest, but the words caught in his throat.

"My pleasure." Volt's hand glowed white as he pulled magic from Alden.

CHAPTER TWENTY-THREE

ALECIA

Alecia's gaze remained fixed on Lucius as he stepped into the bookstore, with Max trailing closely behind him. It had been two damn days since his memory returned, and he hadn't spoken one word to her. It was frustrating, even though she knew he had no reason to trust her.

She missed their friendship. She enjoyed their camaraderie over the last century, even though she knew they were lies. They had never been truly friends. She had only gained his trust to keep a close eye on him as instructed. Unfortunately, most of their friendship was based on memories that weren't true, but somewhere along the way, she began to believe it was real.

"I don't know what you did, but sulking about it will not make him talk to you," Michael stated as he sat on the counter reading through her tome of information.

"I know, trust me. He will talk to me when he is ready, and the day that he does, I actually dread. I am just grateful I am not locked away in the dungeon as Alden is."

"Yeah, well, count your days because the way he has been storming around here, we all just might end up there," Michael muttered as he continued to read.

Circe and Ian came up from one of the aisles of books. "Better than yesterday, but you need to remember to thrust more and move your feet more," Circe instructed.

Ian nodded, listening to her until his eyes landed on Michael. Alecia saw the moment when he tuned her out and all thoughts were on Michael. Even after all these years, they were still very much in love. It warmed her heart and made her long for something she would never have.

Ian walked straight over to Michael and lifted his head to kiss him.

Max groaned, emerging from a different aisle with a book in his hand. "Oh, come on, get a room," he muttered.

"Don't mind if we do." Michael smiled, closing the tome and jumping off the counter. "We will be back," he said before Ian tugged him away.

Shaking his head, Max walked over to Circe. "Lucius asked if you knew where we could find this?" He pointed to a picture in the book.

"Alecia would know more about this than I," Circe said.

Following in Lucius's footsteps, Max hadn't spoken a word to Alecia either, and she wasn't sure why he would be upset with her, unless Lucius had told him, but she didn't think so. He may be pissed at her, but he wasn't one to tell secrets that were not his.

Alecia looked down at the book she wasn't really reading as he walked over to her. Without a word, he placed his book over hers.

She looked up at him with a frown. "That's rude. I was reading that."

"Where can we find this?" he said, tapping the book.

Alecia glanced at the picture. "You are looking for the Malice of Phoenix-al?"

"Yes. Do you know where it is?" he snapped.

"Possibly, if you would ask nicely." She slammed the book closed and then lifted her novel from underneath it, letting it fall to the floor.

With a huff, he picked up the book as she walked away.

"You know, you have to answer my question, especially if you know where it is," he demanded.

"I don't have to answer to you. The only person I will answer to is Lucius, so if he wants something from me, he can come and ask me himself."

"Alecia, you must have a death wish if you want that."

"Maybe. I. do," she sneered, climbing to sit on the stool behind the counter and lifting the book to her face.

It was silent for a few moments. Then she heard Max walk over to the counter.

"I'm sorry. This is all a lot for me. I don't know what memories are real and which were either implanted or manipulated. And Lucius has been reluctant to talk about anything."

"You could have—"

"He said you can't be trusted," he added.

Of course, she was the liar and the traitor. How was he ever supposed to know her side of the story if he wouldn't even listen to her? All she wanted to do was help. With Alden locked away, Lucius clearly didn't believe him, so even though Alden's motive was not in the right place, he still was trying to protect Odessa from that villainous creature. The only thing she could do was prove herself to him. Then maybe he would realize that she wasn't the enemy.

This could also be the opportunity for Max to finally see her. At least until his memories returned, then she knew she would have no chance to get near him.

"Well, we will just have to change his mind then. Ethel has the Malice of Phoenixal, but if he thinks he can summon and control Samuel with it, he's got another thing coming. Ethel has tried several times, but it hasn't worked." She slid off the stool and joined him on the other side of the counter.

"You let Lucius worry about summoning Samuel," Max said as she gazed into his devastating green eyes. "We just need to get it into his hands. Will you take me to her?"

How she wished... wished for a different life with him. Sighing, she replied, "Does that mean I'm allowed to leave?"

"Only with me. If you are thinking of running, I would advise against it. You don't want his wrath, especially now." He turned away from her and strode to the door.

"Trust me, the last thing I plan to do is run."

Lucius

Lucius sat in Max's office trying to make a list of all the supplies they still needed, but his mind kept wandering to thoughts of Mae, his wife.

This was all so strange to him. For him, it felt like it had only been months since this all started, but to learn that over a hundred and fifty years had passed still put his mind through the wringer.

He also couldn't believe how close he had been to his wife. She still looked the same, except for her eyes which were golden instead of their normal silver. He was curious to learn why. It was the only thing that had been different about her. Almost like a veil had been covering his eyes and with the return of memories, it had finally lifted.

Even now, the presence of their soul bond lingered, allowing him to sense her emotions. And right now, he felt a surge of happiness from her, which sent a shiver down his spine. Why would she be happy in a situation like this? The only logical explanation was that Alazar had tampered with her memories, leaving her oblivious to the dangers surrounding her. The uncertainty gnawed at him, amplified by the frustration of his failed attempts to send messages through their bond. He could only hope she could still sense him, even if he couldn't be sure anymore.

Lucius dropped his pen and pushed away from the desk. He would never get anything done like this. This waiting was killing him. All he wanted to do was go after her, but he needed to have a plan and gather his own army.

So far, they had the Clawfields, Berons, Knights, and Clares, four of the largest vampire clans, willing to give them five thousand soldiers each. He was able to cash in all the favors, but Lucius still didn't think it would be enough. He met with the full council yesterday and told them Alden was officially out of commission and that he would be taking his seat back. He opened the floor to challenge, but not one coward stepped forward.

Nothing had changed much in all these years.

The hardest part was that he couldn't get hold of more soldiers without openly declaring war against the demons. It was risky enough that he was able to obtain this amount. The demons weren't his enemies, only fucking Alazar. This army was only a precaution, but he needed more soldiers to prepare for whatever hell he might throw at them.

He could figure this out. He just needed a moment to clear his mind, but his wife drifted into his thoughts as he leaned back.

His hunger for her was growing. Their blood bond had sated his appetite for a while, but he wasn't sure how much longer he would last. If he didn't get her back soon, he would need to have Grey make him a Hiltina, a blood serum to stave off his hunger. Even that would only hold him so long.

Only her blood would sate his thirst, and his body craved to restore their connection to its fullest. No other blood would do.

His thoughts drifted to her, hoping to distract himself from the hunger pains. He still remembered when she infiltrated his estate a week after she got herself invited to the Clan Offering. He had still thought she was a vampire then, but now everything within that cabin made more sense to him.

He had come from an argument with his father, who disapproved of his efforts to convince the vampire clans to set up their home in Eviathian or in Evictus, but his father was determined to follow in his great-grandfather's footsteps of making the Silverlands their home.

The moon was high in the sky when he took his horse from the stables and raced across the field of his parent's estate in anger.

He had been approaching the border of his father's land when he heard a scream. Without any hesitation, he rushed off in the direction of the cry and found Odessa lying on the ground with blood running down her face, unconscious. He checked her for a wound, but it had already closed.

Gathering her into his arms, he brought her to the nearby gamekeeper's cottage. It had been empty, since the last one ran off with the cook's daughter. When she finally woke up, dawn was approaching. She looked quite confused about finding herself with him.

Now, he knew she had just been pretending, trying to get closer to him.

"Where am I? How did I get here?" She innocently sat up, rubbing her eyes. He stood to approach her when he suddenly found himself pinned against the wall with a dagger to his throat. "I know we danced at the Clan Offering last week, but that doesn't mean you can kidnap me, Mr. Cordovan."

Lucius couldn't help the smile that formed. He wanted to kiss her just as he wanted to that night.

"I heard a scream and found you unconscious on the ground. I brought you here so you wouldn't be caught in dawn's first rays."

She slowly stepped back and unpinned him, finding his answer satisfactory. The dagger was the last to leave his throat once she took another step back.

"I was riding in the meadow trying to break in my new fiery stallion, and I looked away for a moment to fix my stirrup. I didn't see the devil of a horse run me right into a damn branch. Damn the stable boy for not fixing my stirrup properly." She looked quite adorable when she was upset. She went to the one window in the room but realized it was sealed tight by the shutters. "Dawn is here. My sister must be worried sick."

"She will be fine. She will be happy to see you alive and well tonight." He approached her, but she stepped back.

"I take it I am at the Cordovan Estate," she said, sitting in the only available chair, forcing him to lean against the wall by the fireplace.

He didn't dare to go near the bed. He shoved away thoughts of undressing her and seeing what she had under that petticoat. Such was improper.

Admittedly, Lucius had been dreaming of this woman since she chose him at the Moonharvest. He had tried to get her into his clutches at the Clan Offering, but she escaped when he had to perform his duties.

"Don't get any funny ideas," she scolded. "I can see the gears in your head turning, and I don't plan on going anywhere near that bed. If you do think of anything funny, you will swiftly find this dagger in your side." She firmly gripped the dagger in her hand and pointed it at him.

Lucius couldn't help but think that the table would do just nicely, not to mention the floor. She may have been pointing the dagger at him, but her eyes betrayed her as she moved her gaze up his body, stopping at his lips.

Lucius laughed. She wanted him just as badly as he wanted her. He would have to play the waiting game. He had a feeling he would outlast her.

"You have nothing to fear from me. I will only touch you when you ask. And trust me, you will *ask."*

She raised a brow in challenge, but there was a ghost of a smile on her lips.

An hour later, he had her on that table.

"Fuck, Lucius," she gasped as he pinned her against the wall.

They had been talking about horses and switched topics to breeding, and then, before they both knew it, his lips were on hers.

He pulled back and lifted her up so she could wrap her legs around him as he brought her over to the table. He laid her down, then lifted her petticoats.

When he found her without undergarments on, it should have raised a red flag or a warning, but he didn't care then. All he wanted was her—to touch her, to taste her.

"I need to taste you. Let me taste you." He ran his tongue over her. "Fuck, you taste delicious."

A shiver went through her as his tongue darted out to flick her clit, sending pleasure to her core before his mouth ravaged her pussy, licking and sucking everything but her nub, driving her crazy. She gripped his hair in frustration.

Finally relenting, he sucked her pulsing clit into his mouth.

Odessa moaned and arched her back as he sucked, bringing her nub deeper into his mouth, then his tongue moved in swirls and loops, creating a design that drove her wild.

He loved it when both her hands were buried in his thick black hair.

She completely came undone when his fingers entered her, and she squeezed tight. She was close.

"Come for me," he demanded. "Let it all go and come for me." His voice filled with need. "I am going to bite you. Don't be afraid."

"Fuck! Lucius!"

Her sweet blood poured into his mouth as her orgasm ripped through her, and he knew then that she would be his.

When he woke that evening, he found his brother standing over him. "Mother is pissed you stayed out all day. She thought the sun's rays had turned you to ash. You know how dramatic she can be."

Ignoring his brother, Lucius searched around the room and found it empty. "Where is she?"

"Oh, you mean the female who ran out of here like a bat out of hell? She went that way," He pointed to the east. "She nearly knocked me over."

Lucius needed to see her again.

It seemed like such a long time ago. A part of him wished he could go back to that day to savor her all over again.

"Sorry to interrupt your daydream," Volt said, appearing in the chair in front of his desk.

Lucius sat up, not surprised to be interrupted by Volt. "What did the witch council say?"

"You can ask them yourself. They are standing in your foyer," he retorted before disappearing.

"Shit." He didn't expect them to come in person. When he sent Volt with a message for them, he expected a 'fuck you', not for them to show up at his doorstep.

Volt reappeared by his door.

"Also, Selene has returned," Volt said before disappearing again.

Lucius stood and grabbed Luzia, securing her to his back. His fight was no longer with witches, but if they came into his home to fight instead of help, he would show them this Ragana Zidakas.

CHAPTER TWENTY-FOUR

DAPHNE

Daphne sat at the large glass dining table, trying to stifle her laughter. She picked up her wine glass and took a sip, hoping it would cover her laugh, but Estelle turned to glare at her.

Alazar had been ignoring her for the past two days, and when she received a special invitation to dinner this evening, she had thought it would just be her and Alazar.

Daphne was going to burst her bubble right then and there to tell Estelle that she had received the same invitation this morning, but she thought it better for her to find out for herself.

When Estelle walked into the east dining room, one of Daphne's favorite rooms because of the natural rock waterfall protruding from the left wall, with the tightest blue dress Daphne had ever seen her wear, she wasn't sure how or if she was even breathing in the thing.

The saddest part was that Alazar didn't even glance at her. His eyes were on Odessa, who walked in behind her in a simple white summer dress.

Estelle sat down in a huff as Alazar walked over to Odessa and guided her to sit on his right side, which was usually her seat, and she didn't dare to sit on his left which was Jezabel's seat even though she never joined them for dinner. She was forced to sit next to Odessa, which made Daphne snicker.

Thankfully, this sickening dinner was almost over. Their last course of deviled Philababe eggs was already served. She hated them. Black eggs stuffed with red goo that made her want to throw up every time she came in contact with their retched smell. Alazar thought they were a delicacy, and he usually forced her to eat them. She was grateful for Odessa distracting him.

"It is so wonderful to finally have my Odessa home," Alazar said, kissing Odessa's hands as she looked at him like he was the air she needed to breathe. "Soon we will be wed, and our kingdoms will be one."

"Yes, we are almost done with the preparations. I just only wish my sisters could be here."

"No worries, my love. I am working on getting some of them there."

More like he was working on trying to enslave a few witches in the same way he had enslaved Daphne. Jezabel had been working on replicating her cuff, but so far, she has failed. As long as they never got their hands on any brass from the realm of Cortofa, then they would never be able to replicate it. Luckily, Daphne destroyed the only book with the information years ago.

"Oh, really? Oh, Alazar. I couldn't be happier. Then I must prepare for more arrivals just in case. Come, Daphne," she said, jumping up.

Daphne managed to swallow down the rest of her wine before Odessa yanked her from her chair and started to pull her from the room. She saw Estelle's face light up when she thought she would have a moment with him, then rage contorted her expression as Alazar disappeared without a word.

This time Daphne laughed out loud, and Estelle turned her furious gaze on her, promising retribution later.

That didn't matter. She didn't plan to be here much longer if everything went according to plan.

◆◇◆

Lucius

"Arietta, Evangeline, and Isiadora," Lucius greeted the three Silverlands witches who were also the heads of the witch council. They stood in the middle of his foyer, not at all happy to be there if the frowns on Arietta's and Evangeline's faces were any indication. Isiadora smiled at him, always kind.

It had been a long time since Lucius had last laid eyes on them. The last time he had seen them was in the Silverlands when they were helping to fortify its borders and bringing witches to safety within Eviathan. They used to be allies but now, all they remember is that he killed and slaughtered their sisters in cold blood.

Lucius thought he hated that damn demon before. He hated him even more now.

"Ragana, next time you send that Khedian as a messenger, he will be returned to you in pieces," Evangeline spat.

A deadly warrior in her own right with an imposing presence that commanded attention and respect. She stood at an impressive 6'5" commanding stature that struck fear into the hearts of both men and women alike. With a lithe and agile form, she moved with remarkable grace and precision, a force to be reckoned with on the battlefield. With chiseled features and piercing gold eyes that held both determination and a hint of wariness, she exuded a sense of fierce resolve. Her long, flowing locks cascaded down her back, framing a face that bore the marks of battles fought and victories won. Scars, reminders of past encounters, adorned her skin, each one a testament to her resilience and indomitable spirit. It didn't help that she carried the Axe of Hollia, which once belonged to the Demon God Hollis, on her back.

"Now, what do you know about Alazar?" Arietta demanded, getting straight to the point. Stern and assertive, as always.

She wore her silver hair in a long braid that cascaded down her back. Her sharp features and piercing silver gaze exuded an air of calculated intensity, as if she were constantly analyzing the world around her. With a slender frame and an upright posture, she carried herself with an imposing presence that demanded attention, even though she still walked with her false cane, the Rod of Karagon. With one stab, she could either kill you or send you to the caves of Karagon, where he would make a meal of her foe.

Interesting, so they knew about Alazar. What else did they know?

"We are aware he has taken over Askaria and is trying to claim the throne of Evictus. He already has control over the Hokima and plans to release Lilith," Isiadora answered. He had forgotten she was an Etherealic, a mind reader. He quickly lifted the barriers of his mind, pushing her out.

You can only keep your secrets for so long, Zidakas, she whispered through his mind.

"We have been looking for the king and queen," Arietta informed him.

"Then you have come to the right place," he said, then turned to see the king and queen walk down the stairs.

"I see. We have much to talk about," Arietta replied as the royal family joined them in the foyer.

"Agreed. I believe we would be more comfortable in the sitting room." He gestured toward the front parlor.

Once they all took their seats, Queen Circe wasted no time. "What exactly do you know about Alazar?"

The witches sat in silence, too stubborn to fess up any information that would allow their enemy an advantage over them or give away any of their precious secrets. If they only knew that Alazar already knew them all.

Lucius knew they wouldn't budge without an olive branch. "You came for a reason, and it wasn't to just answer my message. Believe it or not, we are not your enemy, and a war is coming. We will both need to help each other if we want to stop Alazar before he frees his mother, Lilith."

All three pairs of eyes widened in surprise.

"Lilith had a child? You lie. The Goddess would have told us," Arietta said with disdain, raising her chin.

"Not if she did not know," Circe retorted.

Evangeline raised a brow, waiting for her to explain.

Circe turned to look at King Kieran. "I did not know Lilith was pregnant until she was giving birth to our children and even then, I was in denial that they were mine until I saw the Daimones Rune on their wrists. Then and there, I tried to take them from her, but she hid them away in Enoch. After Lilith was locked away, I searched for them, but when Circe became pregnant, I gave up my search. Truly, I thought them to be dead since so few survive Enoch."

"And how did Alazar come to take over Askaria?" Isiadora asked gently.

"He worked his way through the ranks of my army. Until he gained enough strength and influence that it was easy for him to slip into power once... we left to search for our son." His expression darkened at the memory.

"Yes, we heard of this son of yours, Michael. He is friends with that powerful witch. What was her name?" Arietta asked the others.

"Patrice," Evangeline said.

"*Patience*," Isiadora supplied. "We asked her to join the Sentinels, and she refused us. I stopped you from cursing her. She had a particular aura."

An aura that seems to match yours, vampire.

Lucius tried to keep his emotions in check to learn they almost tried to curse his wife, but he couldn't help the anger that showed.

"Seems we have struck a nerve."

"Who is she to you?" Isiadora asked as she stared intently at him.

"She is the witch who has been trying to help me gain entry into Askaria. She is the one who brought Selene to me. And indeed, she is a powerful witch who is now in the clutches of the enemy."

"The truth, but not quite the whole truth," Isiadora challenged, looking at him curiously.

Lucius was tempted to let his barrier down, but he did not believe they were ready for that truth yet.

"Alazar has the witch, and you are only informing us of this now?" Arietta stood in anger, glaring at Lucius.

He could feel the hum of Luzia on his back, begging him to strike her down.

"She didn't seem to be a concern of yours when you left her without a coven even though you knew how powerful she was. You wanted to enslave her to be one of your fucking guards and when she refused, you had her labeled an Abberant." Lucius hadn't realized he had stood until he was toe-to-toe with Arietta, who gripped her Rod.

"If you are going to stab me with *that*,"—he gestured toward her Rod—"you'd better kill me because I will survive Karagon, and when I am done killing him, I will be coming for *you*," he threatened.

"He's *been* killing us. We are the only Silverlands witches left. With the Goddess gone, we are the only chance of them getting into Askaria and making sure Lilith stays locked away," Selene revealed, walking into the room and coming to stand next to Evangeline. "The most important thing is we need to get Patty. Her powers, I have felt them. If he manages to turn her against us, it will take more than the four of us to take her down. We need to work together because I don't think the Goddess will save us now."

"We believe he may have the Goddess locked away," Evangeline chimed in. "He may use her to get us to open Lilith's prison."

"We will prepare for that possibility. For now, if you agree to work together, we need to focus our efforts on raising an army. We already have about twenty thousand vampiric soldiers, but it won't be enough. We are trying to recruit more, but they don't see this as their fight."

"We will speak with the Covens," Isiadora announced as she stood. "Vampires and witches have much to lose if Lilith is set free."

She was right. If Lilith was released, both sides would suffer causalities that they would not be able to come back from. Lilith would use the vampires to create an army to invade the Silverlands, the place that held the source of all magic. A place she thought was her damn birthright. She had done it before, and they barely made it out alive.

With Lilith safely locked away, he and Mae had left the land in the safekeeping of the Hallows and the witches. Now, they would have to return. They needed his wife back now more than ever.

"Sisters, we must go home. We must protect what is left of the Silverlands. She must not get to the crown or the source," Arietta declared before she finally took a step back from Lucius and looked to Evangeline, who stood and nodded.

"Agreed."

"Now, where is the other son? And do not lie to me. I can hear him," Isiadora said with a mixture of authority and curiosity.

There was no need to lie. "We have him. He is here. Locked away."

"Show him to me," she commanded Lucius. "Sisters, please stay here. I will only be a moment."

He glanced at Kieran and Circe, who nodded. "Follow me."

Lucius led her down the stairs to the dungeon as she quietly followed behind him until they reached the last cell on the far end.

"You hold many secrets that you do not want me to see. What is it you are hiding?"

"Some things you are not ready to believe." He whispered the spell and drew the unlocking symbol. The door clicked open.

"Yes, that may be true for my sisters, but not I. If you will not tell me the truth, show me."

The door swung open, revealing Alden with his head hanging chained to the wall, defeated. He slowly lifted his head.

"Isiadora?"

She ran to him, wrapping her arms around him. "Alden, my love, what have you done?"

CHAPTER TWENTY-FIVE

Daphne

Daphne realized what she needed to do. She needed to tell Odessa the truth.

Twice now, she had caught Odessa staring at her with concern, and she had also caught her staring at her left leg where the Cuff of Anu'un lived. She may not remember who she really was, but somewhere in there was a powerful witch who cared for others.

That was something Alazar would never be able to take away from her, manipulated memories or not.

"Now, we need to add at least twenty more chairs. I'm not sure how many he will be able to get, but I just want to be sure we have enough space." Odessa looked at the floor plan for the garden atrium where the ceremony would take place.

She would get married in front of the portal she was kidnapped through, and she had no clue. Daphne planned to change that, but how could the subject be breached?

"Do you think if we moved these flower arrangements to the back, maybe near the entrance, we could squeeze more chairs on the left side?" Odessa asked, but Daphne did not hear, too lost in her thoughts on how to tell her. "Daphne? Daphne, what do you think?"

When Daphne still didn't respond, Odessa turned and walked over to her, tapping her shoulder. "Is everything okay?" Odessa asked with concern.

Blinking a few times, Daphne gazed up at Odessa.

"Is everything alright?" Odessa asked again.

This was it. This was her chance. She could confess it all and pray the Goddess would answer her prayers.

"N—"

"Ah, here you two are. I have been looking all over for you," Estelle said as she burst into Odessa's sitting room, where she had turned in her wedding workstation.

Daphne swore she saw a glimpse of annoyance on Odessa's face before she plastered on a smile.

"Oh, Estelle, thank goodness you are here. I need help with this seating arrangement."

"Of course. Of course, show me."

Damn, she had hoped Estelle would be helping Jezabel for the evening. That is what she usually did when Alazar rejected her. She would go help Jezabel torture one of the innocent creatures of Evictus or experiment on one of the prisoners of Euphoria.

If she weren't doing that, she would always try to make Daphne clean up any mess she made. Thankfully, with Alazar and Odessa around, she hadn't bothered her much.

Sighing, Daphne stood, debating whether to leave, but as much as she wanted to go hide in her room or curl up in her favorite spot in the library, if Alazar or Jezabel found her lazing about, they would put her to work in Euphoria, forcing her to use her magic to train—a.k.a. torture—its prisoners. She was better off staying here and helping Odessa. No one seemed to bother Daphne when she was with her.

Daphne went over to the swatches Odessa had laid out, trying to figure out what tablecloth and napkin combination she wanted. She picked up a few colors and began to match at random.

"Estelle, do you mind going to check in with the dressmaker to see the progress on my dress? I know they want to do one last fitting in the morning, but they never told me the time. Oh, and I also need the shoes and my corset picked up."

Daphne waited to hear Estelle refuse, but to her surprise, she agreed.

"Of course, anything."

"Oh, Estelle, you are perfect." Odessa clasped her hands together gleefully.

Daphne could not help the laugh that burst from her lips. She tried to cover it with a cough, but when she turned to glance at them, Estelle glared.

Shit.

"I'll be back."

"Take your time," Odessa said as she went back to writing on the floor plan. Daphne returned to matching the swatches.

She heard the door click, but she didn't hear Odessa walk over to her.

"I like the purple and blue. It will match the hydrangeas in the garden," Odessa spoke near her ear, startling her. "Oh, I'm sorry."

"No, it's okay, and I agree. It will look beautiful." Daphne moved the other swatches out of the way and laid the light purple and dark blue next to one another.

"Now that that has been decided, it is time for you to tell me what is going on."

Daphne raised her brow in surprise. She didn't expect her to simply ask her. Now, she felt like she shouldn't say anything.

"Daphne, I know something is going on. Why do you have the Cuff of Anu'un on your leg?" Odessa asked, her eyes moving to look at her left leg even though the cuff was hidden inside her boot.

Daphne turned suddenly nervous. *What if she doesn't believe me?* No, this was her chance. She had to tell her now. She didn't know when she would get another opportunity like this. It was best if she just spit it out. Taking a deep breath, she closed her eyes and said the words, "I am being held prisoner here... and so are you."

She was afraid to open her eyes, but the silence was killing her. Cautiously, she opened one eye at a time and found a scowl on Odessa's face. *Oh no, she doesn't believe me.*

"My Alazar? Holding *me* prisoner?" Odessa laughed. "You jest. Let us try on your gown again."

Daphne's heart sank as she looked away from Odessa, and she did not see her move to the wall to place her hand against it. Light shot from her fingers as her magic quickly sealed the cracks to keep Alazar's spies out, then she moved back to Daphne.

"Prisoner? Is it just us he is holding prisoner?"

Daphne's head shot up as her eyes widened in surprise.

"I'm not dumb, but I can play the ditz very well." Odessa took her hands and led her to the couch to sit down.

"You know?"

"I suspected, but you confirmed it when I saw the cuff. Ever since I woke, my magic has been limited, and my mind has been foggy. I thought I was just going crazy, but my memories are erratic and murky. I remember bits and pieces of certain things, like when Alazar asked me to marry him, but I don't remember where exactly he asked me. And when I asked him to tell me what color I was wearing that night, he vaguely said he believed it was blue."

In all his planning, he forgot to make sure he knew the details of her memories.

"It was silver to match my eyes. How long have we been prisoners here?"

Without any hesitation, Daphne replied, "You have only been here for about a week, and I have been here since I was a child. Alazar told me he saved me from when I was left abandoned in the realm of Enoch, but I'm not sure if that is true, even though all I remember is him being there. Though, I do remember being alone in the dark."

"Oh, Daphne." Odessa wrapped her arms around her, pulling her into a tight hug. "You are not alone anymore."

She had never been hugged before, so the feeling was foreign. The only thing that was familiar to her was Odessa's vanilla scent, which held a hint of honeysuckle. She wanted to bury her head behind her neck and get lost in her warmth, but she didn't know how much time they had left.

Daphne pulled back out of her arms. "We need to get out of here. You can't marry him. He wants your power or at least to control it like he can with mine."

"I never planned to marry him, but I don't know how to get out of here. My magic is limited, and I believe yours is too?"

"Yes, it is, but there is a portal to Eviathan in his office. We just have to find a way in... or steal the key."

"And how do you expect to do that?"

Daphne stared at Odessa, not wanting to say it out loud, hoping she would conclude herself.

"You want me to get the key by..." Odessa stared back at her. "Seducing him."

Alecia

"The malice is here?" Max asked when Alecia pulled up to a red brick building with no windows and a simple black door. They were in the darker part of Orendale, where there were plenty of dark alleys for all kinds of sinister creatures to sneak through, even during daylight hours.

Luckily, they still had a few hours until sundown. The sun still burned even in the shadows.

"Yes, where else would you think we would find Ethel?" She put the car in park and climbed out. The street was quiet, but she expected nothing less. She knew the Florans, gargoyles, were watching their every move, and if they deemed them to be trouble, they would never make it near that door.

"Ethel? Like Ethel the *Sediesse*?" Max gawked at her in disbelief as they approached the door. "Doesn't she eat males?"

"Yup, the very same one, and she only eats the ones that piss her off, so if I were you, I wouldn't piss her off," she retorted, knocking thrice and then tapping once. The door instantly slid to the side, and Alecia grabbed Max's hand, pulling him through before the door slammed closed behind them.

"Pleasure or pain?" an eerie voice asked as they stood in a hallway vacant of light.

Alecia truly hated this part of the experience. She wasn't claustrophobic, but it was almost like the walls were closing in on her and the air was being sucked from the room.

Suddenly, Max placed his hand on her back, and she could find her voice. "Pleasure. We want Sediesse."

"You know the price you must pay." A gold bowl appeared before them with a knife within. Alecia easily picked it up and was about to cut her hand when Max stopped her.

"The price is blood?" he stammered.

She quirked a brow. "Why are you surprised? Isn't that always the currency for secrecy? Besides, if I would have said pain, you would have lost a limb." She cut her hand and let a few drops of blood drip into the bowl before she placed the knife back in. The bowl disappeared, and a door to their left opened to reveal stairs. "Come on, she doesn't like to be kept waiting."

As they moved toward the stairs, Alecia couldn't help mourning the loss of his hand as he slipped it from her back.

"Whatever you do, don't touch anything, and don't drink or eat anything offered," she ordered as they came upon a pair of red double doors. "I mean it, Max. I am not explaining to Lucius how you got caught in a nymph trap and won't be back for a few days."

"Days?" he gasped.

"Max," Alecia scolded.

"I got it. I got it," he said, raising his hands innocently. "I won't touch anything. Promise." He smiled.

Alecia had a feeling he was going to get them into trouble by the end of this night. The double doors opened, and the sweet sound of Hadley, the Singi poured through, luring them in with her seductive voice.

Alecia walked through first, leading the way through the thick, clear plastic tables filled with lustful males. Half of them had their dicks in their hands as they stared at Hadley on stage, in her bright pink v-cut dress, caught in her trance. Alecia was about to turn to tell Max not to stare into Hadley's large amber eyes, but she thought better of it, thinking he would do the opposite of what she said.

She continued walking through the tables, keeping her own eyes on the stain-filled carpet that used to be a light green long ago but was now a darker forest green. She ignored the moans of the creatures that could be heard over Hadley's singing.

A young nymph with neon-blue hair and eyes to match approached with a giddy smile and mini skirt. "Welcome to Havoc, where all your fantasies can be explored," she said excitedly, blocking her way with a cocktail in her hand. "Would you like a drink?"

"No. Let Ethel know Alecia is here to see her."

"I am sure we can fulfill your every desire. We have plenty to offer here." The nymph tried to offer up the drink again, but Alecia pushed past her and continued on.

It wasn't until she reached the door to Ethel's dungeon that she realized Max wasn't behind her. She growled in frustration as she scanned the place. He was nowhere in sight.

Retracing her steps, she found him surrounded by a group of karnal-nymphs. They were ravenous bitches who sucked the lust right out of males and if they really liked him, they could enslave the male to only want their pussy.

Max let out an uneasy laugh. "Ladies, you're going to get me in trouble. I must find Alecia. She will be very upset that she lost me."

"No, my prince, stay with us. You don't need her. You need all of us to keep you sated and warm," one of the karnalnymph's said, climbing out to his lap and placing his hands on her ass.

Alecia had a strong urge to grab her hair and begin to beat the shit out of her. Controlling herself, she called out to him.

"Max, I thought I told you not to touch anything. That included the realm trash."

Four pairs of eyes all turned to glare at her. Alecia wished they would try something. She was looking for a fight, and beating up four nymphs seemed like the perfect place to start.

"Sorry, ladies. I must go," he said, removing the nymph from his lap and standing. "Maybe I will come back and play another time."

"Yes, my prince. Come back to us."

Alecia scoffed as she grabbed Max's arm and led him to Ethel's door. The small rectangular black window slid open.

"Is Ethel expecting you?" a pair of vibrant green eyes asked.

"No, but tell her Alecia is here to see her."

The window closed. They waited. Alecia knew she could let go of Maxim, but she didn't realize how much she missed touching him and just being near him. She didn't know when she would get a chance like this again, so she would savor it as long as she could. The window slid open, and the pair of eyes peered out.

"She will be available momentarily. She is finishing up with a client. You can sit and enjoy yourselves." The window quickly slid closed before she could say anything in response.

Max didn't seem to care about the wait since his attention was fully on the bodacious nymph sliding down the pole in the far corner.

Jealousy perked its bloody ears up for the second time that night. She didn't understand where this was coming from. She had gotten over the possibility of her and Max so long ago. She still remembered the day she had returned and Alazar asked her to give Estelle her wedding ring.

"Plans have changed. Estelle will be better at controlling Maxim and keeping an eye on Lucius."

She could see the vindictive smile on Estelle's face as she stood behind Alazar.

"But you said it would be better if I stayed with him in case the memory spell didn't work. I would still be able to stay because I would be familiar," she defended.

"No, I think it would be better for your sister to be there. I have other plans that would be more suitable for you," Alazar said nonchalantly as he closed the book he was reading.

"Sister, it is for the best. Besides, I know how much you hated being around Max and felt your skills could be put to better use." Estelle smiled sweetly.

"Give her the ring, now."

Alecia had wanted to protest, but if she turned on them, there was no stopping them from capturing her and giving her to Jezabel to experiment on. How Jezabel would love to get her hands on a half-vampire, half-witch. Reluctantly, she pulled off her ring and handed it to Estelle.

It took every ounce of her not to cut off her sister's finger once she slipped it on. Now, she had it hanging around her damn neck.

"You seem tense," Max asked in the present, looking at her.

Without thinking, she grabbed a shot of brown liquid off one of the passing trays and downed it, praying it was just alcohol.

"Whoa. I thought you said not to drink or eat anything," he exclaimed, raising a brow in surprise.

She let the liquid burn down her throat before she answered. She had been able to stay sober all these years because her sister had been gone, for all intents and purposes, and she had been able to at least see and talk with Max without having her sister pawing all over him. Now just the thought of having to do that again made her want another drink.

"I said don't drink or eat anything offered." Another waitress walked by, and she grabbed an additional shot, this one the color of amber. She knocked it back and regretted it as soon as it hit her throat. "Fuck. Don't drink anything, Max."

"Alecia, this is unlike you," Max admitted. "I don't know what is happening, and Lucius won't tell me much, but you know that I am here for you. You can talk to me."

The sad part was she knew he was being sincere, but if Lucius wasn't talking then neither was she. She wouldn't do anything to risk his wrath. He was her only saving grace right now.

"Thanks, Max. I'm fine. Lucius will tell you what you need to know when you are ready." She walked back over to the door and banged.

"Open up or I start killing people." After a few seconds, the door opened. "Max, let's go." She marched through and made sure that Maxim was behind her this time before she went down the few stone steps before her.

They strode down a small stone hallway until they reached a large open room. Hundreds of sexual toys and devices of all shapes and sizes were displayed on the velvet walls. Different sexual contraptions and torture devices were scattered around the room. A wooden X with straps hovered above the king-sized bed with silky red and brown sheets.

Ethel, a voluptuous dark nymph known for the beauty of her midnight skin and ravishing blonde hair, walked from a door to their left. "You sit in there and think of all the naughty ways I am going to make you come if you are a good boy. Now, be quiet while I entertain my intrusive guests," she ordered her hidden client before closing the door.

Alecia immediately grabbed her silk black robe from the bed and walked over to Ethel, holding it out to her so she would cover her nudeness.

The nymph harrumphed. "So, I see this isn't a pleasure visit after all. How disappointing."

Usually, Alecia didn't care who knew that she liked this kind of sex, but she didn't know how Max would take it. Before they were just beginning to explore this, and now she was unsure. She glanced back at him, but his back was turned.

"Such a gentleman. I am as dressed as I will get, sir," Ethel said when the robe was fully secured around her. "Alecia, darling, why have you interrupted me if you aren't here to play with me?"

"We need the Malice of Phoenixal."

Ethel laughed before she walked to a side table and poured herself a drink. "Would either one of you care for one?" she offered.

Alecia was tempted, but she shook her head, afraid to speak.

"How about you, gentlemen?"

Alecia looked at Max, ready to speak for him, when he responded.

"Thanks, but no thanks."

"You both are no fun. You come here asking for my most precious gift and you refuse to play with me and refuse to drink with me. Tsk, tsk." She took a sip of the blue liquid she poured herself. "Next thing you know you will tell me you came baring no gift and nothing in exchange."

Alecia and Max both looked at each other. She hoped he had brought something to give in exchange but reading the look in his eyes, he had thought the same thing as her.

Damn. "We have nothing but ourselves." *Shit.* She didn't mean to say it like that.

Fuck, she was in a playful mood. She didn't even want the malice since she couldn't get it to work, but she wouldn't just give it up. The nymph wanted something in return and with the way she was gazing at the both of them, Alecia realized this was about to turn into a wild night. She couldn't tell if she was afraid or filled with anticipation.

"Excellent. Now show me how much this malice is worth to you. Strip."

CHAPTER TWENTY-SIX

LUCIUS

Lucius was confused. This had to be a trick. He had never known Alden to have a lover… well, except one, but it was not Isiadora.

"What game do you play, witch?" he demanded, drawing Luzia from his back.

"Stay your blade, Lucius. This is no trick. I can explain all if you just unchain him," she said, cupping Alden's face and kissing his forehead.

"Not happening. He may be weak, but his power still flows. He stays there."

"Then just listen. Alazar has perfected his use of the Orb of Gilean for a long time. He has been experimenting with its mists to alter memory. Alden was his first victim."

Lucius lowered Luzia but did not sheathe her. He was willing to listen because he knew Alden was not an evil man, and Isiadora being so close to him proved it. "I'm listening."

"I met Alden the same night he met you and Odessa. Yes, I remember everything and apparently, so do you."

Lucius finally sheathed Luzia and continued listening.

"I knew I would meet someone that would change my life that night. I just didn't think it would be someone I would fall completely in love with. He tried to fight it but eventually, I wore him down," she said, continuing to cup Alden's face as he drifted in and out of consciousness.

"It took him a while to open up about everything, especially since he didn't want me to get hurt because he knew that if Alazar ever found out about me, I would be in danger, so we hid our relationship from everyone, even Odessa."

Isiadora sat back and ripped the end of her dress. She wiped the blood on Alden's brow and lip.

"When Alazar finally got his hands on the Orb of Gilean and Alden learned of his plan, he came to me and told me that he was going to go to you and Odessa with the truth. But he was going to stop his brother first. I begged him to go to you first, but he refused. He thought it would be too late and he had the best chance to stop him. That was the last night I saw him as my Alden." She turned and looked at Lucius. "It was the very next night when everything changed."

"How are you able to remember?" Lucius asked, curious.

"I was in the waters of the Silvers doing my monthly cleanse. I believe I was protected by the waters since my mind was not on this plane."

Lucius nodded, knowing she was speaking the truth. Odessa had told him about how Isiadora had to cleanse her mind once a month to clear out all the negative energy she absorbed and to clear her mind of all the voices she heard daily. He wanted to ask her why she didn't come to him, but then he remembered he would have tried to kill her, or her people may have even seen her as a traitor if they found out she had come to him.

"I can't let him go. Not until he fully remembers who he is. I can't risk him trying to take Odessa away or warning his brother."

Isiadora kissed Alden's forehead one more time before she stood. "His memory may not be fully returned, but I know he remembers me. I have been working on a spell to return his memory, but I need Odessa to make it work."

"Well, that is what we are trying to do. Get my wife back."

Looking at Alden one more time, Isiadora stepped from the cell, then Lucius closed the door. "I can help Selene open the door to Askaria. Just promise me you will not hurt him anymore."

This changed everything. Silas had been only trying to get information from Alden, but now he knew why he was not forthcoming. He didn't know anything. *Shit.* The beatings would stop. Clearly, they would not be getting anything from him.

"He will not be harmed, but he will have to be drained of magic since he seems to have an endless fucking supply."

"Just as Odessa does," Isiadora said pointedly.

He was aware that Alden and Alazar were Lilith's children, so it was possible that they had access to the source of power within the Silverlands. It could also be that Alazar may not have access and wanted to keep a hold on his brother so he could use him.

Either way, Volt would continue to drain him every few hours until they got his wife back and she could help to sort this all out.

They walked back up the stairs to find her sisters waiting in the foyer.

"What have you seen, sister?" Arietta asked.

"I will stay here with Zidakas. They will need my help in creating the portal to the demon world. They have the brother captured but only the witch, Patience, can help him."

"Then will go and talk with the covens and convince as many as we can. We will send a message with our numbers. You stay safe, Dora," Evangeline said before she walked out the door. Arietta nodded, but Lucius knew she spoke in her thoughts based on her intense stare before she too walked out the door.

"Isiadora," the king said, nodding his head toward her.

"It has been a long time, Kieran. It is good to see you too, Circe," Isiadora greeted, bowing slightly.

"You as well, Isiadora. Selene is waiting for us in the library. She knows how to open the portal."

Circe led the way to the library as they followed. Lucius would be seeing his wife soon. He couldn't wait to hold her in his arms. It had been too damn long.

Alecia

"Seduce him."

The look of disgust on Odessa's face told Daphne that they might have to rethink the plan. So far, Odessa had been a great actress, but she didn't know if she could get through it.

"I can't sleep with him. Bad enough he has kissed me twice already. Each time, I've had to control my gag reflex. I can't do that. I know you're desperate to get out of here, but that's too far."

Daphne's eyes widened in surprise. That wasn't what she meant.

"You don't have to sleep with him. I didn't mean that. Can't you turn on your feminine wiles and make him go crazy?"

Laughter burst from Odessa. "You watch *way* too many movies. Where does he keep the key on him?"

"It is always on a chain in his left breast pocket. It is a formidable chain of helix, so it cannot be broken. The only way to get it would be to get him to take the jacket off, which he never does." Daphne had tried several tactics to get him to take off that damn jacket. She even brought him to Dyinal, the realm of Scorching Suns, lying to say she had a lead on Odessa, but they were in the realm for hours and not once did he remove the damn coat. She had almost died of heat when he saved her, bringing her back here.

"And you think if I seduce him, he will remove the jacket? Have you ever tried to drug him and simply take the jacket?" she asked like it was so simple.

"I have tried to drug him and poison him ten times over the past years, but every time he knows, I am punished. I stopped years ago, not being able to face his wrath."

Sympathy filled Odessa's eyes, and Daphne hated seeing it there. She didn't want her sympathy; she wanted out of Alazar's clutches. She wanted to experience life and maybe find whatever family she may have left.

"Where have you gotten the drug or poison from?"

Daphne stood, beginning to pace as they talked. "When he lets me out, I buy some from different apothecaries."

"And how do you get back into this realm with the stuff?" Odessa probed.

"I use the portal in Jezabel's... lab. You think the portal is rigged?"

"Yes," Odessa said as though the answer was obvious. "It would only make sense to make sure you aren't coming back with any weapons or anything to harm him. Whatever we use has to come from this realm."

"We can't. All the drugs are in Jezabel's lab, and she would know if we took any of them."

"Okay, so we make our own. The garden should have what we need."

"I don't know. I never thought of that. Tomorrow, we will go for a stroll in the garden." Odessa held her hand up then placed her finger to her lips. "Shhh... someone is coming. Here, go into the bathroom and pretend you tried this on." Odessa quickly snatched Daphne's dress off the couch and handed it to her. Then she went to the wall.

As Daphne entered the bathroom, she left the door slightly ajar and saw Odessa absorbing light into her hand. It was a deliberate act, a way to seal off Alazar. With his eyes and ears everywhere, Odessa must have found a way to keep him out, to protect herself from his prying influence.

She closed the bathroom door and returned to it, listening to see who came in.

"There you are, Odessa. I found these beautiful pieces that I thought would go great with your centerpieces. Do you want to come and take a look at them?"

"Oh, how wonderful. Of course. Daphne is just changing—"

"This will only take a second. We don't want the carinbals to steal them, now do we..." Estelle trailed off as they left the room.

Daphne gave it a few more seconds before she stepped out of the bathroom. She made a show of looking around and calling out Odessa's name before she put the dress down. As much as she wanted to talk with Odessa more, she didn't feel like incurring Estelle's wrath tonight. She felt better knowing Odessa was now on her side, and they had started a plan. They could formulate the rest of the plan tomorrow because now her bed was calling her.

She left Odessa's room and headed down the hall to her room, but halfway to her room, Estelle's words hit her. Cairnbals. Shit. Fuck.

Daphne turned and ran as fast as her combat boots would allow her.

The carinbals were fiendish little devils who were adorable and sweet until someone touched their silver eggs. Then they became ravenous little demons who ate flesh. Fuck, if Estelle took her to their cage, she would be eaten alive if she touched one of those eggs.

Taking the stairs two at a time, Daphne finally reached the dungeons. She always hated coming down here. It was mostly because she got lost down here for days when she was younger. The beginning of the dungeons resembled an ordinary stone hallway adorned with various devices of torture that sent shivers down Daphne's spine every time she passed them. Yet, as the corridor curved, it transformed into a labyrinthine network of caves capable of disorienting even those who had traversed the halls for years.

Though unfortunate, she had become intimately familiar with its twists and turns. She took two rights and the third left. Voices echoed through the halls.

"See? Aren't they adorable? The eggs are over there. Don't you think they would make a great addition to your centerpieces?"

"I don't know if I should touch those."

"Please go ahead. They love it when we take them. They practically pile them up like that for us to take."

Daphne wanted to yell, but she couldn't risk waking up any of the other demons down here, especially those who weren't in their cells. Moving more swiftly, she finally reached the entrance to their cave just in time to see Odessa walking over to the eggs. All the cairnbals were watching her.

"Odessa, don't," Daphne warned just before she was about to lean down and touch the egg. She snatched her empty hand back up.

"Daphne, go away. This is none of your business. Odessa, you are fine. You can grab an egg."

"Don't do it. Odessa, as soon as you touch one of those eggs, they will tear you apart. Look at their faces."

Odessa looked at the faces of the cairnbals and saw their angry eyes. She slowly took a step away from the eggs.

Estelle glared at Daphne. "You will burn for this," she hissed. "I guess I will have to do this the hard way." She reached into her pocket and threw something silver toward Odessa, but a hand caught it before it could reach her.

Jezabel. This is one time that she was grateful for her. With her long raven hair and pale skin, she stood near Odessa in her black leather armor set. Her crystal blue eyes briefly glanced at Odessa before moving away.

The cairnbals snarled and slowly moved toward her. Daphne pulled her whip from her knee-high leather boots and cracked it through the air. The creatures scattered. They wouldn't dare touch her.

"What the hell do you think you are doing, Estelle?" Jezabel's raspy voice said, filling the cave.

Estelle stood rooted to the spot. Daphne swore she saw a bead of sweat drip down her ashen face. Taking a breath, she tried to answer. "I—"

"It looked to me like you were trying to kill our king's queen," Jezabel seethed, peering at Estelle.

"Never. I was simply giving her a tour of the dungeons."

Jezabel stared at Odessa.

"Yes. It was my fault. I had to stop to see them and thought the silver eggs would make great additions to the centerpieces for the wedding. I didn't think they would mind."

"There is no need to lie for her. I know she brought you down here."

Jezabel always knew who entered her domain. That was something she could never lie to her about. That was why it was so hard to steal anything from her. She would know instantly.

"I don't want her to get in trouble. I know it is just a misunderstanding."

"Daphne, escort Odessa here back to her room. I will deal with Estelle."

Daphne nodded and walked over to grab Odessa's hand to lead her out quickly. They didn't speak until they stood in front of Odessa's door.

"Who is she?"

"Jezabel. His general. She is also, what she likes to call herself, a scientist. Let's just say you never want to be her experiment." Daphne shivered thinking about how the scariest demons cowered in her presence because of the screams that came from the lab where they see their brethren go but never return. "Luckily, she stays in the dungeons, so she is easier to avoid, but now we must keep a watchful eye on Estelle."

"Will she hurt her?" Odessa asked, curiosity evident in her voice.

"Yes. I'm not sure what she will do to her, but she tried to kill what was not hers to kill, and she trespassed into her territory. Jezabel hates when people break her rules and enter her domain without permission."

"Oh," Odessa said. "I will be sure to remember that. Go get some sleep. We have a busy day tomorrow."

Daphne watched Odessa enter her room and waited until she heard the lock click before going into her own room.

Locking her door, Daphne carefully removed her boots and clothes, setting them aside. She exchanged them for a comfortable night-shirt and shorts, preparing for a restful night's sleep. The book she longed to read lay untouched on her nightstand, overshadowed by the multitude of worries that raced through her mind. The main one being what would happen if Estelle successfully killed Odessa.

As she settled into bed, Daphne's thoughts swirled, burdened by uncertainty. Initially, Odessa had merely been a means of escape from this place, but now Daphne had come to appreciate her as a kind-hearted person genuinely. Living in Askaria for all these years had meant surviving in a harsh and unforgiving environment, where the air was thick with malevolence and the very essence of darkness seemed to seep into every crevice.

Daphne had witnessed unimaginable horrors, her soul etched with the indelible marks of suffering and torment. She had seen the depths of the demon's power and the depths of his depravity.

Kindness always came hand in hand with cruelty. It was a contradictory existence, where constant fear and oppression overshadowed moments of respite. Alazar was capable of kindness even though he often veered into acts of unspeakable cruelty. His whims dictated the fates of those unfortunate enough to be caught in his clutches. She had been subjected to his whimsical nature, enduring his sadistic games and relentless torment more often than not. She had become intimately acquainted with pain, both physical and emotional, as she danced on the precarious edge of survival.

So, she recognized that Odessa didn't deserve to be imprisoned any more than she did. She didn't deserve to be subjected to his cruelty and that kind of pain. The fleeting moments when the demon would show a glimmer of compassion. He would offer a tender touch, a soothing word, or a rare act of generosity that temporarily softened the jagged edges of their existence. These moments were deceptive, however, as they only deepened the torment. Daphne couldn't help but yearn for more, clinging to the fragments of kindness like a drowning soul clutching at a flickering lifeline.

Finding a way to free herself was challenging enough, but the notion of rescuing them both seemed almost insurmountable. Still, the fear of losing Odessa gnawed at Daphne's heart, and she knew she couldn't bear such a loss. She would have to figure out a way to get them both out before Estelle managed to kill her because she wasn't sure her heart would be able to take that kind of loss.

Daphne pushed the thought aside, not wanting to go down a list of possibilities. Instead, she closed her eyes and let the thoughts of what her freedom would look like lull her to sleep.

CHAPTER TWENTY-SEVEN

ALECIA

Alecia waited for Max's reaction.

She could probably negotiate with something else if he refused, but the nymph would not let them leave without giving her something she wanted.

"And what exactly is it you want us to do?" Max asked, surprising Alecia.

"I want you to fuck her while I watch."

Alecia couldn't help but observe his face as she said the words. As he turned to look at her, the desire she saw almost brought her to her knees.

She swallowed over the lump in her throat. "Max, we don't have to."

"And if I fuck her, will you give us the malice?" he said, not moving his eyes from hers.

"Only if she reaches an orgasm. Then yes, I promise to give you the malice," Ethel said with a sweet smile. Alecia glared at her. She knew what she was doing. She fed off this kind of desire. It was her favorite kind.

She was so busy glaring daggers at Ethel that it caught her off-guard when Max walked up to her. His mere nearness was going to make her crumble in this moment.

"What about Estelle?" she questioned, her voice tinged with a mix of anxiety and vulnerability. The mere thought of him still harboring feelings for Estelle sent a pang of unease through her heart. The anticipation weighed heavily in the air as she waited for his response, her gaze locked with his, hoping for reassurance.

"I lost hope of ever finding Estelle a long time ago. Only a small spark had remained but knowing she betrayed us, it is extinguished," Max confessed.

The hope that bloomed within her was bittersweet, a delicate flame flickering against the backdrop of uncertainty. It whispered promises of possibilities, igniting a spark of longing within her. Yet she couldn't help but feel the weight of her own foolishness, aware that her mind had wandered into a realm of dreams and wishful thinking. The clash between reality and desire tugged at her heart, casting a shadow over her fleeting hopes.

"I know you said you and Christian aren't married, but are you together?" he asked, gazing into her eyes.

She tried to hide her longing, but she was sure he could see it in her eyes.

"We haven't been together in years," she breathed as she tried to keep control of her thoughts. "I use Ethel more than him.

Desire flared in his eyes as he grabbed the sides of her head. "Then you won't mind if I do this." His lips pressed to hers in an unexpectedly furious kiss as his tongue pushed its way past her lips, eager to explore every crevice of her mouth.

There was no room for tenderness in his kiss as he sucked her lips and enjoyed her mouth fully. Needy and desperate to get his fill of her like a man starved.

Alecia let him take it all.

It had been so long since she had felt this desire flood her system. She became so lost in his kiss she didn't realize her back hit the wall until he was lifting her legs to wrap around his waist.

She wanted him to be closer; she hated the clothes between them. She needed to feel his flesh.

She pushed off his coat as he continued to devour her mouth, then she ripped open his shirt, sending buttons flying across the room. Wetness pooled between her legs when he groaned as she touched his chest. She remembered every curve and scar-like it was just yesterday.

He firmly pushed her back against the wall and used his leg to hold her up as he pulled her shirt over her head, exposing her breasts. He cupped her left breast and covered the nipple with his mouth, sucking hard and then licking it.

"Fuck. Yes," the words involuntarily escaped her lips.

The button on her pants became undone before he slid his fingers in, easily parting her pussy lips and finding her nub. He circled it a few times before moving past it and gliding his fingers into her. She moaned as pleasure coursed through her body. She would come before he was even inside her.

Max's mouth let go of her nipple and kissed his way to her ear. "Alecia, baby, I need you to come for me. Let me feel your juices all over my hand so my dick can slide right in you."

His thumb located her nub and began a steady rhythm as his mouth found hers. When his ring finger poked at her asshole, she came hard in his hand.

Before she could completely come down from her orgasm, he pushed down her pants and turned her around to face the wall. She heard his belt come undone, and then his pants hit the floor before he found her hole and thrust into her in one swift motion. They both let out a moan.

"Fuck, Alecia. You feel good," he grunted. "Too damn good."

Max bent her over further so he could seat himself more deeply in her as he began to thrust slowly and steadily at first, sending Alecia's already frazzled brain into overdrive as his thrusts became faster and faster.

Their moans and groans filled the room, turning her on more as she felt her second orgasm teetering on the edge. His hand reached around her and touched her pussy, finding her nub. As his finger skillfully danced upon her sensitive core, each movement resonated like the delicate strings of a fiddle, playing a melody of pleasure. The rhythm of his thrusts aligned perfectly with her desires, striking that elusive spot that ignited an intense cascade of sensations.

Wave after wave of ecstasy washed over her, rippling through every inch of her body as her orgasm unfurled with undeniable intensity. Stars swam in front of her eyes as she let the pleasure move through her. He continued to pound into her until he found his own release. Her muscles continued to squeeze and milk him as he groaned.

The removal of his warmth brought her back to reality.

"Now, that was downright delicious. Alecia, darling, you are going to have to bring him back here so we can all play together."

"The malice," Max demanded as he pulled up his pants, buckling them. Alecia did the same, suddenly feeling vulnerable.

Alecia heard the malice fall to the ground near them. She still hadn't turned around, not ready to see his eyes. She wasn't sure what she would see, which scared her the most. She scanned her surroundings for her shirt but didn't see it until Max reached out his hand, holding it.

"You okay, Alecia?" he asked gently.

"I'm fine." She grabbed the shirt and quickly put it on, along with her discarded jacket. Once she was fully clothed, she finally turned to face him.

He gently smiled at her, then picked up the malice. As she mustered the courage to meet his gaze, she braced herself for a glimpse of repulsion or disappointment. But to her surprise, those emotions were absent from his expression. Instead, he appeared unfazed, as if their passionate encounter held no significance. It was as though the remarkable pleasure he had granted her, giving her two of the most extraordinary orgasms she had ever experienced, meant nothing to him.

The absence of any visible reaction stung her deeply, surpassing the pain she would have felt had he displayed disgust or disappointment.

She looked away for him and searched the room for Ethel.

"She went back in the room with the client."

"Of course she did." Alecia marched over to the door and opened it. She wasn't surprised to see a male with his hands tied behind his back with a blindfold on eating Ethel's pussy.

"You are a complete bitch for that." The male stopped and turned in her direction.

Ethel laughed, and Alecia slammed the door.

She stormed past Max, not caring for his look of surprise and maybe regret. She went straight to the bar. A shot wasn't going to do. She needed a bottle. It would be the only thing to numb the stupid pain that was threatening to surface.

Lucius

"I can't get her out of my head," Max said as he paced back and forth in front of Lucius for the 100th time in the past twenty minutes. Clearly, he needed to talk.

Lucius placed his pen down and set aside his book. He had been trying to study the map of Evictus and strategize the best plan to get his army there. He wanted to get the advantage against Alazar, and it was better to have the fight in Evictus. The repercussions of involving too many humans in their world were too great, and the truth was, they simply weren't prepared to handle its intricate complexities, not at this moment anyway.

He went over to Max's liquor cabinet and found his stock low. He had been trying to stay away from alcohol since his other self had a real problem with it, but one glass wouldn't hurt. Besides, he knew Max needed it more than him. He found a bottle of green vodka made by the Elves. Not the best alcohol, but it would do for now.

He popped the top and turned away as the horrific smell hit his nose. He poured them both two fingers full, then brought it over to Max.

"Here, drink this and sit." Max stopped his pacing, then without hesitation downed the drink.

Lucius did the same, hating the way it hit the back of his throat and slid to his stomach.

"Shit, that's disgusting." He placed the glass on the table, then sat in the leather chair near his small fireplace. Lucius leaned back against the table.

"Alright, spill, Max. What the hell happened? Who can't you get out of your head?"

For the third time in their friendship, Lucius was met with a quiet Max. The last two times this had happened was in his cabin when they first met, and the second time was when he met Alecia again. Since he was with her earlier, Lucius was guessing it was about her again.

"Did Alecia do something?" he probed. "Max?"

"She didn't do anything. More like what I did to her. Or what we did together," he said quietly.

Lucius thought back to earlier when Max came in. He knew his shirt looked off, but he hadn't thought about it because he was trying to help Selene find more veridian. Now that he thought about it, he realized his shirt didn't have buttons.

His eyes narrowed. "Max. Talk now."

"We needed the malice. She wouldn't give it up unless we exchanged something."

"She is a Sedisse. Of course. You slept with her. Alecia."

Max nodded, his cheeks flushing.

Lucius rubbed his hand down his face and grabbed the vodka, pouring them both another drink. Maybe it was time he told him the truth at least about this.

"Max—"

"I know she is a traitor and a liar. I need to stay away from her, but you know I have always had a soft spot for Alecia. I've kept my distance because of Estelle and Christian. I also didn't know if she reciprocated my feelings." Max downed his drink.

"Max, she is your wife," Lucius confessed. It was time he knew the truth, even though he wasn't ready for it, but he needed Max to have a clear head.

"What?" Max stared at him in shock.

"She is your wife. Not Estelle," Lucius revealed.

"Lucius, don't play with me." His disbelief and possibly, hope, was written all over his face. "Things are complicated enough with all this memory shit."

"I'm telling you the truth before Alazar changed everything. You were married to her." Lucius walked around his desk to sit.

"Wait, I don't understand. Then how did Estelle and I...? Wait, we aren't... are we...?"

"That is something you have to ask Alecia. I am not sure what happened there. What I do know was that you both were happy until she kidnapped my daughter."

Max stared at him in surprise. "You really did have a daughter. I thought that was a lie. That you never had a child. Like they said, your wife died."

"She was seven years old when they took her. Her and Estelle. I did not know Estelle at that time, but I did know Alecia, and when I found out she took my child, I vowed to kill her, but I stayed my hand because of you."

"Where-Where is your daughter?"

"Unfortunately, I don't know. That is the one thing I can't fully remember." Ever since Lucius returned to his true self, he had been trying to remember. That night was still blurry to him. He wasn't sure if he believed Alden, who claimed Jezabel took her to the Anthralls. Especially since learning his memory was altered as well. He couldn't focus on that now. On the possibility.

"Lucius, I'm sorry. Maybe there is a chance. Have you tried to ask Alecia? There has to be a reason why she betrayed us."

"No. I can't trust anything she says. From looking at the memories from over these past few years, we were friends and from what I am learning now, if I am piecing things together correctly, then I believe she did it for her sister which unfortunately, I could understand. Right now, Max, the only thing that matters to me is getting Odessa back. I know this is a lot. It is the reason I was reluctant to talk to you, but in the end, it is up to you to figure out what to do with Alecia. Just know I do not trust her."

"I understand," Max said, his voice heavy with a sullen tone and a hint of resignation.

He let Max wallow in his thoughts while he went back to creating his strategy. Lucius needed more information and unfortunately, the king and queen could only give him so much since they had not been to Askaria for years. He knew they had about a little over a hundred Hokima assassins, possibly more, but Kieran wasn't sure if he had accessed that part of Euphoria yet.

"Volt," he called out, knowing he was within the house.

"You called?" Volt appeared by the door.

"How's everything going in the library?" Lucius asked without looking up from the map he had in front of him.

"I believe they will have the portal open soon. They just got the combination right, but that's not why you called me here," he stated.

Lucius glanced over at Max, who still gazed into the fire. He was sorry, but he needed information. "I need the king and queen... and Alecia."

Volt disappeared. Max's head whipped around to stare at him.

Lucius sighed, "I'm sorry. She has information. I am not going to hurt her, just ask her a question. You don't have to stay."

"It's fine. I will be fine," he said, pouring himself another drink. "Oh. My. God. I am turning into the brooding you. Fuck." He drank down the glass anyway, then threw the bottle into the fireplace, making the flames burst.

Lucius continued to look at the map and mark it with places he thought would give them an advantage. Max came to stand next to him.

"Do you think we have a chance?"

"Yes. This is just a precaution. If we can get into Askaria and kill Alazar, we will not have to result to this, but we must be ready. We need to have the soldiers in position before we step through that portal because we are not sure what we will find."

The door opened, and Kieran followed as Circe walked through the door. Volt appeared with Silas by the desk. "I was able to get another twenty thousand from the Carmichaels and Garcias. Also, the Portens offered their soldiers, but they wouldn't get here in time unless we asked the witches to transport them, but I figured you would want their energy put to use in other places."

Lucius nodded. "We will need the witches to concentrate on getting most of the soldiers to Evictus. We know there are portals here and here." He pointed to the two caves that laid in the Curvus Territory.

"I take it you have the malice of Phoenixal," the king stated.

Lucius nodded.

"Samuel will be surprised to see you alive after all his years of freedom."

Lucius offered a sinister smile. The vindictive ogre had enough years of freedom. It was time he repaid the debt he owed his wife. He would only free him when and if she deemed he had served his sentence.

"We will need the witches to help bring in the rest of the soldiers. We should hear from them soon. The only wish I have is to know what we're actually dealing with in numbers. I know there are hundreds of demons locked away in Euphoria, but it would be impossible for them to have released them all or to have control over them."

Alecia chose that moment to stroll into his office unannounced, Isiadora and Selene not far behind. Lucius tapped the map twice, and his markings disappeared.

"You must have something you need to say," Lucius muttered.

"Jezabel has been gaining control of them," Alecia said, her tone carrying a mix of concern and urgency.

"So Jezabel is alive?" Circe asked, looking at Kieran with concern.

"Yes, she is very much alive, and she is now the general of his army."

Lucius wasn't surprised. They had never found a body. A small part of him was glad she was alive. He looked forward to giving her another scar, and this time he would see her fall. "What I need to know is numbers. How many?"

"I don't know specifics. Sorry to be a disappointment, but what I do know is that Jezabel has control over every demon in Euphoria, except for Xenalia.

She is currently hibernating in her cell at the bottom of the Euphorian Trench."

"She is waiting for the return of the king," Circe whispered. "We can use this. Once Michael touches his wrist to the throne, she will awake and Jezabel will no longer have control. We thought she was killed, but I knew your sister could not be so easily defeated."

"I have not felt her for a very long time," King Kieran confessed.

"You said the same about our son, who is very much alive," Circe said pointedly.

"Bătrâne, ești din ce în ce mai încet cu fiecare vârstă," *(Old man, your age is showing)* Lucius said with a grin.

"Spune cel cu probleme de memorie," *(Says the one with the memory problems)* Kieran chided as a grin appeared then disappeared.

"Let's assume he has control over all the demons, plus the Hokima and your general army. Is it safe to say he has access to—"

"Over sixty thousand soldiers," Alecia supplied.

"Fuck. We are going to need as many witches as possible," Max sighed.

"My sisters have gotten back to me. They will be able to send between fifty to sixty witches from every coven, except two who refuse to work with you. With over eighty covens, that will give you access to almost five thousand witches," Isiadora added.

"But will it be enough power with only four Silverlands witches and your Goddess missing?" Max stated, raising a brow.

Lucius felt Isiadora's gaze on him. He met her eyes. *Don't say it.*

"We do have Alden," Isiadora said cautiously. "His powers would add greatly to ours."

"He can't be trusted. No," Lucius said with a finality that left no room for questions. "Alecia, out."

Alecia grumbled something intelligible before storming out the room.

He gave her time to walk away. He could not trust her with this information. He still was not sure which side she was on. Once her footsteps faded, he double-tapped the table. His markings appeared before he continued, "We don't have nearly as many soldiers as I would like, but time is of the essence, and we need to start getting them into position."

Lucius glanced over the map once more. As much as he wanted to get more soldiers, he wanted his wife back more. He didn't know what Alazar was doing to her, and he was afraid in what shape he would get her back in.

Lucius still wasn't sure if her memories would return, but he had to put his fears aside and forge ahead. He would get her back and figure it out from there.

Resolved, he started to give orders. "Silas, tell the Clares, Berons, and Clawfields to prepare their soldiers to go through the Verlunian Cave. Volt will make sure their path is clear."

Volt and Silas both nodded, before Volt grabbed the latter and disappeared.

"Isiadora, having the witches and vampires in the same place will be tricky. The hate in some of them runs deep. It is going to be an interesting world once everything is righted. For now, we will keep them separated. We will have them appear on this ridge."

Lucius pointed to the ridge that was between both cave entrances but far from each.

"Elemental witches should be in the front and the rest should be in the back. We will need to create a barrier that won't allow so many creatures onto the battlefield in at the same time, we will need your strongest witches here to fortify it because if this falls, we will be slaughtered."

"I will make sure your instructions are conveyed and followed," Isiadora said with a nod.

"Circe. Kieran. You will stay here—"

"No," Kieran boomed. "I will not stay behind while you fight for my kingdom."

"If he manages to kill you, he will come for Michael."

Kieran's eyes filled with defiance as he simply said, "No."

"Nu fi un prost încăpăţânat. *(Don't be a stubborn fool).* You have been down three times in the past week. You are not agile as you used to be. You have been away from your throne too long."

"N—"

"We will stay and protect our son. Kieran has much to teach him before he can take the throne," Circe said curtly. Kieran looked like he wanted to say something, but he wouldn't go against her wishes, especially since she was clearly still pissed at him.

"Max, I need you to get in touch with the Knights, Carmichaels, and Garcias to be ready to have their soldiers to go through Cervus's Cave."

Max nodded before moving to his desk.

"We will be ready to go into Askaria within the next twenty-four hours. Volt, Silas, and Max will go with me to Askaria. If anything goes wrong, Volt will return with instructions on what to do next."

Lucius felt good about this. He just hoped it all would be unnecessary.

"Selene and I will have the portal ready for you," Isiadora said before she disappeared. Circe stormed out with a weary Kieran following behind. Knowing Circe, the king was about to get an earful.

Lucius ran his hands over his face and prepared himself for what he had to do next. He walked over to Max's small bookcase and stooped down.

"Lucius, what are you doing?" Max asked with a little panic in his voice. Lucius smirked; so he was right. He reached out and debated which book to pull. He listened to Max's heartbeat. Its rate picked up when he moved closer to his least favorite book. Typical.

Lucius removed the book and heard the click. Max was right next to him as soon as he slid the case aside.

"How did you know? Never mind. You remember."

Lucius reached in and pulled out his dagger holder before beginning to fill it. "No worries, I am not the raged lunatic anymore."

Max nodded and went back to his desk. Lucius grabbed a few more weapons, then slid the case back. He grabbed Luzia and placed her on his back, then picked up the malice.

"I will be back." He touched Luzia and disappeared.

Lucius reappeared in a dark, dank cave. Bones were scattered and crushed everywhere, and some still had flesh on them.

Lucius walked through until he found what he was looking for. A large figure was asleep against the cave wall. Lucius pulled out his malice.

"Samuel."

CHAPTER TWENTY-EIGHT

Daphne

Daphne hadn't seen Odessa all day.

She went to her room in the morning like she normally did. She found it unlocked and empty. Panic didn't set in until an hour later when she still hadn't shown up.

Daphne decided to walk around to see if maybe she got lost looking for her or something. She searched all the places she commonly went, but she was nowhere to be found.

She thought maybe she went back to the dungeons, but then she saw Estelle walking up the stairs. Daphne hid behind the statue by the window at the top of the staircase. She peeked through the statue's armhole. What surprised her was how unhurt she appeared. Jezabel had never let her get away with trespassing before. Her somber look should have given her some clue, but it wasn't until Estelle reached the top landing and turned left toward her bedroom that Daphne saw the real damage.

The back of Estelle's dress was torn and bloody. She had several whip marks down her back which created a maze of mess. She would clearly be scared badly.

Daphne almost felt bad for her, but she deserved it. Waiting until she had fully disappeared down the hall, Daphne continued her search. She finally ended up in the garden atrium where they had already started the setup for the wedding. As she watched the mindless humans set up, a thought occurred to her.

Did she escape without me?

The thought raced through her mind, filling her with a mix of anxiety and hope. The possibility lingered, fueled by the knowledge that Odessa now had access to magic, especially since Alazar had allowed her access.

No. She wouldn't do that to her. She believed her when she said they would get out of there together. Besides, Alazar would be in an uproar by now. If she did indeed escape and everything seemed to be moving along like normal.

Daphne took a walk around the garden, having no choice but to wait and pray for her return. She began to look at the flowers and plants to see if she could figure out which of them would be useful for their plan.

Having traversed this garden countless times, she had never considered utilizing its plants to create a poison. The knowledge of what the ingredients looked like in their current form eluded her, although she could have searched Jezabel's books on flora or herbalism for guidance. Yet, the risk of being caught rummaging through Jezabel's belongings deterred her from attempting such a venture.

She continued her leisurely stroll, her eyes wandering until they landed on a striking red plant with intricate black veins. Its unfamiliar appearance intrigued her, leaving her wondering about its potential properties. In the vicinity, she also spotted an unusual plant with blue veins and a purple flower with a white stem that she had seen many times. She was about to reach out to pluck some of the petals off of each when she heard yelling.

"How dare you, Alazar?" Odessa screamed.

"My love, she means nothing to me."

"Nothing? You were fucking her," Odessa cried, her voice dripping with venom. "The day before our wedding! How could you?"

Daphne quickly pulled off a few petals from each plant and stuffed them in her pocket before she revealed herself in the garden. "Odessa, is everything alright?"

Alazar's red eyes narrowed on her. He wasn't in his human form. It was strange seeing his hardened demon form pleading with her. His blackened skin and curled horns didn't seem so menacing seeing him like this. "Take her to—"

"That woman tried to kill me, and you were screwing her. The wedding is off," Odessa pulled off her engagement ring and threw it at him before she ran off.

"Fuck," he said in frustration, then he took a deep breath to calm himself. He picked up the ring. "JEZABEL!" he shouted.

She appeared at his side within seconds. "Yes?"

"I will need more mist. Just enough for her to forget the events of the past twenty-four hours." He glanced at the ring before he slipped it into his pocket.

"As you wish, but it may damage her memories. We don't know what she may have done to her own, and this could fracture her mind."

Daphne tried to keep her face neutral as she heard Jezabel's words. Shit.

"That is a risk I am willing to take. Prepare it. And also get the bonding spell ready. We will wed tonight. Enough wasting time."

She couldn't let this happen. If he got that mist in Odessa's system, she wouldn't remember their plan. Daphne had to reach her before they did.

Jezabel disappeared, and Alazar was about to walk away when he called her name. "Daphne."

She cautiously approached.

"Go and keep her from doing anything irrational. Try to keep her calm until I can bring the mist."

She nodded her head and was about to walk away when he stopped her. "Daphne."

Slowly, she turned back toward him. "Yes?"

"I'm sorry. I don't hate you," he said as his eyes grew soft. "I was just upset."

She looked away. She hated when he was sweet toward her. "I know, Alazar."

"Good girl. Now go."

Daphne turned and walked away but when she knew she was far enough away from him, she ran down the halls until she reached Odessa's bedroom. Stopping to catch her breath first, she walked into the room.

"Odessa?" she called out cautiously, not seeing her in the sitting room.

"I'm in here, Daphne."

Daphne moved quickly to the bedroom and found her with a pair of scissors in her hand. Her wedding dress was sitting in front of her.

Placing the scissors in the nightstand, Odessa then pressed her hand to the wall. Daphne watched as light shot from her hand and zoomed around the room, filling in all the crevices and creating a sealed bubble.

"I was going for dramatic, in case he came after me. The fucking bastard. I was up early this morning exploring and trying to find his office. Admittedly, I got lost, but then I saw the bastard hoping he would help me find my way back, but something told me to just follow him. I saw Estelle walk into a room, and then he slipped in after her."

Odessa stood and began to pace.

"As he walked in and closed the door, I knew what he was doing, so I waited until I knew they were well into it, and then I stormed through the door. I thought it would help to delay the wedding."

Daphne watched as she paced, but what hit her the most was when she saw the tears coming down her face.

"I know none of this is real, but I can't help feeling betrayed and heartbroken."

Daphne went over to her and did something she never thought she would do to another person. She wrapped her arms around her and hugged her tightly while she cried.

"I understand, but you must push those feelings aside. We have to get out of here now."

Odessa lifted her head and quickly wiped away her tears. "Why? What happened?"

Daphne reluctantly let go and took a step back. "He plans on using the mists on you again and marrying you tonight. He has a spell he plans to use on you to create a bond."

"Fuck. What are we going to do?" Frustrated, Odessa sank onto the bed and buried her face in her hands.

"The worst part isn't that you'll forget everything in the last twenty-four hours, but it is also possible that it may fracture your mind."

Odessa ran her hands through her curls, thinking, then placed her head in her hands.

Daphne pulled the plant from her pocket. "I found these in the garden. The red and black one I haven't seen before, but these two have always been there. I am not sure if they will help."

Odessa lifted her head and examined each petal. She took them from her hands and gazed at them closely. "You said you found these in the garden?"

"Yes, why? Can we use any of them?" Daphne said, trying not to put too much hope in her voice.

Odessa, considering the options, responded dismissively, "Not this one," and promptly tossed the purple flower into the crackling fire. Daphne observed as sparks danced from the burning petals.

"It could have been useful," Odessa added, "but extracting the poison would be too time-consuming." She examined the red and black petals before discarding them.

"Ah yes. Now this we can use," she declared as she held up the petal with the blue veins. "This is findle. It doesn't have much use, at least not until… you dry it out. Can you get your hands on clay and tinctive powder?"

Daphne thought about it for a second. "Jezabel has them, but they are in her lab. We can't get them. She will know as soon as we walk in and even if we made it, she would instantly know something was missing, and I am always the first person she comes looking for."

"We don't need to go anywhere."

Taking the leaf, Odessa grabbed the fire poker and stuck the leaf to it, then using the fireplace gate, she leaned it over it so the head could dry it out. She next grabbed the metal shovel and laid it underneath so it could catch any falling pieces.

Odessa pulled Daphne to sit on the floor, but not before she flicked her hand toward the door. Daphne heard the lock click.

"We don't want any unwanted visitors." They sat crossed-legged on the carpet. Odessa grabbed her hand. "Now, I need you to relax and trust me. This will work, okay? We are going to summon the items to us."

"You can do that?" Daphne asked skeptically.

"Yes, but she will know they are missing, although I am doubting these are her everyday items, so hopefully we will be long gone before she finds them missing."

Daphne nodded and squeezed her hands. "Do you really think we can get out of here?"

Odessa pulled her in close and looked her straight in the eyes. "Yes. We are leaving here today." She reached behind her and pulled a chain from her pocket, then opened it and let the key drop.

Daphne's eyes widened. "You got it! How?"

"He was too busy screwing. He left his jacket on the floor by the door. I snatched it before I started yelling. Did you notice that he did not have it on?"

Daphne thought back to earlier and realized for the first time ever he was only in his dress shirt.

"He left it on the floor too busy chasing after me and if my instincts are correct, then Estelle won't let him put the jacket back on until they finished what they started. Now, we have to hurry. This leaf will allow us the perfect distraction. Close your eyes."

Daphne closed her eyes, excitement beginning to pump through her. She had never been so close to freedom before, not even when Alazar sent her into Eviathan. She always knew Jezabel wasn't far, but this gave her hope, almost too much.

"Concentrate on the items. Think about where they are first, and try to be as exact as you can. Concentrate on one item at a time, thinking of its place. Do you have them?"

Daphne remembered seeing the clay in a small container on the third shelf on the right wall in the wooden cabinet, and the tinctive powder was sitting in the ingredient cabinet under her metal desk. "I have them."

"Okay, think about the clay. Pinpoint exactly where it is and what it looks like down to its very last detail."

Odessa's hands began to warm and tingle in her hand. Taking a deep breath, Daphne focused on the details of the clay container.

"Good. Now I want you to do the same for the powder."

Daphne thought about the powder then Odessa's hands grew cold. She opened her eyes.

"You did it!" Odessa exclaimed. Daphne turned to see the clay container and the powder both sat next to her.

Odessa quickly got up and grabbed a decorative white bowl. She retrieved the spoon from her discarded tea, then took the leaf off the poker. Placing the leaf in the bowl, she handed it to Daphne. "Crush this up."

Standing, she took the bowl and sat on the couch. She started to mash the leaf. Odessa picked up the powder and clay and placed them on the table near Daphne.

"How long have you had that cuff on?" Odessa asked her, sitting down next to her.

"Umm... since I turned twelve. He gave it to me as a gift and told me it was to protect me. It was after I showed him how I didn't need to use portals to move places like he did. I wish I had kept my mouth shut."

"Can he use it to track you?"

"Not that I know of. Anytime I went out, Jezabel or Estelle were never far."

Odessa stood and grabbed her wedding dress. She tore off a piece, then grabbed her tea. Dipping the cloth into the lukewarm liquid, Odessa closed her eyes, and Daphne watched as it glowed in her hands then faded. Odessa pulled out a dry cloth.

Walking over, she kneeled down and wrapped it around her leg right where the cuff was. "This will shield the magic of the cuff and any locater spell it might have on it."

After tying it securely, she opened the clay container and began to knead it.

"Okay, what's going to happen next is probably going to happen fast, so listen in case something goes wrong."

Daphne nodded, turning toward her to listen carefully. Odessa opened the tinctive powder and added it to the bowl.

"Mix it together slowly. Now, once we combine the clay and the mix, I am going to send it to the garden. As soon as the boom happens, you are going to lead the way to the office. You will not stop. No matter what happens, you get to that office, and you go through that portal."

Daphne stopped mixing. "You want me to go through even if you are not with me."

"Yes, once you are in Eviathan. You have to find... Lucas or Mike."

"You mean Lucius or Michael?"

"Yes! You know them? I hear their names in my memory, but I can't see their faces. What I do know is that they are safe. They will help you."

"I only know *of* them, but I can find them." Daphne couldn't believe she remembered them. Maybe she was right, and their bond wasn't broken after all.

"Good. I plan to be with you every step of the way, but if they come, I want you to run to that office. Do you understand? Promise me."

Sadness swelled within her, making her want to cry at the thought of leaving Odessa behind, but she could not waste this opportunity. She promised herself that if they both didn't make it out, she would come back for her.

"Yes, I understand. I promise."

"Good." Odessa pulled the key from her pocket. "Take this."

Placing the bowl down, Daphne grabbed the key and put it deep into her pocket so it would not fall out.

"Alright, are you ready?"

She was as ready as she was going to be. Daphne almost thought about going back to her room to grab a few things, but they weren't worth it.

The only thing she had of value and that she cared about, she had given away at that damn bookstore for those books that didn't tell her shit. She had planned to go back to get her necklace, but then everything happened. Maybe there was still a chance to get it back.

She nodded. "Yes."

"Okay." Odessa pushed her fingers in the middle of the clay to make a small hole, then she took a careful pinch of the mixture and placed it in the hole. Gently, she pressed it shut. Odessa then closed her eyes, and Daphne watched as the clay disappeared.

As soon as it was gone, Odessa grabbed Daphne's hand and the fire poker and went to the door. Letting go of her hand for a moment, Odessa pressed her hand to the wall and absorbed her magic back, unsealing the room.

They silently waited to hear the boom.

Just when Daphne's heart was about to sink, a loud explosion could be heard in the distance. A tremor went through the entire place.

"Move, now."

Daphne quickly unlocked the door and started heading in the direction of Alazar's office. She wanted to run, but it would be too suspicious until they got closer.

A pair of mindless humans came running down the hall towards them. Odessa let go of her hand and hid the fire poker with her leg as they ran by.

Shit. Alazar would know they came this way. They were going to have to move faster. "We have to run. They will tell Alazar."

"Alright, let's go."

Daphne picked up her pace until she was running. She hated the twists and turns of this damn place, but she knew it like the back of her hand. His office was just around this last turn. She didn't slow until his office came into view, then she looked behind her to find Odessa gone.

Daphne was about to turn back when she remembered what she had just promised her. She would come back for her.

She moved quickly but cautiously toward the door, pulling out the key. This was it. Her freedom was just on the other side; all she had to do was insert the key and turn. Her heart pounded in her chest, the excitement and anticipation mingling with a hint of fear. The key felt heavy in her hand. It felt surreal, as if the weight of her past struggles was pressing against her, urging her to take this final step. Her hand shook as she moved toward the door. Taking a deep breath to calm her nerves, she inserted the key and turned the lock. The sound of the click was joy to her soul. She reached for the handle to turn the knob.

"You treacherous little bitch. How did you get his key?" Estelle screeched, rushing toward her and grabbing her hair. "Oh, wait till I tell him what I caught you doing. You little thief!"

Daphne grabbed at her hands, but Estelle only pulled her hair tighter and began to drag her backwards. The pounding in her head intensified, matching the rhythm of her racing heart. Each word that escaped Estelle's lips felt like a dagger, stabbing deep. Tears welled up in her eyes, blurring her vision as she struggled to hold them back. She couldn't let Estelle see her weakness, couldn't give her the satisfaction of witnessing her pain.

With every step that took her further away from the door, a sense of helplessness washed over her. The dream of freedom was slipping away, replaced by a stark reality of continued captivity. The world seemed to collapse around her as Estelle's relentless rant echoed in her ears, drowning out any shred of hope that remained.

Then Estelle stopped abruptly and let go of her, causing Daphne to drop to the floor. She quickly scrambled away from her, then looked at Estelle. The black metal fire poker protruded from her eye as Odessa stood over her lifeless form on the ground.

"Is she dead?" Daphne gasped.

"I fucking hope so," Odessa spat, then held out her hand to her. Daphne took it, and Odessa lifted her up. "Sorry, I saw her back there. I wasn't sure if she was running to tell him, so I went after her only to follow her right here. Come on, let's hurry. We don't have much time left, especially if Estelle is here. He has his jacket on. He will know it's missing and come straight here."

They ran towards the office door. Odessa turned the handle and tugged them into the office. She pulled the key out and slammed the door closed, locking it.

Daphne scanned the room. It looked like a normal office with a mahogany desk and old books on the walls but no mirrors in sight. Did she get it wrong? Was this not where the mirrors were?

"I don't think they are here. Shit. I got it wrong." The wetness on Daphne's cheek let her know her dam was about to break wide open.

"Keep it together, Daph. The mirrors are here. I can feel their powers humming." Odessa moved around the room, her hands gliding over various objects, searching for something, anything that could offer a clue or a hidden secret. Her fingertips brushed against the books on the bookshelf behind the desk, and as she made contact, a surge of magical energy tingled through her fingertips. She allowed the magic to guide her, trusting her instincts. The sensation intensified when her hands landed on a red book, pulsating with a faint enchantment.

Without hesitation, she pulled the book, and as if responding to her touch, the bookshelf silently shifted, revealing a room.

A loud boom echoed through the office, causing Odessa and Daphne to jump in surprise. Something heavy collided against the door, reverberating with a powerful impact. Her heart raced, and a mix of fear and anticipation coursed through her veins. She quickly turned her attention toward the door.

Odessa cast her a wary look and urged her on. "Daphne, come."

Daphne moved toward her and grabbed her outstretched hand, then pushed them through the shelves into a room with two mirrors. The mirror to the left had black veins crawling up the wall. The dark glass rippled, then cracked and became smooth again.

"We are not going through there," Odessa said, moving to the mirror on the left as another boom echoed through the office behind them.

The mirror on the right looked completely normal. It wasn't active like the other mirror. "You said you would use another portal to get to Eviathan."

"Yes. Is it always active, or is there a word someone says to activate it?" Odessa asked as they both ignored the third boom, but what made her heart jump was the crack of the door. Odessa flicked her wrist and the bookshelf closed, sealing them in. There was no turning back now.

Daphne took a moment to wrack her brain. Were there words that Jezabel had said? Yes. But what were they? Dammit.

"I think it is, *Aperi ad notum ostium in Eviathan*." The mirror lit up and the glass rippled. Daphne's heart soared, but at the same moment, the bookcase blew open.

Wood splintered everywhere. Odessa shielded her before she grabbed Daphne, pushing her through the mirror. Odessa tried to let go, but Daphne wasn't having it; she was not going to leave her. She pulled Odessa through with her.

They tumbled through darkness until they landed on a sofa in the middle of someone's living room. They were in a house. A house that was a potential trap.

Daphne quickly moved, knowing they needed to get out of this house and onto the street. She grabbed Odessa, who looked a little dazed, and ran for the front door. She thanked the Goddess when the door effortlessly opened and sprinted down the front steps into oncoming traffic. She dodged two cars before they made it down the street far from the house.

"Daphne, slow down. My head is spinning." Odessa pulled her hands from her and leaned against a fence to catch her breath.

"I'm sorry but we needed to get as far away as possible—Odessa, you're bleeding."

They both looked down at her stomach where there was blood spreading over her shirt. She lifted the hem. An inch-long wooden splinter protruded out. Daphne turned her around and found six inches of wood sticking out of her back.

Odessa moaned in pain. "How bad is it?"

Horror rippled through Daphne. "We need to get you to a healer." She turned her back around. "Can you walk?"

Odessa tried to walk a little, then stumbled. Daphne grabbed her arm and put it around her neck to help carry her weight. They only made it a block before Odessa tumbled forward, completely falling to the ground.

"Shit. Odessa. You have to get up. Odessa?" Daphne looked at her and realized she had passed out.

The humans were starting to stare. This wasn't good. What the hell was she going to do? She didn't have a phone, and she couldn't let them take her to a human hospital. She would be too vulnerable, and humans asked too many questions.

"Odessa," a voice said from behind her. Daphne froze for a minute, thinking it was Alazar until the man came into view, stooping down in front of her. "What happened?"

"We escaped. She must have gotten hit when the bookcase exploded open."

He checked her pulse, then her wound. He had the most beautiful silver hair she had ever seen. She wanted to reach out and touch it until he lifted his head and gazed into her eyes. His silver eyes were filled with nothing but concern.

"I need to take her to Michael," he said, easily lifting Odessa into his arms. "Grab hold of my arm."

Daphne hesitated. She didn't know who this man was. It could be a trap.

Her thoughts went to all kinds of conclusions until he said, "You are safe with me. I promise. Trust me."

She could see the truth in his eyes. She nodded and grabbed onto his arm. She just prayed to the Goddess that her instincts were right.

CHAPTER TWENTY-NINE

LUCIUS

Lucius forgot how stubborn Samuel could be.

"Now, Samuel. There was no need to make this so difficult," Lucius said, gripping the Malice of Phoenixal. He swung up, knocking the giant ogre against the cave wall for the fifth time. "Do you submit to me? I can do this all night if we must, but you and I both know that eventually you will submit to me."

The stubborn ogre climbed back to his feet. "Samuel submits to no one!" he roared.

Lucius smiled and charged toward him. The malice lit in his hand, knowing who its master was and giving him the strength to defeat its enemy.

The ogre tried to dodge out of the way, but Lucius was faster at knocking his legs out from under him. He landed on his back with a thump that shook the entire cave. Stunned, Lucius took the opportunity to tighten the collar he had managed to loosen, then he put the malice on the ogre's chest to weigh him down.

"Sam, submit. You know this is a tireless game. Submit."

The ogre let out a final roar before he turned his head away and held out his hand. Lucius lifted the malice and laid it against his wrist. The malice lit, and Sam's wrist glowed as a cuff appeared.

Lucius lifted the malice once it was complete. "Now, see? That wasn't so hard."

Sam huffed as he sat up and turned his back on him.

"I know you are mad, but I need you to listen. Soldiers will be coming in from the portal. You cannot kill them."

Sam thundered but kept his back turned.

"But what you *can* kill is anything that tries to harm them."

Samuel's ears perked up. "Samuel gets to kill."

"Only those that harm the soldiers, do you understand?"

Samuel peeked over his shoulder and nodded, then turned his face back to the wall. Lucius knew he would forgive him as soon as he saw the nice cow and sheep he had brought to his den. For now, he was satisfied that the ogre would obey.

Exhausted, he touched Luzia and transported himself home.

As soon as he appeared, he knew something was off. There was no one in the house. He quickly made his way to the library to confirm and found it empty.

He was about to turn to go check the office for Max when Volt appeared in front of him.

"Lucius. We have her." Volt didn't explain any more, just grabbed his arm and transported them. They appeared inside GreyJoy's bookstore.

Kynigos, she has returned, Grey said to him, but he couldn't understand it. All he saw were her silky curls and blood. Michael and Circe were standing over her, and he was pushing magic into her.

Finally snapping out of it, he moved into action. He set the malice down and moved over to her. There was a piece of wood sticking out of her stomach, and her heartrate was slowing.

"I don't understand. Why is it not working?" Michael cried.

"It's because of the wood. We have to remove it, but it is going to bleed out fast." Lucius kneeled down next to Circe and lifted her shirt to look at the wound. "We need to roll her onto her side."

They worked together to gently push her to her side. He examined her from the back and concluded it would pull out clean.

"Max," he called, knowing he was there without even having to look. Max came to his side and kneeled. "I'm going to need you to pull out the wood fast. Michael, as soon as he pulls it out, you need to push your magic into her to heal her as fast and forceful as you can."

Lucius looked Michael in the eyes. "You can do this. You have saved her many times before. Trust me, this is not even the worst time."

Michael's eyes widened, but he gave a slight nod.

"Alright on the count of three. One... two... three." Max pulled the spike, and Michael's hands glowed as he pushed his magic into her. Luzia hummed to life as her magic drifted from her and added to Michael's.

Lucius watched as Odessa's wound slowly closed, and her heartrate picked up.

When it was completely healed, they laid her back on the floor. A pillow and a blanket formed under her.

"Will she be alright?"

Lucius looked beyond Volt at the young woman next to him, and everything in him froze. Lucius blinked a few times, but she was still there. She wasn't an illusion or a figment of his imagination. He slowly stood and walked over to her.

He gazed into her eyes which were the same color as his, silver-grey. His eyes told him what his heart already knew to be true. He didn't know how it was possible, but she was alive and standing in front of him.

"Sabine," he breathed.

Confusion then fear filled her eyes; she didn't know who he was to her. She probably only knew him as the Ragana Zidikas. He wasn't sure how much her memory may have been altered.

"There is no need to be afraid. No one here is going to hurt you. You are safe." The relief Lucius saw in her eyes brought joy to his heart but sadness that for even one second, she thought he would hurt her.

"Is she going to be alright?" Daphne asked again.

He realized he had never answered, too stunned at seeing her here. His eyes were still wide in disbelief.

"Yes, she will be fine. She just needs to rest. You look like you need rest, as well." It was taking everything Lucius had not to pull her into his arms and hug her tight.

"I'm fine. I actually should get—"

"No, you will stay here with us. Odessa will be upset if she finds that we let you go, especially without her seeing you," Circe said, walking up to her. "Besides, Lucius speaks the truth. You are safe here. Eat. Rest. Gather your strength."

Circe was a blessing. Lucius was more grateful for her presence than ever before.

"Volt... can show you where you can lay down?" He cast a questioning look towards the male.

"Definitely. This way." Volt led her through the aisles full of books, but she looked back at the door and then at Lucius. He smiled, hoping to put her at ease. He felt better when a small grin appeared, and then she continued to follow Volt.

Kynigos, they both are here. Finally. Grey couldn't have said it better. Lucius's family was finally home.

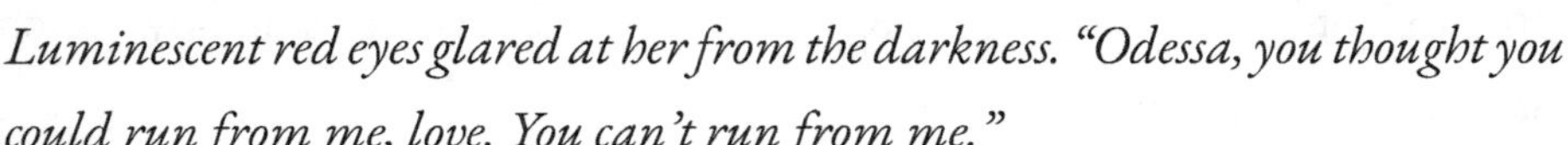

Luminescent red eyes glared at her from the darkness. "Odessa, you thought you could run from me, love. You can't run from me."

Odessa looked around her. Darkness surrounded her as she struggled against her restraints. She was tied to a bed. "Please let me go," she begged, pulling at the ropes restraining her wrists.

His wretched laugh filled the room as he walked closer to the bed from the darkness, revealing his full form in his alabaster suit. "Never."

He stopped at the foot of the bed where she was laying. Naked.

Starting at her toes, he slowly dragged his finger up her leg, briefly stopping at the apex. Hunger sprung into his eyes as he continued his ascent, making his way up her chest. Stopping at her breasts, he made slow circles around both of her nipples.

She hated her body for involuntarily responding to him. A knowing smirk appeared on his face. He knew this was killing her.

Continuing his torture, he dragged his finger up to the pulsing vein in her neck, tracing it with glee. He took his time in making his way up to her lips. He smiled down at her as he outlined them with his finger. Happy to have finally caught his prize.

"You are mine. Forever."

"Let me go and I promise to make your death swift. You lying bastard."

He threw his head back and laughed. "You are mine. My queen. You will return to me."

Fear gripped Odessa as she struggled against the rope. She tried to tap into her powers, but she could not access them. She screamed and struggled in frustration.

"Shhhh... no need to struggle. I will be gentle. I have waited a long time for this." He moved his hand down her body, caressing her. His touch burned, killing her soul with every caress. "You are mine," he whispered in her ear.

"Let me go!" she screamed, struggling to get away. She wouldn't let him have her. She had to get out of here.

"Never. You will never escape me, my love. We are meant to be."

Odessa opened her eyes, jolting awake.

Jumping up, she ran. She didn't know in what direction she was going, but she had to get away. Alazar couldn't find her. She wouldn't go back to him.

She ran until she realized it was books she was running past. She slowed herself, catching her breath. It had just been a dream. She was here in reality. Finally feeling a little better, she moved through the shelves.

At one point, she stopped and checked her stomach. Did she dream the wound too? No, that had to have been real. Daphne must have found a way to heal her.

Odessa continued to walk until she came to a sitting area.

"Daphne."

She sat on one of the sofas talking with a strange male with silver hair. Daphne stood and ran over to her, hugging her tightly. "I thought I had almost lost you."

"No, still all in one piece. Thank the Goddess. Who's your friend who is staring at me strangely?" The male's silver eyes bored into her with a bewildered expression, as if she had grown an extra head.

The male stood, looking immaculate in his green suit. He ran his hands through his hair before striding over to them.

"Odessa, this is Volt. Volt, this is Odessa. He rescued us and saved your life. Though, he still won't tell me how he knew we would be there," Daphne said, glaring at him playfully.

It was nice to see that she felt safe enough to be playful. It was such a change.

Odessa smiled. "Thank you for saving my life, no matter how you found us there."

"Anytime. It is just good to see you safe and well."

A tug at her core spooked her, then a sense of home spread through her. "Do you feel that too?"

"Feel what?" Daphne asked, staring at her curiously.

"I think someone is coming." She turned to look behind her. A male with brown hair and hazel-blue eyes came to stand before her. "Patience."

"Huh? Patience for what?" she asked him.

Laughter filled his eyes, lighting up his face. "I'm sorry. I forgot the whole memory thing. Odessa. I'm Michael."

She didn't know why, but her heart soared when he said his name. She threw her arms around him and hugged him so tightly, she never wanted to let him go.

He smiled against her hair. "The feeling is mutual. I have missed you too."

"I don't understand. Who are you?" She pulled away and wiped the tears from her eyes.

"I'm your best friend, silly."

Odessa laughed. She could see how they were friends. There was just something about him that made her feel at ease and like she was home.

"I don't understand. Why can't I remember you? I know your name from pieces of my memory, but I can't place you." Odessa hated being in the dark, and she felt a tremendous loss of not being able to remember any of their friendship.

"Oh, we have so much to explain. There is a lot that I don't remember either."

She felt some relief at hearing it wasn't just her with memory issues. There had to be a way to get the mist from her system so she would be able to remember everything. What she really needed was a kitchen, some herbs, and a book on memory spells.

"Do we have any idea how to fix it?"

"Not yet, but we were hoping with you back, you would be able to help us. We have Selene and…"

Odessa tried to concentrate on what he was saying, but her mind couldn't focus. There was someone coming. He was moving toward her, determined to find her. For a moment, she thought it was Alazar but no, this was different. Stronger.

A tug pulled at her core from behind her.

Odessa froze as all sound faded away. All she could concentrate on was the tugging and the presence approaching her. She knew the moment he was behind her. She was afraid to turn around.

"Odessa," his voice vibrated through her, going straight to her very soul.

Slowly, she turned around and met silver-grey eyes that saw right through her. "Who are you?" she asked, already knowing the answer.

"I'm Lucius. Your husband."

CHAPTER THIRTY

ALAZAR

In a fit of rage, Alazar swept his arm across the table before him, toppling it with a forceful motion. The delicate silverware and porcelain dishes cascaded to the floor, creating a cacophony of clattering and shattering sounds. The once neatly arranged table now lay in disarray, a chaotic scene mirroring the turmoil within Alazar himself. The scattered debris bore witness to his anger and frustration.

They think they have won. They may have escaped my clutches, but they haven't won. This is only the beginning.

He paced back and forth and waited for Jezabel, who finally walked through the door. "Will she live?"

"Yes." Jezabel threw a gold talisman at him. He caught it. "You will be able to control her and her magic with that. She will need time to recover, but then she is all yours."

"Good." When he found Estelle near his office, the rage that poured out of him was pure. He thought her to be dead, but when he came back from trying to retrieve Daphne and Odessa, Jezabel told him she would live with a few modifications. He would give her anything to fix his love.

His foolishness had almost gotten her killed—the female who would be his true queen as soon as he freed his mother.

He needed to capture both Odessa and Michael. They were the keys to securing both Evictus and the Silverlands. He would sit on the throne here, and his mother would finally take her place on the throne in the Silverlands once Odessa gave him the power. She would make him king, and then he would kill her. Then, he would concede the throne to his mother, and they would rule both lands.

Now that Daphne and Alecia were with them, he planned to use them to get exactly what he wanted, but first, he would need to find out where the hell his brother was.

It wasn't usual for him to disappear for weeks at a time, but now he was beginning to worry. He would never have stayed away from Odessa this long.

"Jezabel, I need you to ready the army and send the Hokima out to find Alden."

"Is it time?"

"Yes, we need a distraction, and sending demons into Eviathian seems like the perfect plan." Their laughter echoed through the room, filled with a shared sense of madness and delight. Alazar couldn't help but be captivated by the unhinged symphony of their laughter, recognizing in that moment why they were the perfect pair.

———◆◇◆———

Zarius

Zarius eased in and out of the shadows as he moved through the vacant halls.

The explosion had finally given him the opportunity to slip through their fortress walls. He had been waiting for this opportunity for a long time, training for it, preparing for it, and killing for it.

He needed to free her. She begged him to free her. Years and years of torture and pain had brought him to this very moment. Finally, he would be free of her. She would get out of his head and leave him alone.

He continued silently moving through the halls, following her instructions pouring through his head.

Yes, you are so close. I am down here. Come to me, Zarius.

He wished he could rip her voice from his head, but he couldn't no matter how much he tried. The pain didn't stop until he started to follow her instructions, so he did. Now, he was here. She promised that if he set her free, she would leave him alone.

Quietly, he maneuvered past a flurry of servants who hurried towards the sound of the explosion, descending the stairs that led to the dungeon. Her voice grew increasingly demanding as he navigated past row upon row of cells. The imprisoned eyes watched him intently, their gazes following his every move, yet none dared to reach out or impede his progress.

No one wanted to invoke her wrath. Their queen would be free soon.

Zarius kept moving through the halls until the smooth stone turned into the rough rockface of the interior of a cave. Deeper and deeper he went. He found a sleeping female, but she wasn't the voice he sought. He kept going until he discovered where her voice became the loudest.

He slid through the aperture and stood in front of the ancient door. *You have found me*, she purred. *Now let me out!* she roared into his head.

Zarius pulled the dagger from his back and sliced his hands. He placed them against the door and repeatedly spoke the words she forced him to say.

"Acum Esti Liber. I grant you your freedom."

The ground trembled as the doors opened, and red eyes peered out at him.

"Hello, Grandmother."

TO BE CONTINUED...

GLOSSARY

Weapons/Objects

Anduril Blade – used to kill the Tral'goth demon

Astral Coins – Will buy a creature three questions from Umber, an Eviathan Troll

Axe of Hollia – Once belonged to the Demon God Hollis and now belongs to Evangeline. Gifted to her by the Goddess.

Bastion Tree – sacred tree in Valen that holds a natural portal between realms

Blades of Flux – Used to kill hokima assassins.

Blade of Valhal – double-edged sword used by hokima assassins

Blade of Sapience – Created by Calla T'elair, a Stoven, Master of the Blade for Queen Nulna of the Fairy Trolls. A purple double-edged blade created to be used in the ceremony of Trolady to cut spiral herbs and to shed the blood of the magna. Also can sever unwanted magical ties when used with the Spell of Seperatus.

Blanket of Hildan – Blanket made of Truesilk. Found in the forest of Nolice.

Bluegrog Horn – Blown by the selkie guards of Amare to announce visitors.

Bracelets of Noribus - Two titanium bracelets spelled so bearers can't to harm the other

Ceamallia – shimmering purple flowers on the wall of the Atrium in Amare.

Cloak of Overance – a silken cloak used to conceal powerful weapons or objects

Damascus – a full-length magical stone mirror.

Dolem Talisman – used to spell a specific bearer. It paralyzes the bearer's magic and lulls them into a deep sleep. Only the one who spelled the talisman can wake the person. A silver metal circle with red glass and a silver five-pointed star in the middle. The earth, fire, air, water, and magic symbols were etched into each point of the star.

Fleece of Gilahein - the fleece gifted to Michael by the Queen of the nymphs. Made of Truesilk.

Glopinian – Red velvet pouch used to contain powerful objects like the soul gem

Gutrend spike – a poisonous spike used by the hokima to render a being powerless

Malice of Phoenixal – Used to summon and control Samuel, the ogre.

Mense Petals – sweet smelling flowers of gray and pink only fold in Valen.

Orb of Gilean – can control and manipulate people's memories. Lost in the dark realm.

Rod of Karagon – With one stab, the wielder could either kill you or send you the caves of Karagon, where he would make a meal of them. Gifted to Arietta by the Goddess.

Shadowsteel cuffs – used on Alden - thick unbreakable black steel cuffs

Truesilk – used to slow a hokima assassin.

Quary Leaves – Veiny darker green, almost black-like leaves found in Valen.

Silks of Neadle – Cloth made of Truesilk. Gifted to Michael by Toussels.

Sphere of Erogonian – a magical sphere that implants the memories the wielder created into the chosen victim/s.

Victus Blade – A jagged blade. Deadly when used with omicron poison on the blade to paralyze the victim.

Magic

Blessing of Ashes - The blessing was a curse. Cursing the bearer to never have children or create other creatures.

Blood bond – when blood is exchanged with a vampire within 24 hours. Can be broken, if one party is killed. Grows stronger with each sexual encounter or blood exchange.

Calamene – sleeping potion

Crimson Clutch – a deadly poison meant to hold its victim's death at bay by giving them long slow agonizing death

Elixir of Lovia – a powerful potion known for its ability to induce intense feelings of love and infatuation

Glendale weed – erases magic residue

Hiltina – a blood serum used to stave off blood hunger temporarily.

Simental stones – stones known to hold the feelings of loved ones and sometimes even memories if the magic was strong enough.

Soul-bond – exchanging of half their souls. Giving half of one soul to another and vice versa. If one being dies, the other will die too.

Spell of Seperatus – Can sever unwanted magical ties when used with the Blade of Sapience.

Water d' Silver – a precious and revered healing liquid derived from the mystical Silverlands, possessed extraordinary rejuvenating properties. This elixir held the power to restore vitality, which would accelerate the healing process and ensure the toxins had left the body.

People/Creatures

Aberrants – Witches who were not part of any coven because they chose not to conform. Patience is labeled one unwillingly.

Absergo - a devourer of magic – is found in the dark forest by a creature with four arms and no eyes. Realm unknown.

Arachnias – spiders who live in the realm of Enoch

Ashmore – The malevolent beast who stalks the cavern of Valen who hasn't been seen for centuries.

Bolrag – a cross between a warthog and a rhino

Canaan – a powerful draconian steed found in Valen.

Dracul – great-great-grandfather of Lucius and Ian Cordovan

Demon king – Kieran, King of the Evictus. Father of Michael and co-creator of vampires.

Drath - half vampires who denounced their witch ancestry. Only a few have magical abilities.

Ethel – A Sedisse, a creature who feeds on pleasure and enjoys pain.

Ganton - a hideous-looking gray creature with three arms

Goddess- Goddess of the witches. Possibly a descendant of a Silverite. Currently, missing.

Grenchen hounds – demon hounds with two mouths and luminous green eyes

Daimones – Michael and King Kieran are daimones. Ancient demons were thought to be extinct. Go through two transitions that make them powerful demons. Need a soul gem to complete the second transition.

Dragonistes – shadow creatures with sinuous bodies and razor-sharp teeth

Etherealic – a rare mind reader

Etherians - non-humans

Florans – gargoyles

Hadley – a Singi. Her songs enthrall her clients giving them pleasure which she feeds off of.

Half demon – Alazar, son of Lilith. He is trying to set her free. Unknown Etherian. Currently, has taken over Askaria.

Half witch- Alecia and Estelle are half-witches.

Hallows – Guardians of the Silverlands. Currently, lying dormant waiting for the Goddess to return.

Hokima – Guardians of Askaria commanded by the being who sits on the throne.

Irza – God of Iranti, God of Memory

Jezabel Elixiaire –The admiral of Lilith's army. It was said she was killed by the Hallows. She now works for Alazar creating his army of demons. Deadly with a whip.

Khedian – a creature with the ability to move undetected and has a photographic memory.

King Kieran - King of Evictus. See. Demon King.

Kynigos – means friend. What Jafa calls Lucius.

Lilith – Mother of all vampires and the mother of Alazar and Alden.

Lockhart Demons – grey-skinned creature with long red-tipped talons and pure black eyes

Milchan coven – Coven cursed to kill themselves over and over. Patience saved them.

Makas – little troll servants that do the bidding of Umber

Maladrias – the commanders of the Amarian army and the personal guards of the queen

Mastria – Teachers of Magic

Nasagals – A dark, ghostly creature with hollow eyes and a ravenous appetite. Nothing lived in Carmarthen because of them.

Novarians - skilled warrior assassins, part of the nation of Sabia that was lost long ago in the realm of Enoch. The city of light in the realm of darkness. Lilith destroyed their kind.

Phantoraros – a keeper of all knowledge. There are different kinds in each of the realms.

Ragana Zidikas – translation: Witch Hunter. Lucius Cordovan, an infamous witch hunter who slaughtered witches for over a century.

Seckor – Little ball of light and pathfinder

Sediesse – a creature who feeds on pleasure and enjoys pain.

Samuel – the ogre who guarded one of the largest portals to Evictus.

Sentinel of Light - a Guardian of the Witch's Council

Silverlands Witch – The first people to receive magic from the Goddess.

Spunkak demons – creatures with illuminated yellow eyes and razor-sharp teeth dripping with venom.

Silverite – first to use magic to create

Strainlin creature – a stonebreaker

Tarnok – They were shadow demons that carried sickness and death wherever they went. Eight thick horns adorned their rugged heads as they emerged from the shadows. Their hard, fibrous bodies were riddled with gaping wounds showing the infernal fire that burned inside them as their whip-like tails snapped behind them.

Tral'goth - Four thick-horned reptilian demons. Hokima's creature.

Umber - an ancient Eviathan Troll, legend had it he was around before the humans habituated the realm. His Makas kept their ears to the ground and gathered the information for him. A person with the correct currency would divulge certain information to the right questions. He covets Astral coins which would buy any creature about three questions.

Vampire Council – made up of ruling members of the vampire clans. Maintain laws.

Vasteri – Askarian Mountain, where Blades of Flux were forged.

Witch Council – members of each witch coven are elected to sit on the council to maintain laws.

Xenailia – a demon hibernating at the bottom of the Euphorian Trench

Zokarian – dangerous creatures who wreaked havoc on everything and everyone they encountered until they finally killed the ones they were summoned to go after. They were hard to capture and even harder to kill. Almost damn near impossible, in fact.

Enchantments/Charms

Allure of Souls – Lure charm. Used to attract humans to certain Etherian feeding grounds.

Black ankh - vampire emblem found on vampire establishments.

Nyonian Diamond – used to keep the Nasagals at bay. They are afraid of its light.

Whisper of Soul's charm - Used on technology (via website) to lure humans

Places/Languages

Aznarian – Language of the Phantoraros (GreyJoy)

Amare – the realm of the Selkies/Sirens

Askarian – Capital of Evictus

Astrona - the realm of lightning

Argian – Language of the Silverlands

Calidium – Territory within Evictus ruled by Sucora, a Demon Goddess

Carmarthen – the Shadow Realm, where the Nasagals ruled.

Caves of Astrona – known for their labyrinthine nature, with tunnels that twisted and turned in unpredictable ways.

Curvus Territory – a territory in Evictus outside the boundaries of Askaria.

Devilians – vile creatures known for their insidious nature and deadly attacks

Elderwins – Tree Sprites in the Sarewin Forest in the Silverlands

Epati - the language of Morian warlocks.

Enoch - dark realm. Birthplace of Lilith, Alazar, and Alden.

Evictus – Demon Realm

Eviathan – Realm to humans, vampires, witches, and other Etherians. Ruled by vampires and witches.

Euphoria – Prison in Askaria where Lilith is locked away.

Euphorian Trench – a deep crevice below Euphoria where Xenalia hibernates on a stone.

Helemal realm – Realm where the Mornes is located.

Igoria – Realm of the lost, where Patience found Michael.

Kilborn Academy – First school of witchery

Kavarian – Nomad Etherians of Calidium

Pools of Eden – shimmering pink pools in Amare where the sirens seduced their victims

Misthos – creatures known for their illusions and trickery

Mornes – the place between realms. A gateway located in the Velvidem Forest.

Sarenwin Forest – Sacred forest where the Elderwins live in

Silverlands - the realm in which the Goddess lived and the source of all magic and the place that connected all the realms.

Valen – the Acidic Realm, known for its acid rain, where most of its creatures lived underground in caverns.

Valenious – a chamber deep in the Silverian Mountains in the Silverlands.

Velvidem Forest – Sacred forest within the Helemal realm. Home to the Guardians of the Mornes.

Wailing Mountains – Mountains in Enoch

ALSO BY CHARLEY BLACK

Within the Darkness Trilogy
Entwined Within the Darkness
A Dance Within the Darkness
Forever Within the Darkness - TBA

Coming Soon...
The Elite: the Fall of Celearius

About the Author

Charley Black is an up-and-coming writer and author who has been creating stories since she was twelve years old. Her early short stories dabbled in different genres, but her passion for romance novels — paranormal romance in particular — always shone through. Charley currently resides in Rhode Island, with her family and works at a local university. Entwined will be the first of three novels set in the Within the Darkness universe.

You can connect with me on:

- facebook.com/authorcharleyblack

- instagram.com/authorcharleyblack/

- twitter.com/AuthorCharleyB

- tiktok.com/@authorcharleyblack

Subscribe to my newsletter:

www.charleyblack.com